PENGU
The Perfu

Fiona Schneider lives in Cambridgeshire with her German husband and three children. She graduated from Cambridge University with a degree in English, and in 2000 moved to Ireland to complete an M.Phil. in Creative Writing at Trinity College Dublin. *The Paris Affair* was her English-language debut.

By the same author

The Paris Affair

The Perfumer's Secret

FIONA SCHNEIDER

PENGUIN BOOKS

PENGUIN BOOKS

UK | USA | Canada | Ireland | Australia
India | New Zealand | South Africa

Penguin Books is part of the Penguin Random House group of companies
whose addresses can be found at global.penguinrandomhouse.com

Penguin Random House UK
One Embassy Gardens, 8 Viaduct Gardens, London SW11 7BW

penguin.co.uk

Penguin
Random House
UK

First published 2025

001

Set in 12.5/14.75pt Garamond MT
Typeset by Falcon Oast Graphic Art Ltd
Printed in Great Britain by Clays Ltd, Elcograf S.p.A.

The authorized representative in the EEA is Penguin Random House Ireland,
Morrison Chambers, 32 Nassau Street, Dublin D02 YH68

A CIP catalogue record for this book is available from the British Library

ISBN: 978-1-405-95880-6

For my mum, Susan, my brother, Mike,
and my niece, Mia.

'Make me a fragrance that smells like love.'
— Christian Dior

℃ଓ

Prologue

Iris – Melun, near Paris, December 1946

'I want it to stop,' Iris cried. The pain was unbearable. Outside the cell, the prison guard stood watch by the closed door. She gripped the edge of the scratchy blanket. It barely covered the bulge of her stomach.

The doctor, a kindly old man who treated the women at Melun with dignity despite their crimes, shook his head. 'Not possible, I'm afraid. This baby is coming whether you're ready or not.'

Iris shook her head. 'I just want this to be over,' she moaned as a huge surge broke over her body. 'It hurts so much.'

The doctor lifted the blanket to examine her. 'It won't be long now.'

Iris stared up at the ceiling. Plaster peeled in the corners where it was damp. She wanted to see the baby that had grown inside her these long, difficult months. But when the baby arrived, everything would change, and she'd never be so close to the child again.

A contraction came; her belly tightened. Deep inside, a pressure was building.

'We're nearly there,' the doctor said.

'I can't do this,' Iris said, teeth clenched in pain.

'Keep your breathing steady. Picture yourself far away from here, somewhere safe where you feel at peace.'

Iris screwed up her eyes. Unbidden, an image of the perfumery at Penhallam's floated into her mind. The bottles on the shelves, the large mahogany desk, a hint of scent in the air, the limitless possibilities offered to create a perfume from her imagination. It was like sitting down to a blank page and feeling excited to write on it. That moment, when ideas bubbled up and the perfume came into being inside her head, was the most peaceful moment she could think of.

'In a minute, when I tell you, you're going to push into the contraction,' she heard the doctor say. 'As soon as I can see the baby's head, I'll tell you.'

Iris opened her eyes. The baby's head. The vision of Penhallam's vanished. She gripped the doctor's hand. 'But is everything ready?'

He nodded. 'We've followed your instructions to the letter.'

His words renewed Iris's energy. She was nearing the end of this nine-month journey. In the prison, with its strict routines and endless monotony, Iris had little control. But she would ensure that her baby would have the freedom and life it deserved.

She clenched her fists. The painful contractions overpowered her. The cell disappeared. Instead, she was struggling in a stormy sea, cresting each wave, hoping it was the last, only to feel another one, larger and more forceful, crashing down on her. Far off, she heard the doctor's voice telling her to push.

Iris bore down and emitted a howl that seemed to come from a primal source. She pushed again, and again. As her cries ebbed away, they were replaced by another sound. A baby's cry.

Iris opened her eyes, astonished. The pain vanished, the sea was unexpectedly calm. The doctor smiled down at her. He held a baby in his arms, red and scrunched up, but perfect.

'It's a boy,' he said. 'You can hold him for a moment. There's time.' He cut the cord and gently wrapped the child in a blanket.

'I can't.' Iris turned her head away, imagining the sweet weight of him in her arms. If she so much as reached out and touched him, if she inhaled his scent, it would make this unbearably harder.

But she couldn't resist looking at him, his eyes sealed shut, lips pursed as if in the middle of a perplexing thought, fingers curled round in a tiny fist. She wanted to hold him more than anything, but it was impossible.

The doctor sighed. 'All right. Sign here, then.'

Iris took the fountain pen and the document, the final piece of paperwork that could be completed only once the baby was born. She scribbled her name and stared at the ink drying on the page. There. She'd done it. Signed away the only living thing she'd ever made. But what else could she do? The child deserved the chance of a better life. A life that Iris could never offer.

'Please, take him away,' she said, a sob catching in her throat.

The doctor hesitated for a moment, then asked the prison guard to open the door.

Iris's heart began to fracture. The urge to snatch the baby back, to feel him snug and safe in her arms, was almost more than she could bear. The doctor walked out of the cell carrying her child. A stab of pain tore through her. No, it was *their* child, Iris's and the man she'd loved.

The door closed with a deadening bang. The baby would never know what she'd done. Never miss her. Never know his true father.

Now Iris must try to forget that the child had ever existed.

La Scintilla
(The Spark)

Top Note
Rosemary and Lavender

☙

Heart Note
Jasmine

☙

Base Note
Cedarwood

☙

I

Stella – London, May 1996

Stella closed her eyes and silently went over the main points of her presentation. She needed to be convincing. Nerves fluttered in her stomach, but she was good at hiding them. Once she was in front of the stockists, she would hopefully exude confidence. She had to secure orders for next year or the perfumery that had been in her family for decades was going to struggle.

She tried to concentrate, but a scent wafted in through the first-floor window, distracting her thoughts. Irises. They grew outside the old perfumery on the ground floor. It was a scent used in one of Penhallam's classics. It reminded her of that glorious evening when her father was away, and Claudine, the last perfumer at Penhallam's, had inducted Stella into the wonders of the perfumery. She'd been ten years old, fascinated by the array of amber bottles which, when opened, unleashed magical scents on to the white-paper test strips.

That had been twenty years ago now. Since then, at her father's insistence, she'd devoted herself to the business side of things. It had become more cost effective to shift production off site five years ago when Claudine had retired. Since then, the perfumery had stood empty, used as a makeshift storeroom. Stella went over and dragged the sash window shut with a bang. She'd closed off her sense of smell long ago.

'This company has been in the Penhallam family for five generations,' her father, Richard, used to say. 'We need to keep it that way. Your great-grandfather and his father before him were perfumers, but the rest of us have always been businessmen. That's how we've kept Penhallam's going. As my only child, you'll need to take on the mantle when I'm gone.'

Richard had died last year after a car accident and Stella had taken on the mantle sooner than expected. She'd worked at Penhallam's since finishing her business degree, save for a secondment to the luxury goods company GPL. It had been a bid for freedom, but then her father had died and Stella had returned to Penhallam's as the managing director and sole owner to pick up the pieces.

In theory, it shouldn't have been too difficult. Since her grandfather's day, Penhallam's had had a tried-and-tested business approach. Instead of taking a risk and creating new scents, Charles had simply commissioned the factory to produce the established scents from their old ledgers. Penhallam's had a base of loyal customers who had been coming to Jermyn Street to buy their favourite scents for years, but as they got older their numbers were dwindling, and the cost of business rates and other expenses meant that Penhallam's was only just breaking even.

Stella put her note cards into a pile. Fingers crossed she could convince the big London department stores to keep stocking Penhallam scents. Sales and orders had been down and today was an opportunity to change that.

There was a tap at the door and Arnold's friendly face peered round. He'd been her father's accountant for years and had agreed to stay on and support Stella as she took the reins. His hair was thinning, but he looked very smart in his Savile Row suit and horn-rimmed glasses. He hadn't changed much over the years he'd worked for the family.

'They're all here and having coffee,' he said. 'Are you ready?'

Stella nodded. She'd done plenty of presentations over the years; she knew it was all about preparation. Her navy-blue blazer and matching trousers, Red Berry lipstick and heels were all part of the performance. She flicked through her notes. Hopefully, she could pull this off.

'You're going to be fine,' Arnold said. 'Good luck.'

'Thank you,' she said, glad of his support.

The weight of the company was a lot to bear. It had been founded in 1870 by her great-great-grandfather, Felix Penhallam, who was succeeded by her great-grandfather, Alistair, in 1918. On his death, Stella's grandfather, Charles, took over in 1937, and then passed it on to Richard, Stella's father, in 1986. Now here she was, the first woman in charge of Penhallam's, and desperate not to let the company fail on her watch.

'Promise me you'll never let the company fall out of family hands,' her father had said, in the final hours before he died of his injuries. Stella could only stand by while the medics tried frantically to staunch his wounds. She'd been allowed only a brief conversation with him before the operation the doctor hoped would save him, agonizingly aware that it might be their last. Stella had squeezed his hand, her eyes blurred with tears, and promised Richard that she would never let Penhallam's go. It was the last thing she ever said to him.

Her mother, all the way over in Australia, where she'd moved with her second husband, had warned Stella that Penhallam's was a burden too great to bear. 'That business ruined our marriage. It took everything out of him and left no time for anything else. I don't want to see that happen to you,' she'd said. But Stella was determined not to let her father down.

Now she walked into the meeting room, anxious not to give any hint of the troubles Penhallam's was facing.

'Good morning, everyone, thank you for coming today,' she said, keeping her voice steady. She'd kept this presentation to only the key buyers from the top London stores. The idea was to make the event feel intimate and exclusive, as though they were the only people in the world to be offered another piece of Penhallam's history. 'As you know, at Penhallam's we believe in the heritage scents that my great-great-grandfather and great-grandfather, both expert perfumers, created. But we know that customers today want to buy a product that looks "of the moment".'

She gestured to the samples of new packaging that were already on display on the table. 'We have listened to customer feedback and used the services of a design company to repackage our much-loved perfumes for the modern day.'

There was no need to tell them that Arnold had brokered an investment loan from a lending institution to commission the feedback and redesign work at great expense. As she observed the faces of the buyers, Stella hoped it had been worth it.

'Together with a new-look counter and shelf display, we intend to relaunch these fragrances next year and bring the classic Penhallam scents to a new customer base. You can see by the design that we're aiming to appeal to a younger audience with the vibrant colours. I think you'll agree, this radically overhauls our somewhat out-of-date image and attracts the eye with a more up-to-date look.'

Stella scanned the room. It was hard to tell what the buyers were thinking. One woman jotted notes on her pad. Stella handed out the new packaging. Personally, the lime and red patterns and angular perfume bottles weren't to her taste, but the branding expert recommended by her boyfriend, James, had been very convincing. Stella had met James while she was at GPL on her secondment. He still worked there now, overseeing the US market. She wouldn't exactly say their relationship was anything serious – he was away a lot of the time – but it was handy having someone in the business to talk to about it all.

'So, to summarize,' Stella said, hoping she'd done enough to turn things around, 'Penhallam's has a solid product portfolio with decades of history, but its exquisite perfumes now have a new setting. We hope you will consider placing orders for next year.'

From the back of the room, Arnold gave her the thumbs-up. Other than James, he was the only one who knew about the dire financial situation she faced.

'Any questions?' Stella said.

'Are there any new scents in the pipeline?' the buyer from Liberty asked.

Stella cleared her throat. 'As you know, the unique selling point of Penhallam's is that the lineage of each scent can be traced back for years. Our back catalogue is our main asset.'

'Ah,' the woman said. 'I was afraid you'd say that.'

A bald man cleared his throat. He was from House of Fraser; they'd stocked Penhallam's for years.

'Forgive me, but isn't the lack of new scents your problem?' he said. 'I appreciate what you've done with the new bottles and boxes, but it isn't enough.'

Stella gripped her notes. 'As you know, my father, Richard Penhallam, was adamant that quality will always prevail over novelty where the actual contents of the bottle are concerned,' she said firmly. 'It's our heritage that people look for . . .'

The man from House of Fraser replied, 'I'm sorry, Stella. We're exploring new lines for next summer as the older scents aren't selling through as strongly any more. Our customers are looking for something new, more modern. You can assert your heritage all you like, but it's innovative scents that keep customers coming back for more. Your father never did understand that. I'd hoped you might usher in a new era at Penhallam's.'

The room went quiet. A siren blared a few streets away. Stella swallowed. He'd put her on the spot.

'I'm sorry to hear that. House of Fraser has always been a valued client,' she said, her throat dry. She had to think of something. Thoughts scrambled in her head. She plucked one out. 'We do have *some* ideas in the early stages of development, but nothing I could share with you today. Perhaps I could be in touch, if you can keep that window open for us just a little longer?'

The man nodded. 'We place our Christmas orders at the start of September, as you know. That gives you three months to come up with something convincing.'

His words signalled the end of the meeting. Stella was collapsing inside, but she put on a brave face, shaking hands and promising to send samples of a new perfume in a couple of months. Everyone was very polite, but she could sense their attention waning, and they soon left.

Stella closed the door and slumped down into one of the chairs. 'That was awful.'

Arnold came and sat next to her. 'It could have been worse. You managed to salvage something there at the end.'

'But I don't have any new scents. I panicked and made it up.'

'You used your instincts. A new line is exactly what Penhallam's needs.'

'Of course it is, but we don't have the money to hire a perfumer or develop new perfumes from scratch. Besides, there still has to be some link back to our past, or what's the point of our brand at all?'

Arnold sighed. 'Have you thought about what James said?'

James had hinted that GPL would be prepared to buy out Penhallam's. Stella shook her head. 'It will never happen,' she said. 'I won't be the one to lose Penhallam's. When I worked at GPL, I only met the CEO, Andrea, once, but she struck me as formidable. I have great respect for what she's done at GPL, acquiring failing luxury goods companies and turning them around, but I couldn't think of a worse fate for Penhallam's.'

'But if you don't consider some kind of help and sales remain stagnant or drop even further, you may have to look at selling Penhallam's anyway.'

Stella sat up straight and flicked her hair back. 'I will never do that,' she said firmly. 'It would be a betrayal of everything this family has stood for. I know things are difficult. I've discounted stock as much as I can and taken a massive cut in wages myself. There's not much left I can do. But I'm determined to think of something.'

Arnold took off his glasses and wiped them on his tie. 'Well, you need to think of it quickly. We can't take the loss of a big client like House of Fraser. It'll be the final straw. Penhallam's is running on fumes as it is.'

'I know.' Stella stood up. 'I'm meeting James for a drink tomorrow. He's over from New York, so I'll pick his brain for suggestions. Whatever happens, I'm not giving up.'

Arnold smiled. 'Your father would be proud of you.'

'Thank you. I don't know what I would have done without your support.'

Stella returned to the office. Her father's portrait hung on the wall. Next to it was her grandfather Charles's portrait. Their eyes looked concerned. For better or for worse, this company was in her blood. She had to find a way to turn its fortunes around or Penhallam's would be lost.

2

Iris – London, July 1939

Iris Penhallam gripped her satchel in one hand, and her gas mask in the other and crossed the road at Grosvenor Place. The trees abutting the high wall around Buckingham Palace Gardens glowed green in the afternoon sunshine. Before she turned on to Hyde Park Corner, Iris glanced back at St James's Secretarial College. At last, she was finished. Never again would she have to set foot inside, except to collect her certificates. Bookkeeping. Correspondence typing. Note-taking. She was done with them all. She'd also kept up her language skills, at her brother Charles's insistence, perfecting her French and Italian so that she was nearly fluent. Charles would have to make good his promise now, and appoint her as the first apprentice perfumer at Penhallam's. A surge of elation put a spring in her step as she headed towards Jermyn Street.

It was impossible to stay happy for long, however. Along Piccadilly, newspaper sellers called out the headlines. The papers were full of the news that Neville Chamberlain had reaffirmed his support for Poland. It was clear that Britain would intervene on Poland's behalf if Germany continued its expansion across Europe.

Iris hurried along the pavement. Outside the Ritz, sandbags were piled up against the windows. London had been preparing for hostilities for months. Anderson shelters had been distributed. Blackout material purchased. War was all anyone talked about; a shadow on the horizon, creeping closer and closer.

She turned into Jermyn Street. The sight of the cobbled narrow road was comforting. The rest of London seemed to be holding its breath, but here the flower sellers were out as usual by the railings of St James's Church. Number 79 Jermyn Street came into view. The five-storey building housed the Penhallam perfumery and was also Iris's home. She'd lived here since she was born. Following the sudden death of her father, Alistair, two years ago from a heart attack, the perfumery had been managed by her brother, Charles, twelve years her senior. A new perfumer, Marcel, had been employed to take on her father's role.

Iris sighed. The large windowpanes of the shopfront shone back her reflection. She and Charles had never been close. He'd seemed to resent her bond with their father, the long hours she'd spent with him in the perfumery concocting scents and discussing ingredients. Charles had always been distant, disdain hovering in his eyes.

She took a deep breath. Well, she'd done what Charles had asked: two years at secretarial college. It hadn't been easy. If her father had still been alive, she was sure he'd have taken her on as his apprentice perfumer when she turned eighteen. But Charles had been adamant. 'You need to learn the business side and be useful,' he'd said. 'We've got Marcel, so we don't really need an apprentice. But I promise, if you get your qualifications, I'll seriously consider you to be Penhallam's first one.' Hoping to appease him, to glean some recognition from him, Iris had agreed.

She pushed open the door and walked into the perfume

shop. Glass-fronted cabinets purchased by her grandfather glittered with mirrors and perfume bottles. A delicious waft of scents set her nostrils tingling. A long wooden counter stood on the left-hand side. Marcel was there, counting up the takings.

A kindly man in his early sixties, Marcel had a bushy grey beard and sympathetic brown eyes. From the moment he'd arrived at Penhallam's, Marcel had seemed to understand Iris's yearning to create scents. When she had time free from her studies and Charles was out at his club, Marcel had been willing to teach her. It wasn't anything like what she'd learn as an apprentice, but his patience and kindness had ensured she'd kept up her natural talent for making perfumes.

Iris lifted her bag and gas mask on to the counter, glad to be free of their weight.

'Good afternoon, Marcel,' she said, noticing the notes and coins on the counter. Takings had been steadily decreasing all year. The prospect of war had turned perfume into a luxury that not many could afford. 'That doesn't look good.'

Marcel shook his head. 'I'm afraid it isn't.' He scooped the coins into a bag. 'Charles was at the bank this morning and, judging by his mood when he returned, it didn't go well. He cancelled lunch with Jane, saying he didn't have time to meet his fiancée on a day like this. Henri is up there now. You'd better prepare yourself, my dear.'

Ah, Henri Levèque. Charles and Henri had been best friends at Eton, where Charles had got a scholarship and Henri had been sent to broaden his connections and improve his English. Henri had joined the Penhallams every year at their house in Mougins in the south of France.

Iris had hopelessly adored him from afar in her early teenage years. Any conversations had been brief, full of stuttering and blushes on her side and detached amusement on Henri's. But lately something had changed. Iris couldn't quite put her finger on it, but it was as if he saw her as a woman now, rather than a child. The change was unnerving. She always felt a flutter of anticipation when he visited: his admiring gaze and flirtatious tone made her nervous.

Henri came over from Paris regularly to see Charles, but she hadn't realized he was coming this week.

'Why do I need to be prepared?' Iris asked.

'I know what today means for you,' Marcel said, concern etched on his brow, 'but you have to consider the current circumstances. I fear the apprenticeship might not go ahead, Iris.'

'What do you mean?'

Iris reached into her pocket and clamped her hand around a tiny perfume bottle. It was the scent she'd been secretly working on over the last few months. The glass was cool against her palm. Working in the perfumery was the only way to stave off the grief of losing her father. Without it, she wasn't sure she could keep going.

'You'd better head up and see him yourself,' Marcel said.

Iris picked up her bag and ran up the stairs from the shop to Charles's office on the first floor. Her heart felt like it was going to explode. The apprenticeship *had* to go ahead. Just before she reached his door, she slowed her pace. Her brother hated outbursts of emotion. Reason was the only thing that Charles understood.

Iris smoothed down her skirt. Besides, Henri would be there. She wanted to keep her composure in front of him. She took a deep breath and rapped her knuckles on the door.

'Come in,' Charles said.

Iris opened the door and entered the study. The window was ajar and a soft breeze ruffled the papers on Charles's vast mahogany desk. The stern face of her grandfather stared down from the walls. A new portrait of her beloved father was underway.

Charles sat at his desk. His hair was grey at the temples; a frown etched his forehead. Henri sat in one of the leather chairs by Charles's desk.

Henri smiled at Iris, his gaze sweeping down her body. 'You're looking beautiful today, Iris. I'm glad to see you again.'

'Thank you.' Iris's heart beat a little faster. Whatever she had to say, she would have to say it in front of Henri. 'Charles, Marcel says the apprenticeship might be in doubt, but I hope he's mistaken. I've just had my last day at secretarial college, doing the course you asked me to undertake. You can't go back on your word.'

Charles linked his fingers together. 'I only promised to consider it, Iris.'

His tone was irritatingly superior. It reminded her of countless moments when, as her older brother, he'd held the upper hand.

'But I've been talking about the apprenticeship for years,' Iris said. 'You know how much it means to me. Out of respect for you, I was willing to learn the other aspects of the business, but being a perfumer at Penhallam's is all I've ever wanted.'

Charles motioned for her to sit. She sat down in the leather chair next to Henri's.

'I'm sorry, Iris, the apprenticeship isn't going ahead now. I've looked at the matter from every angle and decided this is what's best for the perfumery,' Charles said with a helpless shrug.

Henri folded his arms, clearly not wanting to get involved. But he gave Iris a sympathetic smile.

'But Marcel will need a successor one day,' Iris said. 'Who better to take over from him than me?'

Charles fiddled with his fountain pen.

'There's no question of your talent,' Charles said. 'I remember when you were only seven years old and had wandered into the perfumery. Mother was frantic with worry, but she found you sitting with Father, sampling ingredients, and describing them with such precision that Father was astounded.'

Iris remembered that day too. The amber bottles, each containing a different scent, were like notes of music. She could look at them and imagine a symphony in her head. It was the first time she'd been allowed to compose, and she'd loved every minute of it. It was then that her father had given her the perfumer's notebook that she kept with her always, jotting ideas and formulas down on the pages.

'But that's why I need this apprenticeship,' Iris said, sitting up in the chair. 'I have the perfumery in my blood. It's been my obsession all my life.'

Henri raised his eyebrows. 'That is true, Charles. Iris and that old perfumer from Paris, Raffaele di Fiore, were inseparable every summer in Mougins.'

Raffaele di Fiore was a renowned Italian perfumer who had relocated to Paris in the 1920s. He'd become a good friend of Iris's father and hired a cottage in Mougins next door to the Penhallams' house every summer. Raffaele and Alistair spent the evenings talking about perfume, Iris hanging on their every word. Sometimes, Raffaele's sister, Francesca, had come to visit from Venice with her little boy, Jacopo. A talented perfumer in her own right, Francesca had been patient with Iris's many questions about blends and ingredients. Over the years, the two families had got to know each other very well. Now Raffaele was in his late sixties. He had been very upset about Alistair's sudden death.

'Raffaele's in London this week,' Iris said. 'He's making a speech at the Perfumers' Convention. I was hoping to be able to tell him the good news. He knows how much Father wanted me to do this.'

Charles shook his head. 'It was a mistake for Father and Raffaele to encourage you. It wasn't an appropriate way to prepare you for the world. Look at how you fared at school,' he said. 'If you hadn't been so obsessed with fragrances, you might have fitted in better.'

Iris rubbed her forehead. She didn't like to think of those days.

'It wasn't the perfume-making that made me different,' she said. 'It was having a father who they scorned for owning a shop, the fact that I loved science. There were a hundred reasons why the girls at school didn't like me. Making perfume was a refuge from all that, not the cause. Perhaps if Mother hadn't died when I was so young, things might have been different.' She reached into her pocket and took out the little bottle. 'Just smell this, Charles. Tell me it isn't good.'

Charles shook his head.

'Oh, go on, Charles, one sniff is hardly going to kill you,' Henri said. Henri lifted the bottle out of Iris's hands and inhaled the scent. 'Actually, that really is good.'

Iris flicked through her perfume notebook, encouraged. She opened the pages to the middle of the book, showing Charles. 'Look, you can see the ingredients. I'm trying for something different. The old scents in the ledgers are very heavy and floral. We could pioneer something new. Maybe even take it to the Perfumers' Convention.'

'It's worth listening to what she says,' Henri said.

'Let me handle this, Henri,' Charles said, waving away the bottle.

Henri gave it back to Iris with a shrug.

Charles reached for his cigar box, took one out and lit it. Smoke filled the air. The earthy, woody scent combined with a slightly sweet note hinted at leather and spices. It reminded Iris of her father. She gripped her notebook. She wished he was here now to fight her corner.

'I'm sorry, Iris, but the apprenticeship cannot go ahead,' Charles said. 'Penhallam's doesn't have the money to pay you. With war looming, we need to shore up our liquid assets. The cost of ingredients from Europe and the Far East has risen exponentially. Put simply, we can't afford an apprentice.'

Iris flung up her hands. 'But Charles, that's no obstacle at all. I'm family. I wouldn't want to be paid. All I ask is that you let me devote all my time to being taught by Marcel.'

Henri nodded. 'That's a good point.'

Charles scowled at him. 'There are other reasons,' he said. 'I don't think perfumery is a suitable occupation for Iris to pursue. It's time she settled down and got married. Marrying well is the best way to honour Father's memory.'

Henri nodded. 'Also, a very good point.'

The air was suddenly too smoky. Iris went over to the window and wrenched it open, gulping in the fresh air. Her stomach felt sick. Charles had no right to decide her life or make her feel that she would be dishonouring her father if she went against his wishes.

'Charles, please,' she said, turning to face him, 'I've done everything you asked for.'

Charles shook his head. 'I'm sorry, Iris. Ultimately, the decision is beyond my control. War is coming. I've decided to enlist. Father did the same thing during the Great War. Marcel will keep things going here as much as possible. Jane is going up to her parents in Scotland and I want you to go with her. That way you'll be safe and out of the way.'

'Scotland?' She couldn't leave London. Jane was a nice, straightforward girl and Iris had been delighted when Charles got engaged to her, but sit out the war with her up in Scotland? Impossible. 'Please, let me stay in London and help Marcel. I'll be more use here.'

'No, it's decided,' Charles said. 'With the way things are, we've all had to adjust our plans. You are no exception.'

Iris opened her mouth to protest, but no words came out. What could she say? Charles was going to do his duty and enlist. Her plight was nothing compared to what was happening in Europe, with thousands of people already displaced from Austria and Czechoslovakia. And if Hitler continued his expansion, things would only get worse. That's what war did. It blighted the future of everyone who was swept into its path.

Charles tapped the cigar against the ashtray. 'Now, if you don't mind, Henri and I have got more important matters to discuss.' He picked up his papers, his mind elsewhere.

Iris nodded. All at once, she was ten years old again, an annoying little sister just getting in the way. She put her notebook and the bottle back in her bag. 'I'll leave you to it then.'

Henri rose and walked her to the door. 'Let things settle,' he whispered. 'He's got a lot on his shoulders, right now. The finances aren't good. The news from Europe is, frankly, terrifying. I'll help as much as I can, but he's not in the mood for compromises today.'

'I can see that,' Iris said, with a brief smile.

Henri lifted her hand to his lips and kissed it gently. 'That scent you've created is truly outstanding. If you need anything,' he said, 'anything at all, I'm here for you.'

He stared intently. Warmth rippled across Iris's skin. She had always longed for him to look at her this way. She'd seen him charm women before at dinner parties, but here he was, casting his spotlight on her. Thank goodness she knew not to take him too seriously.

'Come on, Henri. I need your eye on this contract,' Charles called.

Henri smiled and closed the door.

Iris went downstairs. So many thoughts swirled inside. The hopes of that morning had evaporated. War was imminent. Like many others, she had been overjoyed when Chamberlain had come back from Munich last year waving the agreement with Hitler in the air. And yet, just six months later, the Germans had invaded the Sudetenland. Iris could no longer hide from the reality of what was happening. She shivered. The shadow of war was almost upon them. Her plans, and the plans of so many others, were about to be torn apart.

3

Stella — London, May 1996

Stella woke up in the flat on the second floor of 79 Jermyn Street. Light seeped in through the thin curtains, illuminating the packing boxes that stood around her camp bed. When her father died and Arnold had revealed the extent of Penhallam's financial woes, Stella had decided to give up her apartment and move into the empty flat above the shop to save money.

She flung back the covers. She should really sort her stuff out, but there was no time for anything any more. Penhallam's absorbed her every thought, night and day.

Yesterday afternoon, she'd gone for a walk along Bond Street to clear her head and wandered past Fenwick's. There was a striking perfume display in the window. On one side, CK One by Calvin Klein was displayed in an understated way with its plain bottle and unisex appeal. On the other, Angel by Thierry Mugler, sparkling and vibrant in a blue-glass star-shaped container. Stella had wandered in and sprayed a sample of each on her wrists.

Now, as she got dressed, she smelled the fading perfumes on her skin. Penhallam's had nothing to compete with iconic scents like this. CK One had a fresh aquatic scent of musk, bergamot and violet. Angel, by contrast, combined patchouli with notes of chocolate, honey and cotton candy to create a new category all of its own: 'gourmand'. Penhallam's lacked aquatic and gourmand scents and desperately needed something that made it stand out from the crowd but didn't compromise its historic past. Stella had lain awake for hours trying to think of how to solve this conundrum but had got nowhere.

The doorbell rang downstairs. She knew it couldn't be Amy, the shop assistant; she didn't start for another hour. Stella tucked her shirt into her work trousers, popped on a black blazer and hurried downstairs. It would be Bruno. She opened the door and there he was, standing in the street, two coffee cups in his hand.

'*Buongiorno*, Stella,' Bruno said, handing her one of the cups.

'You really don't have to do this every day,' Stella said. The coffee smelled delicious though. She took a sip. Bruno came into the shop, and she closed the door. It wouldn't be opening time for a couple of hours, but Bruno was an early riser, just like her.

'I know, but the instant coffee you have here is terrible,' he said, his chestnut-brown eyes twinkling.

Bruno was about Stella's age, with olive skin, a dusting of stubble on his face and dark brown wavy hair falling over his eyes. He'd arrived from the University of Venice two weeks ago to do some research in the Penhallam archives. He was writing a book about the development of perfume in the 1930s and 1940s.

'The basement is looking so much more organized, by the way,' Stella said. 'Even Arnold remarked on it.'

'Well, you said I could look for material for my book so long as I catalogued everything and organized the archives. Also, this makes them less of a fire hazard and more of a resource.' He smiled. 'You've been working hard too. We both deserve a good coffee.'

Stella smiled. She should stop staring at him, but it was hard not to be drawn in by his presence. His faded jeans, worn T-shirt and cardigan radiated ease. Stella straightened her blazer.

'Anyway,' she said, 'I'd better let you get on.'

'Do you have any time free later on?' Bruno said. 'I've found a couple of things you might be interested in.'

Stella shook her head, though it was tempting to think of spending time in Bruno's company. 'I'm afraid I'm rather busy at the moment. There's lots of things to sort out. Maybe tomorrow.'

Bruno nodded. 'Of course, you're the first to open up and the last to leave. It must be hard to live and work here every day,' he said.

Unsettled by his perceptive remarks, Stella shrugged. 'Oh, I'm used to it.'

He raised his eyebrows, clearly not convinced. 'Well, enjoy your coffee. I'll leave you in peace.'

Bruno headed to the door that led to the basement stairs. A scent lingered in the room. Stella wondered what aftershave he'd been wearing. Lime. Ambergris. Earthy but fresh. It reminded her of creating scents in the perfumery all those years ago. Mixing ingredients and trying to find the right combinations to re-create a feeling or a moment had been intoxicating.

Stella took another sip of coffee. The caffeine woke her up. She wandered to the back of the shop until she came to the door that led to the perfumery. It had been abandoned for the last five years and was piled high with stock.

She opened the door a little and peeped through the gap. There in the perfumery were the wooden cabinets, the old desk and, beyond, the perfumer's organ, displaying bottles of ingredients. It was sad that the perfumery was no longer in use. Her father had deemed it a waste of money and said that creating bespoke scents was no longer profitable. When Claudine left, they'd saved money by not replacing her and by outsourcing production. It was tantalizing to think what new scents could have been created in this very room. But there was no point lingering here now. Stella closed the door. She needed her business mind to find her way out of this; she wouldn't find the answer in idle dreams.

That evening, Stella went to meet James. She'd spent the day on the phone to the utility companies, trying to negotiate better rates. It hadn't amounted to much of a saving, but it was better than nothing. She'd also looked into cutting down on production, but it felt like a step too far. She'd only consider it if she really had to.

James had been in London for two days on a business trip to the UK headquarters of GPL and this was the first opportunity Stella had had to meet him.

The flags above the entrance to Claridge's fluttered in the evening breeze. Stella hurried up the marble stairs, smiling to the doorman as he opened the heavy brass and glass doors. Her heels clattered on the floor and she took a breath, slowing her pace. She didn't want to look flustered.

James was already at the bar, chatting to the bartender and looking very smart in his dark blue suit. He'd been a kind shoulder to cry on since her father had died and somehow the relationship had progressed from work colleagues to something more.

'There you are,' he said. He cupped her face and kissed her cheeks. 'Would you like a negroni? They do a great one here.'

'All right. Thank you,' Stella said.

He nodded at the bartender. Stella perched on the stool. The drinks came and Stella took a sip. 'It's felt like ages since I've seen you,' she said.

'I know. Me too. Work has been really busy lately. I've been doing everything I can to stay on top of things.'

'How come?'

James took a gulp of his drink. 'There's a drive to ramp up profits and they're looking to make some acquisitions.'

Stella stirred her drink with the straw. 'Don't start on about selling Penhallam's again.'

'Why not? It could be good for the company, and for you too. It's been a millstone round your neck since you had to go back there.'

Stella frowned. 'I know you mean well, but I'm not abandoning the company my family worked their whole lives to build.'

James held up his hand. 'All right, I'm sorry. I won't mention it again.'

'But there is something I'd like to ask your advice about.'

James laughed nervously. 'I thought we were done talking shop.'

'It's never bothered you before.'

'No, it's just . . .' He hesitated. 'There's something I need to talk to you about too.'

That sounded ominous. Come to think of it, James didn't look quite his usual ebullient self. His eyes were dusted with shadow and his suit jacket was creased. Perhaps it was the jet lag.

'What's going on?'

James took another swig of his drink. 'No, you go first. Tell me what's on your mind.'

'Okay,' Stella said, still concerned about what he had to tell her. 'Well, I took out that loan from the lending company you recommended. I've used it to try and find a solution, but Penhallam's profits have continued to decline. To make matters worse, one of our biggest clients has hinted that they might not renew their order for the next season.'

James sat back and gave a low whistle. 'Wow, it's worse than I thought. Which client?'

'House of Fraser. It would be a major blow.' Stella twisted her glass in her hand. 'I'm really worried. I can't repay the loan right now, and I need to borrow some more money to find a sustainable solution for Penhallam's future.'

'What kind of solution, then, if you don't want to sell?'

'I need something big and innovative to excite the clients again,' she said. 'But I'm struggling to work out which direction to go in. I don't want to contradict the heritage of Penhallam's that Dad wanted so desperately to protect.'

James swirled the ice around in his glass. 'From what I've seen, small perfumers are delving into their past and finding discontinued scents that capture the imagination of a modern-day customer. If there's a story or history attached to them, so much the better. GPL are impressed with some of the ideas that your competitors have in that direction.'

'Really?' Stella said.

'There are all sorts of deals going on, and, as you know, GPL are interested in taking on more artisan perfumers,' he said. 'The next big trend is reviving a forgotten vintage line of scents and giving them a new twist.'

Stella sighed. 'All our vintage scents are already on the market. We need something undiscovered.'

'Why not have a look in the Penhallam archives? You might be surprised by what you find down there.'

The word 'archives' made Stella think of Bruno, his mussed-up hair and sun-kissed skin, the scent left in the room when he'd gone. The image was incongruous, sitting opposite the immaculately groomed James, but somehow it caught her breath. Bruno. Whatever he was doing down in the archives, it was unlikely that he'd find something to save Penhallam's. But maybe she needed to get more involved in the research.

James rattled the ice in his nearly empty glass. Stella's mind circled back to what he'd said earlier. 'What was it you wanted to tell me?'

James rubbed his hands together nervously. 'Look, I'm sorry, Stella. It's been great this past year. I've loved spending time with you. But I need us to cool off for a while.'

Stella stared at him. 'That's a bit out of the blue. I mean, I know there's nothing serious between us, but I thought we were both fine with that.'

James reached for her hand. 'Of course, and I wish it could continue but, between you and me, there's talk of me moving back permanently to London and working on the perfume portfolio. Andrea has said I could really make something of the role and advance my position, but I need to keep my nose clean.'

Andrea was often profiled in magazines as a dynamic and inspiring CEO. There was a time when Stella had certainly looked up to her. If Andrea had said this to James, it was something he had to take seriously.

Stella sat back. 'Ah, I see.'

'I don't want to jeopardize my chances by blurring the boundaries. It would be seen as a conflict of interest, you see, if I carried on our relationship.'

'And when you worked in menswear it was all above board?' Stella said, raising her eyebrows.

James ducked his head. 'I know we talked a lot about your business and my work, but it was all just chat. There's a real chance I could become a director. Andrea has warned me that I need to get things in order. Otherwise . . . well, I need to maintain my credibility with the perfume industry going forward.'

Stella sighed. It wasn't like this was going to break her heart, but something sounded off in his reasoning. 'But this industry is riddled with relationships that criss-cross the boundaries. I'm not sure why you need to be so careful.'

James leaned over and twirled a strand of her hair around his finger. 'Taking a break from you isn't something I want to do, Stella,' he said. 'In fact, it's the opposite of what I want to do, but the powers above have hinted that it might be best if I don't mix business with pleasure. For now, at least.'

'I see, and then I suppose, when you feel like it, you'll give me a call and we'll pick up where we left off?' she said, unable to keep the sarcasm out of her voice.

Not that there was much to pick up on. Meeting in fancy hotels and having what felt like a one-night stand every few weeks wasn't exactly what Stella would call an intimate relationship.

'Don't be like that,' James said.

Stella finished her negroni. 'Look, it's fine. I understand that business comes first. To be honest, I need to devote all my energy to Penhallam's right now. If anything, you're making the right call for us both.' A thought occurred to her. 'Just promise me you'll keep what I've told you tonight to yourself.'

She didn't want word getting out that Penhallam's was in difficulties, and maybe James wouldn't feel the need to be so loyal if they were no longer together.

'Of course. I really do hope we can see each other again, down the line.'

'Maybe.' Stella stood up and straightened her skirt. Part of her longed for a soulmate. But she'd never really thought of James like that. 'Anyway, no hard feelings. I hope you make a success out of whatever GPL has in store for you.'

She kissed him briefly on the cheek and picked up her bag. Maybe it was for the best things were over. Now she could focus on the only thing that mattered in her life. Saving Penhallam's.

4

Iris – London, July 1939

The next evening, Iris sat in front of her dressing table and got ready for the Perfumers' Convention, which was to be held at Claridge's. The tabletop was littered with perfume bottles and objects collected from her trips to France. The most recent letter she'd had from Raffaele lay in front of her, expressing his delight in coming to London and seeing Iris again.

Iris took a string of pearls from her jewellery box and fastened them around her neck. In their correspondence, she had shared her hopes and dreams with Raffaele. She knew he would be disappointed for her about the apprenticeship, and she wanted his advice.

But as she glanced down at his letter, Iris knew that Raffaele had more worrying things on his mind.

I've been trying to arrange for Francesca and Jacopo to come and live with me in Paris, but the authorities don't look kindly on immigrants from Italy at the moment, especially Jewish ones. I'd hoped the fact that I took on French citizenship a year ago might help, but unfortunately it hasn't. Not that Francesca is willing to leave Venice. You know how stubborn she is. But things are getting very difficult there for her and Jacopo.

Since February, a new bill limiting Jews from owning real estate and conducting commercial activities has meant she can no longer

operate the perfumery. She is having to teach Jacopo at home as Jewish
children are banned from going to school. I fear I've left it too late to
get them out. I'm haunted every day by what might happen to them.

Iris studied her reflection. The pale blue dress was beautiful and complemented her blue eyes and blonde hair. But somehow, her appearance didn't give her any satisfaction. The world felt very vulnerable. As if everyone was teetering on the brink of hell, and some people were already there.

Jacopo must be eleven years old by now. She couldn't bear to think of him suffering. He was a bright, lively boy who should've been at school with his friends, a promising future ahead of him. Instead, he was being denied all this because he was Jewish.

Iris picked up the smooth grey pebble daubed in pink and red hearts that she kept in pride of place on the dressing table. She and Jacopo had spent hours collecting pebbles on the beach in Nice during that last visit in 1937 when her father was still alive. They'd decorated the stones in the kitchen at Mougins. At the end of the holiday, Jacopo had gifted her this one.

'Don't forget me, will you?' he'd said, wrapping his arms around her. He'd smelled of lavender soap and pain au chocolat, which they'd had for breakfast in the garden. 'Of course I won't,' Iris had replied, holding him tightly.

Iris placed the pebble down and sighed. That was the last time she'd seen him. Raffaele had begged his sister to remain in France and not return to Venice. But Francesca was adamant that she wanted to stay put in the city that was her home.

'I'll fight for our freedom if I have to,' she'd said as they parted at the train station. Raffaele had shaken his head. 'That's what worries me, my dear.'

Now it seemed that his worst fears had come true. Iris had read with horror of the imposition of anti-Jewish laws in Germany and the lands it now occupied. Italy had signed the Pact of Steel with Germany in May, and now Raffaele's homeland was imposing the same laws. No wonder he was terrified for Francesca and Jacopo.

The taxicab dropped Iris and Marcel off at Claridge's at eight o'clock. Even this illustrious hotel was preparing for war. The kerb had been painted white in case of blackouts and the lower windows were boarded up.

Charles had declined to attend as planned, saying he had too much work to do. Henri had gone back to Paris. In some ways, it was a relief to be here independently. That way she could have a proper talk with Raffaele.

Iris climbed the steps, carrying her gas mask and her evening bag, weighed down by her perfume notebook and the bottle of perfume. She hoped to consult Raffaele about it. Her heels click-clacked on the marble and the beads on her dress shimmered as she walked past the doorman. Marcel followed her to the French Salon, turning left down a wide corridor with black-and-white marbled tiles on the floor. Mirrors glimmered in the lamplight and neatly dressed waiters hurried past with glasses of champagne.

'Who's paying for this convention?' Iris asked.

'Mostly the French perfumers,' Marcel said, 'but they consider it worthwhile. The aim is to foster a spirit of cooperation among the artisan perfumers. With war looming, the committee decided to bring the date forward. It's a chance for people to show their latest products and discuss developments in the perfume world. Ernest Beaux, the man who made Chanel No. 5, was supposed to be coming. But he's pulled out. Some people prefer to stay close to home at the moment.'

A hubbub of conversation emanated from the door of the salon. A waiter handed Iris a glass of champagne and she took a gulp. The air was heady with a medley of scents, all vying for attention. Around the room, on tables covered with black cloths, stood tantalizing bottles and discreet signs displaying the names of artisan perfume houses. Iris had wanted to create a new scent with Marcel to exhibit here too. But Charles had vetoed the idea.

As she crossed the room, Iris smelled amber fragrances, chypre and mosses, citrus and woody notes all mixed together. The effect was dizzying but it set her senses alight. Marcel disappeared into the throng, leaving her to look around for Raffaele's familiar face.

There he was. Sitting quietly in the corner, understated as ever, despite his celebrated talent. Iris weaved through the crowd towards him. He had long white hair and a white beard. He looked older than when she'd last seen him, bowed down by his worries, but his face lit up when he saw her.

'My dear,' he said, 'I would hardly have recognized you. You've grown up since I last saw you in Paris and have blossomed into such a beauty.' He leaned forward and kissed Iris on both cheeks, glancing at the champagne glass in her hand. 'I'm glad to see you're celebrating your apprenticeship. Once I've got this damned speech out of the way, I want to hear all about it.'

Iris smiled and nodded, knowing that this wasn't the right time to tell him what had happened. His face was pale, and she knew how much he hated public speaking.

He'd felt obliged to accept the invitation to address the convention as it was such an honour.

A woman came over and gestured towards a raised dais at the end of the room.

'Wish me luck,' Raffaele said. He leaned on his stick and headed over towards the lectern.

Iris stayed at the side of the room, sipping her champagne. The chatter died down as the woman took to the stage.

'Good evening, and thank you to everyone for attending, especially those who have come over from the continent,' she said. 'I'm sure you'll agree that we are most fortunate to have Raffaele di Fiore here tonight from Paris. For twenty years, he has dazzled that city and beyond with his hand-crafted scents. We look forward to hearing his thoughts about how the artisan industry can survive, and indeed thrive, while facing the combined uncertainty of political and economic circumstances.'

The audience, who stood in clusters around the stage, applauded as Raffaele came forward to the lectern. Iris noticed a young man standing not far from the front. He was tall with broad shoulders that stretched the seams of his blue shirt and dark brown hair that was combed back. At that moment, his head turned and his eyes met hers. On the left side of his forehead ran a long scar. It reached from his hairline down to the edge of his eye. Strangely, it made him even more handsome. He was different to Henri, who seemed to flaunt his good looks. This man held a world of depth in his eyes. For a second the air around her seemed to vibrate, then he looked away, back to Raffaele.

Iris shook her head and finished the rest of her champagne, startled by her reaction. She fixed her eyes on Raffaele and focused on what he was saying.

'Thank you for letting me share my story,' Raffaele said, 'when it seems that, at the moment, a great many people are unwilling to listen to or empathize with others. Indeed, that is what sets us artisan perfumers apart from those who make scents in a factory. We have to interact with and listen to the people for whom we make them. Clients come to us with their stories – of love, loss, childhood, anniversaries, memories – and we attempt to capture them in a perfume. You see . . .' He paused and squinted at his notes. 'I mean . . .'

Iris watched anxiously. Raffaele appeared to have lost his thread. He cleared his throat. 'I'm sorry, I . . .' He tugged at his collar, his skin paled, and he swayed alarmingly.

The handsome man that Iris had noticed rushed forward. He gripped Raffaele in his arms, trying to steady him. The woman ushered them both off the dais and through a side door. She came back a moment later. 'I'm sorry, Signor di Fiore has been taken ill, I hope only temporarily. Please continue with your drinks and, hopefully, we can resume shortly.'

Iris put down her glass and rushed through the crowd. She'd never seen Raffaele looking so weak. What could be the matter with him? She opened the door through which he'd gone and found him lying on a sofa.

'Raffaele,' she said, kneeling at his side. 'What's happened? Are you okay?'

He smiled at her faintly, his lips dry. 'I don't know what came over me.'

The young man was still there, hovering uncertainly. Iris turned to him. 'Could you get him a glass of water, please? And perhaps something stronger too.'

The man nodded. 'Of course,' he said. Iris detected an Italian accent. 'I just wasn't sure what to do.'

'I can imagine. It's a shock to see him like this,' Iris said. 'I'll stay here while you go.'

The man headed out. The fresh scent of cologne lingered in the air. Iris detected cedarwood and another note, white moss perhaps, together with mandarin. It was an unusual combination but one that worked.

Iris turned back to Raffaele. 'How do you feel?' she said. She reached over and gently loosened his tie. 'Is that better?'

Raffaele closed his eyes. 'I don't know what came over me. One minute I was standing there, the next minute my notes were swimming in front of me and I couldn't catch my breath. It's so embarrassing.'

'It doesn't matter,' Iris said. 'The main thing is your health. Has this happened before?'

Raffaele nodded. 'A few times. I'm just exhausted.'

'And full of worries,' Iris said. 'Francesca and Jacopo's situation must weigh heavily on your mind.'

'It does,' Raffaele said, clutching her hand, 'but a weak heart doesn't help either. The doctor has been on at me for months to slow down. That's why I've hired an apprentice, although, with business booming, he has his work cut out.'

'You mean . . .' she said, glancing in the direction the young man had gone. That's why he had stepped forward so quickly. He must be Raffaele's new apprentice.

The young man came back into the room with two glasses in his hands. He crouched down beside Iris. '*Ecco, Signor di Fiore, beva prima il whisky, ti aiuterà a ristorarti.*'

Iris knew a little bit of Italian from spending time with Raffaele, but it was the man's tone of voice that struck her more than his words. It was full of care and kindness. He held the whisky glass up to Raffaele's lips. Raffaele took a sip and gradually the colour returned to his cheeks.

'*Grazie*,' Raffaele said. 'Iris, this is Alessandro Mori.'

Alessandro stared at her with interest. 'Raffaele has spoken of you often. I understand that you too have a passion for making perfumes.'

Iris smiled, her skin warmed by his interest. 'I do,' she said, feeling the heat of his attention. 'Although I have not been so fortunate as you. The apprenticeship that was supposed to come my way has not transpired. You are lucky, indeed, to have Raffaele to teach you.'

'But I thought it was all agreed,' Raffaele said. 'You finished your secretarial studies, surely, just as Charles demanded?'

Iris shrugged. 'I did everything he asked for, but Charles is planning to enlist and scale down the perfumery, and he wants me to accompany his fiancée to Scotland,' she said. 'I can't really blame him. As Charles pointed out, what's happening in Europe changes everything.'

Raffaele sighed. 'It certainly does.' He edged himself up to a sitting position. Alessandro was at his side, bolstering him with a cushion. 'But your skills are extraordinary. It seems a shame to waste them.'

'It would,' Alessandro's eyes dusted her lips, then flicked back to her face. 'I would love to see some of your work. Signor di Fiore is a great believer in learning from other perfumers.'

Raffaele patted his back. 'Indeed I am.'

'I *have* been working on a new scent,' Iris said shyly. 'But I'm not sure it's ready yet.'

'Have you got it here? I'd love to smell it,' Raffaele said.

'You need to rest,' Iris said. 'They're still hoping to hear your speech.'

'Ah, they can wait,' he said. 'And I'm feeling much better. It would do me good to see what you've created.'

'All right then.' Iris took the perfume out of her bag with trembling fingers and handed it to Raffaele.

'I wanted to re-create those summers in the south of France,' she said. 'The sunshine and the sea, the warm nights and the jasmine-scented air, that feeling of us all being together, before things changed. I didn't want it to be heavy. I'm aiming for something that's fresh.'

'I see,' Raffaele said. He opened the bottle and inhaled.

Iris waited with bated breath. Raffaele's signature scent, Vedendo, was world renowned. She trusted his judgement, but she also feared it.

Raffaele inclined his head. '*Non-male*,' he said. 'I can certainly picture the south of France. It's very unusual how you've created this marine-like smell.'

He handed the bottle to Alessandro, who sniffed the perfume and raised his eyebrows. 'Fascinating. Almost like a cologne. How have you done that? I feel like I'm smelling a sea breeze mixed with all the other scents of the night.'

Iris blushed. 'It's a bit unorthodox, I know. Marcel wasn't sure – it's not overtly feminine. The freshness comes from rosemary and lavender.'

Raffaele nodded. 'Very interesting. But this is just the beginning. You've set the scene – by the sea on a summer night – now you need to dig deeper into the story.'

Iris's heart sank. The scent wasn't good enough.

'Don't worry,' Raffaele said, 'it shows great potential. It just needs developing.'

Iris shook her head. 'But how can I do that stuck up in Scotland, miles away from anywhere? It's so frustrating. If only Charles would let me stay and help Marcel. There's so much I want to learn.' A thought struck her. She stared at Raffaele. 'I've just had a splendid idea. You need more help at the perfumery in Paris. I want to learn perfume-making. Why don't I come to Paris and work at your perfumery instead of going to Scotland? It's the perfect solution.'

It *was* the perfect solution. Charles would take some persuading, but she'd work on that later. If only Raffaele was willing to give her a try.

Raffaele frowned. 'I'm not sure. Charles wants to keep you safe from war. With the way things are, it might be a risk coming to Paris.'

Alessandro didn't look enthusiastic either. 'I'm not sure we need another apprentice,' he said. 'We've managed quite well, just the two of us.'

'Please,' Iris begged. 'I'll work hard. If there's the slightest sign of trouble in France, I can come home. I just want a chance to do what I'm passionate about.'

Raffaele rubbed his chin. 'It would depend on a few conditions. Much as I want to help the daughter of my friend and take more rest, I don't want to upset the balance in the perfumery.'

'There's certainly a lot to consider,' Alessandro said.

Iris bit back her frustration. Why was Alessandro so against it? Perhaps he feared the competition. Here, at last, was a flicker of hope. She had to convince Raffaele it was essential he took her on. And that meant reassuring Alessandro.

'I'm sure you're doing an incredible job,' she said. 'I wouldn't be there to undermine that. But you must know how it feels to want to follow your passion. I desperately want that chance too.'

Raffaele patted Alessandro's arm. 'Of course he knows. Alessandro was earning decent money as an attendant on the *Orient Express*, but he knew he wanted more. He'd been learning in his spare time with Francesca in her perfumery.

She contacted me and, the next thing, Alessandro was hanging up his blue-and-gold trimmed uniform and heading to Paris.'

'So, you must know Jacopo, Francesca's son,' Iris said, hoping to find a common bond.

'Yes.' Alessandro smiled. 'Such a wonderful child. He loved playing cards with me after my lesson with Francesca. He beat me most of the time.'

Raffaele looked thoughtfully at the two of them. 'You know, maybe this could work, if Charles will permit it. Another pair of hands, especially as skilled as yours, Iris, would help enormously.'

'Oh, thank you,' Iris said. 'I won't let you down.'

Raffaele put up his hand. 'Not so fast, my dear. I said there would be conditions. If I'm going to take you on, I need to know that you and Alessandro can work together, that I can trust you to cooperate in the perfumery.'

He looked at his watch. 'I'd better return to the convention. I suggest you get your travelling perfumer's case, Alessandro, and take Iris to the Fumoir bar. I want you to work together to bring her scent up to the standard I expect.'

A test. Iris clenched her jaw. She had to pass it. She had to show Raffaele she had what it took to perfect the scent and work with Alessandro.

'Very well,' Alessandro said, clearly still uncertain about the situation.

Raffaele stretched out his hands. Iris took one arm, Alessandro supported the other, and together they lifted him up. 'So, Iris, let's see what you can do. While you two work, I have a speech to give.'

*

The Fumoir bar was empty. Iris chose a spot in the corner. Alessandro put his case on the table and sat down. 'So, I suppose we'd better see what we can do,' he said. 'May I smell the scent again?'

Iris handed him the bottle. He was probably doing this because he had to rather than because he wanted to. 'What do you think will improve it?'

It wasn't that she really wanted Alessandro's advice, but that's what Raffaele had instructed. She only needed to prove that they could work together and the apprenticeship would be hers.

Alessandro took a test paper out of his case, dipped it in the perfume and closed his eyes to inhale the scent. 'It is very good,' he said, grudgingly.

Iris flushed. 'Maybe, but there's obviously something missing. I understand what Raffaele means. This scent could be any holiday. With Vedendo, you can tell that the scent started off as a unique memory for Raffaele.'

Alessandro nodded. 'He told me the story of Vedendo the first time I met him. He said that the scent encapsulates the night he fell in love with someone he could never have,' he said. 'In one sentence, he paints a whole picture, and from that he makes the most complex and intense scent imaginable.'

Iris took the bottle and inhaled the contents again. 'So that's what I need,' she said. 'A sentence.'

Alessandro sat back and folded his arms. 'I can't really help you there,' he said. 'This scent is based on your memories. What precise moment do you want to focus on?'

His questioning was surprisingly helpful, though she wouldn't have admitted it. Amid the sunshine, the picnics, swimming in the sea and family dinners, which moment had clung to her heart? All at once she knew.

'I want a scent that encapsulates the moment I realized that I wanted to be a perfumer,' she said.

'Still too vague,' Alessandro said, 'Raffaele will want you to be more specific.'

Iris hesitated. The memory was so deep, so personal, she wasn't sure if she could share it. But for the sake of the apprenticeship, she must.

'All right, I'll try,' she said. She thought for a moment. 'We were in Mougins. The air was still warm, the heat bringing out the scent of the jasmine. I noticed a man and a woman sitting on their balcony talking.'

She pictured it in her mind, almost forgetting that she was sitting in Claridge's with a man she hardly knew.

'What happened?' Alessandro said.

'He whispered something to her, and she laughed, but he didn't smile. He looked very serious. He lifted her wrist, drinking in her scent, then kissed it, and she stopped laughing and simply gazed at him. There was such intensity between them, like a bright spark.' Iris hesitated, remembering. 'I realized that as a perfumer, you can make a scent that is present at the most intimate moments of a person's life. That's what I wanted to do.'

That day had changed her life.

Alessandro cleared his throat. 'I see,' he said. '*La scintilla*. That spark when you are with someone or find something you're passionate about, and just know.'

Iris blushed. 'Is that the Italian word for it? Yes, that's what I mean. That couple knew they wanted each other. I knew that all I ever wanted was to be a perfumer.'

'Well, I'm sure Raffaele will be impressed.' Alessandro opened the case of ingredients. 'You just need to build on the scent you've created.'

Iris looked at the bottles. She read the labels and separated out the ones that might be useful. She needed scents that smelled earthy: indole, which was musky, and cedarwood oil.

Alessandro cast his eye over her choices. 'You've gone for ingredients that conjure the physical sensations,' he said.

He glanced at Iris's wrist, then looked away. She was suddenly aware of him not as a reluctant work colleague and perfumer, both of which he still was, but also as a man.

Time was running out. There was only half an hour left according to the clock behind the bar. Iris focused on the scent, taking out her perfume journal and making notes. Without weighing scales, she'd have to measure with drops, an imperfect method due to the varying weights of the liquids, but it would have to do. She sniffed each ingredient as she worked.

'Indole, three drops, and four of frankincense,' she said, making a note on the page.

She shook the bottle, then inhaled the scent. 'Do you think it's nearly there?' she said.

Alessandro closed his eyes and inhaled. He took his time, which gave Iris an opportunity to look at his face. The slight rise on his nose where he'd probably broken it once. The long scar, the skin tight and stitch marks visible. Then he opened his eyes, and she realized there were flecks in his dark brown irises that were like gold filigree. She blushed, embarrassed to be caught staring, but he didn't seem to notice.

'You need more cedarwood,' he said. 'That should dominate as the base note.'

'But won't that take it off balance?' Iris asked.

'No. I think it's needed, the warm and spicy, fiery spark

to balance out the aqua notes. It will linger on the skin and fits with what you described. Maybe a drop of lime for the top note,' he said, sitting back, arms folded. 'But it's up to you. You don't have to take my advice.'

Mindful of Raffaele's words, Iris did as Alessandro suggested. To her amazement, when she tried the scent, it was exactly right.

'Goodness me,' she said with delight. 'That's it! Here, you smell it too.'

She held a fresh test strip under Alessandro's nose.

'That's perfect,' he said.

The clock on the wall behind the bar chimed. 'Raffaele will have finished his speech. We'd better get back.'

Alessandro shook his head. 'I'm going to stay here and have a drink. You can go and take the glory for yourself,' he said.

There was still a hint of resentment in his voice. He was probably just as ambitious as Iris and wanted to be the sole apprentice.

'Look, I meant what I said,' she said. 'I'm not trying to take your place or anything.'

Alessandro sighed. 'Perhaps not. But if our income drops, Raffaele won't be able to keep us both on. You obviously have a close relationship with him. I'm no fool – he's not going to leave you out in the cold. It's my career that will suffer.'

'I don't think that's the case. Why are you so determined to see my coming to the perfumery as a negative thing? You should have more confidence in your own abilities.'

She picked up the bottle with the modified scent. Alessandro had no reason to take against her. She put her notebook in her bag and stood up. She wouldn't let his attitude get in her way.

'Wait,' Alessandro said, standing up too. 'You're right. I've only been working with Raffaele for a few months. I *do* doubt myself. Francesca said it was always my one drawback.'

Iris smiled cautiously. 'Only one drawback?' she said, with a laugh to her voice.

'Well, obviously, I'm not perfect.' He bit his lip. 'You deserve a chance, Iris. I'm sorry I haven't been more encouraging.'

She nodded. 'Thanks.'

He reached out and touched her elbow briefly. A warmth lingered where his hand had been. 'Look, you need to give the scent a name. Raffaele will expect it.'

Iris thought for a moment. Only one name came to mind. She was loath to give Alessandro the credit, but the name fitted perfectly.

'I'll call it La Scintilla,' she said. 'If you've no objections.'

Alessandro smiled. 'That's the perfect name,' he said. 'Good luck. If you can persuade your brother, I think we'll be working together in Paris soon.'

'We will.'

Iris walked out of the bar with the new perfume in her hand, certain that Alessandro's eyes were burning into her back. She resisted the urge to turn round. If she got this apprenticeship, it would mean working with Alessandro every day. Unexpectedly, he had played a crucial part in helping her towards achieving her dream of being a perfumer's apprentice.

5

Stella – London, May 1996

Stella walked back from Claridge's, thinking over her conversation with James. It was a mild evening and the trees in Berkeley Square rustled in the breeze. She waited for tears to come, to feel something about their relationship ending. But there was nothing.

She crossed the road at Piccadilly and headed past the Ritz. Black cabs pulled in and out by the entrance, and men and women, dressed to the nines, were gathered on the steps, presumably arriving for some function. Stella dodged between them and turned into St James's Street. Over the years, she'd always managed to keep her boyfriends at arm's length. It was better that way, especially when things didn't work out. But, somehow, the lack of emotion about James made her feel that she was missing out on something. How could she ever find a soulmate if she wasn't willing to take a leap of faith and trust someone? Stella's parents' unhappy marriage, which resulted in her mother following her new partner to Australia, wasn't much of an inspiration. It seemed that her father had been unable to run Penhallam's and have a meaningful relationship at the same time. Stella feared having a similar fate.

The sun had nearly set when Stella arrived back at the shop. She locked the door behind her and stared around. Usually, the sight of it never failed to calm her nerves.

The dark polished wood, the clean lines of glass bottles arranged on the shelves, the domed cloches under which scented wax emitted a taster scent. She loved it all. But this evening it made her panic. The heavy wooden cabinets that had stood for decades seemed burdensome in her mind.

Then she noticed that the light on the basement stairs was still on. Bruno must have forgotten to turn it off. She'd have to speak to him about being more careful. Wasting electricity was only going to make the finances worse.

As she made her way down to the archives and rounded the shelves, there, standing on a stepladder, was Bruno. He was getting a box down from the top shelf, his arms stretched out, his muscles taut.

'Bruno,' she said. 'What are you still doing here?'

He turned towards her, startled. The box toppled on to the floor and he struggled to keep his balance. Stella rushed over to hold the ladder steady. He gripped her shoulders, laughing.

'*Dio mio*,' he said. 'You gave me a shock.'

He climbed down just inches away from where she stood. Static buzzed as his arm brushed hers. The air pulsed with the scent of his aftershave.

'Sorry,' she said, stepping back. 'I didn't expect you to be here so late.'

Bruno straightened up the fallen box. 'I'm only here a couple more weeks,' he said with a smile. 'I want to get it sorted before I go.'

The basement really did look better. Things had been stored down here for years, since before her grandfather's time: files and old perfume-making equipment. She also noticed evidence of Bruno's presence. A bottle-green cardigan hung over the chair by the desk; on it, books splayed open, handwritten notes on a pad, a scattering of photographs.

James's advice about the perfumery came into her mind. *Why not take a dive down into the Penhallam archives? You might be surprised by what you find.*

'So, what exactly are you researching?' Stella asked. Perhaps she should have taken more of an interest before. These papers were Penhallam's property, after all. 'You said your book was about perfumes before and during the war.'

'Yes. Everyone knows about the big names – Bourjois Paris, Chanel No. 5, Narcisse Noir, Shalimar, Femme, Bandit – but it's the artisan perfumeries I'm looking at. The ones in London and Paris.'

'Were there many?'

'There were a few. I'm particularly interested in an Italian-Jewish perfumer called Raffaele di Fiore.'

'I'm not familiar with him. If you find any information, what will you do with it?' Stella asked.

'It'll form the basis of my fourth book. I've got the summer left for research and then I need to head back to Venice for the autumn term. If my book is a success, there's a permanent position I'm hoping to get.'

So, despite his casual attire, Bruno was actually quite ambitious. But Stella still didn't quite understand his motives for coming to London.

'And remind me, what has Penhallam's got to do with your project?'

'I didn't think you had time to talk to me about it,' Bruno said, raising his eyebrows.

Stella blushed. 'Sorry if I've given that impression. Things have been rather trying recently. Penhallam's isn't doing too well at the moment, and I was hoping there might be a solution down here.'

Bruno folded his arms. 'It's long overdue for a sort-out,' he said. 'Some of the papers go back years. The conditions down here aren't ideal. It's damp too. You need to get waterproof storage boxes.'

Stella nodded. 'It's been neglected, I know. The archives were never of any interest to my father, and I suppose I've had my work cut out since he died.'

Bruno's eyes crinkled sympathetically. '*Scusi*,' he said. 'It must have been a very difficult time for you. I'm sorry.' He reached out his hand and briefly touched Stella's arm. It was fleeting, no more than a second, but the warmth of the gesture startled her.

'It's fine,' she said. The feeling of his touch burned on her skin. 'Maybe I can get some better storage containers. It's just the perfumery is a bit strapped for cash at the moment. But I'll see what we can do.'

Stella picked up one of the black-and-white photos on the desk. Three people stood on a platform, a steam train in the background. An older gentleman stood leaning on a stick, next to him a clear-eyed young woman looked warily at the camera and, next to her, a young, handsome man scowled.

'Who are these people?' she asked.

Bruno stood close to her as he looked at the photo and she was hit with *that* scent again. She almost closed her eyes to savour it. James had always had such a clean, fresh smell, all citrus and herbs. At first it had seemed dynamic. But, inhaling Bruno's deeper scent, she realized that James's had been rather bland.

'I came across it when researching in Paris,' he said. 'Raffaele di Fiore is the old man on the left. He was a perfumer in Paris in the twenties and thirties. I'm not sure of the identity of the young man on the right. But the woman in the middle is your great-aunt.'

Stella looked at him, surprised. 'My great-aunt?'

'Yes, Iris Penhallam. Look, it says so on the back.' He turned the photograph over. Her name was written on the back, along with a date: 1939. 'It's fascinating to see her with Raffaele. That's why I knew I had to come to Penhallam's.'

Stella stared at the photo. She'd never met Iris. A family estrangement after the war meant that her grandfather had never wanted to hear her name mentioned. She'd only heard snippets about Iris, but it seemed that the falling-out had been irrevocable on both sides. The woman who stared out at Stella from the photograph looked very young. But her eyes had a steely determination about them. 'I don't understand,' Stella said. 'Where was this taken?'

'The Gare de Lyon, I believe, judging by the ironwork,' Bruno said. 'It proves a connection between the London and Paris perfumers. One of the themes of my book will be how they influenced each other.'

Bruno went to the desk and picked up a yellowed piece of paper. It was a letter, written in neat, sloping handwriting with a fountain pen.

'This is what I wanted to talk to you about. I found this down here the other day,' he said. 'It's dated 1955, and it's from a man called Jacopo to Charles Penhallam, your grandfather. It shows that Iris didn't just know Raffaele, she went to work for him, as an apprentice.'

Stella listened as Bruno read the letter out loud.

Dear Mr Penhallam
Please forgive my writing unannounced like this, but I will be forever

indebted to your sister, Iris, and what she did for me in the war. Her efforts, along with those of Alessandro Mori and Tommaso Ricci, saved my life.

I would be very grateful for your help with two matters.

The first concerns Iris herself. I know there has been some trouble for her since the war ended. I don't know the full extent of what happened, only what I've gleaned in the papers, but please can you tell her that I bear her no ill will. I most sincerely hope that you will pass that on to her. I wish she had contacted me at the time. I might have been able to help with my version of events.

The second matter is somewhat more complicated. During the brief time that I was with Iris in 1939, she and a man named Alessandro Mori were both apprentices of Raffaele di Fiore, my uncle. They were working on a collection of five scents.

Iris and Alessandro were kind enough to let me sample some of the perfumes, and I have to say, since that day I've not been able to get the memory of them out of my head. Perhaps it was because of the intensity of those days, or because I've come to associate those scents with freedom, but I find myself longing to smell them again.

Do you perhaps have the original perfume bottles? Could they be replicated and sent to me? Or do you have any information about the perfumes' whereabouts? Maybe Iris might know where they are. Unfortunately, I have not been able to find any trace of Alessandro Mori. I wish I could come and search in person, but I'm indisposed and unlikely to be able to make the journey over to Europe for the foreseeable future.

I was parted from Iris and Alessandro in very difficult circum-stances, but I owe them both my life. If there is anything you can do to help me trace the perfumes, I would be eternally grateful.

Yours sincerely

Jacopo Calvetti

'I had a hunch that I'd find out more about Raffaele at Penhallam's,' Bruno said, pointing to the letter. 'But this is incredible. The letter proves that your great-aunt Iris definitely was his apprentice, and it looks like she was involved in creating a collection of five perfumes for him.'

Stella stared at Bruno. Iris had been a perfumer. Stella had had no idea. None of the old ledgers made any mention of her creations. Questions burst into her head. Why had she gone to Paris? What kind of perfumes had she created? The mention of five scents and the mysterious story that lay behind Jacopo's words set her thoughts alight. This was exactly the kind of archival material James had been talking about – a narrative that could sell perfume in huge volumes. She looked around the basement. Perhaps the perfumes were somewhere right here in this room.

'What do you think?' Bruno said.

'I think this is incredible,' she said. 'It's just that . . .'

Stella had never met Iris. From what she'd gathered, Charles and Iris had become estranged after the war. Stella had grown up thinking that Iris must be bad news for such a rift to have occurred. No one spoke well of her, not even her father. She thought back to the first time she'd heard Iris's name.

It was Christmas, and Stella was thirteen. Her grandfather had drunk a few too many sherries and was recounting the ups and downs of Penhallam's.

'Of course, I blame Iris,' he'd said. 'She had the talent and wasted it. She was an extraordinarily gifted perfumer but never knew where her limits lay. She left us and ran off to Paris. She preferred to stay in France. Instead of helping her family, she nearly ruined us. She was a disgrace.'

'Who is Iris?' Stella had asked timorously. Her grandfather was not an easy man to talk to, but she was curious. She knew the word 'iris' as a flower, not as a person. There were irises growing under the perfumery window.

'Iris was my sister. Your father's aunt. *Your* great-aunt.'

'Why don't I know about her?'

'She's not worth knowing about. She failed us, Stella, never forget that. Too interested in serving her own vain ambitions. Never a thought for anyone but herself.' He'd downed the rest of his glass, his red face moving closer to Stella's. 'We've got to keep people like that out. This business is ours: mine, your father's – and one day it'll be yours. People like Iris don't deserve anything.'

'What are you talking about?' Her father had come in from the kitchen and caught the tail end of the conversation.

Her grandfather sat up straighter in his wing-backed chair. 'Oh, nothing. Just my disappointing sister.'

'I don't think that's a good idea.' Her father gave Charles a warning glance. 'Your long-lost sister has no place in our lives now, after everything she did.'

'What did she do?' Stella asked.

Her father and grandfather exchanged a knowing look.

'Never mind,' her father said. 'It's not worth spoiling Christmas Day for.'

'But I want to know.'

'No,' he said, his voice weary. 'Just drop it, Stella, please.'

Sensing that another question would push his patience too far, Stella said no more.

Whoever Iris was, she had clearly behaved badly. Not long after that Christmas her grandfather had died and the burden of running the business had passed to her father.

Stella had tried raising the subject of Iris once again, after her father discovered her searching for correspondence between Charles and Iris in the office desk drawers. He'd shaken his head, a sorrowful look in his eyes. 'You won't find anything. Your grandfather burned all the letters when I was a child,' he had said, his face pained. 'She brought shame to this family. She did unspeakable things during the war that could have tainted the Penhallam name forever. That's why your grandfather cut her off after the war ended and he found out what she'd done. All you need to know is that we must never have anything to do with Iris again. Your grandfather was very clear on that. Do you understand?'

Stella had nodded, her curiosity piqued even further by the mystery of her disgraceful great-aunt, but not wanting to upset her father. Even now, staring at this letter, which must have remained buried down here forgotten, ideas ran through her mind about the five scents. She felt guilty as to what her father and grandfather would have said if they knew Stella was even entertaining the idea of looking for the scents to save Penhallam's.

'Are you all right?' Bruno asked. 'I know it's a lot to take in. To think those scents might be right here in the archives.'

It wasn't Bruno's fault. He wasn't to know that Stella was still burdened by her father's words not to get involved in anything to do with Iris.

'I'm not sure Iris Penhallam is the answer I'm looking for,' she said.

'But that letter is fascinating – it's just begging to be explored further,' Bruno protested. 'Since I've been down here, I haven't stumbled upon anything half so interesting.

Believe me, I've done enough of these research projects to know when I've struck gold, and this is it.'

'It's complicated,' Stella said, putting the letter and the photograph in her pocket. 'You see, there was a big rift between Iris and my grandfather that started just after the Second World War ended. The animosity carried on through my father. We had no contact with Iris at all. It would go against his wishes, and those of my grandfather, to risk linking Penhallam's to Iris.' Stella rubbed her forehead. It suddenly felt hot and airless down here.

'Why don't we go upstairs and take some fresh air?' Bruno said softly. 'Being down here can drive you crazy.'

'Yes,' Stella said. 'Let's get out of here.'

She followed him upstairs, through the perfumery, and into the little courtyard garden, fringed with lavender and irises. It seemed ironic that irises grew here, named after the very woman whose scents she felt honour-bound not to explore further. It was a clear night. The moon shone and the sky was orange with the glow of the city. Stella sat down next to Bruno on the wooden bench and took a deep breath.

'Sorry. I don't know what came over me,' she said, embarrassed at letting him see her in a state.

'What happened between your grandfather and Iris?' Bruno said.

'Like I said, I don't know much, but Iris apparently brought disgrace to the Penhallam name during the war,' she said. 'She and my grandfather were permanently estranged from the end of the war right up until he died. She must have done something terrible because even my father refused to countenance any contact with her.'

'But does that have to prevent you from finding out

more?' Bruno said. 'These five scents could be useful.'

Bruno rested his arm on the back of the bench, his hand almost touching her shoulder. For a moment, Stella wondered what it would be like to lean against him and feel his arms around her.

'It's hard to explain,' she said. 'It probably sounds ridiculous to you. But the way my grandfather and father talked about Iris, as if she was a bitter enemy of the family, I'd feel like I was going against their wishes. I'm sorry if I've wasted your time.'

'You haven't.'

For a moment, he contemplated her steadily. It was the strangest feeling, but for a few seconds, looking into his eyes, Stella forgot about Penhallam's and all her responsibilities. Then it all came crashing back in.

'I need to get some sleep,' she said.

Bruno nodded. 'Good idea. I'm going to pack up downstairs and head back to the hotel. I can lock up.'

'Thank you.'

'But surely there's no harm if I at least look for the scents while I'm clearing up the basement?'

Stella sighed. The weight of her grandfather's and father's disapproval lay heavily on her shoulders. Despite what they'd said, her curiosity about Iris had still lingered. The scents probably wouldn't be there anyway. 'Okay, you might as well see.'

Upstairs in her room, Stella knelt down by her camp bed, took out the photograph and letter from her pocket and laid them out in front of her. They weren't the answers she'd been looking for, but, staring at the photograph, it was impossible not to wonder about what they meant.

Whispers from a past about which she knew nothing. And Bruno had found them. She tucked them away again. Bruno's presence here was unsettling, in every way.

6

Iris – London, July 1939

The high, open ceilings of St James's Church were flooded with sunlight. Iris loved the crisp white walls and gold stucco. As a child, sitting here with her father on one side and Charles on the other, she'd liked to imagine the church was decorated with icing.

The church was empty now. It was Wednesday afternoon, and she had finally plucked up the courage to speak to Charles about the apprenticeship at Raffaele's perfumery. Raffaele had been delighted with La Scintilla and pronounced that the alliance of Iris and Alessandro had promise. He'd offered to talk to Charles before he went back to Paris, but Iris preferred to speak to him herself.

Charles was hunched over in the pew as if in prayer or deep thought. Iris had a moment's hesitation and then clenched her fists. Somehow, she had to make him understand.

She slid on to the pew next to him. Charles gave her a look of annoyance at the unexpected interruption. 'What are you doing here?' he said.

'Father always loved coming to this church,' Iris said. She looked over at the wall where Alistair's memorial plaque had been placed.

Charles nodded. 'Yes, he liked the smell of the incense, said it helped him feel more spiritual.'

Iris nodded. 'I know what he means.' She clasped her hands together. 'I have something to tell you, if you've got a moment.'

Charles narrowed his eyes. 'What?'

It was best to be direct. 'I went to see Raffaele the other day. He's aged considerably and isn't in the best health. He's taken on an apprentice, but there's still too much work, so he asked if I could go to Paris and help him,' Iris said. This wasn't strictly true, but it seemed the most persuasive way of explaining things.

Charles shook his head. 'Absolutely not. It's out of the question.' He picked up his coat and stood up. 'Now, if you'll excuse me, I've got two weeks before I head off to training camp. And I believe you have some packing to do for Scotland.'

Iris touched his arm. 'Wait. Just listen for a moment. I accept what you say about Penhallam's and not taking me on as an apprentice. In fact, after thinking it over, I fully support your decision. Father left Penhallam's to you because he trusted your judgement,' she said. 'But I can't bear the thought of going to Scotland. Jane is lovely, but I don't know her family and I'd have nothing to do up there. This way, I can be useful. Raffaele was one of Father's dearest friends. Father would be glad that I was helping him.'

Charles pressed his hand to his forehead. 'Iris, you've read the papers, you're not blind. War is coming. You won't be immune from that over in Paris. In fact, you might find yourself in the firing line. I can't allow it. It's my job to keep you safe and ensure that the unblemished reputation of the Penhallam name is upheld. I can't do that if you're over in France.'

Iris stood up. 'If things turn complicated in Europe' – Charles raised an eyebrow – 'all right, even *more* complicated, I promise I'll come home. I can be back from northern France at the first sign of trouble. Please, Charles. I will be perfectly safe, and I won't disgrace the Penhallam name, I promise.'

'I'm not going to discuss it any more,' Charles said. He turned on his heel and walked down the aisle.

'Charles, wait . . .' Iris hurried after him. Outside, by the railings, she tugged on his sleeve. 'I need to do this. You go into the church and sit there quietly to be close to Father. I create perfumes for the same reason. I beg you, please let me go and help Raffaele. Surely we can come to some compromise. I'll do anything if you let me go.'

Charles folded his arms. The scent of the roses and freesias wafted over from a vase near one of the graves.

'No, Iris,' he said. 'You think being an apprentice is the be all and end all. But other things are more important.'

'What do you mean?' Iris said, puzzled by his words.

A group of children led by a governess, each carrying a gas-mask box around their necks, wandered towards the church door.

'We can't talk here,' Charles said. 'Come on, let's go to my office.'

Iris followed him over to Penhallam's, anxiously wondering what this was all about. Charles climbed the stairs to his office in silence and then closed the door behind them. Iris sat down in front of the desk. Charles opened the sash window and turned to face her.

'Well, what's more important than the apprenticeship?' Iris asked.

'Marriage,' Charles said. 'Father always wanted you to

marry well. You were the apple of his eye, after all, and do you know who he had in mind as a suitor?'

Iris shook her head. 'No, he never said.'

'He thought you and Henri would make a fine match.' Charles gave a weak smile. 'Sometimes I think Father saw more of himself in Henri than in me.'

Henri was the one who swam furthest, ran fastest, walked with a swagger and held his own at any party. Charles had never had those gifts, but her father had always compared him to Henri.

'Charles, I'm sure it wasn't meant unkindly . . .'

Charles waved his hand. 'It doesn't matter. It's all in the past. If, God willing, Jane and I are lucky enough to have a son, I would do things differently, but that's beside the point. The point is that Father was right about one thing. If you married Henri, it would be a very good thing for you . . . and for Penhallam's.'

'I don't understand.'

Charles came over to his desk and sat down in the leather chair. 'This building is leasehold. That means, in a couple of years, when the lease that our great-great-grand-father took out is finished, we'll need to purchase a new one. Except we don't have enough money. With the war coming, our income is likely to decline even further.'

'Then why are you enlisting when you don't have to yet?' Iris said. 'Surely it would be better to stay here and do all you can for Penhallam's until they bring in conscription, if war does break out.'

Charles rubbed his temples. 'I'm enlisting because I need to feel useful again. Here, I'm fighting a losing battle. Penhallam's is failing, and I'd rather wind down the business for the time being and save money than watch it happen.'

Iris gripped the arms of the chair. 'But what if there's no business left in a few years?'

'That's where Henri comes in.' Charles tapped his fingers on the desk. 'I happen to agree with Father that the two of you would be a good match. Our families know each other well, and you are bright, skilled, intelligent, beautiful in your own way. I believe Henri thinks so too.'

Iris stared at Charles. 'Surely not?' she said, astonished.

'He's hinted as much,' Charles said, leaning forward. 'Henri's a rich man. If you married him, you wouldn't just be following your heart and Father's wishes, you'd be securing Penhallam's for future generations.'

Future generations. The phrase caused a dull ache in Iris's chest. Her adoration of Henri belonged to the past. She'd sensed a change in him, gleaned hints that he admired her, but marriage? Surely that wasn't his intention. He was a seductive charmer, but Iris couldn't picture him proposing. Of course, as a child, she'd made up stories about Henri sweeping her off to his castle like a princess, but she'd never really believed it would happen. She still didn't believe it. But Charles seemed to, and perhaps that presented her with an opportunity to convince him to let her go to Paris.

Iris went over to the open window and gazed down at the courtyard and the haze of purple lavender in the flowerbeds. Last time Charles had asked her to do something, she'd obeyed unquestioningly in return for an apprenticeship. This time, he didn't even think he needed to offer anything to her. He thought marrying Henri would be all that she wanted.

Iris closed her eyes. The breeze wafted over her face. It was up to her to fight for her independence. Charles would never grant it. And, right now, she held the key to something Charles wanted: Henri's money. She'd never really stood up to her older brother before. But now it was time.

She went over to his desk, her feet planted firmly on the Persian rug.

'Charles, I want to help Raffaele. He needs me. And truth be told, I need him too. I'm sorry that you don't agree with my plan. But I do believe there is a compromise to be reached if, as you say, Penhallam's would benefit from me marrying Henri one day.'

Charles shifted in his chair. 'Go on.'

At least he was listening. Iris hoped her thudding heart didn't make her voice waver.

'It's true I have always adored Henri from afar. But I was a child. I am willing to consider marrying him, in a year or two, but not without knowing him better. So, this is what I propose. You let me go to Paris and work for Raffaele . . .'

Charles opened his mouth to protest. Iris put up her hand to stop him. 'And, in return, I will stay with Henri and his mother. That way there's no disgrace attached to me being in Paris alone, Henri will keep me safe in your stead and we can get to know each other.'

'And what happens if I refuse your compromise?' Charles said.

'I have my own will, Charles. It's time you recognized that.'

Charles narrowed his eyes. 'Doesn't the future of Penhallam's mean anything to you?'

'Of course it does,' Iris said. 'But I won't be a sacrificial lamb. Let me have the apprenticeship I deserve and, I promise, I will consider the idea of marrying Henri while I'm in Paris.'

Iris was determined not to look away. The silence length-ened. If he didn't agree, there was precious little she could do other than scrape her savings together and run away.

Charles sighed. 'You're tougher than I thought, Iris,' he said, a note of grudging admiration in his voice. 'All right, you have one year. After that, I expect you to marry Henri.'

'Very well.' It was easy to say yes because Iris was certain Henri had no such plans in mind. She let out her breath. She'd done it. She was going to Paris.

7

Stella – London, May 1996

A week had passed since the discovery of the letter and the photograph of Raffaele, Iris and the unknown man. Bruno had been combing through the archives for Iris's scents, but so far he'd found nothing. Stella hovered between relief and disappointment. Not finding the scents meant avoiding the question of going against her family's wishes. But there were literally no other legitimate vintage scents to be found either, and with each day that passed, Penhallam's teetered on the brink of collapse.

The contents of the letter drifted through Stella's mind, a thousand questions making it impossible to concentrate on her work. Had those mysterious perfumes ever been made? If so, did they still exist? And what of Iris, the great-aunt Stella had never met? Was she still alive?

She looked up at the family portraits. It was no good: she had to at least find out why Iris had been off limits to the family for so long. Averting her eyes from her father's reproachful stare, Stella turned to her computer. Maybe she could glean something about all this from the internet. She typed in a search for Iris Penhallam, but nothing came up. What was the name of the perfumer that Bruno had mentioned? Raffaele di Fiore. She typed in his name.

Pages of results came up – all based in Italy. She scanned

through several entries, but they were just men with the same name. The search needed to be more specific. Stella narrowed the search down by adding 'Paris' and 'perfumer' to his name.

Only two results came up this time. The first was an eBay listing for an empty bottle of a perfume by Raffaele di Fiore called Vedendo. The bottle was black with a gold chain around the neck. The starting bid was £400. That was an enormous sum of money. Ten times what they'd charge for a thirty-millilitre bottle at Penhallam's. No doubt it was a rare find: scarcity in vintage perfumes tended to drive the price up. Stella returned to the search results.

The second listing directed Stella to a website archive of past copies of *Le Figaro*. The link went straight to one particular issue: Mercredi, 6 Septembre 1939, page trois. Stella stared at the tiny printed script. War had been declared against Germany by Britain and France only three days earlier. The headlines were full of news about the troops and the Maginot Line.

In among the other news a small headline tucked on the bottom-left-hand corner of the page caught Stella's eye.

Signor Raffaele di Fiore announces a new collection of perfumes

Di Fiore apprentices Iris Penhallam and Alessandro Mori are travelling to Milan on the Orient Express *to create three new scents inspired by the journey. These will be added to the two scents that have already been composed by these talented apprentices – La Scintilla and Primo Bacio – to make a stunning collection of five scents. Signor di Fiore commented, 'In these uncertain and troubled times, I want to make sure that nobody forgets what really matters:*

*the human capacity for love. We are going on a journey to capture
what it means to fall in love.'*

*Di Fiore's perfumery at No. 23 rue Bayard will unveil the full
collection, entitled The Perfumer's Secret, in early 1940.*

Stella sat back in her chair. There it was. The first official
mention of the lost perfumes that Jacopo had cited in
his letter. The idea for the collection was stunning. Stella
knew instantly that these perfumes could be a hit for
Penhallam's. The romance of the journey and the idea of
capturing what it meant to fall in love: surely that would
appeal to stockists and customers. Stella's mind got to
work, thinking of how the perfumes could be packaged
and marketed.

A knock at the office door startled her from her
thoughts. Arnold came in. He worked a couple of half
days in a little room next to Stella's. Before the financial
problems, Stella had employed an administrator, so the
calls still went through to that phone.

'It's Andrea from GPL,' he said, raising his eyebrows.
'Says she needs to talk to you.'

Stella's stomach somersaulted. What did Andrea want?
Save for that one brief conversation at a work function,
Stella had never properly spoken to Andrea before; she
had been far too high up at GPL to notice Stella. She took
a deep breath and picked up the phone.

'Good morning,' Stella said apprehensively.

'Hi, Stella,' Andrea said in her warm Californian accent.
'Sorry to call you out of the blue like this, but it couldn't
wait. I hear House of Fraser isn't likely to renew their order
with Penhallam's.'

Stella sucked in her breath. Christ, how did she know about House of Fraser? The only person who could have told her was James.

'You must have heard wrong,' she said, keeping her voice firm. 'We have a long-standing relationship with House of Fraser and our other stockists.'

'So, House of Fraser isn't dropping you, is that what you're telling me?'

'No,' Stella said. But there was no point lying if James had already told Andrea what she'd told him in confidence. 'Not yet, anyway. The market is tough for small businesses at the moment, but Penhallam's is finding a way through.'

'Ah,' Andrea said. Stella heard the rustle of papers down the telephone line. 'I see you were with us for a couple of years before moving back into the family firm.'

'Yes,' Stella said cautiously, wondering where this was going.

'You've taken on quite a lot, I imagine.'

'Nothing I can't handle.'

Andrea laughed. 'Look, I believe James has already floated the idea of a buyout. I want to make that offer concrete; I'll email over the terms. It's a very generous offer, considering Penhallam's situation.'

'I've already told James I'm not interested.'

'Stella,' Andrea said, a hint of steeliness in her tone. 'Your family business is struggling, and GPL is the best option you've got. Which would you rather have? No Penhallam's and be out of a job, or a Penhallam's supported by GPL and run by you as managing director? I'd be willing to grant you that for a trial period. Your track record with us shows you have promise.'

Stella swallowed. Andrea had a reputation for being determined. It was easy to see why. 'I appreciate your interest, but Penhallam's isn't for sale. I'm handling this in my own way and I'm confident we'll survive.'

Andrea sighed. 'I admire your pluck. But you're running out of options. No doubt you've already taken on a loan?'

Stella's chest tightened. Had James told her that too? 'That's none of your business,' she said.

'If you say so,' Andrea countered. 'But I warn you, be careful of trying to refinance your way out of this. It won't end well. I've seen it before with a dozen family businesses. Clinging on while the ship goes down isn't good for anyone.'

'It's not like that,' Stella said. 'Why do you want Penhallam's, anyway, if your sources say it's doing badly?'

Andrea chuckled. 'Because I can make it turn a profit. GPL has the resources and expertise to bring Penhallam's back to life. You won't be able to do it on your own.'

Her words cut deep. Stella was starting to lose faith in herself too, but she refused to let Andrea see that. 'I can at least try.'

'We'll see,' Andrea said. 'I'll be keeping an eye on things, Stella. I don't give up easily on something I want.'

Abruptly, Andrea put the phone down and the line went dead. Stella held her breath, trying to make sense of the knots she'd tied herself in. How could James have told GPL's CEO the things she'd told him in confidence? This was why James had broken things off with her. It all made sense now. He needed to prepare the ground for a formal offer from Andrea.

A moment later, Arnold came in. He must have been hovering by the door. 'Everything okay?'

Stella shook her head. 'Andrea knows about House of Fraser. James must have told her. She made a direct offer this time. Said outright she wants to buy us. The sharks are circling.'

Arnold sat down. 'It's worth considering, Stella. We've nearly used up that loan and the repayments are adding to our expenditure.'

'Could we get another loan to tide us over a bit longer?'

'Probably, but it's only going to put off the inevitable unless you can come up with something to turn things around.'

Stella tried to muster her thoughts. She was damned if she was going to give Andrea the satisfaction of being right.

'The factory is going to extend our credit limit,' she said. 'And I was thinking of reducing Amy's hours. I could take over her shifts at the weekend. But I'd feel terrible. I know how much she needs the money.'

'Those aren't solutions, they're sticking plasters,' Arnold said. 'Unless you have a credible solution to pursue, there's no point taking out another loan. You've got a few days' grace, and then you'll have to make a decision. I'm sorry.' He patted her hand. 'I'm heading out to a meeting now, but let me know if you want to talk it through.'

After Arnold had gone the beginnings of a headache pounded in Stella's temples. How could things have come to this? All her business training and she couldn't even save her own family's business. The idea of five mysterious scents was alluring, but there were no details to go on. Stella rummaged in her bag for a paracetamol. The packet was empty. The faces of her ancestors glared down at her. Suddenly she couldn't bear to be at Penhallam's any longer. The walls seemed to be closing in.

Downstairs, Amy was tidying the shelves. Stella felt awful just looking at her – how could she even have thought of reducing her hours? Amy depended on this job.

'I'm just going to the chemist,' Stella said. 'Can I get you anything?'

'No, I'm fine,' Amy said. 'By the way, this was delivered earlier. I didn't want to disturb you while you were on the phone.' Amy went behind the counter and took out a small parcel.

Stella didn't recognize the handwriting on the brown-paper package. The postmark read: Paris. She took it from Amy and popped it in her bag. 'Thanks. I'll be back soon.'

After she'd been to the pharmacy in Mayfair, Stella walked down to Green Park. She couldn't face going back to the office yet. It was lunchtime and people were lying in the sunshine on the grass or sprawled in deckchairs reading the papers.

Stella made for one of the shaded benches under the avenue of trees. The parcel had weighed down her bag the whole way and she was eager to open it. Stella took it out, curious as to what it might contain. The handwriting was old-fashioned, slanted to one side and wavery, as if written by a shaking hand.

Stella carefully peeled back the Sellotape and unwrapped the paper, breathing faster as the contents were revealed. Inside was a small notebook that fitted into the palm of her hand. The cover was decorated in blue and silver swirls. Where had it come from? Stella opened the book. On the flyleaf was written: *My Perfumes, by Iris Penhallam.*

Stella stared in amazement. Iris's perfume journal. It was as though the universe had heard her pleas and answered them. She stared out across the park. Two boys threw a

Frisbee back and forth, stretching and ducking to catch it. After all this time, here was another sign of Iris. And not just a mention of her name in a letter but something much, much more. Her actual book of perfumes. Stella smoothed her hand over the page. How odd that this should come now.

She opened the book, her heart thumping. The first half of the book was taken up with copious notes about perfumes and jottings of formulas. In the middle, Stella noticed a change. The handwriting was neater and Iris had added dates to her entries. The first dated entry was for July 1939. It was incredible. A whole new world of Penhallam's perfumes opened up in front of Stella's eyes.

She turned the page, the sense of anticipation growing inside her. There, at the top, Iris had written: *My first perfume for Raffaele, with Alessandro's help, of course. It's called La Scintilla (The Spark).*

This was exactly what she'd been hoping for – some unexpected perfumes from the past. These must be the perfumes mentioned in the letter and the newspaper article. It seemed too good to be true.

The boys had packed away the Frisbee and were now kicking a football between them. The sight of the ball going back and forth was almost hypnotic as Stella tried to take in what she had in front of her. So many questions burned inside her, but, above all, she wondered where on earth this notebook had come from and why it had arrived now.

Stella turned back to La Scintilla. In neat, cursive handwriting – different to the hand that had written the address on the packaging – Iris had set down what must have been her thoughts for a scent. The first few lines were crossed out.

Sunshine on the beach at Nice. Dinners on the terrace. Ciccadas
throbbing. The hills above Grasse at midday. Picnics at the edge of
the lavender fields. Endless. Carefree. Fresh.
The memory needs to be more specific. So here it is:
He lifted her wrist, drinking in her scent, then kissed it, and she
stopped laughing and simply gazed at him. There was such intensity
between them, like a bright spark. As a perfumer, you can make a
scent that is present at the most intimate moments of a person's life.

Stella leaned back against the bench. Even the description,
brief as it was, was powerful enough to transport her to
another time and place. What must the scent itself have
been like? Stella glanced at the ingredients. Rosemary and
lavender. Jasmine. Cedarwood. Unfortunately, there was
no proper formula, no mention of quantities and intensity. It looked like a page was missing. Stella saw the frayed
edges where it had been ripped out. It would be impossible
to re-create without the formulas or the original perfume
as a guide.

Stella flicked through the remaining pages and counted
four more perfumes. Then she noticed that some more
pages had been torn out. It looked as if the formula for
each perfume had been removed, but why? It was perplexing. Here in her hands lay, potentially, the answer to
Penhallam's problems. Brand-new scents that could be
traced back to 1939, and linked to Iris, Raffaele and an
unknown man called Alessandro and a journey they took
on the *Orient Express*. Already, Stella's business mind was
whirring – the glamour of the era, the mystery of this notebook, not to mention the beautiful perfumes themselves.
And yet, there were no formulas.

As she came to the end of the book, a small business

card fell out of the pages and on to the ground. Stella bent down and picked it up.

Printed on one side was an address for a convalescent home in Paris: *EHPAD Korian Magenta à Paris, 54–60 rue des Vinaigriers, 75010 Paris 10.* Stella turned the card over. Written in the same handwriting as on the packaging, she read the words: *From Iris Penhallam.* That was it. No explanation. No instructions. But the meaning was clear. Iris wanted Stella to come and find her. Why else send the notebook and an address?

Stella wrapped up the notebook and thrust it into her bag. This find was tantalizing, yet part of her wished it had never come. It made everything more complicated. A notebook without formulas but with just enough information to make it an undeniably exciting prospect. Her estranged great-aunt seeming to expect Stella to come to Paris. The opportunity to heal a rift that had stretched on for decades. All while Stella was up to her eyes in debt and struggling for ideas.

Stella got up and started walking back to Penhallam's. How could she go to Paris now? Not to mention how disloyal she'd feel to go against her father's instructions never to get involved with Iris. As Arnold had pointed out, there were only a few days left before the loan money was gone. She'd have to take out another loan if she was going to pay the staff and the factory this month. Iris's perfumes were the only option on the table and, sooner or later, Stella would have to make a choice about whether to pursue them or not.

The Penhallam's shop was depressingly empty when she got back. The walk and the paracetamol had done little to clear Stella's head.

'Bruno wondered if you could pop down to the archives when you got back?' Amy said.

Stella checked her watch. She could spare a few minutes. 'Okay, and then I'll cover your break.'

Stella headed down the stairs. She ducked her head to get through the doorway and gasped in astonishment. The room had been transformed. Bruno had labelled everything, and boxes now stood in chronological order on the shelves. She found him sitting at the desk wearing his familiar green cardigan, his aroma hanging in the air. She would miss that sweet, woody scent when he was gone.

'It looks amazing,' Stella said. 'Thank you. I appreciate you sticking around and not leaving the job half done.'

Bruno smiled, his hair hanging over his eyes. 'I wanted to honour my promise to get the archives shipshape before I left.'

'Well, you've definitely done that.'

'I also found this while I was sorting it all out.' He picked something up and came over to where she stood.

'It was in a cardboard box full of bottles and stoppers.' He opened his hand and there in his palm was a tiny bottle of scent. 'It's half full. I'm not sure when it was created or who by, but perhaps it might be useful.'

He gave the bottle to Stella. It had a brass lid and was only a few centimetres wide and two inches high. A label was stuck on to one side. La Scintilla, it read.

Stella's eyes widened. Impossible. She undid the stopper and inhaled. A shiver went through her. There it was. The spark. The exact moment Iris had described. The warmth of the wrist. The scent above the pulse. The intimacy of the man's gesture.

It was breathtaking. What was more, Stella had the

strange feeling that she understood its composition. This scent was all about the base notes. She could detect indole, but it was dominated by cedarwood. Stella felt an urge to head to the perfumery and start mixing accords. Without a formula, deconstructing the scent from an actual sample was the next best thing. But, of course, the perfumery was no longer usable.

Stella hadn't felt this inspired in years. Not since her father had rubbished her first composition and told her to stick to learning business. First the letter, then the notebook, and now this. Three signs pointing to Iris. It was too much of a coincidence to be ignored.

She caught Bruno's eye. He was regarding her with a puzzled expression on his face.

'Are you okay?' he said. 'Your face is glowing.'

Stella hesitated. Should she tell him about the notebook? He'd been decent enough to respect her wishes about Iris and sort out the archive. And over the last few weeks they'd been on a friendly footing with chats every now and then, and the daily coffee he brought her. Surely it couldn't hurt and, of all people, he would understand her excitement.

'A parcel came today,' she said. 'I've only just opened it. Inside was Iris Penhallam's perfume notebook with entries from 1939. Can you believe it? I've heard barely anything about Iris for years, and then, just now, when Penhallam's is in trouble, her name is everywhere. It's like someone is trying to tell me something.'

Stella took the notebook out of her bag to show him.

Bruno stared at her. 'A perfume notebook? Belonging to Iris?'

'There aren't any formulas in it,' she said, leafing through to show him. 'Only titles, notes and descriptions. But I think this scent you've found is the first one she mentions: La Scintilla.'

'But Stella, this is incredible,' Bruno said, his eyes lighting up.

'I'm still in shock,' Stella said. 'The scents are written in the book. They must be the ones that Jacopo mentioned in his letter.'

'Where did it come from?'

'Paris. Look, I found this inside.' Stella handed him the card. 'According to this, it was Iris who sent me the notebook. That means she must be still alive.'

Bruno read the address and the wording on the back. 'Maybe she heard that Penhallam's is in trouble and wanted to help,' he said. 'This note is so brief. Still, there's an address. It has to be worth following up.'

He picked up his notebook from the desk and scribbled the address down.

'What are you doing?' Stella asked.

'I'm going to head to Paris and see if I can find who sent you the notebook. Iris might still be alive and, if she is, I can interview her for my book. It would be invaluable material. A first-hand account of Raffaele di Fiore by someone who worked with him.'

'Wait a minute. This is my great-aunt we're talking about.'

Bruno nodded. 'Of course, sorry. It's just that I thought I'd hit a dead-end with finding out about Raffaele, and now this revives my search. Surely it makes a difference to your business problems too. I'd assumed you'd want to go to Paris. We could go there together.'

'I don't want to rush into anything,' Stella said. He was speeding ahead. She hadn't even got her head around the existence of the notebook itself, let alone the idea of meeting her long-lost great-aunt. 'I told you about the situation with Iris. I need to think this through first.'

Bruno folded his arms. 'Stella, from what you told me, the issue was between Iris and your grandfather, and it must have happened years ago,' he said. 'You don't even know the reason for the estrangement. Somewhere in Paris, right now, is your great-aunt. She's sent her perfume notebook to *you*. That has to mean something. Forgive me, but what is there to think about?'

Stella's chest tightened. 'It's not that simple.'

'Isn't it?' Bruno said. 'I know it's hard for you, but avoiding the issue of Iris is perhaps what's holding Penhallam's back. That letter from Jacopo suggests Iris saved his life in the war. You're holding her amazing perfume in your hand. There's clearly more to Iris than your grandfather and father have told you. How will you know the truth if you don't throw caution to the wind and go in search of it yourself?'

Stella stared at him. He was right. She *was* afraid. The presence of her father and grandfather permeated the building. The weight of ancestry had stunted that little girl who only wanted to play with scents. But now she was in charge of Penhallam's. Its first female owner. Maybe it was time to find out about Iris, the other woman in the family. This could be the opportunity Penhallam's needed, and a chance for Stella to meet her great-aunt at last. She could get Arnold to arrange a second loan and take a risk on these perfumes being the answer to Penhallam's prayers.

Stella took a deep breath. Was she really going to do this? Somehow it felt right to forge her own path and take a different route to that her father and grandfather had taken. The classic Penhallam's perfumes were no longer so popular. The business was in a dire state. Neither her father nor her grandfather was here to rescue it. Nor were they here to question Stella's choices or be disappointed in her or disapprove of her going to meet Iris. The task lay on Stella's shoulders right now and the only solution was this one. Maybe meeting Iris and talking to her about her scents would save the company.

'Okay, let's do this,' she said.

Bruno reached out to shake her hand. The gesture was formal, but the press of his hand around hers felt anything but. He held on to it a fraction too long and, for a moment, she imagined him turning it over and pressing his lips to her wrists, as in Iris's description of La Scintilla.

Then he let go as if anxious to restore things to a more professional footing. 'Well, it looks like we're off to Paris.'

Primo Bacio
(First Kiss)

Top Note
Orange Blossom

☙

Heart Note
Wisteria

☙

Base Note
Frankincense

☙

8

Stella – Paris, June 1996

Waterloo was teeming with people dragging luggage and pausing to look up at the departures boards. Stella pulled her suitcase, striding after Bruno, who carried a battered rucksack over his shoulder and flask of coffee in his right hand. He glanced back and smiled at her, pointing to their carriage. The last few days had been a whirlwind of preparation. She was still grateful that Bruno was accompanying her, but now that they were on their way, it did feel strange to head off to Paris with a man she'd only known for a few weeks.

'It's a shame you couldn't get us seats together,' Bruno said as they edged their way down the aisle.

'It was all so last minute,' Stella said. She checked her ticket. 'This is my seat.'

Bruno held out the flask. 'Here, you take it.'

'No, really, I wouldn't want to deprive you of caffeine this early in the trip.' She smiled.

'I've had enough this morning,' Bruno said. He folded down the little table and placed the flask on it. 'Enjoy.'

Stella settled into her seat with the *Financial Times*. He really was very thoughtful. It would have been nice to have sat together and talked about Iris on the journey. Left to her own thoughts, Stella was more anxious about the whole thing. Bruno had an upbeat, encouraging way about him that made her feel more hopeful about the decision to go to Paris.

Arnold, however, had been rather pessimistic about it when Stella told him. It was his job, though, to sound a note of caution.

'Are you sure you want to do this?' he'd said. 'There's no guarantee of success.'

'True, but I have to try,' Stella had replied. 'I might be on a train back tomorrow – I don't know what's going to happen when I see Iris. But I'd be really grateful if you could base yourself in my office and hold the fort until I'm back.'

Arnold had nodded. 'Very well. I'll let you know when the second loan application is accepted.'

Now Stella took a peek over at Bruno. He was reading a book and seemed oblivious to two young women sitting opposite him who kept glancing at him surreptitiously. He was good-looking, of course, if not so well presented as James. He wore that threadbare cardigan with a black T-shirt that seemed to have shrunk and faded in the wash. Stella imagined leaning against his shoulder and inhaling the unsettling yet attractive scent that was unmistakably his. At that moment, Bruno looked up and caught her eye. She blushed and gave him a jaunty wave. What was she thinking? This was a research trip, purely business. Nothing else.

Three hours later the train pulled into Gare du Nord. Stella found a taxi to take them to the convalescent home near the St Martin Canal. The street looked like any normal Parisian residential area, made up of grey Haussmann buildings. She'd expected to see a purpose-built home, but it seemed as if this one had been adapted from a house. Bruno paid the taxi driver and got the bags out of the boot.

Stella looked up at the building. Somewhere in there was Iris.

'Are you okay?' Bruno asked, coming to stand beside her. 'This must feel strange.'

Stella nodded. 'It does. I wish I'd been brave enough to ask more questions about her at the time.'

Bruno smiled. 'Well, today is your chance to ask her anything.'

Stella sighed. 'I hope so. I just feel a bit guilty even being here, given how my grandfather felt about Iris, and my father too. In my head, I can rationalize it because of the perfumes: seeing Iris is potentially critical to the fate of Penhallam's. It's not like I have to strike up a lasting friendship with her. I just need her help to find the perfumes.'

'I see,' Bruno said, raising his eyebrows, 'and is that what I am, part of the plan to save Penhallam's, or do you think you can call me a friend by now as well?'

Stella's cheeks glowed. 'Maybe a work colleague slash new friend might be a better description,' she said. 'You found the letter and the perfume bottle and have been very supportive, but this is still a work trip, after all. Your book and my family business are the priority here, and I'm grateful for your help.'

Bruno smiled, and the warmth of it radiated over Stella. 'I'll take work colleague slash friend . . . for now.' His eyes stayed fixed on hers and her heart skipped under his gaze.

Stella picked up her suitcase to deflect the intensity and prayed her cheeks didn't betray her thoughts. 'Well, let's hope we make some progress today,' she said. 'For both our sakes.'

Inside the convalescent home, a whiff of cleaning fluids filled the air. Dihydromyrcenol, one of the synthetics, Stella thought, surprised at how quickly the name came to her. She must have taken in more from Claudine over the years than she'd realized.

'Hello, I rang yesterday,' Stella said to the man on the reception desk, 'about coming to see Iris Penhallam. I'm her great-niece, Stella Penhallam, and this is my colleague, Bruno Silvestri.'

The man looked at the computer in front of him. 'Ah yes. Do you have some ID, your passports, perhaps?'

Stella and Bruno handed their passports to the man. Stella caught a glimpse of Bruno's photo. He had longer hair and a bushy beard.

'My student days,' Bruno said with an embarrassed smile, tucking the passport into his rucksack. He caught sight of Stella's photo. 'Yet you looked just as beautiful then as you do now.'

Stella put the passport back into her bag. 'Thanks,' she said, thrown by his compliment. 'So, is it okay if we go and see Iris?' she said to the man.

'Ah yes, she's on the second floor,' he said. 'Head up in the lift and someone will buzz you through the double doors.'

Stella bit her lip as she waited for the lift. Even Bruno looked nervous. The notebook and bottle of La Scintilla were stowed in her bag. Her stomach was doing somersaults at the thought of meeting the woman her family had fought so hard to keep hidden. Part of her was excited, the other part wishing that Iris had never sent her the notebook in the first place. What would her grandfather and father have said about all of this?

Bruno touched her elbow. 'You're thinking of your family again, aren't you?'

Stella nodded.

'Your father is no longer here; nor is your grandfather. This is *your* past now, not just theirs. It's yours to do with what you will. Meeting Iris might be exactly what you need.'

'You mean for the business?' Stella said, getting into the lift and pressing the button for the second floor.

Bruno gave a small nod before saying, 'But also, it might be good for you too. Iris is the last one of her generation left in your family. She's going to be delighted to see you.'

Stella smiled. His words were comforting. 'Fingers crossed you're right.'

The lift stopped and Stella walked out, her legs feeling weak. Bruno pressed the buzzer and a nurse opened the door. She was small with black bobbed hair and a friendly smile.

'You must be Stella,' she said. 'My name's Monique, I'm in charge of this floor. We're so pleased that someone has come to see Iris. She's been here for two weeks now and you're the first visitors. I was surprised to hear that a family member was finally coming.'

'I had no idea she was here,' Stella said. 'I don't know her at all, really. We've never been in touch. But she sent me a book and the address to this place, so I'm hoping she's pleased to see me.'

'I did tell her that you were coming after we got your call yesterday,' Monique said. She hesitated. 'I'm afraid she didn't take it too well. Let's just say that Iris has good days and bad days. It's taken her a while to recover after what happened.'

'What did happen?' Stella asked.

Monique sighed. 'She was visiting Paris and a fire started in her hotel – in her room, in fact. Apparently, it was faulty electrics. She was treated in hospital and then moved here to recuperate. We often take patients for the medium term who need care and support before they can go home. She could barely speak at first. Her voice has improved, but the smoke inhalation has really damaged her vocal cords. She was badly burned too.'

'That's awful. It must have been traumatic. Are you sure she's all right to see me?'

Monique nodded. 'She can manage a short visit. It's this way.'

Bruno touched Stella's arm. 'Shall I wait here?'

Now the moment had come, Stella didn't want to go in on her own. 'I'd rather you came too.'

She took a deep breath and followed Monique into the room, Bruno by her side. A smell of patchouli hung in the air. The sweetness of the scent mingled with the serenity of a thin old lady lying in the bed, seemingly asleep. She had long white hair, pinned in a loose bun, and wore a soft blue bedjacket. Her arms were covered in bandages, and she had a square of gauze on one cheek.

So, this was Iris, her great-aunt. She appeared so frail. It was hard to see how this little old woman had caused such a rift in the family. A bunch of flowers stood in a vase on the bedside table.

'I thought the flowers might cheer her up,' Monique whispered. 'Not that she can smell anything. That's why she slept through the fire almost until it was too late. She suffers from anosmia.'

Stella shivered. It must have been terrifying to wake up

in the middle of a burning room. Iris had clearly had a lucky escape.

'I need to check on my other patients,' Monique said. 'I'll be back in a few minutes. She'll probably wake up in a moment.' She slipped out of the room.

Stella hovered at the end of Iris's bed. Should she say something and introduce herself? Bruno shrugged, clearly also unsure. Stella scoured Iris's face for glimpses of a family resemblance. At that moment, Iris opened her eyes. They were bright blue like the flame of a pilot light and straight away Stella saw the likeness to her grandfather, Charles.

'Stella?' Iris said, her voice weak and croaky. She began to cough, deep, racking coughs that shook her body. Stella passed her a glass of water from the bedside table and Iris took a sip.

Bruno nodded encouragingly.

'Yes, I'm Stella,' she said. 'I'm your great-niece. Your brother, Charles, was my grandfather; his son, Richard, was my father.'

Iris put the glass down slowly. 'My great-niece?'

'I'm afraid this might come as a bit of a shock to you, but I'm sorry to tell you that neither my father nor your brother is alive any more.' It seemed best to tell Iris this straightaway, in case she thought they were still alive.

'I know,' she said. 'We may not have had good relations, but I did keep an eye out for news about Penhallam's in the English newspapers.' Her eyes were moist. 'It must have been very hard for you.'

Stella nodded. 'It has been a difficult time. Grandfather was old and he'd been ill for a long time. But my father—' She stopped, emotion catching in her throat.

The police had called round to her former flat in Clapham to tell her about the accident. From the minute Stella saw their grave faces, everything became unreal. For the first few hours, her father had been in pain but lucid, extracting the promise from Stella to look after the perfumery. But his internal injuries had got the better of him, and during the operation he had slipped away. To cope, Stella had focused on the details: organizing the funeral, leaving GPL, taking over Penhallam's, moving out of her flat. It sounded crazy, but in some ways Penhallam's problems had been a godsend. They distracted her from the loss of her father and the grief that threatened to overwhelm her.

Iris stared at her, her eyes filled with understanding, and something else . . . a kind of pain at Stella's sorrow, perhaps. 'I'm so sorry you had to go through all of that. But I don't understand. Why have you come to see me after all this time?'

Stella felt a stab of unease. 'You sent me the perfume notebook. It was such a coincidence, but it arrived just when I needed it. I'm sorry we've never met before. I've got so many questions . . . about you, and my grandfather, and this book.'

'The notebook?' Iris said. Stella nodded, took it out of her bag and handed it to Iris. Iris picked it up and thumbed through the pages. 'I thought it had been lost in the fire.'

'You've been through such a terrible ordeal,' Stella said. 'But I don't understand. I thought it was you who'd sent the notebook. It arrived a few days ago at Penhallam's.'

Iris kept hold of the notebook. 'It wasn't me,' she said, her voice hoarse. 'I imagine it was the fire service, or the hotel where I was staying.' She coughed again.

'But there was a card inside with this address on.

Look . . .' Stella showed it to Iris. 'Don't you think that's odd? When did you last have the notebook?'

'I'm not sure. I fell asleep reading it on the bed in the hotel. The next thing I remember is being out in the street on a stretcher, and the notebook was nowhere to be seen.'

Bruno touched Stella's arm. 'I'll go and find Monique,' he said. 'See if she knows anything about this.'

Stella swallowed. What was going on? Iris claimed she hadn't sent the notebook. And she seemed to know nothing about the address card sent with it. Had Iris even wanted her to get in touch?

She cleared her throat. 'I'm so sorry if my arrival has come as a surprise,' she said. 'I honestly thought that sending me your notebook was a sign you wanted me to visit. I'm as perplexed as you are about how I got it.'

'It doesn't matter. It's here now. I'm glad to have it back.'

Stella glanced at the notebook, tight in Iris's grasp. 'Is there any way I could borrow it for a while?' she said tentatively. 'You see, Bruno and I were hoping to find out more about the perfumes inside.'

'Bruno. Is that the man who was here a moment ago? Is he from Italy?'

Stella nodded. 'Yes, Bruno's from the University of Venice and he's researching the perfumer Raffaele di Fiore so that he can write a book about him. We were hoping you might be able to help us track down some perfumes you made with Raffaele during the war. The ones you mention in the notebook.'

Iris fiddled with the necklace around her throat, a silver chain and locket. 'I don't want to talk about them,' she said. 'You should never have been sent the notebook. I'm sorry you've come all this way for nothing.'

Stella sat down on the chair next to the bed. 'It isn't all for nothing – I've had the chance to meet you for the first time, and that alone is something,' Stella said earnestly. 'Look, I realize this might all be a bit much, but I really need your help. Penhallam's is struggling. It needs a new collection of perfumes to boost its sales, and when we found the letter from Jacopo and he mentioned five scents made at the start of the war, it seemed like the answer I'd been praying for.'

Iris closed her fingers around the locket. She didn't seem to take in the information about Penhallam's. 'You had a letter from Jacopo?' she said.

'It wasn't sent to me,' Stella said, hastening to explain. 'It was sent to your brother. Jacopo said that you had saved his life. And he talked about the perfumes.'

'Your grandfather would not want you to get involved with me,' Iris said hoarsely.

'Maybe not, but he's not here any more.' She took Jacopo's letter out of her bag in the hopes that it would appease Iris. 'Look, Jacopo writes: *I will be forever indebted to your sister, Iris, and what she did for me in the war. Her efforts, along with those of Alessandro Mori and Tommaso Ricci, saved my life.*'

'Jacopo said that?' Iris said.

'Yes, and more.' Stella turned back to the letter, reading it aloud. '*I know there has been some trouble for her since the war ended. I don't know the full extent of what happened, but please can you tell her that I bear her no ill will. I most sincerely hope that you will pass that on to her.*' Stella paused, trying to gauge Iris's reaction. 'You obviously did something very brave to help Jacopo. Did Charles ever tell you that Jacopo had written to him?'

Iris's eyes filled with tears. 'No, he didn't. We were

estranged in 1946 just after the war ended, and never spoke directly to each other again. I would have very much liked to know how Jacopo felt.'

Stella reached out and touched Iris's hand. 'This must be very upsetting for you. We don't have to continue right now, if it's too much. I'm in Paris for a few days. I hope it's okay if I come and visit again.'

Iris shook her head. 'I'm sorry. I don't want to delve back into the past or have anything to do with Penhallam's.'

There was a knock at the door and Monique and Bruno came into the room. Monique went to tuck Iris's covers in.

'Did you find out who sent the notebook?' Stella asked, coming to the back of the room, where Bruno stood.

Bruno shook his head. 'No, no one could account for it. The hotel had never seen it. The hospital had it down as one of Iris's possessions when she was admitted, but it was never logged as an item here.'

Stella sighed. 'I'm not sure what to do. Iris is keeping hold of the notebook and is clearly very upset by the whole thing. It's probably best if we let her rest and come back tomorrow. I'm worried me coming here has stirred things up for her.'

Bruno took Stella's hand. His grip was firm and strong. At that moment, it was exactly what she needed to feel. 'I think that's a good idea,' he said. Then, as if seeming to realize what he'd done, Bruno let go of her hand. 'Sorry. I forgot we're more work colleagues than friends.'

'It's okay,' Stella said, not wanting to act like it was a big deal. But the touch of his hand was imprinted on her skin.

Iris seemed to have drifted off to sleep; at least, her eyes were closed, but her hands were still firmly gripped around the notebook.

'Come on,' Stella said. 'We'd better go.'

Monique escorted them down the corridor and opened the double doors leading out of the ward.

'As I say, she has good days and bad days,' she said. 'Maybe she'll feel more like talking tomorrow.'

'Thank you,' Stella said.

She'd have to be patient with Iris, which wasn't easy, not when Penhallam's was urgently in need of help. Today had been a first step, not just in finding the perfumes but in understanding her own family history. Iris was Stella's relative, and yet her great-aunt was completely unknown to her. A missing piece of the family jigsaw. Stella pushed the button to summon the lift. She wouldn't give up, not yet. She just needed to convince Iris to confide in her.

9

Iris – Paris, August 1939

Iris stepped off the train. She'd been travelling all day. After docking at the Gare Maritime in Calais, she'd boarded *La Flèche d'Or* and had now arrived in Paris at the Gare du Nord. The station was crowded. Soldiers bustled on the platform. There were signs showing the location of the nearest air-raid shelters. Just like London, Paris was preparing for war.

Throughout the journey, Iris's stomach had been churning. Did Henri know about the bargain she had struck with Charles? Did he approve, or was he perhaps angry that she'd used him as leverage? It might make things very awkward. But there was no time to wonder. There was Henri, striding through the crowds in a dark blue suit and white shirt, his expression unreadable.

'Well,' he said, raising his eyebrows, 'here you are, Miss Penhallam.'

Iris swallowed. 'Yes, thank you for letting me stay with you and your mother.'

A smile played on his lips. 'All part of the deal you made with Charles, I believe?'

Iris nodded. 'I'm sorry, I should have consulted with you first.' It was difficult to find the words to explain. 'I wanted so desperately to come and learn with Raffaele that I'm afraid I took advantage of Charles's harebrained notion that the two of us should marry.' She laughed a little nervously. 'I hope you don't mind.'

Henri smiled. 'It's all right, Iris,' he said. 'I'm actually rather proud of you. You negotiated the best outcome for yourself. But I have to tell you, I don't think it is such a harebrained scheme, hence my agreement to you staying with Mother and me. I like the idea of getting to know you better – if that's what you want too.'

His blue eyes focused on her as if she was the only woman in Paris. 'Oh,' she said, not sure if he was teasing her or being serious. 'Well, I suppose we'll inevitably see more of each other as I'm living under your roof. Thank you for understanding.'

He reached down and picked up her suitcase. He offered his other arm to Iris, and she adjusted the strap on her gas-mask box to stop it getting in the way and linked her arm through his. Iris noticed other women glancing at Henri as they walked out of the station, but it seemed that Henri had eyes only for her. She'd believed that Charles was mistaken about Henri having any serious regard for her. But as they crossed the road and Henri pressed her hand, Iris wondered anxiously if there was more to his feelings after all.

The next day Iris woke to a peal of church bells sounding the hour. The Levèques' house was in rue Rimbaud. It was strange to be back here in the room she always stayed in on visits with her family, with its familiar white stucco ceiling, blue flocked wallpaper and large carved oak armoire, whose depths used to terrify Iris when she was little. Iris and her father and brother used to stay in Paris with the Levèques when picking Henri up to take him down south with them to Mougins. Henri's mother was often bedbound due to her nerves. Henri's father had been killed in the Great War and she had never got over the loss. Henri had been only too glad to climb into Iris's father's grey Standard Ten and motor down with them to the south of France every year.

Today was the first day of Iris's apprenticeship. She'd barely slept, in nervous anticipation of what the day would bring. She got dressed, drew back the curtains and opened the window. Black railings outside framed a little balcony. It wasn't big enough to stand on, but a pot of red geraniums brightened up the spot. They smelled like roses and violets combined, with a hint of earthy leaf scent thrown in.

Downstairs in the breakfast room silver trays with lids stood on hotplates. Henri was already at the table, reading the paper and eating toast and eggs. He looked up when Iris came in and smiled.

'*Bonjour.* I hope you slept well. There's coffee arriving shortly, which should fortify you for the day ahead.'

'Thank you,' Iris said. She lifted one of the lids, spooned out scrambled eggs, then took some toast and sat down.

Henri folded away his paper. 'So, your first day at di Fiore's perfumery. Are you excited?'

Iris buttered her toast. 'Yes, but also a little nervous.'

'I must say, I do admire this new independent streak in you. I never noticed it before.'

Iris smiled. 'I surprised myself by confronting Charles, but I am twenty-one now. It's time I stood up for myself. He has quite a traditional view of what a young woman should do with her life.'

Henri laughed. 'He does, but I can understand Charles's traditional values. I know what it means to carry the mantle of your ancestors on your shoulders. I was brought up to continue the family business too,' he said. 'But the world is changing. If war is coming, there are opportunities to be had if a person has talent and energy. Charles, I fear, lacks both, and so is floundering. But you, my dear, appear to possess them both in abundance.'

A maid came in with a silver pot of coffee and filled a cup each for Henri and Iris. Iris pondered Henri's words. Surely it was a little disloyal of him to criticize his friend like that.

'Well,' she said, taking a sip of coffee, 'it remains to be seen how abundantly I have them. Marcel was always very kind, and Father praised me to the hilt no matter what concoction I made in the perfumery. Although I've come here to help Raffaele, he will no doubt expect me to live up to his exacting standards.'

Henri smiled. 'I'm sure you'll find a way to impress him. He always had a soft spot for you, as did his sister. When Jacopo had a tantrum in Mougins, you seemed to have the knack of calming him down.'

Iris nodded. 'I was still a child myself. I knew how it felt to be surrounded by adults, having to be on your best behaviour. Jacopo loved making perfume potions and playing in the garden. It was easy to soothe him.'

'Well, if it doesn't work out with Raffaele, perhaps there might be other options for you.'

'What do you mean?' Iris said, placing her cup on the saucer.

Henri leaned forward, his elbows on the table. 'As you know, my father made his money growing flowers and distilling oil. The business now supplies and trades in raw materials for perfume ingredients. We're at the coalface, shall we say? We supply the essentials but leave the creating, the glory, to others.' He rubbed his moustache. 'It's my intention to change that.'

Iris stared in surprise. The Levèque company traded all over the world, supplying Penhallam's and other perfumers in London, Paris and beyond. But she hadn't known that Henri had aspirations to own a perfumery.

'You'd like to make perfume?' she said. Already she was seeing Henri in a new light.

Henri took a spoonful of sugar and stirred it into his coffee. 'Well, not me exactly – I'm more of a business-man – but it's certainly an ambition of mine to have a Levèque scent to our name. There might be opportunities in the future to take over some existing perfumeries. If you find di Fiore a hard taskmaster, you could join me.'

Iris smiled. 'Thank you, Henri, that's very kind of you. But at the moment I still have a lot of learning to do.'

Henri reached out and touched her hand. It was cool and dry.

'Of course,' he said. 'Just remember that di Fiore isn't the only judge of what's good in the perfume world. In fact some might say it's time that people like him learned to accept their place in the world.'

Iris slid her hand out Henri's grasp and took a bite of her toast. 'What does that mean?' she said.

'You know he's a Jew, don't you? I'm just saying that, generally, Jews have too high an opinion of themselves.' He raised his eyebrows. 'There's no need to look so dis-approving. I'm not saying anything terrible. In my line of business, I work with lots of Jews. It's just something I noticed, that's all.'

Iris wasn't sure how to take Henri's words. He sounded so reasonable, but there was something about his tone that she didn't trust. She thought of Raffaele's letter, about the persecutions Francesca and Jacopo were facing because they were Jewish.

'I've never noticed anything with Raffaele, and if he does have a high opinion of himself, then it's entirely justified. He is an outstanding perfumer,' she said.

Henri drank the rest of his coffee and stood up, tucking his paper under his arm. 'That's good to hear,' he said. 'I thought he seemed all right when we met him in Mougins. One of the good ones.'

He gave Iris a wink and headed out of the room. Iris swallowed her toast. If this was Henri's casual attitude, how many others here in Paris shared his view? All at once, the fears she had for Francesca and Jacopo seemed much closer to home.

Iris hurried towards rue Bayard, not wanting to be late on her first day. Raffaele had written to her about the demonstrations that had been taking place in the last year, of the unrest between the Front Populaire and Action Française. Thankfully, the streets were quiet today. At rue de la Chaussée d'Antin, she went into the Métro and took the train to Rond-Point des Champs-Élysées.

The trees along the Avenue Montaigne were in full leaf. Iris remembered coming here sometimes when they stopped off in Paris on the way back from Mougins. Haussmann buildings stretched on either side, their grey-clad roofs matching dark against the blue of the sky. Once, Raffaele had shown her father and Iris around his perfumery. Tucked away behind the illustrious designer boutiques of the Champs-Élysées, the establishments along the rue Bayard were more eclectic and modest. The di Fiore perfumery – a four-storey building where Raffaele also lived – was sandwiched between the premises of an antique dealer and a silversmith. Now, just like in London, there were sandbags piled up on the pavement. People were going to work with an air of urgency, gas masks in hand.

Iris crossed the road and headed over to the perfumery. A plaque on the wall read: *Raffaele di Fiore, Parfumier*. The shop was locked this early in the morning, so Iris rang the doorbell. From the back, a familiar figure emerged. Raffaele opened the door and smiled warmly.

'Come in,' he said. 'We're just getting set up. I'm afraid it's full steam ahead today. I don't know if it's the threat of war or the fear of scarcity, but we've never been so busy.'

Iris stepped into the shop. Unlike Penhallam's, with its dark wood display cabinets, Raffaele's ground-floor shop was light and airy, with white marble floor tiles and countertops, and pristine white walls.

Before they entered the perfumery, Iris touched his arm. 'With everything that happened in London, I never got a chance to ask you about Francesca and Jacopo,' she said. 'Have you heard anything more from them?'

Raffaele shook his head. 'Post is sporadic at best. I wrote to Francesca last week. Hopefully I'll get a reply soon.'

'And are things okay for you here in Paris?' Iris said, thinking of Henri's words.

'Things are very tense – they have been for years,' Raffaele said. 'The influx of foreign Jews, refugees fleeing the Nazis, has put a strain on everything: jobs, tolerance, housing. People accuse the Jews of wanting France to go to war to settle a score with Germany. Shops have been looted in the north of Paris. So far, I've escaped such treatment, but it's very worrying. Perhaps Francesca is right to stay in Venice.'

His eyes were anxious, his face pale. Iris took his hand. 'You've had to contend with a lot,' Iris said. 'Well, Alessandro and I are here to protect you now.'

He squeezed her hand. She followed him through a door at the back. The perfumery was equally bright, with natural light flooding in from large windows that overlooked a garden. Alessandro sat at the bench, using a pipette to drop liquid into a test tube.

'Good morning,' he said. 'Did you have a good trip over?'

'Yes, it's lovely to be in Paris again,' she said.

'Good.' He studied her for a moment, as if wanting to say more, then went back to his work. Iris hoped that the doubts he'd had about her coming had gone.

Raffaele went over to the workbench and cleared a space for Iris. 'You can work here. The natural ingredients are over there in the cupboards, empty bottles under the counter. Feel free to treat this place as your own.'

'Thank you,' Iris said. 'I can't wait to get started.'

She hung her coat on the stand and stowed her bag in the cupboard. At last, she was where she belonged: in a perfumery.

'Now, take a seat next to Alessandro, Iris, and I'll run through a few things. It's important to me that you both get along. The aim is that you work as a team – that is how we succeed or fail. Understand?'

Iris nodded. She tried to concentrate on what Raffaele was saying about the daily routines of the shop, what they'd be learning, their individual responsibilities, but it was hard with Alessandro just a whisper away. He studiously avoided looking at her. Whenever she sneaked the odd peek at him, his jaw was clenched, his focus fixed on Raffaele.

It was hard to tell if he was still uncertain about her being there. Or if he was simply shy. Iris concentrated on Raffaele's words. Things with Alessandro would hopefully sort themselves out.

The first day flew by in a flurry of activity. Iris helped on the shopfloor, advising customers and getting to know Raffaele's signature scents. She took turns with Alessandro to be in the perfumery in a two-hourly rotation, which meant the only contact she had with him was when she had to pass him in the doorway.

The shop was interesting, but Iris preferred the moments one to one with Raffaele in the perfumery. He explained the composition of his scents and showed Iris how to make repeat orders of bespoke perfumes using formulas he had recorded scrupulously in his ledger.

He took some bottles down from one of the shelves. 'I use a small number of synthetics to bring out the jasmine notes.'

'Marcel swears by naturals,' Iris said. She took one of the bottles and inhaled the contents. 'But I can see the advantage of isolating the molecules. It's like using herbs in a dish to bring out the flavour.'

Raffaele nodded. 'Yes, I was reluctant myself, but after seeing what Ernest Beaux achieved with Chanel No. 5, I knew I had to keep up with developments. I have a rule that I only use synthetics to augment or garnish the naturals, never to replace. You'll see that most of this formula is tuberose, jasmine and lavender. Your task is to recreate it.'

Iris nodded, slightly daunted. 'I'll try,' she said, 'but can you tell me the brief that inspired you to make it?'

Raffaele observed her over the rim of his glasses. 'An astute question,' he said. 'I remember that quality in you.

The customer wanted a perfume to celebrate thirty years of marriage. But I could tell by her tone of voice and the story she told me of how she met her husband that she also wanted to recapture the early magic of their relationship.'

'How were you so sure?'

'Intuition. Perfume is a magic potion that laces a person's life with the dreams they once had.'

'But what if those dreams didn't come true?' Iris asked.

'It doesn't matter. The dreams are still there in a person's soul nonetheless, and that's what they want a scent to revive. Dreams don't die just because they don't come true. They die because we don't honour them.'

By the end of the day Iris was exhausted. She gathered up her coat and bag. Alessandro was tidying up his work bench.

'Did you enjoy your first day?' he said.

'Yes. I hope I can remember everything.' Iris peered through the open door into the shop, where Raffaele was closing up. 'He seems better than he did in London.'

Alessandro nodded. 'That trip was too much for him, but I believe the thought of you coming has eased the pressure on his mind.'

'That's good,' Iris said, touched by his words. With the sunlight shining in through the window, the skin around Alessandro's scar looked tight. She wanted to ask him how he got it, but he looked away, as if conscious that she was observing him.

Raffaele came into the perfumery. 'Iris, you've done well,' he said. 'Perhaps you could escort Iris back to the tenth, Alessandro?'

'Oh, no, there's no need,' Iris said, certain that Alessandro wouldn't be keen on the idea. 'I was planning to visit Le Jardin du Palais-Royal.'

But, to her surprise, Alessandro nodded. 'I can walk you there too.'

Raffaele smiled approvingly. 'It's good to have you both here.'

By the time Alessandro and Iris reached the gardens it was nearly six o'clock. The air was still warm, and Iris carried her coat over her arm. The gardens were quiet at this time of day. The street noises seemed to fade, and she felt the calmness lap over her. Even Alessandro seemed to relax beside her.

'Why did you want to come here?' Alessandro asked.

'It was my father's favourite place in Paris,' Iris said.

'I'm sorry. When did he die?'

'Two years ago,' Iris said. 'He loved the Pierre de Ronsard roses. Look, you can see them everywhere, heavy pink petals drooping languidly on the trellises. They inspired one of his bestselling scents. He made it for my sixteenth birthday and then sold it at Penhallam's. Whenever we visited Paris he'd bring me here to sit and drink in the smell of the roses.'

Alessandro tucked his hand under one of the flowers and bent his head towards it. The gesture was unexpectedly tender and intimate. His nose and lips brushed the petals, his eyes closed and he inhaled deeply.

'You must miss him,' he said softly.

'Yes, very much. Making perfume is a way of belonging to the world he once inhabited. One that he shared with me,' Iris said. Alessandro kept his eyes on her, as if waiting to hear more. But Iris wanted to know about him. 'How did you get into perfumery?'

They set off strolling along the gravel walkway, heading towards rue de Beaujolais.

'My father was a glassblower. Francesca used to come to his workshop for perfume bottles. I was intrigued, and she invited me over to see the perfumery. I was eighteen. It had been . . .' He hesitated, then smiled briefly. 'Well, it had been a difficult time, and making perfume was a good way to recover. When I got a job on the *Orient Express* with my friend Tommaso, I continued learning with Francesca whenever I could.'

Iris wondered if the difficult time had anything to do with his scar. A small unit of soldiers walked past. Their boots crunched on the gravel. They looked out of place in the elegance of the garden.

She was about to ask more when she heard a familiar voice. 'Ah, Iris, there you are.' It was Henri. He strode towards Iris and kissed her cheek. 'Raffaele said you'd headed this way. I must have just missed you.'

'You didn't say you were coming to meet me,' Iris said. Henri stared pointedly at Alessandro. 'Henri, this is the other apprentice, Alessandro. Alessandro, this is . . .' She hesitated, unsure how to describe what Henri was to her.

Henri reached out his hand. 'Let's just say I'm a hopeful suitor, with more than enough reasons to believe he will be successful,' he said, with a hint of an edge to his voice.

Alessandro shook his hand. 'I see.'

Iris winced inwardly. Did he have to be so blunt, as if he needed to stake his territory? Nothing had been decided, and Iris had certainly not given Henri reason to hope he would win her hand. And yet, despite Alessandro's obvious discomfort at the implications of what Henri had said, he held his ground, an aura of calm around him, in contrast to Henri's slight agitation.

Alessandro bowed his head. 'Well, I have a meeting to get to. It was nice to meet you, Henri. Iris, I'll see you tomorrow.' He walked back the way they'd come, heading to the river.

'Odd fellow,' Henri said. 'Must be one of Raffaele's Italian communist friends. I can just picture the kind of meeting he's going to, over in Montmartre, or some other quarter where foreigners have taken over. There'll be a lot of bluff and bluster about ridding Italy of Mussolini, but it's all talk, while they lie low in Paris rather than taking action.'

Iris watched Alessandro disappear through the arch at the end of the garden. 'Don't be silly, he's nothing of the sort. He's a perfumer.' She shook her head. 'There's no reason for you to take against him like that.'

Henri frowned. 'Isn't there? The two of you looked to be having quite a tête-à-tête.'

'About perfume,' Iris said. The idea of Henri being jealous was rather unsettling. She'd never imagined she would have been capable of rousing it in him.

'So long as that's all it was.'

'Of course. There was no need for you to go on like that about being my suitor. I told you, despite my bargain with Charles, I'm not looking to marry at the moment,' Iris said.

Henri smiled. 'But perhaps I am. There's no harm in making sure fellows like Alessandro know you're almost spoken for.'

'Henri,' Iris said, batting his arm, not quite sure if he was joking or not, 'you don't have to worry about Alessandro. He's just a work colleague, that's all.'

And yet as Henri took her arm the memory of Alessandro's tenderness when he held the rose lingered in her mind.

10

Stella – Paris, June 1996

Stella and Bruno had booked a hotel near Canal Saint-Martin, which lay to the north-east of Paris, not far from the Place de la République. It was a leafy stretch of water that felt more laid-back than the boulevards of central Paris. That afternoon, after visiting Iris, Stella unpacked her few belongings and opened the window. A barge was negotiating its way through one of the lock gates, the tourists on board taking photographs. Sunlight sparkled on the water and the barge's engine throbbed.

It was hard to imagine what Paris would have been like for Iris – 1939 was so long ago, and Europe would have been on the cusp of war. And yet Iris had set off to work with Raffaele in the middle of it all. How had she managed it? Stella wanted to get the answers, but it was clear that the memories of that time were too upsetting for Iris to recount.

Stella turned back to the room and looked through her clothes. Bruno had suggested going out to get something to eat. He'd made it sound casual, as if it was just a sensible idea, but Stella couldn't help but feel a twinge of excitement. There was something about being here in Paris and the moments that flashed between them that Stella couldn't put her finger on. To be honest, Bruno was neither work colleague nor friend. It was hard to categorize him and, in many ways, Stella didn't want to attempt it.

After trying on several outfits, none of which seemed to suit the occasion – too corporate or too dressy, Stella settled on jeans and a silk shirt.

At seven o'clock she headed down to Bruno's room. She was about to knock on his door when she heard his voice. He appeared to be talking to someone on the phone. He sounded perturbed. Stella leaned closer to the door.

'I know that's what we agreed, but I've decided I no longer want to be involved with this project . . .' she heard Bruno say.

There was silence as, presumably, he listened to the person on the other end of the line. Stella stood still, unable to tear herself away.

'I'm not interested in how much you're willing to pay,' Bruno said. 'I didn't realize the full extent of the task you were asking me to undertake. Now that I do, I don't want any further part of it.' He paused. 'Well, there was no official contract. I told you, I don't care about the money. I don't want anything more to do with it.'

It sounded like something to do with work. Hopefully, being in Paris wasn't causing him problems. Stella hesitated. If she knocked, he'd know she'd been listening and it would be awkward. But what else was she supposed to do? She waited a moment, until it was clear the call had ended, and then rapped her knuckles on the door.

Bruno came out wearing a dark blue shirt, open at the collar, and dark blue jeans. 'Sorry, I just need to get my jacket.' He headed back into the room. Stella glimpsed a pile of books on the desk, his rucksack by the bed.

'Right,' he said, looking more relaxed, 'shall we go? The receptionist recommended a bistro round the corner so I've booked us a table there.'

'Great,' Stella said. This felt like a date. Except that it wasn't, she reminded herself. Stepping out on to the Quai de Jemmapes, where couples were strolling under the trees or sitting with their legs dangling over the canal sharing a bottle of wine, it was impossible to escape the fact that this trip meant spending a lot of time with each other.

'Do you know Paris well?' Stella asked.

They climbed over the steep green metal bridge that crossed the canal.

'A little. I've been to conferences here at the university, sometimes a research trip.' He smiled. 'Nothing like this, though. I'm usually in dingy libraries. It's nice to have a change.'

At the bistro, Stella and Bruno chose steak and a bottle of red wine. After the waiter had brought it over and filled their glasses, Stella took out a copy of the article she'd found online in *Le Figaro*.

'I'm guessing you already know about this article,' Stella said. 'I found it on the day the notebook arrived, but in the excitement of the perfumes and La Scintilla I forgot all about it.'

Bruno leaned forward to read the text. 'Yes, I've seen this.' He nodded. 'It's partly what led me to Penhallam's. What do you make of it?'

One thing had struck her as unusual. 'It's odd they were heading out on this trip just as war was declared. Poland had already been invaded. Surely it was reckless for them to travel east across Europe.'

'It is strange timing,' Bruno said. 'It's also interesting how this makes it clear that Iris and Alessandro created these perfumes together for Raffaele di Fiore.'

Stella sighed. 'Iris was very distressed today. I'm not sure if it's the trauma of the fire, or the past, or both. I'd like to go and see her again tomorrow.' She paused, taking in the enormity of the task that faced her. 'At this rate, I might not have a company to go back to.'

She ducked her head, aware that her voice sounded panicked and frightened. Tears smarted in her eyes. Bruno reached out his hand and took hers. He turned her palm upward and smoothed his thumb across her skin. The effect was so arresting that she held her breath. Time seemed to stand still.

'Stella, listen to me,' Bruno said. 'No one is going to take your business if you don't want them to . . .'

'James has told GPL that Penhallam's is struggling. If word gets out, it won't look good.'

Bruno tilted his head. 'I don't understand. Who's James? And what is GPL?'

'James works for GPL. It's a massive company that wants to buy out Penhallam's.' She paused, wondering how much to share with Bruno. 'James and I had been seeing each other on and off, but recently we broke up – he was worried about a conflict of interest. Andrea, the company CEO, rang the other day to make an offer, so now I know why James got cold feet. His chances of promotion rely on him getting this deal.'

Bruno let go of her hand. 'But he has no right to interfere. And you need to tell GPL the company isn't for sale.'

Stella smiled and rubbed the base of her wine glass with her finger. 'Oh, I have,' she said. She might as well tell him the whole sorry story. 'But I've taken out a second loan to pursue this idea about Iris's perfumes. If it doesn't pay off, I might have to consider taking drastic action.'

'Surely not,' Bruno said. Stella was surprised to see how passionate he was about it. 'I've seen you these last few weeks, running that place single-handedly. GPL couldn't do what you do. You've given your all to that company. It's yours, no matter what happens.'

'Not if it keeps losing money.'

'Then we have to find these perfumes and prove that you can turn the business around.'

Stella was used to shouldering the burden of Penhallam's alone. It felt good to have his support. 'I've already started drawing up a timeline of how we could develop, produce and advertise a set of scents like this. But it might take weeks, or months, for Iris to want to confide in me, and I can't get started until I have samples of all the perfumes for a proper collection and work out how they're made.'

'The best way is to retrace Iris's steps one step at a time and not get in a panic about all the other details,' Bruno said calmly. 'This all started when Iris came to work for Raffaele. Look at the last sentence in the article: *Di Fiore's perfumery at No. 23 rue Bayard will unveil the full collection, entitled The Perfumer's Secret, in early 1940.*'

Stella nodded. 'You're right – one step at a time,' she said. 'Number 23 rue Bayard. That's where we need to go tomorrow.'

The next day, Stella and Bruno left the hotel early. When they reached the address, Stella was dismayed to discover that the perfumery was no longer there. Number 23 rue Bayard was now a designer clothes store. The interior had been stripped of any historical features. Black and white panels and spotlights adorned the walls. It was hard to imagine that this had once been a perfumery. The building itself was old: the stone was a honey-cream colour, and garlands of fruit and vegetables had been sculpted on the outside wall. Ornate black cast-iron fencing skirted each window, and the building stretched up over six floors.

'What shall we do?' Stella said.

'We might as well go in and enquire about Raffaele. I doubt they'll know anything, but it can't do any harm.'

The manager of the shop was a tall woman with dark hair who seemed genuinely sorry the perfumery had gone. Her name badge said she was called Lorraine. 'When the owners bought the building ten years ago everything that remained here went to the Musée des Arts et Métiers. There were several boxes of stuff from the basement. They used some of it for an exhibition.'

'It was a long shot to expect that it would still be here,' Stella said.

'The building was in use as a perfumery until the late seventies,' Lorraine said. 'Then it stood empty for a while until my boss bought it.'

'Do you know what kind of things were in the boxes?' Bruno asked.

She shook her head. 'No, I'm afraid not. You'd have to ask the museum.'

'Does anything remain of the old perfumery?' Stella asked. 'My great-aunt was an apprentice here before the war. I'm trying to retrace her footsteps. I'd love to catch a glimpse of those times.'

Lorraine smiled. 'There is something I can show you.'

Stella and Bruno followed her through double doors at the back of the shop. 'We store the stock in the basement,' she said, 'but this is our staff room and informal office space.'

The doors opened on to a light, airy room with a high ceiling. Large windows at the back looked out on to a courtyard. Along the edge of the room, under the windows, was a wooden workbench. On the right-hand side were heavy wooden shelves stocked with stationery.

'The bench and shelves are some of the original fittings,' Lorraine said.

Stella imagined the shelves full of amber bottles. The room swirling with different aromas. Iris and Alessandro seated at the benches, just like Claudine when she was composing scents. Stella felt a powerful connection with the room: if she half closed her eyes, she could be transported back to that time. Raffaele's words in the newspaper article – *'In these uncertain and troubled times, I want to make sure that nobody forgets what really matters: the human capacity for love. We are going on a journey to capture what it means to fall in love.'* – would have surely ignited their creativeness. Stella could feel her own ideas whirring at the thought of scents to evoke such a journey. The question remained, however, why travel at such a fraught and dangerous time in history?

'It's beautiful,' Stella said. 'The perfumers would have worked here, overlooking the flowers in the courtyard.'

'It's like stepping back in time,' Bruno said, his eyes meeting hers. He felt it too, the thrill of being in this place, where it had all begun for Iris and Alessandro.

Lorraine nodded. 'Yes, we're lucky to have it. The courtyard is a real sun trap and a lovely place to have lunch.'

'Maybe we could find the exhibition pieces in the archives of the Musée des Arts et Métiers,' Bruno said. 'Although the artefacts are probably not in the museum any more. There's a new building in Saint-Denis that houses the museum's reserves. We might find something there.'

Stella gripped Bruno's arm. The excitement at perhaps finding a lead had bubbled up and it seemed only natural to express it to him. 'Let's go after we've seen Iris.'

They thanked Lorraine and Stella followed Bruno out of the shop. She could never have done this alone. It was nice to have someone her own age to work with, someone who seemed as passionate about this search as she was. But as she climbed into the taxi, Stella knew he was here to find material for his book, nothing more. She needed to be careful not to let her search for the perfumes spill into a search for something else.

Monique led Stella and Bruno down the corridor to Iris's room. Most of the doors in the corridor were closed, but through one open door Stella caught sight of a man and woman — family members, she presumed — visiting an elderly gentleman. It pained her to think that Iris had been on her own here, with no one to come and see her. Her fingers tightened on the bottle of La Scintilla in her pocket. It wasn't just the mystery of the perfumes she wanted to know about. It was the reasons behind the family estrangement too.

'She's still very weak, but I think today might be a good day,' Monique said as they approached Iris's room. 'She's sitting up and has been talking a little more than usual. She's even asking when she'll be discharged. I get the impression she's impatient to go home.'

'Where's that?' Stella asked.

'Somewhere in the south of France, I believe. Now, here we are. Can I get you a coffee?'

'Thank you,' Bruno said, 'I'll come and help.'

Stella smiled at him, grateful for his tact. She knocked

at the door and then opened it slowly. Iris was sitting up against a bank of pillows, wearing a pale blue dressing gown. She had the perfume notebook in her hands and was leafing through the pages.

'Good morning, Iris,' Stella said. 'How are you feeling?'

'So, you've come back,' Iris said, her voice croaky. Stella wasn't sure if Iris was pleased or not. 'I feel much the same. Monique says it could be a few weeks before I can go home.'

'That must be hard. There's nothing like being in your own place,' Stella said. When she got back to London, she really needed to unpack all those boxes and make her little room at Penhallam's feel like home.

Stella sat down in the chair next to the bed. On the way over here, she'd decided that the best way to approach Iris was as if she already *did* know her and just to behave normally. Yesterday she'd been too blunt. Iris had been caught off guard. Stella felt quite protective of the frail woman, who was regarding her now with a pair of intensely blue eyes. But to her surprise, it was Iris who started the conversation about the past.

'Did your grandfather ever tell you why we didn't speak?' she said.

Stella shook her head. 'Not specifically. He said that something happened just after the war and from that moment he wanted nothing more to do with you.'

Iris nodded. 'And your father . . .' She stopped again to clear her throat, the effort clearly painful from the way she winced. 'What did he say about me?'

Stella paused, unsure of what to say and how honest to be with Iris. She didn't want to hurt her feelings, but she also instinctively knew Iris wouldn't appreciate a lie.

'Nothing, really, it was just understood that you were no longer part of the family.' She paused, fiddling with the cuff of her cardigan. 'But you see, you and I are the only Penhallams left. That's why I'm here. My father entrusted the running of the business to me, and I don't want to let him down, and I suppose in the back of my mind I was always curious about you, given that we'd never met.'

Iris began to cough. The coughing fit went on for a long time. By the time it had finished, Iris looked exhausted.

'You did meet me, actually,' she gasped, resting her head back on the pillow. 'Just once.'

'Really?' Stella said. 'I've no recollection of it.'

'You were only three,' Iris said, her voice strained. 'Your father brought you to see me when I lived in Chantilly.'

Stella's eyes widened. 'He brought me to see you. Here in France?' He'd never said anything about it. What had led him to visit Iris? Curiosity? The same impulse that Stella now felt to trace her family. 'I'm guessing my grandfather didn't know about it?'

Iris took a handkerchief out of her sleeve and wiped her mouth. 'No, he didn't. It was your father's attempt at building bridges, apparently,' Iris said. 'Nothing ever came of it.' She smiled for a moment, as if remembering. 'You ran around my garden, smelling the flowers. You had a gift.'

'I don't understand,' Stella said.

'A gift for scent,' said Iris, coughing into the handkerchief.

'Me?' Stella said. 'That's impossible.'

Iris shrugged. 'That depends. A gift needs to be appreciated. You need to make it possible.'

'I'm not a perfumer,' Stella said. 'I'm like my father. Or Charles. I work in the office and run the business from there. We don't have a perfumer any more. It's never been my role.'

Iris reached out for Stella's hand. The gesture was unexpected. Her hands were papery and soft. Stella felt the jolt of a connection that she couldn't explain.

'Are you quite sure you don't have the urge to be a perfumer?' Iris said. Her blue eyes seemed to see right through Stella.

Stella slid her hand away. 'Yes,' she said. 'Quite sure.' But as she said the words, Stella experienced a moment of doubt.

Bruno came in carrying a tray of hot drinks. 'Morning, Iris,' he said. 'I've just been teaching Monique how to make a proper Italian coffee.'

Iris raised her eyebrows. 'I can't imagine she enjoyed that.' She took the cup that Bruno handed her and had a sip. 'But I must say, that's very nice. I always did prefer it on the stronger side.'

'Is that how Raffaele made it?' Bruno asked. 'Or Alessandro, perhaps? I'd love to talk to you about those days, if you feel up to it.'

'Ah yes, Stella mentioned your book,' Iris said. She put the mug down on the bedside table. 'I'm afraid those days are long gone now. In fact, I can hardly remember them.'

'I've got something that could help you remember,' Stella said. 'You see, when Bruno was clearing out the archives in the basement at Jermyn Street, he found a bottle of perfume.'

Stella took out the bottle of La Scintilla. Iris's eyes widened.

'It's one of the first perfume you mention in the notebook,' Stella said. 'I thought perhaps the scent might have spoiled, given all the years that have passed, but it's crystal clear.' Stella undid the lid. 'Would you like to smell it?'

Stella held it out towards Iris. The glorious scent filled the air. A brief flicker of recognition flitted across Iris's face. Could she smell it? Even a little? Iris reached out her hand to take the bottle, then stopped.

'Put it away,' Iris said, her face twisted with anguish. 'My anosmia won't let me smell it. Do you know how it feels not to smell properly? It's like the colours have gone out of the world. Instead, there's just a blank page where all the scent and memories should be.'

Stella put the lid back on the perfume, her cheeks reddening. 'I'm sorry, it must be terrible.'

Iris closed her eyes. 'You can't imagine what it's like,' she whispered. 'Instead of using your gift, you ignore it. Coming here, telling me you want my perfumes to rescue Penhallam's. Why would I help you? Charles wanted nothing to do with me, and neither did your father. I don't owe Penhallam's anything.'

Stella glanced anxiously at Bruno. This wasn't going well.

'I don't know why you and Charles fell out,' Stella said. 'But surely you must feel some loyalty to the business that your grandfather started.'

Bruno cleared his throat. 'We don't wish to distress you, Iris,' he said, 'but if you could tell us more about the perfumes, it would really help us both.'

Iris closed her eyes.

'Could you at least tell us if they exist, if the other perfumes were ever made?' Stella said.

Iris's breathing seemed to slow. The room stood still – the noise of the traffic outside and the ticking of the clock on the wall were amplified by the silence.

Iris opened her eyes. 'They exist,' she said. 'But they are

lost to me. And I want them to stay that way.' Her eyes were glazed with sorrow. 'I'm sorry I can't help you.'

There was nothing else to say. Stella didn't want to force Iris into talking. 'I understand,' Stella said. 'I'm sorry if we've upset you. Perhaps it's time we went.'

'I'm sorry too,' Bruno said. 'We'll let you get some rest.'

As Stella closed the door she glimpsed Iris run her locket along its chain, clearly agitated. There was so much of the family's past locked inside her. So many words that might help Stella, if only she'd release them. But Stella would need to work harder at convincing Iris to trust her.

11

Iris – Paris, August 1939

A week after Iris had started at Raffaele's perfumery, Henri insisted on walking Iris to work in the morning sun.

He had put on his smart trench coat and held out his arm for her to take. Iris didn't want a chaperone.

'Honestly, there's no need,' Iris said. She put on her cardigan and lifted her bag on to her shoulder. 'I'll be fine going by myself.' She enjoyed the early-morning walk through Paris and the ride on the Métro. It gave her a feeling of independence.

She opened the front door, but Henri stuck his foot out and jammed it. He stood very close, the citrussy blast of his cologne hitting Iris's nostrils.

'I've been thinking that perhaps I need to make my feelings clearer,' he said.

'What do you mean?'

'My feelings towards you,' Henri said. 'I want to marry you, Iris.' He came closer. 'As each day goes by, I find our proximity in this house maddening. Surely you feel it too?'

Iris stared at him, flustered. 'I thought Charles had got it wrong. I never thought you'd actually want to marry me.'

Henri smiled. 'Well, I do. I thought you'd be pleased. I don't think it's possible to wait a year for you, Iris. War is coming, and I want to marry you as soon as I can.'

She could feel his breath on her cheek. 'I don't know . . .'

Since the walk back from the gardens, she'd been more conscious of Henri's eyes on her. The intensity of his gaze, over dinner or in the morning, was disconcerting.

'But that's why you wanted to stay with me in Paris, isn't it? To get to know me better. I know the apprenticeship was involved, but I just assumed you were too embarrassed to let me know you wanted me too,' Henri said, twisting a lock of her hair in his fingers. 'I remember how you used to look at me when we were at the beach in Nice. I noticed you, Iris, more than you realized. I still notice you.'

Iris blushed. 'Henri, you are a very good friend to Charles, but there's no need for you to indulge his idea that we should marry. You were always surrounded by a flock of beautiful women in Mougins. Why on earth would you want to court Charles's little sister?'

Henri regarded her intently. 'Ah, well, let's just say a combination of things has conspired to make you the woman I choose.' He bent down and kissed her cheek, his lips warm against her skin. 'And who says you're not beautiful?'

Oh God, what had she done? In her haste to convince Charles to let her come to Paris, Iris had forgotten one thing. Henri was not a man to be toyed with. In Mougins, he was determined to win every card game, debate and race. It seemed he was determined to win her, too, and that made things here more complicated.

'So come on,' he said, removing his foot and offering her his arm. 'I insist that you let me walk you to work.'

Henri left her at the door of the perfumery and continued on to his office. Iris stood for a moment, relieved that he hadn't insisted on coming in. She watched him stride along the pavement, without a backward glance. What was she going to do? She was dependent on Henri's goodwill to stay here in Paris. She would have to tread carefully.

'Are you going in or not?' Alessandro stood behind her.

'Oh, sorry,' Iris said, her train of thought broken. She searched in her bag for the key. 'It's in here somewhere, just a minute. Damn, I can't find it.'

Alessandro touched her arm. 'Are you okay?'

He'd been more distant since the day Henri came to meet her in the gardens. Now he regarded her with concern. She didn't want him thinking she needed his pity.

'Yes, I'm fine. Here it is.' She shoved the key in the lock and opened the door. 'After you.'

Iris entered the shop after him, inhaling a mixture of floral and spicy scents. Worries about Henri didn't belong in here; this was her safe space. She pushed them from her mind. She needed to stay focused on Raffaele's teachings. That's what she was here for. Somehow there had to be a way for her to stay true to what she wanted.

Raffaele was in the perfumery. 'I need you both to visit a client for a bespoke perfume,' he said.

'Both of us?' Iris said. Part of her liked the idea of spending more time with Alessandro, but she was concerned about Raffaele being left alone in the shop. 'Wouldn't it be better if just one of us went?'

Alessandro raised his eyebrows. 'I suppose you mean you.'

'No, I didn't,' Iris said, 'although I have done a consultation before, with Marcel.'

'And so have I, with Francesca.'

'Then you go,' Iris said, wondering why he was so defensive. 'I'm just trying to think what's best for Raffaele.'

Raffaele furrowed his brow. 'I expect harmony in my perfumery. I need you to work together. Otherwise, how can I . . .'

'What?' Iris asked, distressed by his tone.

'Nothing. It's just that I fear I will need all my strength for the horrors that might lie ahead if this war comes to pass. I was forced to join up when Italy entered the Great War. I've seen fighting, and I know what destruction it wreaks.'

Alessandro took his arm and guided Raffaele to a chair. 'I'm sorry. You need to rest. I'm so grateful for this opportunity you've given me. I don't always believe that the good things that have come my way will last.'

Raffaele patted Alessandro's hand. 'You need to trust your ability. I'd like you both to see Madame Geffroy. We'll close the shop for a few hours. Making a bespoke scent is a great responsibility. You worked well together on the scent in London. I want you to use those skills and co-operate again.'

'Of course we will, won't we?' Iris said. She nudged Alessandro, and he nodded. 'If you give us the address, we'll go and see her right away.'

Raffaele smiled at them both. 'Thank you.' He jotted it down. 'Remember, the best way to help me is if you work together.' He headed upstairs to the flat above.

'Being here obviously means a lot to you,' Iris said to Alessandro.

'This last year has been quite difficult. Things haven't worked out as I'd planned. Raffaele took me in, but everything seems precarious. If war breaks out, Italy is certain to take Hitler's side. The Pact of Steel demands it. The French will want us here even less.'

Iris sighed. 'Then perhaps the only thing to do is lose ourselves in making perfume. It's what I always do when the pressure gets too much.'

'Me too,' Alessandro said. He smiled briefly. 'I'm sorry about arguing with you. I've been used to being the only apprentice here up to now, and you . . . well, you're obviously very talented, from what I've seen, and I suppose it's made me nervous.'

Iris raised her eyebrows. 'I'm equally intimidated by your skills.'

Alessandro shook his head. 'I find that hard to believe. You're from a different world. A family of perfumers. A rich suitor.' He dropped his gaze. 'You could run this place single-handedly.'

Iris swallowed. 'No, I couldn't, and Henri isn't exactly my suitor,' she said. 'He's my brother Charles's oldest friend, and I'm staying with him and his mother while I'm here. It was the only way to persuade Charles to let me come.' It seemed important to explain this to Alessandro.

Alessandro reached for his travel bag of ingredients. 'It's none of my business,' he said. 'I just meant to say, I'll put my insecurities to one side from now on. You were right. We need to do our best to help Raffaele.'

Mme Geffroy lived in an old mansion on the outskirts of Montmartre. The white dome of the Sacré-Cœur sat on the hill just above the house and shone in the morning sunshine. A maid ushered Iris and Alessandro into an elegant drawing room with light yellow walls and a large Persian rug on the wooden floor. A lavish flower display stood on a grand piano. Whoever lived here had exacting standards. Iris hoped she and Alessandro would be able to meet them.

A woman who looked to be in her seventies came into the room and sat on one side of the coffee table, gesturing for them to sit on the other.

'I was hoping for Raffaele,' Mme Geffroy said, looking unimpressed.

'Raffaele has entrusted us with this commission,' Iris said. 'We work very closely alongside him at the perfumery.'

She eyed them suspiciously, before saying, 'That might be true, but I'll only pay if I'm happy with the end result.'

'Of course,' Alessandro said, a hint of nerves in his voice. 'Perhaps you could describe the scent you're looking for?'

'I would like a scent that reminds me of my first kiss,' Mme Geffroy said defiantly.

This was a surprise. 'Can you tell us more?' Iris said, mindful of Raffaele's advice to get the story behind a client's wishes.

Mme Geffroy sat back in her chair. 'It was 1890, and I was twenty-one and on my first visit to Paris. It was glorious – the sun always shining and the city so vibrant. One day my mother was ill, and I was supposed to stay in my hotel room, but instead I sneaked out and went into the city alone. Young people were milling about on the steps of the Sacré-Cœur, there was a procession, incense burning, and I got carried along through the cobbled streets, wisteria blooming on the houses.'

As Mme Geffroy spoke, her face was transformed. Iris caught a glimpse of the beautiful woman she must have been.

'I got hopelessly lost. A young man noticed me looking distressed. Without any hesitation, he took my hand and led me back to the Sacré-Cœur. We walked through some gardens behind the church, sat down on a bench and talked for hours. He moved closer, and then . . .'

'What?' Iris said, captivated by the story.

'He kissed me, and all the scents and sensations mingled together in a moment that set my skin alight. That first kiss was like nothing I'd ever experienced before.' Mme Geffroy blushed. 'Well, I seem to have got a little carried away,' she said, patting her hair.

'Did you ever see him again?' Iris asked.

'Two years later we were married.' Mme Geffroy smiled. 'But that's another story. All I want you to capture is that first kiss.'

Iris caught Alessandro's eye. His cheeks reddened. Was he thinking of his first kiss? Had it been as magical as the one Mme Geffroy had just described? Iris looked away and made notes in her book.

'Very well. First kisses are very special. This scent needs something to make your heart pound and your senses open,' Alessandro said. 'I'm sure we can manage that, can't we, Iris?'

Now wasn't the time to admit that she had never had a first kiss. It wasn't something she wanted to divulge to Alessandro.

'Of course,' she said. 'This needs to capture the surprise and freedom you felt that day, Madame Geffroy. Along with the wisteria, and incense, is there anything else you remember?'

The scent needed a top note, something to blast the senses with the first inhalation.

'Yes,' Mme Geffroy said, 'I do remember another smell, although it's more of a taste. We drank fresh orange juice from a stall. I tasted that orange in his kiss.'

'Then we have the pillars of this perfume,' Iris said, tapping her notebook with her pen.

'*Merveilleux,*' Mme Geffroy said. 'I'm grateful for how well you've picked up my thoughts.'

'Shall we talk through some suggested ingredients,' Alessandro said, 'and we'll jot down your reactions? Just a moment while I get the bottles.' He scouted through the perfumer's case for the natural oils and lifted out wisteria, a selection of citrus fragrances and frankincense.

He opened the wisteria, dipped in a test strip and handed it to Mme Geffroy.

'Take a deep breath and inhale,' he said. 'This will be overly strong by itself and smell like a mixture of other scents – jasmine, lily of the valley, lavender and rose, along with a touch of clove. This wisteria floral will be the heart note.'

Mme Geffroy nodded. 'Yes, I like that, but in the background, perhaps.'

Iris jotted notes. Alessandro was good at this, leading Mme Geffroy through the complex ingredients. One by one, he handed her the bottles. 'You said about the hint of orange,' he said, 'so perhaps we could use orange blossom, and have it as a top note?'

Mme Geffroy smiled. 'That sounds ideal,' she said. 'You know, I was a little startled when I saw you here instead of Raffaele, but it seems you both understand what I want.'

Alessandro smiled, glancing briefly at Iris. She caught his eye, and he surprised her with a quick wink. She quickly looked back down at her notebook.

'Why don't we make up some blends and we can come back the day after tomorrow for you to sample them?' Iris said.

'Wonderful,' Mme Geffroy said.

*

Alessandro and Iris walked down the cobbled road. It was mid-morning and the air was still fresh and cool.

'That seemed to go well,' Alessandro said.

'Raffaele should have told her he was sending his apprentices. But I think, by the end, she was pleased. We made a good team.'

They reached the end of the road. Steps headed up to the Sacré-Cœur. She'd been up there long ago with her father and Charles.

'Shall we climb up and look at the view? I've never been up there before, and maybe it will help inspire us,' Alessandro suggested. He shifted the perfumer's case from one hand to the other. 'That is, if you're not in a hurry to get back.'

'No, I'd like that,' Iris said. She smiled shyly, flattered that he wanted to spend more time with her. Henri wouldn't approve, but right now that wasn't her concern.

Iris lost count of the steps up to the Sacré-Cœur. Her legs ached as she followed in Alessandro's footsteps. Every so often he looked back, as if to check she was still there. 'Not far now,' he said encouragingly.

He reached out his hand to help her up the last step. She took it, the firmness of his grip, the smoothness of his palm, reassuring. But also, something else. He held her hand a moment longer, and her skin seemed to tingle. His cheeks reddened and he let go. They sat down on the steps and looked at the view. The whole of Paris stretched out in front of them, a cloudless sky above. The Eiffel Tower stood proud above the skyline.

'Incredible,' Alessandro said.

In the distance, a hum of planes. The crowd of people milling on the steps grew silent and watched the planes fly past, black specks on the empty sky.

'They're gearing up,' Alessandro said. 'It's been happening a lot recently. A few weeks before you came there were practice manoeuvres in the city streets. *Le Monde* has reports of German troops massing on the Polish border. It seems like it's only a matter of time.'

The planes disappeared out of view. 'It would have been so different when Mme Geffroy was here,' Iris said. 'Funny how that chance encounter changed her life.'

Alessandro smiled. 'Admit it, you were a little taken aback when she said she wanted a perfume that reminded her of her first kiss. Your face was a picture.'

'Nonsense,' Iris said, smiling back. 'It was you who was surprised. I could tell by your flowery language. What was it you said? *First kisses are very special. This scent needs something to make your heart pound and your senses open.*' Iris exaggerated the words as she said them. 'It was pure poetry.'

Alessandro laughed. 'I thought it was very perceptive of me,' he said. 'She certainly appreciated it. And anyway, that's what a first kiss does feel like, or at least mine did.'

'I suppose so.' Iris's inexperience prevented her from saying more.

Alessandro glanced at her. 'I presume you've had a first kiss?'

'Do you?' Iris said, wishing he would drop the subject.

'Of course. Henri.' His voice sounded flat.

Iris wrapped her cardigan around her. It was breezy up here. 'Actually, no, not Henri.'

Alessandro tilted his head. There was no point pretending.

'If you must know, I haven't had a first kiss yet. Unless you count the young man at a school dance who tried to accost me.' She shrugged. 'I'm afraid I poured my lemonade over him. But it doesn't mean I can't empathize with what Mme Geffroy told us. A perfumer needs a good imagination.'

'I can tell you about my first kiss, if you like,' Alessandro said. 'It was at a carnival, and I'd had my first taste of wine at our neighbours' house and my head was spinning. I went outside to get some air and the neighbour's daughter, Roberta, followed me, and we stood side by side, looking at the moon on the water, and we both turned to each other at the exact same moment, and . . . well, it was fleeting, and not quite what I'd expected.'

He'd described it so clearly Iris felt like she was there, in Roberta's place, standing next to him. And yet the thought of him sharing that moment, a moment she'd never experienced, with someone else, was strangely disconcerting.

'Well, I'll have no need of a first kiss, what with your description and Mme Geffroy's.' She stood up and brushed down her skirt.

'Iris, I didn't mean to upset you.'

She forced a smile. 'You haven't. It's just that it's getting late. We should get back.'

They headed back down the stairs in silence. It was ridiculous. She'd always longed to have a first kiss. In her dreams, growing up, it was Henri she'd imagined kissing. Iris sighed. *He kissed me, and all the scents and sensations mingled together in a moment that set my skin alight.* It made no sense that it was Alessandro's warm, curving lips she pictured now.

12

Stella – Paris, June 1996

The next morning, Stella and Bruno headed to the Musée des Arts et Métiers. The taxi sped out of Paris and into the industrial estates of Saint-Denis, the Stade de France looming in the distance. The taxi turned right and down a side street which led to a huge building made of curved grey metal, resembling an army barracks.

Stella and Bruno went up the steps and into the small reception area. A man looked up from a computer. 'Can I help you?' he said.

'I hope so,' Stella said. 'I'd like to enquire whether you have any items from the perfumery of Raffaele di Fiore stored here.'

The man consulted his records. 'Yes, I believe we do.'

Stella smiled at Bruno, relieved. At last they were getting somewhere.

'Please could we come in and take a look at them?' she said.

The man frowned. 'Do you have an appointment?'

'No . . .'

'Are you a visiting academic on our register?'

'No,' Stella said. 'My great-aunt worked at the perfumery as an apprentice just before the war and I'm trying to find out more about her life.'

The man shook his head. 'Then I'm afraid I can't help you,' he said. 'Unless you have a university card or academic status, I can't admit you at such short notice. My apologies.' The man turned his attention back to the computer.

Bruno reached into his jacket pocket and took out his wallet. He handed a card to the man. 'It's my University of Venice identification card. This should be enough to allow us to access the museum reserves today.'

The man sighed. 'Fine. Let's sign you in.' He handed Stella a slip of paper with the location of Raffaele's items.

'Thank you,' Stella said. Without Bruno, she'd never have got in.

Inside the warehouse-sized caverns of the reserves, artefacts and papers were stacked on shelves six foot high. There was no natural light inside the building. Bulbs hung down on long chains and the air was cool and musty.

Bruno held the slip of paper. 'Aisle Y, shelf 48.'

They walked along the smooth concrete floor. Archivists were working in some of the aisles, cataloguing boxes and crates.

'Almost everything has been moved here while they're renovating the building in Paris. It looks like they've got as far as M, which hopefully means that Raffaele's objects will still be untouched.'

At last, they came to row Y.

The light was dimmer at this end of the warehouse, the murmur of the archivists quieter. She followed Bruno down the aisle. He turned round to look at her, a grin of excitement on his face. She wanted to reach out and touch him, sharing his enthusiasm, but she curbed the impulse.

Shelf forty-eight. She stopped next to Bruno and peered up. There were two thick cardboard boxes next to each other on the shelf. Stella reached up and lifted one down. It was heavier than she'd thought. Bruno grabbed the sides to steady it, his body pressing against Stella's, his hand brushing hers. The touch of his skin was like a jolt of electricity.

'Sorry,' he said. Had he felt it too? His cheeks were red. 'I'll get the other one.'

'Let's take one box each and have a good look through,' Stella said briskly.

For the next half an hour, they were silent, sifting through the boxes. In Stella's there was a jumble of equipment — pipettes, empty bottles, jars, letterheaded notepaper. In Bruno's were a pair of weighing scales and a set of accounts from 1928.

'There must be more than this,' Bruno said. 'I'll go and ask while you finish going through these.'

His footsteps receded. Stella lifted out the test tubes and papers. Underneath, she caught sight of a glass bottle. She reached in and took it out. It was the same shape as the bottle of La Scintilla. It had the same distinctive gold top and glass body. Sure enough, when she turned it over, she found a label: Primo Bacio. First Kiss. The second perfume in Iris's notebook. She unscrewed the lid and lifted the bottle to her nose.

The smell was like nothing she'd experienced before. An intense hit of orange blossom, like an assault on the senses, followed by the complex sweetness of wisteria. Underneath, frankincense, powerful and mysterious. It was incredible.

Stella dabbed some on her wrists. The power of a first kiss. How had Alessandro and Iris created it? It was like a mixture of dark and light, passion and fury, masculine and feminine. She inhaled again.

Something clicked in her mind. This perfume was written in a language she could understand. A code she could decipher. It was as if, all these years, her sense of smell had stood dormant, waiting for this moment. Suddenly she understood what Iris meant. Stella did have a gift. But far from feeling delighted about this, she felt only frustration. Her job was simply to find the perfumes, not to interpret them. Once she got back to London the business would claim all her attention, as it always did.

There was no one around. Without a second thought, she slipped the bottle into her pocket. She peeped through the gaps in the shelves to the other aisle. No one had seen her. It wasn't really theft. After all, the bottle belonged to Iris, and as her great-niece Stella had every right to take it. If only she could persuade Iris to tell her more. Perhaps the language of the scent would inspire her trust.

Footsteps sounded. Bruno must be coming back. He walked down the aisle.

'Apparently, this is it,' Bruno said. 'Did you find anything else?'

Stella shook her head, not sure if she was ready to share her discovery with him yet.

'Let's pack up the boxes. I'm sorry there wasn't anything here to help us.'

He stopped, frowning. 'What's that smell? That perfume. I didn't notice it before.' He moved closer to Stella. 'It's coming from you.'

Stella blushed. 'I found a bottle of Primo Bacio in the box,' she whispered. 'I tried it, and it's astonishing. I'm taking it with me.'

'You're stealing it,' Bruno said, his eyes wide. 'I can't imagine you doing anything like that.'

Stella smiled. 'Perhaps this trip is changing me,' she said. 'I saw it and I knew I had to take a risk.'

'A risk,' Bruno said, moving closer, his eyes on hers. 'Is that what you think this is?'

'This was the second fragrance that Iris and Alessandro made together. Just smell it.' She reached into her pocket to get the bottle, but Bruno took her hand.

His eyes darkened. 'I don't need the bottle to smell it,' he said. 'I can smell it on you.'

Stella's heart hammered in her chest, aware of the dark shadow at the base of his throat, the curve of his lips, the warmth emanating from his skin.

He gently took her hand and lifted her wrist to his nose. 'It's intoxicating,' he said huskily.

'Is it?' Stella whispered, feeling the burn of his touch.

'You are intoxicating,' he said.

He stared into her eyes for a moment, then placed his hand against the small of her back. Stella felt a rush of desire. She reached up and put her arms around him, the perfume mingling with his scent. His lips came closer, so close they almost seemed to brush hers. She closed her eyes, yearning to feel his touch. When it came, she gasped, then kissed him harder. He pressed her up against the shelves. The world stopped for a moment, lost in the fire of an endless kiss.

Then suddenly, he pulled away, breathing hard. 'Sorry,' he said. 'I wasn't thinking. You just looked so beautiful standing there, the smell of that perfume wafting over me, and your smile . . .'

Stella took a deep breath. He was clearly embarrassed, his usual easy-going composure ruffled. The perfume had tipped them both towards the edge of a cliff. She needed to save face and undo the last few minutes.

She touched her lips. 'Maybe we got a bit carried away.'

'I didn't mean . . .'

Now was the time to draw a line under this. Clearly it had been a mistake. Her body begged to differ – a flame lit by his touch was still burning – but her head doused it. 'No, it was a moment of madness, let's just forget it.'

'If that's what you want,' Bruno said. He reached for his box and lifted it back on to the shelf.

Stella breathed deeply, regaining control of herself. She shouldn't have done that. She packed the last few items into her box, passing it over to Bruno to replace on the shelf. They headed back to the reception desk. The perfume bottle was still in her pocket, but the man at the desk simply waved them through.

Out on the street, Stella rubbed her wrist, wishing she could wash off the perfume. It was so full of emotion. She wondered if Iris had felt it too. Working with Alessandro at such close quarters, it was easy to imagine that they had shared a kiss too. How else would they have been able to create such an evocative fragrance?

'Are you okay?' Bruno said.

Stella smiled, unable to bear the concern in his eyes. Was he feeling sorry for her? Or regretting the fleeting impulse he'd felt to kiss her?

'I'm fine,' she said. 'We've got the second perfume, that's all that matters. And it's given me an idea.'

'What's that?' Bruno said.

'I need to go back and see Iris tomorrow,' Stella said, 'and talk to her on a different level. She doesn't want to talk about Penhallam's and the family rift. But perhaps the perfumes themselves, how they were made, might be something she would share. The process of them, rather than the story of our family.'

Bruno nodded. 'Even though you hardly know her, I guess that's one thing you have in common. A love of perfumes.'

'Yes,' Stella said. 'And something happened in there . . . I mean' – she blushed – 'to my sense of smell. Maybe I do have a gift, like Iris said, that I've never acknowledged. Maybe channelling that will enable Iris to trust me.'

'In what way?'

'I looked up anosmia last night. It doesn't necessarily mean that a person's sense of smell is completely gone. Some scents can travel to the olfactory bulb in the fore-brain, under the right circumstances.'

'So, you think Iris might be able to smell something after all?'

'It's worth a try,' Stella said. 'Maybe smell is the way for me to get through to Iris.'

13

Iris – Paris, August 1939

The next day, Iris left the Levèques' house very early, before anyone was up, hoping to avoid Henri. A letter had arrived from Charles the day before. He was still impatient for news of an engagement.

Jane and I got married last week. I decided there was no time to lose. Which makes me think that you should prepare for returning to London. You've had a good run over there, and Henri still seems very taken with you, but even he can't protect you from the chaos that will be unleashed if Hitler marches into Poland in the next few weeks. Unless, of course, you have decided to marry him, in which case I would have no option but to allow you to remain in Paris with your husband. I don't need to tell you how your nuptials would also ease the financial burden at Penhallam's.

Iris clenched her fists as she walked along the Champs-Élysées. All she wanted was a few months of calm to learn as much as she could from Raffaele, but more and more that felt like a naive thing to wish for. Making perfume was a refuge, but it couldn't shelter her from war or Charles' insistence that she wed.

Iris looked anxiously at a faded poster on the dark green Morris column advertising French Infantry Day. A mother holding two children by the hand hurried past, and

Iris watched as she herded the children into the Métro. Perfume couldn't stop bombs, or protect those children either. She was here to help Raffaele, but, Iris realized, she would be prepared to do much more if needed.

When she arrived at the perfumery Iris unlocked the door and went in. It was still early, and she could tell that Alessandro wasn't here yet because the shutters were still closed.

Iris heard a creak on the stairs. 'Who's there?' Raffaele's voice called down from the first floor.

'It's me,' she said.

'You're early. Why don't you come up and have a coffee?'

The kitchen door stood open and a delicious aroma of freshly brewed coffee filled the air. Raffaele was at the stove, lifting the coffee off the hob. The table was set with challah and butter.

Iris had skipped breakfast so the sight of the food made her stomach growl.

Raffaele smiled. 'Come and sit down – help yourself. What brings you here so early in the morning?'

'I couldn't sleep,' Iris said, not wanting to burden him with her worries.

Raffaele put a slice of challah on her plate. 'Try this. I get them from the baker around the corner and they remind me of home.'

'I remember Francesca and Jacopo making these in Mougins,' Iris said. She bit into the thick bread. 'Any news from her yet?'

Raffaele shook his head. 'No. I've sent another letter. If there's no reply soon . . .' His voice faded away. 'It feels as if the noose is tightening on us all. I saw the rise of fascism in Italy. I know what harm it can do.'

Iris cradled her cup in her hand, listening.

'When Mussolini came to power in 1922,' Raffaele continued, 'I had misgivings. And when the socialist deputy Giacomo Matteo was assassinated two years later, I was decided: fascism had no place in Italy. I got involved in writing for an anti-fascist publication in my spare time. The authorities became suspicious and, one night, after a raid, several of my colleagues were captured. I had to escape Italy and continue my training as a perfumer here in Paris. That's why Francesca and Jacopo came over to meet me in the south of France. It wasn't safe for me to go back to Venice.'

A menorah shone in the sunlight on the windowsill. There was a framed photo on the wall of Francesca, her husband and Jacopo, a babe in arms. Now he was eleven. World events had never felt so personal. Charles had enlisted. Francesca and Jacopo were suffering in Italy.

'There must be something we can do to get them out,' Iris said.

'I should have insisted while I still had the chance.' Raffaele's face was pained. 'I send money when I can. This non-aggression pact between Germany and Italy doesn't bode well – even here in France things are getting difficult.'

'In what way?'

'I might have to make alternative arrangements for the perfumery, should anything happen to me. In Holland, Austria and Germany, the laws against Jews are very strict, and some business owners here in France are taking the precaution of handing ownership of their business over to Aryans, who will be protected from such laws if ever the Germans, God forbid, manage to occupy France.'

Iris's blood ran cold. 'But that's unthinkable,' she said. The idea of Nazi boots in France. Surely the Maginot Line would protect them from that. But if it didn't? A shiver ran down her spine. Hitler was intent on expansionism. It was horrifying to think of him setting his sights on France. 'The French government won't let it happen. Jews will be protected.'

Raffaele shrugged. 'It's sickening how governments can legislate against a race of people to the point at which they can barely function as human beings. Hopefully that will never happen in Paris. But I must be prepared.'

Iris thought of Henri's offhand remarks about Jews. 'I wish the world was a kinder place,' she said. 'I don't understand why people hate anyone who is different. How humans can so easily despise what they don't know or fear those with different beliefs. As if there isn't enough to cope with in this world without inventing reasons to ostracize fellow human beings.'

Raffaele patted her hand. 'It gives me heart that you feel that way,' he said. 'We need more people to stand up for what is right.'

For the rest of the day, the shop was busy with customers. Iris thought often of her conversation with Raffaele, wondering what she could do to help. At least with her and Alessandro here he had time to rest. But Iris worried that, upstairs in his flat, he was fretting about Francesca. There was no one she could discuss it all with other than Alessandro, and there was no chance to talk to him as they continued their two-hour rotations in the shop and the perfumery, passing only en route.

Finally, by three o'clock, the shop was quiet. Iris straightened the bottles on the shelves, trying to get a semblance of normality back after the rush.

Alessandro hovered near the doorway. 'I suppose we need to finish that perfume for Madame Geffroy,' he said.

'Yes, we should, although I'm not sure any of it makes sense at the moment.'

Alessandro came into the shop and leaned against the counter. 'Why not?'

Iris sighed. 'Raffaele is really concerned about Francesca. There's been no letter yet. I remember she was quite a headstrong person, but I would have thought she'd have got out of Italy before now, for Jacopo's sake.'

Alessandro rubbed his temple. 'I don't think she really believed things would go this far,' he said. 'We were both there in Venice that day in 1934 when Hitler met Mussolini for the first time. I could barely see either of them in the crowds, but loudspeakers broadcast their words. Hitler declared that Austria belonged to Germany. Mussolini shouted that it was Italy's. It seemed unlikely that the pair would ever find any sort of accord.'

'I wish I could do something useful to help him,' Iris said.

'You can,' Alessandro said. 'We need to finish First Kiss, our first commission. Running this perfumery is what Raffaele needs us to do.'

Iris nodded. 'You're right.'

She put the closed sign on the door and got out her notebook. Alessandro fetched the ingredients they had agreed on the day before and set them out on the workbench. He fiddled with the bottles, clearly something on his mind, then cleared his throat.

'I'm sorry about what I said yesterday at the Sacré-Cœur. I got carried away,' he said. 'My first kiss didn't lead to anything I'm proud of. I wish I'd never brought it up.'

Iris undid the bottle of wisteria oil. 'It's fine. Let's just forget it,' she said. She was determined to keep this businesslike, for Raffaele's sake. 'Why don't we make a few blends separately, then discuss and combine our ideas. It will be easier to work together once we have a starting-off point.'

'So long as you're not making this into a competition,' Alessandro said, raising his eyebrows.

'Of course not,' Iris said with a knowing smile. 'What makes you think I'd ever do that?'

But there *was* a bit of competition; it was unavoidable. Alessandro concentrated intently on his vials. Determined that her scent would be better than his, Iris wrote out a draft formula and made up an accord.

Normally, she could focus. But it was difficult to concentrate with Alessandro there. Every time Iris took a deep breath to inhale the blend she was working on, it was as if she was breathing him in too.

She glanced back at her notes. *He kissed me, and all the scents and sensations mingled together in a moment that set my skin alight.* How was she supposed to capture a first kiss when she had never experienced it herself? Use your imagination, she told herself. What would it be like to kiss Alessandro? His soft, full lips, those strong hands on her body. He looked up.

'Are you ready?' he said.

She swallowed, embarrassed to be caught staring. 'Something's missing from mine.'

'Mine too.' Alessandro touched the amber bottle he'd been mixing. 'I'm struggling with the contrasts. Can I smell your blend?'

'Let's swap.'

Her stomach fluttered at the thought of Alessandro assessing her work. And what if she hated his blend? How could she tell him without starting an argument? Or worse, what if it was so good it put her scent to shame?

'Are you as nervous as I am?' Alessandro said, voicing her thoughts.

She smiled, relieved he felt it too. 'A little.'

'On the count of three,' Alessandro said. '*Uno, due, tre.*'

Iris held the strip up to her nose and closed her eyes. Frankincense and wisteria hit her senses first. The smoky, dark undertones mingled with the sweet flower. It was hard to trace the orange blossom.

When she opened her eyes, Alessandro was looking at her. 'What do you think?' he asked.

Iris shook her head. 'Tell me what you think of my blend first.'

'I like the way the notes build up,' he said. 'It starts gently, with the orange and suggestions of wisteria, then it's as if we go closer, right into the scene, until the dusky current of frankincense carries us away. It's subtle – somehow it holds back, as if the kiss is just a dream.'

He was right. The scent was holding back because she'd never actually kissed anyone.

'Yours is the opposite,' Iris said, taking another sniff of the test paper. 'Everything comes on at once, a contrast of sweet and woody. This isn't a criticism, but maybe there's too much of the physical and less of the dream.'

Alessandro tried the two test strips together. 'I see what you mean. Yours is too subtle; mine is too strong. We need to reconcile these two scents so that the elements are balanced.'

He smiled, his eyes deepening. 'These scents could

almost be a metaphor for what's happening here, between us, don't you think?'

Iris felt her heart quicken. 'What do you mean?' she said, flustered.

Alessandro put the vial down, not taking his eyes off her. 'When I'm working with you, I feel like my ability and energy are doubled. We are different in many ways, but being with you brings out the best in me.'

Iris felt a wave of heat course through her body. Was he just talking about their working relationship? She bit her lip. 'I feel the same. When we're making a scent together, it's like I need to push myself. I think First Kiss is going to be amazing.'

'Maybe it's that passion for perfume and being the best at what we do that connects us, but I can't help feeling it's more than that.' Alessandro swallowed, his eyes locked on hers.

The room faded out and all she could smell was the aroma from the scents, all she could see was his dark brown eyes, deep and full of longing.

His hand slid along the counter until it touched hers. Their fingers entwined and a fire ignited in Iris. Blood rushed in her ears; a pulse of desire flared. She sat still, unable to move, as he came closer, his eyes on her. She closed her eyes. The first brush of his lips on hers, gentle, almost imperceptible, made her want more. The kiss deepened, his hands in her hair now, pressing her closer, her arms reaching up to clasp him tight. His tongue probed and she opened to its warmth. The kiss was like a scent enveloping her, transporting her. For those few minutes in his arms, Iris forgot everything.

Then Iris heard a sound. Someone was banging on

the shop door. She pulled away, her breath ragged, her lips tingling from the kiss. What were they doing? This was Raffaele's workshop. He could have appeared at any minute. And now there was a visitor.

Alessandro swallowed. 'Iris . . .'

Iris jumped off the stool. 'I'll see who that is.'

She hurried out of the room, her face on fire. That kiss had been incredible. A moment of madness. She opened the shop door, still reeling from it. Henri stood on the pavement, a bouquet of flowers in his arms.

'*Ma chérie*,' he said, planting a kiss on her cheek before she could protest. 'You look radiant. It's such a beautiful afternoon I've come to take you out for an early dinner.'

'I'm working,' she said, thrown by his arrival. 'I can't leave now.' Did the kiss show in her face? The desire still lingering on her skin and in her eyes.

'Of course you can,' Henri persisted.

'But . . .'

'It's fine. You go,' a voice said behind her. Alessandro stood in the doorway to the perfumery, his face pale. She watched him take in Henri, his expensive suit, the flowers, the way he'd kept hold of Iris's hand.

She twisted her hand free. 'But we need to finish the perfume,' she said.

Alessandro walked over, carrying her coat and bag in his hand. He must have heard Henri's words and assumed she would leave with him. Or was he regretting what had happened and now wanted her to go?

'I'll make up a blend and we can consult tomorrow before Mme Geffroy comes,' he said.

Iris took her things, hardly able to meet his eye. Just seconds ago, they had been so close, and now it seemed he wanted to get rid of her. 'Please don't do anything without me,' she said. 'I'll get here early in the morning.'

Alessandro nodded and went back into the perfumery. Iris wanted to run after him, explain that Henri was nothing to her, but what would that achieve? Maybe it was for the best that they'd been interrupted. That kiss was unprofessional between two work colleagues. She was ashamed of it. Yet a fire still burned within her, even as Henri took her hand and led her away.

Candle wax dripped down the silver candle holder and on to the tablecloth. Iris pressed a nail into the soft, white wax. That kiss with Alessandro, her first kiss, kept playing on her mind. It was difficult to concentrate on what Henri was saying.

'You're very quiet,' he said. He sat next to her on the banquette in a secluded corner of the restaurant.

Iris smiled at him. 'Sorry, I'm just tired, it was a busy day.'

The waiter brought their main courses. Iris had a beef steak and Henri had pork belly. But Iris wasn't really hungry – her mind still lingered on what had happened in the perfumery.

Henri ran his finger around the base of his wine glass. 'I've written to Charles and told him everything is going well here. I also enclosed a cheque to tide him over.'

That got Iris's attention. 'You've lent him money?'

'Well, the threat of war is starting to bite. It's a long-term investment, and it's not just for him, it's for you too.' He smiled and touched her hand. 'Business is doing well for me, and I wanted to show you how much I care about your family . . . and you.'

Iris slid her hand out from under his. 'Charles thinks

you're helping him, but really, you're buying a stake in Penhallam's?' she observed.

'Don't be like that,' Henri said, frowning. 'I'm thinking of your future, of our future. Don't forget that.'

Iris was silent for a minute, picking at her food. She didn't understand what the hurry was. Henri seemed to assume their marriage was a done deal, and yet he'd only broached the subject with her yesterday.

'You're lucky that business is going well,' she said, hoping to appease him.

Henri adjusted his gold watch. 'Yes, things are certainly looking up. I'm making the most of all this uncertainty. Our factories have switched to making armaments as part of the national push to prepare for war. It's proving very lucrative.'

Iris widened her eyes. 'You're making weapons?'

'I know it's not a comfortable topic of conversation, but this is the world we live in. I'm also buying shares in companies that are struggling to help them out. I prefer that to the factory side, but arms pay for the philanthropy.'

Iris took a sip of wine. 'Wouldn't it be better to sign up instead of selling bombs to the highest bidder?'

'There's my asthma, unfortunately, which will prevent me from being conscripted. I'll try, of course, but it's unlikely I'll be accepted.'

He didn't seem exactly heartbroken about not being able to play his part. She wished her father could have seen how brave her brother was in comparison to Henri. 'I see,' Iris replied. 'Then it will be Charles instead who takes the brunt of any bombs.'

Henri raised his eyebrows. 'You're being awfully defiant tonight, Iris. This new-found independence is certainly allowing you to blossom. Unless the view of that communist Italian has influenced you. What did you say his name was? Alessandro?'

'Don't be ridiculous. I've no idea if he's a communist or not,' she said.

'The ones over here are all communists, begging the French communist party to help if Hitler and Mussolini go through with their non-aggression pact,' Henri said. 'I'd steer clear of him if I were you.'

'We work together, Henri, that's all.' She was tired of his opinions, but she didn't want to offend him.

Henri gazed at her in the candlelight. The shadows and light seemed to bring out a weariness in his face.

'I'm jealous of the time you're spending at the perfumery and not with me,' he said.

Iris put down her glass. She had to nip this in the bud. 'Look, Henri, I'm flattered by your attentions and, perhaps one day, I hope to be married, but you must see, right now I'm focusing on this apprenticeship and nothing else.'

Henri smiled. 'I do see,' he said. 'I apologize if I've been overbearing in my courtship. I did rather wonder if I'd scared you off yesterday.'

'A bit,' Iris admitted. 'You've been my staunchest ally lately, and I was worried you might not want to support me if you knew that marriage isn't really on the cards for me at the moment. It's not that I don't value your company. But I don't want to think about marriage yet. I want to run my own perfumery one day, so I need to give this apprenticeship my full focus for the time being.'

Henri stroked her hand. 'Of course,' he said. 'And I will do everything within my power to help you.'

Henri moved his arm around her shoulder. His closeness felt cloying.

'But I won't give up on you that easily,' he said in a low voice. 'You've blossomed into such a jewel. I don't think you realize how much I value you. And as for marriage, I can wait.'

Iris wanted to move her head away, but he loomed over her. She couldn't make a fuss here in the restaurant.

'There's no need to wait for me,' she said.

'Oh yes there is,' he whispered.

He was going to kiss her, Iris could feel it. It was the last thing in the world she wanted, but she couldn't offend him in such a public place. He bent down towards her, and she screwed up her eyes. His lips touched hers and his moustache brushed against her skin. It was a polished kiss, delicate, almost chaste, over before it had begun.

Henri sat back, a smile on his face. Iris blushed and looked away. Her second kiss in one day. What was it about being here in Paris? She had gone from never having been kissed to having been kissed by two men in the space of a few hours.

Iris touched her lips. She had spent her whole childhood infatuated with Henri, but his kiss had not set her skin alight. No, it was Alessandro's kiss that burned in her memory, his touch still alight on her skin.

14

Stella – Paris, June 1996

Stella strode along the pavement to the convalescent home. She could still feel the sting on her lips where Bruno had kissed her. She'd felt it all night. That kiss had been a moment of madness, nothing more, and it was clear he felt so too. He had barely said anything when they'd got back to the hotel. He'd mumbled something about getting started on his book and headed up to his room. It was impossible to know what he was thinking. This morning, instead of coming with Stella to see Iris, he'd gone to visit the National Archives. In some ways, it had been a relief to see him go. But as Stella entered the building and went up in the lift, she wished he was with her.

On the second floor, Monique let Stella in. 'Do you think she'll talk to me today?'

'You can try,' Monique said, 'but remember, she's still very weak.'

Stella went to Iris's room, where she lay in bed, her eyes closed, the window open. A soft breeze wafted the curtains. The newspaper article had clearly stated that Iris and Alessandro had accompanied Raffaele on the *Orient Express*. The photo of the trio at the train station proved it. How had Iris felt about embarking on a journey at the start of the war with Alessandro? Thinking of Bruno,

Stella could easily imagine how being in such proximity to someone like that would be a distraction.

Iris's eyes fluttered open. She stared at Stella for a moment. 'Ah, you've come back,' she whispered.

'I hope you don't mind, but I had to,' Stella said. She sat down on the seat next to Iris's bed. 'I'm sorry if it was all too much for you last time. I'm aware I came across rather . . . strong.'

Iris sat up, shifting the pillows behind her. 'I can understand why you might have questions,' she said, her voice still hoarse. 'I just don't think I'm the right person to answer them.'

'You're the only one who *can* answer them,' Stella said. 'I think it was you that sent me the notebook, and then, afterwards, regretted doing so.'

Iris shook her head. 'I didn't.'

Stella touched her hand. It was soft and papery and felt so delicate. 'Iris, you can be truthful with me.'

Iris looked away. 'It was a moment of weakness,' she whispered. 'That's all. After all these years of staying strong, when they took me to the hospital, I suddenly felt as if time was slipping away. One of the nurses posted the notebook for me.' She coughed and reached for the glass of water on her bedside table, taking a sip. 'But then I realized I'd made a mistake.'

'So, you did want to reach out and get to know me?'

Iris wiped her mouth with her handkerchief. 'For a moment, perhaps, but then it didn't seem fair on you. My connection with Penhallam's is in the past now and that's where it needs to stay. I'm sorry I involved you.'

'But I'd like to get to know you, if you'll permit me to,' Stella said. 'And I need your help. There's only me left to run Penhallam's, and it's so bloody difficult. But I can't give up on finding a solution, because I made a promise to my father.'

Iris frowned. 'What did you promise him?'

'That I would keep Penhallam's going, no matter what. That's why I'm here, and you're the only one who can help me.'

Iris nodded. 'That's a big promise. You've taken on a lot of responsibility. I saw how much the business troubled Charles . . . and then I imagine it was a burden to your father, and now you.'

'It was what I was brought up to do,' Stella said. 'The same with my father. A business degree seemed the obvious choice. I actually quite enjoy the strategic side of things, especially if I'm selling something I believe in, like perfume.'

Iris smiled. 'Charles convinced me to go to secretarial school and said that in return he would think about offering me a perfumer's apprenticeship at Penhallam's. I hated every minute. My shorthand was atrocious. But I did it in the hope that he would let me make perfumes.' She squinted at her notebook on the bedside table. 'He didn't let me, of course. That's why I had to come to Paris and work with Raffaele.'

Iris's expression had relaxed a little. Stella didn't want to push her too far, but her words invited more questions. She'd take it gently though.

'I wanted to make perfumes too, when I was little,' Stella said, 'but Dad wasn't keen on the idea, nor was Grandfather. They were worried that if I got lost in scents I wouldn't go to university. In many ways, I'm glad they did encourage me. I had a wonderful time studying economics at Cambridge, and found I had a real flair for the business side of things too.'

Iris's eyes brightened up. 'You went to Cambridge?' she said. 'How marvellous. That must have been an incredible experience, and you are clearly a very smart young woman. There weren't those kinds of opportunities for girls like me growing up.'

There was a note of pride in her voice. Stella decided to venture further. 'If you don't mind me asking, was you coming to Paris a source of friction between you and Grandfather? Is that what caused the falling-out?'

Iris shrugged. 'It didn't help, but no, it wasn't the reason.'

'Or was it because you were using your talents to make these perfumes with Alessandro instead of for Penhallam's?'

Iris shook her head. 'It's too complicated to explain. I'm sorry, Stella, I know you want a solution for Penhallam's, but you're not going to find it in my past.'

'This isn't just about Penhallam's, it's about getting to know one of my last remaining family members. You're the great-aunt I never thought I'd get to meet.' She thought for a moment. It was only a hunch, but it was worth a try. 'Then maybe the rift was because Charles didn't approve of you and Alessandro?'

'What do you mean?'

'I couldn't help but wonder if maybe there was something between the two of you. The name of the first two perfumes – La Scintilla (The Spark) and Primo Bacio (First Kiss) – sound like the start of a love affair. And then there's that part in the journal where you describe the inspiration for First Kiss.'

Iris rubbed her forehead. 'Which part?'

'I can't remember properly, I only read it once. May I?' Stella reached for the notebook. Iris nodded. Stella flipped through the pages until she came to the second perfume, Primo Bacio. She read aloud from the journal.

Mme Geffroy described the scent that she wanted Alessandro and me to create. The key sensations encapsulated what Mme Geffroy told us: 'He kissed me, and all the scents and sensations mingled together in a moment that set my skin alight. That first kiss was like nothing I'd ever experienced before.' How do we capture that when Alessandro and I are so different from each other? How do we even try?

Iris's eyes were moist. Stella knew she was right.

'You did capture it, didn't you?' Stella said. 'There was something between you and Alessandro.'

Iris's breath stilled. She touched her silver locket.

'I've smelled the perfume – it told me all I needed to know. I found a bottle of Primo Bacio. Look.' Stella took the bottle out of her bag.

Iris reached out for it, as if defeated by Stella's persistence. 'That's not why Charles and I argued,' she said. 'But meeting Alessandro . . . yes, I'll admit, it changed my life.' She turned the bottle in her hand. 'I can't believe you've found this. After all these years.'

Iris was relaxing her guard. Stella could feel it. 'If you try, you might be able to detect its aroma.'

Iris hesitated a moment, then unscrewed the lid, placing the bottle under her nose and inhaling deeply. Stella saw the same flicker of recognition cross her face, just like it had done with La Scintilla. Iris's eyes filled with tears.

'I never meant for any of it to happen,' Iris said.

'Sometimes I think I can live with it all, but other times . . .' She handed the bottle back to Stella.

'You can smell it?' Stella said.

Iris nodded. 'A little.'

'Iris, I think that, deep down, you want me to discover what happened to you,' Stella said softly.

'No, I don't,' Iris said. 'That's why I regretted sending the journal to you. When you know the truth about what happened, you'll turn your back on me, just like Charles did. Do you know how hard that was to bear? My own brother. Why should you be any different? I don't deserve, nor do I want, your help. That's why I wished I'd never sent you the notebook.'

Iris began to cough, hard, wracking coughs that made her heave to catch her breath. Stella reached for the glass of water and helped Iris to take a sip. She was clearly in torment about the past but somehow couldn't bring herself to face it properly.

Once Iris had recovered, Stella took out the old photograph and showed it to her. 'Do you remember when this was taken?' she said. 'Were you about to get on the *Orient Express* and head to Italy to make a new collection of perfumes?'

Iris took the photo in her hand and stared at it. 'Where did you get this?'

'It was in the archives at Penhallam's.'

'I remember it being taken,' she said. 'Just before we set off for Milan. Alessandro and I look so young.' Her mind seemed to drift into memories that Stella couldn't grasp. Iris put the photo down. 'It was another world, Stella. I don't want to go back there.'

'I wish you could trust me,' Stella whispered.

Iris shook her head. 'I'm so sorry, I just don't have the words to explain it all,' she said, her voice weak. She picked up the notebook and placed it in Stella's hands. 'If you want the perfumes, you'll have to find them yourself.'

'You're giving me the notebook?' Stella said. It was more than she'd expected. Iris couldn't seem to bring herself to tell Stella about the past, but perhaps this was her way of giving Stella permission to explore it further.

Iris nodded. 'I did send it to you, after all. Perhaps I was wrong to regret it. I just don't know. But maybe I should trust the instinct that made me want to give it to you in the first place.'

'Thank you, Iris. I promise I'll look after it. Bruno and I will be very careful with whatever we discover and keep you informed about every step. I'd love to know you better, and this could be the way.'

Iris smiled sadly. 'I'm afraid of you knowing me better,' she said. She turned her head away and closed her eyes. 'Please, take the notebook and go now, before I change my mind.'

Stella walked back to the hotel in a daze, clutching the notebook. True, Iris wasn't ready to tell her about Paris, but this was surely a breakthrough and gave Stella the opportunity to find the perfumes and uncover the story of Iris's past. Iris's words were unsettling, however. *I'm afraid of you knowing me better.* What was Iris ashamed of? Stella felt certain it could be overcome. Iris had given Stella the notebook, after all, so perhaps she wanted the truth out in the open.

Outside the hotel, wooden tables and chairs cluttered the pavement. The sun shone a dappled light through the leaves of the trees that lined the canal. Stella sat down and ordered a glass of white wine. She needed time to digest her encounter with Iris, and she wanted to read the notebook again.

On the other side of the canal, however, she spotted Bruno. He waved and crossed the bridge. Seeing him again, Stella remembered the kiss, and a shiver of anticipation ran through her. The power of his stride, the strength of his body underneath his shirt and jeans. The urge to go to him, to take his hand and pull him in for another kiss, was almost uncontrollable. Stella took a sip of wine and slowed her breathing. No. She wouldn't be the one to crack. He'd given no sign that he wanted more. In fact, he'd done the opposite. She straightened her back and smiled as he reached her.

'Well?' he said, putting his rucksack under the table. 'How did things go with Iris?'

'I'm not sure,' she said. 'She's still very conflicted about meeting me. But on the other hand, she's given me the notebook, which I'm taking as her permission to look into the past. It turns out she *did* send the notebook to me but then wished she hadn't. She can't bring herself to talk about it, but she seems to accept that I want to find out more.'

'That's great,' Bruno said. 'Having the notebook will really help.'

'She still won't tell me why she fell out with my grandfather.'

'Maybe it really is something terrible,' Bruno said.

Stella shrugged. 'Or she's got it all out of proportion. You know how arguments can seem like life or death at the time but, in fact, the reasons that cause a rift between two people might actually be insignificant.'

The waiter came over and Bruno ordered a beer. When he left, Bruno ran his hand through his hair nervously.

'So, in light of everything that's happened so far in Paris, what do you want to do next?' he said.

Stella hesitated. The tone of his voice suggested this was more than just a question about the search for the perfumes. She wasn't sure if she was ready to talk about that kiss just yet. It was easier to keep things matter-of-fact.

'I really want to get to know Iris, but I can't forget that I've taken out a second business loan to afford this trip and that the main purpose for coming was to find a solution that will make Penhallam's successful again,' Stella said. 'So, I should either go back to London and start working on something else, or head to Milan and see if I can find the next perfume.'

The waiter came over with Bruno's beer.

'I see,' Bruno said, his brown eyes, a mischievous glint to them, fixed on Stella. 'And are you interested in what I think you should do? I mean, you probably already know that I'll be going to Milan. I've got a book to write, after all.'

'Of course. I thought you would be – that's your job.'

Bruno twisted the bottle in his hands. 'Yes, but it's not just that. You see, I'm the only one supporting our family and I'm hoping the book will really help with . . .' He paused.

'What?' Stella said.

'I'm not very proud of the situation,' he said, his cheeks reddening, 'but I'm in a substantial amount of debt. My sister is in a specialist clinic to help with her drug addiction. Getting a loan was the only way I could afford to send her there, and having an advance for the book would help to pay for it.'

It was clearly costing him a lot to reveal his situation.

'You have a lot of responsibilities to deal with.'

'Like you,' he said.

'In a way, although my only responsibility is to the family business. I've no family members left to worry about. My mum is in Australia, I've no siblings and my grandfather and father are dead.'

'In some ways, that makes it harder. You're on your own, except for Iris,' Bruno said. 'So it's up to you. Are we continuing this journey together?'

The air swirled around them. Stella swallowed. 'I don't know.'

Her eyes dropped to his lips. The sweetness of that kiss. His lips parted, as if he knew what she was thinking. A moment later, his hand touched hers, electricity crackling as his fingers interlaced hers.

'I'd like us to go together,' he said. 'I haven't been able to get that kiss out of my head. I know it's not what we planned and we're here for a different purpose, and who knows where this might lead, but I don't want you to leave yet.'

Stella felt herself drawn to him, a strong pull that was almost impossible to resist, but she had to keep her feelings separate. This search was for Penhallam's, not for exploring whatever this was that simmered between her and Bruno. She gently pulled her hand away.

'I want to go to Milan with you. I need your help. But maybe it's best if we forget that kiss ever happened and just keep things on a professional footing. Would that be okay? After all, you have a job to do too.'

Bruno contemplated her for a moment, then sighed. 'I can't promise to forget,' he said, 'but I understand what you're saying. We're both used to putting our personal lives on hold for the sake of our jobs, aren't we? I can manage a professional relationship, if you can.'

That should have meant the matter was resolved. Being professional was the sensible thing to do – there was no point complicating things – but as she watched Bruno lift his bottle of beer to his lips, she wondered if it was truly possible. No matter what she said, the truth was inescapable. There was something more to her relationship with Bruno, just as there had been with Iris and Alessandro.

15

Iris – Paris, August 1939

With Primo Bacio completed and delivered to Mme Geffroy, life settled down at the perfumery. Iris could tell that Raffaele was preoccupied by thoughts of his nephew, but he still made time to teach her and Alessandro. He had taken them through nearly all the individual ingredients in his perfumery, one by one.

'Only by knowing the scents can you compose perfumes. It's important to get the building blocks right,' he said.

Iris tried to arrive early most mornings, bringing pastries or hot chocolate to share with Raffaele in his kitchen. He talked about life in Venice and growing up there with his sister. She came to value those companionable moments. He had so much to teach her about life and scent, and in the absence of her father, who had always been Iris's confidant, she found herself divulging her own hopes and dreams to Raffaele.

Life with Henri had become more routine too. The kiss had perhaps confirmed something in his mind and he seemed to take for granted that marriage was on the cards. Iris could tell by the way his hand lingered on the small of her back as they went into dinner, or how he waited for her outside the perfumery to walk her home, that he had not given up on the idea. Iris still had no intention of marrying Henri, or anyone else. A problem loomed on the horizon, but she was grateful not to have to confront it yet.

As for Alessandro, he seemed to have put their kiss firmly in the past. Just like Iris, he was intent on concentrating on his work in the perfumery. Iris wasn't sure whether to be relieved or disappointed, but at least that complication was out of the way, for now.

One afternoon, she was counting the bottles of Vedendo when a voice whispered in her ear. 'Found you.'

Iris nearly jumped out of her skin. It was Henri, a knowing smile on his face. 'You scared the life out of me,' Iris said. 'What on earth are you doing down here?'

'I managed to persuade that surly Italian to let me come down and see you,' Henri said. 'He's not very friendly, is he?'

Iris ignored the question. 'Aren't you supposed to be at work?'

Henri scooped Iris up in his arms and whirled her around. 'Of course I am, but now I'm the boss I can do what I want. And what I wanted was to see you.'

Iris laughed uncertainly. His bold behaviour was rather unexpected. She didn't relish this intrusion into her workplace. He put her down on the floor, but his arms still gripped tightly around her. 'I've hardly seen you lately.'

'You've been busy with work, as have I,' Iris said. He seemed to fill the basement. There was no room to move with the shelf behind her and Henri pressing against her body.

'I haven't forgotten our kiss, you know,' Henri said, bending closer.

Iris wanted to duck away. 'We can't, Henri, not here.'

'Why not?' Henri said. 'I'd say this was the perfect place.'

He pressed his lips against hers. She endured his tongue slipping inside her mouth for a moment and then pulled away. 'Honestly,' she said, forcing a smile, 'I thought you said you could wait.'

'I've changed my mind,' he replied. 'We don't know what the future will bring. Charles brought forward his wedding. We could at least announce our engagement. It would be prudent in the current climate.'

'You make it sound like a business deal,' she said, trying to laugh it off. He was making her uncomfortable. Something about his entitled tone reminded her of when he'd spoken in that offhand manner about the Jews.

'Think of the perfumery I will let you run,' Henri said. 'And how our union will save Penhallam's.'

'I told you: I want to find my own way,' Iris said. She squirmed against the wall, wishing he would move.

'Maybe I can help make it happen more quickly than you'd realized,' Henri said, a glint in his eye. 'You could easily run this place.'

'I want to do this on my own merits,' Iris said. 'Besides, this is Raffaele's perfumery.'

Henri raised his eyebrows. 'For now.'

Iris recalled what Raffaele had said about governments legislating against Jewish businesses. Surely that's not what Henri had in mind. But the hint of cruelty in his voice made her think Raffaele's fears were justified.

'Iris, can you help up here?' Alessandro's voice called from the top of the stairs.

'I need to go,' Iris said. 'I'm sorry, Henri, but I'm not sure about all this.'

Henri took her hand. 'We'll make a good team,' he said. 'You're just like me: ambitious, determined, you'll do whatever it takes to get what you want. I need a woman like you by my side.'

'You make me sound calculating,' Iris said. The thought of being like him alarmed her. She'd always known that Henri had swagger, but his attitude right now was showing a different side.

Henri kissed her hand. 'Not calculating, but pragmatic. You're ruled by your head, not your heart. In time, I hope you'll see that marrying me makes sense on all fronts. Especially when you consider how I can help Penhallam's.'

At the door he gave her a brief kiss on the lips before saying goodbye and stepping out on to the street. Iris was relieved to see him go. His actions and words had made her feel very uncomfortable. She knew that Charles and Penhallam's had a lot to gain by her anticipated union with Henri. Maybe Henri would go back to being his jovial normal self. That was the man she had adored for so many years. Iris felt torn between her duty and her instincts.

'Nice of you to come and help,' Alessandro said, from behind the counter.

Iris looked around the shop. It was empty. 'There's nobody here,' she said.

'That's because I served them all while you were downstairs with that cad.'

'Don't call him that,' Iris said defensively, though she was beginning to think Alessandro had a point.

'What are you doing with him?' Alessandro said, shaking his head. 'You can't seriously like him?'

'I told you, he's an old family friend, and it's complicated,' Iris said, the turmoil inside rising to the surface. 'I don't expect you to understand. If you're going to despise me for associating with him, go ahead.'

Alessandro shook his head. 'If you think I despise you, then you're more blind than I realized,' he said. 'I just wonder why you don't question what's right in front of you.'

Iris flushed. 'You know nothing about what I question and do not question. Just because we've worked together on two perfumes, it does not give you any right to presume you know me.'

Alessandro nodded. 'Of course. Forgive me. You are probably delighted to have the attention of someone like Henri,' he said, with an edge to his tone. 'He'll keep you in the manner to which you're accustomed and ensure that not a hair on your head is out of place until the day you die.'

Iris stared at him, something clicking in her mind. 'Are you jealous?' she said.

Alessandro crossed his arms. 'Don't be ridiculous. In what universe would there ever be a place for you and me to be together?' he said.

His eyes locked on to hers. Iris felt the blood rise in her cheeks. The argument was like a flash flood, emotions rising all around her, but where had it come from? The passion in his voice alarmed and excited her. She'd never fought like this with anyone – so openly, so unguarded.

Alessandro ducked his head. 'I'm sorry. Forget I said any of that – I don't know what came over me. You're free to choose your companions as you please.'

'I am,' Iris said.

'It's just that . . .'

'What?'

Alessandro sighed. 'Nothing. Let's just leave it,' he said. 'I'm going out to get some fresh air. I'll be back soon.'

He turned away. Iris couldn't bear it. 'You make these assumptions about me, but it's not fair. I know you regret that we kissed, but that doesn't give you the right to judge me so harshly.'

Alessandro shook his head. 'I don't regret it, Iris. I haven't stopped thinking about that kiss,' he said. 'But I know that, outside this perfumery, there's no way we could be together.'

What could she say? It was partly true. Charles would never countenance such a match. But a thrill went through her at what Alessandro had said. He hadn't forgotten the kiss either.

Before she could speak, Raffaele came down the stairs. He held his briefcase and walking stick. He hadn't been into the perfumery all day. She hoped he hadn't heard her argument with Alessandro. His face was very pale, dark rings around his eyes. All thoughts of Alessandro and Henri were pushed aside.

'Raffaele, are you all right?' Iris said.

He clutched his briefcase. 'I'm fine. I've got a meeting with my lawyers. There are some urgent matters I need to take care of.'

'Let one of us come with you,' Iris said. 'You shouldn't be going all that way on your own.'

'I'll find a taxi. Don't worry,' he said. 'But if you could meet me tonight for dinner. There's something I need to discuss with you both.'

Iris felt a pang of misgiving. Raffaele didn't seem himself at all.

'I wish you'd let us help,' Alessandro said.

Raffaele shook his head. 'I'll see you both tonight.' The door clicked shut.

'What do you think is the matter?' Iris said.

'I don't know,' Alessandro said. 'Whatever it is, we won't help him by arguing.'

'No.' She wanted to reach out to him. To have him take her in his strong arms and shelter her from all the chaos around them. But as he'd said, they couldn't be together. Instead, she headed to the basement stairs. 'I'd better finish off stacking the bottles and then get home and change for dinner.'

Later that evening, Iris got out of the taxi and stood across the road from the restaurant. There, at one of the tables near the window, sat Alessandro. There was no sign of Raffaele. Alessandro looked up anxiously every time the door opened. He wore the same outfit he wore to work: dark grey trousers and a white shirt, open at the collar. A wave of such longing filled her. She shook her head. Tonight was about Raffaele and whatever it was he needed to explain. She straightened up and crossed the road, her blue dress swishing around her ankles and the string of pearls she wore swinging against her neck.

Alessandro looked up as she walked in.

'Hello,' she said, sitting down. She ordered a Martini and the waiter scuttled off. 'Sorry I'm a bit late.'

'No problem,' Alessandro said, taking in the sight of her. 'You look beautiful.'

'Thank you.' Iris blushed. 'No sign of Raffaele then?'

'No, not yet. I suppose we should wait before we order.'

'Of course.' She put the menu to one side. 'I was thinking about our discussion this afternoon – what you said about Henri – and I wanted to explain my position. He's been a family friend for years, so I don't appreciate you criticizing him. He means a lot to my brother and has stood by him for a long time. Besides, I am perfectly capable of judging people for myself.'

'I know,' Alessandro answered. 'I'm sorry for what I said. I never meant to imply you weren't. I'm not really cut out for living somewhere like Paris. Everyone is frighteningly sophisticated. Henri included.'

The waiter brought Iris's drink. She thanked him and took a sip.

'Do you miss Venice?' Iris asked. The softness in her voice surprised them both. Alessandro tilted his head.

'Every day,' he said, 'There's no place like it. The early-morning mist on the water, the buildings filled with grandeur, the noise as people go about their business. Not to mention the smells. You would love it. Spices arrive from the East and the air is filled with a thousand scents.'

'It sounds beautiful.'

'It is,' Alessandro said. 'Francesca's perfumery is tucked away on a quiet fondamenta. You can hear the water lapping against the walls and smell the sea air. It's very different to Raffaele's perfumery, just a tiny room really, but inside I felt I had access to the whole world through the perfume bottles.'

Iris smiled. 'I felt the same about my father's perfumery. Charles didn't think it was ladylike to be in there so often, but Father didn't mind. He'd explain where each oil came from: the land, the people, the plant, the process and more. He taught me how to associate scent with memory and the imagination.' She sighed, touching her cutlery. 'I miss him.'

'It must have been difficult when your father died,' Alessandro said. Iris looked down at the tablecloth. His hand seemed to move closer, almost close enough to touch.

'Yes, it was. I hardly remember my mother's death, but with him . . . It was very sudden, you see, and there are so many things I wish I'd said or asked. Being here with Raffaele feels like being near my father in some way.'

Alessandro nodded, as if he understood.

Iris felt like she could open up to him, that he was almost asking her to with his gentleness this evening. She was beginning to feel as though she could trust him.

'Penhallam's is struggling,' she said. 'That's why I have to at least consider Henri as a match. My brother bears the burden of the perfumery, its debts and struggles – it's all fallen on him. Henri would have the power to change all that.'

Alessandro's eyes were full of sorrow. 'I see,' he said.

'It's not that I don't see Henri's faults, I do. But I'm not sure I can afford to act on what I see,' she said, staring at him intently. She wasn't sure what she wanted to say but, somehow, she had to make him understand. 'I'm not really in a position to do what I would choose.'

Alessandro swallowed. Had she said too much? Something about the depth in his eyes, the feeling of electricity that flashed between them, told her he had understood.

'Iris,' he said, 'there is always a choice.'

She opened her mouth to speak, but suddenly Raffaele was there. His face was pale and his hand, as he pulled out the chair to sit down, was trembling.

'I'm sorry I'm late,' he said, sitting down.

'What's wrong?' Iris said. 'You look exhausted.'

Raffaele rubbed his forehead. 'I had some horrendous news this morning,' he said, his voice hollow.

'What is it?' Alessandro said.

Raffaele covered his eyes. 'I told Francesca to be careful. The *squadristi* have been clamping down on anti-fascists. But she wouldn't listen. One last protest, she said. But it was a close call. She's telegrammed to say she's fleeing

Venice and heading towards Milan. She's planning to hide in a delivery truck. Some friends have relatives there where she can lie low in a safehouse. She needs my help to get visas and make it to the border.'

Iris's hand flew to her mouth. 'Oh, my goodness, Raffaele, that's awful.'

'She's taken Jacopo with her. I went to see my lawyers and have made arrangements to go away.'

'I don't understand. Where are you going?' Iris asked.

'Milan, of course. I have to help them get over the border. I'll get visas in Switzerland and then meet up with them to help them escape Italy.'

Alessandro stared at Raffaele. 'But you know how dangerous that would be. The idea is unthinkable.'

Raffaele shook his head. 'I'll find a way. There are routes over the Alps if necessary.'

Iris didn't want to offend him, but the task seemed too much for one man. 'Alessandro's right, it will be impossible. And then there's the state of your health and, forgive me, your age. How on earth could you manage such an expedition?'

Raffaele screwed up his napkin. 'But time is running out. If war is declared, it'll make it even harder to get them out. What do you expect me to do? Sit in Paris and do nothing?'

His frustration chimed with Iris's own. She couldn't remain on the sidelines.

'You must let me come with you.'

Alessandro pressed his hand against the table.

'Iris, that's a remarkably courageous offer,' he said, 'but you know as little as Raffaele about getting in and out of Italy. The language, the customs, the risks. No, it has to be me that goes, it's the only way.'

Raffaele studied them both. 'Your offers to help mean so much, but I can't put this on anyone else. Especially you, Alessandro.'

'Why especially Alessandro?' Iris asked.

Alessandro sighed. 'I was arraigned by the *squadristi* too. But I'm not scared about that. I owe so much to Francesca. I wouldn't be here if she hadn't taught me. I'm going with you, Raffaele, whether you like it or not. I still have contacts on the *Orient Express* – we can travel by train to get across the borders.'

'Perhaps it could work,' Raffaele said, a note of hope in his voice. 'We need to think of a reason to explain why we are travelling to Milan. On business, perhaps?'

Iris took a swig of her Martini. If they were both going, she wanted to go too. She cared about Raffaele and his family as much as Alessandro did.

'No one in their right mind would believe Alessandro is a businessman. No offence, Alessandro, but you don't have the charm and polish, and for that you should be thankful.'

'Then what do you suggest?' Alessandro said.

'What is it that you and I excel in?' Iris asked with a smile.

Alessandro hesitated as if he thought this was a trick question. 'Arguing?'

'No,' Iris said, though not able to hold in her laugh. 'We are both incredible at making perfume. And that's what we'll be. Perfumers who have been commissioned to create scents that embody the route of the *Orient Express*. We'll have our bottles and perfumers' organs with us, our notebooks and formulas. You bring the knowledge of Italy, and I'll bring the charm and finesse. Nobody will dare question why we're going to Milan.'

'So, the two of you would come with me to get the visas and deliver them to Francesca in Milan?' Raffaele said.

'Yes,' Iris said. 'We could be in and out within a matter of days.'

'But what about my sister and Jacopo? How will you explain their presence on our return journey?' Raffaele asked.

Alessandro raked his hand through his hair. 'I have a friend who works on the *Orient Express*; he will help us to hide them. The border checks are cursory if you know how to manage the border guards. Give me a few days to organize everything.'

Raffaele sat back and folded his arms. 'I want to think of an objection, but I can't. I can't thank you both enough for doing this. I'll close up the perfumery while we're gone. Perhaps even put an announcement in the paper about our idea for a collection of scents based on the romance of travel. That will explain why we've gone.'

Iris touched his hand. This wasn't about her ambitions or winning the apprenticeship, it was about doing what was right for a man who had meant a lot to her. 'Raffaele, you've done so much for me, it's no hardship to repay you this way.'

'And you took a chance on me when I was desperate,' Alessandro said. 'If I can do you a favour in return, I'm glad to help.'

Raffaele wiped his eyes, which glimmered with tears. 'Thank you,' he said. 'It means everything to me that you would both do this, and I promise, I will be forever in your debt.'

Amanti
(Lovers)

Top Note
Sage

൨

Heart Note
Immortelle

൨

Base Note
Musk

൨

16

Iris – Paris, September 1939

A few days later, Iris sat at Raffaele's kitchen table, the newspaper spread out in front of her. Europe on the brink of war, the headline read. She'd left the Levèques' house early, before Henri got up, leaving a brief note on the sideboard. The train was due to depart at midday and Iris and Alessandro had joined Raffaele in his flat above the perfumery to wait for the impending announcement about the war.

Iris kept her eyes fixed on the clock. In ten minutes, the ultimatum Neville Chamberlain had given Germany, demanding it withdraw its troops from Poland, would expire. At five o'clock, a similar ultimatum by the French government would also run out. By the end of the day, it looked increasingly likely that France and Britain would be at war with Germany, but Iris prayed there would be a last-minute reprieve.

'I don't know what to do,' Raffaele said. 'I can't drag you and Alessandro away if war is declared.'

Iris folded up the newspaper. 'Nobody wants another war. France and Britain aren't prepared. Now is exactly the time we must get Francesca and Jacopo out of Italy, before it's too late.'

'I agree,' Alessandro said. 'Mussolini and Hitler's pact means that Italy is bound to get dragged into this mess.

But right now, Italy is not involved. As Iris says, this might be our only chance to travel.'

Raffaele sipped his coffee. 'Thank you,' he said. 'Your support means a lot to me; I couldn't do this on my own. But I intend to keep teaching you both. Iris, I've got you something so that you can keep creating scents on our journey.'

Raffaele passed her a leather bag about the size of a travelling toiletry case. Instead of brushes and talc bottles, Iris opened the lid to discover a miniature perfumer's organ full of essential oils.

'It's beautiful, Raffaele, thank you. I don't know what to say.' In this bag, she would have a world of creativity at her fingertips.

'You don't need to thank me. It's the least I can do, given what you've offered to do for me,' Raffaele said. 'Alessandro's already got an identical one; I bought it for him when we travelled to London. Between the two of you, you've got about fifty ingredient bottles, representing the main families of scents: Floral, Oriental, Woody and Fresh.'

'Thank you, it really is wonderful, and very practical. Now when inspiration strikes, I'll be able to follow up with some blends,' Iris said, touching the smooth glass bottles.

'I know our main aim is to rescue my sister, but that doesn't mean you need to stop learning,' Raffaele said. 'We're going to journey along a magnificent railway line, through some wonderful places, and I want you to chart the journey in scent.'

'So, our cover will also be useful,' Iris said. 'What's your idea for this collection?'

'I want to create scents that smell like love. People will need to remember the human capacity to love in the face of war. We already have La Scintilla and Primo Bacio.

Think about what comes next. This will be your collection, Alessandro and Iris, with three more scents to add.'

Alessandro caught her eyes and fire burned between them. She didn't dare think about what came next. The scents were already too personal, too intimate. Three more perfumes on the theme of love? It seemed too dangerous to contemplate. But Raffaele looked so pleased with the idea she didn't want to disappoint him.

'That's a wonderful plan,' Iris said, patting Raffaele's hand. 'We'll do our best, won't we, Alessandro?'

'Of course,' he said. He checked his watch. 'It's nearly time.' He fiddled with the radio dial.

The static cleared and the crisp tones of the BBC World Service presenter came out of the speaker. He announced that Neville Chamberlain would address the British people. It was eleven fifteen. Iris held her breath and listened as he spoke.

'This morning the British Ambassador in Berlin handed the German Government a final Note stating that unless we heard from them by 11 o'clock that they were prepared at once to withdraw their troops from Poland, a state of war would exist between us.

I have to tell you now that no such undertaking has been received, and that consequently this country is at war with Germany.'

Iris closed her eyes. Britain was at war. France was sure to follow. Suddenly, the world seemed different: the ticking clock more ominous, the eggs and toast on the table insubstantial, the thought of people going about their daily business incomprehensible.

'Well, that's it then,' Alessandro said. He stood up and rubbed his scar. 'While the world takes a breath to digest this news, we need to be on the *Orient Express* in an hour.'

*

Midday, and the Gare de Lyon felt eerily normal. People milled about on the platform, but no more than usual. A photographer was taking pictures of the *Orient Express* as it stood waiting by the platform. Since the invasion of Poland, refugees had been pouring into Paris, but today it was quiet. Perhaps it was because of the British announcement. Everything seemed now to be on hold until the French deadline later that day.

'Why don't you wait here with our things, and I'll help Raffaele get the tickets?' Alessandro said.

'Yes, of course,' Iris said. They'd each been silent in the taxi to the station, lost in their own thoughts. Now Alessandro touched her arm.

'Are you all right?' he said gently. 'It's not too late to back out. I can accompany Raffaele. Perhaps you want to go back to England to see your brother, or at least stay here, where it's safe. I'd understand if you didn't want to come.'

Iris shook her head. 'I want to help Raffaele. I'm not backing out,' she said. 'Go on, get the tickets. The sooner we're on that train, the better.'

Alessandro took Raffaele's arm, supporting him as they walked towards the ticket office. There were other reasons why she wanted to leave Paris. Henri's attentions, for one. And a strange desire not to be parted from Alessandro.

'Iris,' a voice called.

Marching along the platform was Henri. Damn it. She'd hoped to escape Paris without a fuss. She'd left a note, of course, but planned to be on her way before he read it.

'I came as soon as I could,' Henri said, frowning as he caught sight of the suitcases. 'You simply cannot go on this trip. It's madness. Charles would never allow it, and neither do I.'

'I am going.' Iris clasped the handle of her bag. 'We're creating a collection of perfumes. We'll be there and back before the week is out.'

'Didn't you hear the announcement this morning?'

'Nothing is happening with the war straight away. We'll be perfectly safe.'

'Nonsense,' Henri said. 'There's no need for you all to go. Raffaele can send that Italian chap and have done with it.'

He tried to pick up Iris's suitcase, but she barred his way.

'No, Henri,' she said. 'I'm going, and that's all there is to it. It's important for my development as a perfumer.'

The expression in Henri's eyes soured. 'You're my fiancée, Iris. I won't allow you to go traipsing-off across Europe. In case you hadn't noticed, France will be at war before the day is out. It's too dangerous.'

'I'm perfectly capable of judging the state of things for myself,' she said. 'And I'm not your fiancée, we're not engaged, so you have no right to tell me what to do.'

Henri's expression softened, but she noticed there was still a harshness to his eyes that he couldn't shake. 'I'm only thinking of you, my dear,' he said. 'And Charles too. Imagine how devastated he would be if something happened to you. You owe it to us all to stay safe. It's my duty to protect you.'

She'd avoided telling Charles about this trip; she hadn't wanted to worry him.

'I don't need you to protect me.'

Henri took hold of her hands. 'But I do need to. Haven't you adored me for years? Well, now I adore you too. And I want to do everything I can to rebuild Penhallam's . . . once we're married.'

Iris pulled away. 'But you've already given Charles a loan.'

'Yes, a small one, to tide him over. But he knows as well as you should that the real investment will only come once I am family too.'

It seemed that the fate of Penhallam's was now tied to her decision about whether or not to marry Henri. It complicated things. She had to tread carefully.

'I haven't decided yet,' she said. 'If there's going to be a war, I want to do my bit and help. It's such a precarious time and, to be honest, I'm not sure I'm cut out for being a wife. I want to run my own perfumery, not sit at home and have children. There must be someone more suitable out there for you.'

Henri smiled. 'Everything you've just said, Iris, is exactly why you'd be perfect as my wife,' he said.

He pulled her close in an embrace. The familiar smell of his aftershave enveloped her. He was larger than life, this man she'd been smitten with all her life. Why was it that, right now, when he was offering her everything a girl could dream of, the adoration she'd felt had slipped away?

'You can't stop me going.'

Henri shrugged. 'No, but I can delay the extra money that Charles has asked for to shore up Penhallam's in these difficult times.'

'Are you threatening me?' Iris asked, unable to keep the wariness from her voice.

Henri shook his head, smiling as if her assumption was absurd. 'Of course not. I'm merely reminding you of the advantages of our union.'

From the corner of her eye, Iris saw Raffaele and Alessandro approach. She pulled back from Henri's grip. Alessandro glared at Henri.

'Monsieur Levèque,' Raffaele said. 'I wasn't expecting to see you here.'

'I came to persuade Iris to change her mind about coming with you,' Henri said.

'She's not obliged to come,' Raffaele said. 'It is her own choice to accompany us.'

'She said something about researching new perfumes on the journey to Milan. Is it necessary to go all that way at a time like this?'

'I believe so,' Raffaele said, 'and it won't take long. Having a new collection will help di Fiore's to survive. I'm sure you, as a businessman, can understand that.'

Henri raised his eyebrows and considered Raffaele's words. He seemed to be turning something over in his mind. 'Indeed,' he said, 'and I hope you know, I am keen to support your perfumery. Iris is obviously a very important part in its success.'

He turned to Iris and regarded her carefully. 'Very well, if I am to let you go, you must promise me one thing,' he said. 'I'd like us to be married before the year is out. It's to everyone's advantage if we marry soon, including Penhallam's.'

Iris glanced at Raffaele and Alessandro, embarrassed that they were overhearing this conversation. 'Can we talk about this when I get back, please?'

Alessandro cleared his throat. 'I didn't realize you were engaged,' he said.

'We're not,' Iris said, exasperated at the situation. 'Not yet.'

'Don't be coy, Iris. We're as good as engaged, and you know it,' Henri said. 'Hopefully we'll be able to announce something when you return.'

'Henri, I told you—'

'I insist. It's the only way I'll be able to appease Charles when I tell him where you've gone. If he knows about us, it will put his mind at ease.'

Iris dropped her head, feeling cornered. Henri appeared to take her silence as acquiescence.

'Good. I'll be picking out rings for you to choose from while you're away.' His words would be thrilling to so many women, but to Iris it felt like a threat. He noticed the photographer, who was taking a picture of some of the guests boarding the *Orient Express*. 'Come on, let's have a photograph. I can send it to Charles.'

'I don't think that's a good idea . . .'

But Henri was dragging her over to the photographer. He clamped his arm around Iris, and she smiled for the camera.

'Let's have one of us all too,' Raffaele said.

'If you insist,' Henri replied, without any enthusiasm.

Raffaele stood on one side of Iris, Alessandro on the other. She could feel the fury building in Alessandro, his fists clenched by his side, a scowl on his face. The engine let off steam just as the camera clicked, and there it was. A photograph of them at the start of their journey.

'I'll let Charles know the good news,' Henri said. 'Anything else you want me to tell him?'

Iris opened the travelling case and took out a sample bottle of La Scintilla. 'Send him this too, please. Tell him it's the perfume that convinced Raffaele to take me on. It was inspired by those nights in the south of France. Tell him . . . I hope he remembers how happy we all were, and that I'll see him soon.'

Henri took the bottle and kissed Iris's hand. 'I will, my dear. Now, promise you'll be careful. I'll expect you back in a few days.'

He turned to Alessandro, his lips curled in distaste at Alessandro's plain suit and workman's boots. 'I'm sure you'll agree, Iris deserves the very best. It's only to be expected with a woman of her social standing.'

Alessandro dropped his eyes to the ground. 'Of course,' he muttered.

Raffaele picked up his suitcase. 'We must go,' he said. 'Don't worry, Monsieur Levèque, we will take good care of Iris and bring her back safe and sound.'

Henri narrowed his eyes. 'You will indeed, or you'll have me to answer to.' He bent down and kissed Iris on each cheek. 'See you soon, my love. Be careful.'

Iris let out a deep breath. Alessandro wouldn't meet her eye, but Raffaele touched her elbow.

'Are you ready?' he said.

'Yes,' Iris said. She could put Henri out of her mind, for now at least. Thank God they were leaving Paris. She wanted nothing more than to be on the train and to focus on rescuing Francesca and Jacopo and creating more perfumes. The complications of marriage and Henri could wait.

17

Iris – Paris to Lausanne, September 1939

Iris leaned back on the seat rest and felt the tug of the train as it pulled out of the station. She waved to Henri on the platform, then watched with relief as the train picked up speed and he was no longer visible. Iris breathed deeply. It felt like she was the one escaping.

Raffaele had booked three sleeping compartments. The plan was to stop briefly at Lausanne to collect the visas and then continue on to Milan. The *Orient Express* was like a hotel on wheels. The carriage in which they sat resembled a drawing room with its dark blue velvet curtains and gold tassels, the colours of the Compagnie Internationale des Wagons-Lits. The smooth marquetry on the walls and the cut-glass lamps that shone brightly from their sconces made the carriage inviting. The seat was soft and comfortable, and Iris sank into it, closing her eyes.

But even with her eyes shut she was acutely aware of Alessandro sitting next to her. The buzz of static between them, a consciousness of his presence. She interlaced her fingers, as if to prevent them from following their instincts and reaching over to touch Alessandro's arm. She opened her eyes. She had to shake that impulse from her body. It was the only way to survive this journey.

She turned to the window. They were moving through the easterly suburbs of Paris. Perfume needed to be at the forefront of her mind. She got out her notebook and began making notes about the journey.

A man dressed in the Wagons-Lits uniform came over to their table. 'Alessandro, I've been expecting you. Good to see you again.'

Alessandro stood up and gave the man a hug. He turned to Iris and Alessandro.

'This is my best friend, Tommaso. He's the one who sorted out our tickets and he has kept me on the straight and narrow for more years than I care to count,' he said. 'Tommaso, this is Raffaele di Fiore, and my work colleague, Iris.'

Work colleague. It sounded very businesslike. Iris nodded a greeting to Tommaso. He was shorter than Alessandro, with a friendly expression on his face.

Raffaele shook Tommaso's hand. 'Thank you for your assistance,' he said.

'Not at all,' Tommaso said. 'Anything to help. Although perhaps you should have stayed in Paris,' he said to Alessandro. 'Things are bad in Italy. Mussolini is eliminating his opponents. Now the British have declared war on Germany, it's only going to get worse.'

Alessandro shrugged. 'It'll be fine – we've got you to look after us, Tommaso.'

'I'll do my best. But you need to be careful, Alessandro. Security at the border crossings and stations is tighter now.'

'I thought Switzerland was neutral,' Iris said.

'It is,' Tommaso said, 'but once you're in Italy it's a different story. Anyway, I'll keep an eye on you all. But for now, I need to get back to my duties.'

Alessandro sat back down, wincing slightly as he touched his scar.

'Are you okay?' Iris asked.

He nodded. 'It just feels tight sometimes,' he said with a brief smile.

'What did Tommaso mean about you needing to be careful?' Iris said.

'Nothing. He's just protective of me; we've been friends for years,' Alessandro said.

'Now' – Raffaele seemed keen to change the subject – 'let's think about the next perfume. We're at the beginning of our journey. What do you sense right now?'

The train was moving at pace across the French countryside. Iris filtered out the worries in her head. Henri. Alessandro. The war. She focused on what was immediately around her.

'The smell of polish, the ladies' scents and men's colognes, the wealth: leather, champagne, salmon, velvet upholstery, waxed moustaches.' She paused and smiled. 'It's so overwhelming I don't know how to capture it all.'

'Ah, well, that's where discernment and memory come into it,' Raffaele said.

'To decide what's important?' Alessandro asked.

'Exactly. Imagine you are the client, Alessandro; you want a scent that will conjure the excitement, trepidation and promise of a journey on the *Orient Express*. Forget that war looms over us, or that we have our own quest. Delve into your own memory, for other journeys when perhaps you felt the same.'

Iris watched as Alessandro closed his eyes, slowing his breathing. This opportunity to scrutinize him unobserved was too good to miss. His lips parted. His eyelashes fluttered on his cheeks. She wished she knew what he was thinking.

His eyes opened. 'It's difficult,' he said. 'I can only think of working on the *Orient Express*. I've never really travelled for pleasure.'

'What about you, Iris?' Raffaele said.

'Charles and I had to take *le Train Bleu* down to Grasse once. My father had gone on ahead, so it was just us. It was the start of the summer holidays, and I can remember the air getting warmer as we travelled south and the prospect of being off school, free at last. It filled me with excitement.'

'Anything else?' Raffaele said.

Iris blushed. 'Well, I was only fourteen, still a child really, but there was someone I liked, and I was hoping he would notice me at last.'

'You're talking about Henri,' Alessandro said.

'I was only young. It was an infatuation.'

'But that excitement you felt. It was desire, wasn't it?' Alessandro said, his eyes fixed on her.

'Yes,' Iris said. 'I suppose it was.'

Alessandro folded his arms and looked out of the window. 'I thought so.'

'Every perfume needs that flash of desire,' Raffaele said. He looked at his watch. 'We'll be in Lausanne in seven hours. If you don't mind, I'll leave you two to work on the scent and retire to my compartment. I didn't get much sleep last night.'

'Of course,' Iris said. As soon as Raffaele had walked down the corridor out of earshot, she turned to Alessandro. 'What's going on?' she said. 'Why are you so on edge?'

'We were discussing the scent, and I was merely adding to the debate.'

'By criticizing me,' Iris said. 'I was a child. You can't blame me for what I felt then.'

'And what about how you feel now? I couldn't bear to see you railroaded by Henri. Why don't you stand up for yourself? You have no problem speaking your mind with me.'

'You know that there are financial obligations at stake between the family business and Henri,' she said, thinking of Charles's expectations, of Penhallam's and how Henri could help the family business. 'It's not that simple.'

'Isn't it?'

The air hummed between them. It felt like he could see the conflict in her heart. But she didn't want reminding of Henri right now. She just wanted to live in this moment.

'I know Henri's overbearing, but his heart is in the right place, and there are so many expectations. I don't want to think about it all now. Can't you and I just be here together, working on the perfume, and forget about everything else? Please.'

The fragrance. It was what bound them together, the only thing perhaps, apart from their wish to help Raffaele. She hoped he wouldn't jeopardize that.

'Yes,' he said gently. 'Of course. I'm sorry. Let's not allow the outside world to spoil this time together.' He reached for the notebook. 'Why don't I jot down the numbers for the accord? We could get a rough idea of ingredients and proportions we could use.'

No one else had ever written in her book before. But he was trying to make amends, and this was supposed to be a task they did together.

'All right,' Iris said, 'but make sure you get it all down accurately.'

Alessandro smiled and picked up the pen. 'I will.'

*

Later that day, as the train hurtled towards the Alps, Iris went to her compartment to get ready for dinner. She unfurled her lipstick and attempted to apply it, but her reflection dipped in and out of the tiny mirror as the sleeping car bumped up and down on the tracks.

She wore a red satin gown that she hoped wasn't too over the top. Not that it mattered; no one would think twice about her outfit, given the news. Word had spread through the train just after five o'clock that France was also now at war with Germany. It seemed as if there was no going back, although the *Orient Express* felt like a world apart, immune somehow from what was going on outside, keeping going while everything else fell apart.

Iris smoothed out the folds and looked out of the window, watching the scenery move past. All afternoon, until the news about war, she and Alessandro had worked on perfecting the perfume. The mountains, merely a smudge on the horizon at first, had increased in size until now they filled up half the sky, jagged and snow-capped. The sun had just dipped behind them, and the sky was streaked with pink and purple clouds. By her reckoning, they would be in Lausanne by eight o'clock.

She went out into the corridor as Raffaele emerged from his compartment, putting the finishing touches to his bow tie. Alessandro was already there, looking out of the window. He was still wearing the same suit, but now he wore a burgundy tie. Iris guessed that Raffaele had lent it to him.

The dining car was buzzing with conversation as Tommaso showed them to their table. 'Let me bring you the menus,' he said, 'and a bottle of wine. White or red?'

'White, please,' Raffaele said. He waited until Tommaso

had walked away. 'My contact at the embassy, Isabella, will meet me on the platform when we stop at Lausanne,' he said in a low voice. 'And then, if all goes well, we'll arrive in Milan tomorrow morning.'

Tommaso uncorked the wine and poured each of them a glass.

'It feels strange to be serving you,' he said to Alessandro. He smiled at Iris and Raffaele. 'We're about to cross the border into Switzerland. Normally, it's just a case of passing through, but with everything that's going on we've heard they want to board the train and check papers, so have them ready.'

Iris looked nervously at Raffaele. 'I suppose we have nothing to worry about.'

'Of course not, my dear,' he said. 'We are simply journeying for business, like everybody else on this train.'

The train shuddered to a halt as they pulled into what looked like a small halting place in the mountains. There was no fanfare at this border-crossing post, just a one-storey building and a short platform. Behind it, into what Iris assumed must be Switzerland, a dark forest climbed the hillside. The doors opened and Swiss border officials boarded the carriage, politely asking each traveller to show them their papers before allowing them to travel on into the country.

'*Bonjour, mademoiselle, messieurs*,' the main official of the party said. Iris handed over her British passport. The official nodded approvingly at Raffaele's French passport; he'd lived in France for so long Iris guessed he'd thought it prudent to apply for French citizenship.

At Alessandro's passport, however, the man scowled. 'This stamp says you entered France only a few months ago. Why are you now taking the return journey?'

Iris's stomach clenched. The official's tone was harsh. But Alessandro seemed to be keeping his cool. 'I'm travelling with work,' he said. 'We are perfumers, heading to Milan to create scents for our new collection.'

'I see. So long as you're planning to travel on from Switzerland,' he said. 'We've been told to be on the lookout for communists seeking refuge in our territory. Mussolini will respect Swiss neutrality so long as we don't harbour his opponents.'

'I'm no threat to Mussolini or to the Swiss, I assure you,' Alessandro said smoothly.

The Swiss official stared at him a moment longer, then shrugged and stamped his passport. 'Well, it's the Italian border police you need to worry about,' he said. 'Your name means nothing to me, but they have lists. Be careful you're not on them.'

He slapped the passport down on the table and walked off to the next group of passengers. Iris let out a deep breath.

'I was afraid he was going to throw you off the train, or worse. Why was he so suspicious of you?'

Alessandro shrugged. 'There's no love lost between the Swiss and the Italians, is there, Raffaele?'

'No indeed. I'm glad I had French papers – saves a lot of bother,' he said, with a rueful smile. 'Although, in my heart, I will always be Italian. No amount of paperwork can change that.'

By the time they had finished the main course – roast chicken and seasonal vegetables – the train had reached Lausanne. Lac Leman gleamed like a mirror between the streets. When the train stopped, Raffaele and Alessandro got out to meet Isabella on the platform. The platform was full of soldiers and their equipment. Switzerland seemed determined to defend its borders and its neutral status.

Iris sat and waited, twisting the napkin through her fingers. Through the window, she spotted Raffaele and Alessandro talking to a tall woman with steel-grey hair over by the waiting room.

Tommaso came over to the table. 'Hopefully they won't be too much longer,' he said. 'We're leaving again soon.'

Iris scrutinized the view from the window. Alessandro said something to Raffaele and Isabella and strode back towards the train, a worried look on his face. 'What's happening?' she said when he reached the carriage.

'There's no time to explain now,' Alessandro said. 'We need to get off. I'll go and fetch the suitcases.'

Puzzled and alarmed, Iris hurried to her compartment, gathered her toiletries into their bag, closed the suitcase and grabbed her travelling perfumer's case. Tommaso came to help Alessandro and Iris down on to the platform.

'Talk about cutting it fine,' Tommaso said.

'I know,' Alessandro said. 'I'm sorry. We'll all catch the next train, the day after tomorrow.'

'It's an early one,' Tommaso said. 'It leaves Paris at ten thirty tomorrow night and will be arriving here at 6.26. Don't be late.'

'Thank you,' Alessandro said. He and Tommaso hugged, a clasp and a slap on the back, and then Tommaso gave the engine driver a wave and jumped back on to the train.

Iris watched as the doors slammed shut and the *Orient Express* pulled away in a cloud of steam. She glanced back towards the waiting room. Raffaele and the woman had disappeared.

'Now can you tell me what's going on?' she demanded.

Alessandro loosened his tie. 'Isabella, Raffaele's contact, hasn't got the visas yet. It seems that the new situation with Britain and France declaring war on Germany has got the diplomats in a spin. She's not even sure if she can get them. We're going to have to stay over and sort it out first, before travelling on to Milan.'

'Where?'

'The Lausanne Palace – it's just a four-minute walk from the station. Isabella has arranged rooms for us all. I'm sorry, it's not going to be as straightforward as we planned.'

Alessandro picked up the suitcases. 'Come on, let's go.'

Iris stood for a moment, breathing in the fresh alpine air. The *Orient Express* had gone. This delay would extend the trip but maybe it was what she needed. Some breathing space from Henri. But it also meant more time with Alessandro. She was conscious of a golden thread between them, drawing them nearer to each other. Iris wasn't sure if she had the strength to resist it. She hurried to catch up with him, and only hoped that the visas could be obtained soon, for Raffaele's sake and for her own.

18

Stella – Paris to Lausanne, July 1996

The train to Lausanne was delayed, allowing Stella the chance to call Arnold to see how everything was going at Penhallam's.

'Good morning, Penhallam's of Jermyn Street.' Arnold answered the phone in his reassuring voice.

'Hi, Arnold, it's Stella.'

'Stella, I'm glad you've called. I tried the hotel this morning, but they said you'd checked out.'

'Yes, we're leaving Paris to look for Iris's perfumes. We've already got the first two and are hopeful of finding the rest by following the journey she took on the *Orient Express* to Milan, just after war broke out. Things haven't exactly gone as planned,' Stella said, thinking of Iris's reluctance to delve into the past, 'but Bruno has been very helpful on the research side and we're taking it one step at a time. We might even be able to catch a glimpse of the *Orient Express* before we get on our train, if it's running.'

'And these perfumes,' Arnold said, 'do you really think they present a solution for Penhallam's?'

Stella hesitated. She'd been caught up in things here in Paris – meeting Iris, discovering Primo Bacio and that kiss with Bruno – but she hadn't lost sight of the practicalities.

'Yes, I believe they're the most credible way out of this mess. I've been working on some figures. I'll email them over when we get to the next hotel, but we're talking about five scents that were lost to history, and the story behind them will capture everyone's imagination. And it's not just the story. The scents we've found so far rival anything the other perfume houses are creating. Iris was clearly ahead of her time – there are aqua and gourmand notes and exciting combinations that will impress perfume reviewers. I really think Iris's perfumes could make the difference to Penhallam's finances.'

'What kind of timescale are you thinking here?' Arnold said in his measured voice.

'Development on the perfumes could start in the next couple of weeks, provided we find the other samples. I'll send them to a perfumer so they can work out the formulas and ingredients,' Stella said. Verbalizing the plans that had been swirling around her head over the last few days made her feel more confident. 'If we expedite things and the factory has capacity, we could at least produce something to show House of Fraser by September. It would give them the confidence to order, pay a deposit, and then we've got a bit of breathing space.'

'I see,' Arnold said. He paused. 'I hate to be the bearer of bad news, but I'm concerned we won't make it until September.'

Stella swallowed. 'I thought the second loan was secured,' she said.

'The lending company has refused our application.'

'On what grounds?'

'That the business isn't viable. I've tried talking to the other banks, but it's the same answer. Your idea about Iris's perfumes might pay off, but these banks aren't experts in perfumes, they're just looking at the cold, hard facts.' Arnold sighed. 'I'm sorry, Stella, but we may have reached the end of the line.'

Stella grasped the receiver. No, she wouldn't allow it. Not when there was still hope. She closed her eyes, trying to think through the options. There was one solution. It wasn't what she wanted, but perhaps it would buy her some more time.

'Right, there's only one thing for it,' she said. 'Please can you contact Andrea at GPL?'

'You're going to sell Penhallam's?' Arnold said incredulously.

'No, not if I can help it, but I'd like you to suggest a compromise. Tell her about the perfumes and the timelines I've outlined. Explain that I'll sell GPL twenty per cent of the shares in Penhallam's if she agrees to invest in this idea.'

'She won't accept twenty per cent,' Arnold said. 'It's not worth her while.'

'All right. Do what you can, but don't go over forty-nine. I need to make sure I've still got the controlling share.'

'And if she doesn't agree?'

'I don't know. We'll just have to hope that she does,' Stella said, rubbing her forehead. 'Maybe I should just come back to London.'

'No, keep going. Let me handle the finance side. Give me a call in a few days and hopefully I'll have news. You do know they won't just hand over the cash. They will expect a say in how things are run.'

'I know, but at the moment it's the only chance we've got. At least Andrea understands the business, and from what she said, she appears to trust my judgement. I'll just have to keep my fingers crossed that she'll be on board with what we're doing.'

The sooner she completed this search for the perfumes, the better.

The grey and blue TGV Lyria train to Switzerland stood at the platform. It had two decks and looked taller than a standard train. There had been no chance after all to see the *Orient Express* because it wasn't due into Paris until the next day.

Stella heaved her case on to the train. Bruno stowed his rucksack under the seat, then bent down to take Stella's. His hand brushed hers as he reached for the handle, and immediately goosebumps appeared on her skin, betraying her reaction. Warmth flared between them. Bruno looked away. The kiss lay between them like a burning ember. But so far, they were both doing their best to remain professional.

Bruno had managed to book them table seats on the top deck, so they made their way up and sat down. The journey would take about four hours, heading southeast through Dijon towards Lausanne. As it was nearly midday, Stella estimated they would reach Lausanne by four o'clock.

The train pulled out of the station. Graffiti splattered the hoardings and buildings next to the track. How had Iris felt leaving Paris that day? Right now, Stella felt a sense of unease. Was she right to delay her return to London for something that might not work out at all? It was risky. It would be tempting to confide in Bruno about what Arnold had told her, but she didn't want it to look like she was leaning on him for support. He took a folder out of his rucksack. Was she taking a risk with him too?

'Did you find anything at the National Archives?' she asked.

'I did, actually. There wasn't time to see any hard copies, but I looked at the digital records,' Bruno said. He passed over a sheet of paper. 'I've written a translation on the back.'

It was a photocopy of a newspaper cutting. Written in French, it contained few brief sentences that made Stella gasp.

M. Henri Levèque and Mlle Iris Penhallam
announce their marriage,
which took place on 6th October 1939
at the Hôtel de Ville in Lausanne, Switzerland, with a wedding
breakfast afterwards at the Lausanne Palace Hotel.

The happy couple will reside at the Levèque residence at
24 rue Rimbaud, Paris.

Stella stared at the words. 'But it doesn't make sense. Iris went on this journey with Alessandro, and they clearly had ambitions to launch a perfume line. There's been no hint of another man in her life, just work. Why on earth would she be married a month later to a Frenchman called Henri Levèque?'

'I don't know,' Bruno said. 'I haven't yet checked out who Henri Levèque was.'

Stella stared at the short paragraph. 'This date, the sixth of October, is exactly a month after the article came out in *Le Figaro* about the perfume collection. It's strange that in just four weeks everything seemed to have changed for Iris.'

'It is. And it's something we need to look into on our way to Milan. That's why we need to stop in Lausanne first.'

Stella nodded. 'I agree. We need to locate the marriage certificate and find out more.'

'Exactly.' Bruno smiled. 'You're starting to think like a researcher. I've also emailed someone I know in America. He works at the University of Boston. He's going to see if he can track down Jacopo and get us an address, if he's still alive.'

'That's great,' Stella said. She sat back in her seat. Green fields flashed by, yet inside the train the ride felt remarkably smooth. Bruno took out a pen and began scribbling notes in his book. He really was invested in this journey. It wouldn't have been the same doing this alone. Bruno must have felt her looking at him.

'What are you thinking?' he asked.

Stella hesitated, wondering if she should share her thoughts. But sitting here, his dark brown eyes alighting on her face, she decided to risk it.

'I'm glad you're here,' she said. 'I mean, I know you need the information for your book, but still . . . I'm grateful for your help. Especially when you must be worried about your sister.'

Bruno put the pen down and looked at Stella.

'In many ways, it helps to be busy,' he said.

'Can you tell me about her?' His face looked pained and Stella instantly regretted asking. 'I'm sorry, you don't have to.'

'No, it's okay. I know so much about your family's history. It's only right you should know about mine.'

Stella waited while Bruno found the right words.

'It started with cannabis and ecstasy,' he said, 'but a few years ago it developed into something more serious when her boyfriend at the time introduced her to heroin.'

'Oh, Bruno, I'm sorry.'

'She also has debts that I'm trying to sort out.' He rubbed his temples. 'It's a black hole, really – the debts keep getting bigger and the rehab bills keep coming. I'm at my wits' end. I just want her to get better.'

'What's her name?' Stella asked.

'Anna,' Bruno said. He rolled the pen under his fingers. 'Before all this, she was such a happy person. I used to take her out on our boat along the canals early in the morning at sunrise. Her eyes would light up, watching the sun sparkle on the water. It's heartbreaking to see her now.'

'Is rehab working?' Stella said.

'It seems to go up and down,' he said. 'The doctors have warned us that progress may be slow. The advance for my book has been almost swallowed up. There's nothing I can do but keep paying the bills and hope that one day she'll come back to Venice.'

Stella sighed. 'I hope she will. If we can find the perfumes, maybe your book will get you that promotion and you can ease the burden on your shoulders.'

'Maybe,' he said. He reached out and took her hand. Stella knew she should resist, but the warmth of his palm felt too good to pull away. 'And you will be able to sort out your financial troubles too.' He ran his fingers along each knuckle. 'I don't want you to be burdened either, Stella. You deserve to feel free.'

Stella held her breath, each sensation of his touch travelling deep inside, loosening her senses. She smiled. 'Maybe for now we can forget the outside world,' she said. 'Here on this train, it doesn't seem real. But this journey, it's a moment to savour.'

He nodded and squeezed her hand, releasing it with a thoughtful look in his eye. She was going against her own rules, and yet now he seemed to hesitate. He leaned back and stared out of the window. What had it been like for Iris, travelling with Alessandro? Stella wondered what they would discover in Lausanne when they arrived.

19

Iris – Lausanne, September 1939

Iris went down to the breakfast room. A long window looked out on the lake and she stared, awestruck. Before her was a palette of blues: the cloudless sky, the hazy mountains and the sparkling waters of the lake. Raffaele waved her over. He and Alessandro looked to have already eaten. The waitress cleared their plates away. Iris sat down and reached for a croissant.

'Isn't it beautiful?' Raffaele said. 'It's given me some more ideas about the scent you're working on. La Scintilla and Primo Bacio were just the start. This next one is going to be more challenging. It might mean stepping beyond what you see and smell and exploring what you *feel* about things.'

Alessandro poured Iris a cup of coffee from the pot that stood on the table. 'That's not always easy.'

'No,' Iris agreed. 'And what if our feelings aren't clear?'

'It's your job to make them clear,' Raffaele said. 'You can't be a perfumer and hide from emotions and conflict. That's the kind of passion that will sell fragrances.'

He was right. People bought perfumes because of how the fragrance made them feel.

'It follows on naturally that the next scent should be called Amanti,' Raffaele said.

'What does "Amanti" mean?' Iris asked, taking a sip from her cup.

'Lovers,' Alessandro said, looking intently at her.

Iris blushed and looked away.

'I'm going with Isabella to the embassy this morning,' Raffaele said. 'Why don't you two explore the town and gather impressions for the perfume?'

'I'd like that,' Alessandro said, still with his eyes on Iris. Her heart pounded. Enjoy each moment. That was the challenge she'd set herself. But the word 'Amanti' lingered in her mind. It spoke of something more than mere enjoyment. Iris wasn't sure if she'd have the courage for this scent.

'Are you sure you know where you're going?' Iris said sometime later. She wrapped her coat belt tightly around her.

'I'm pretty sure this is the way,' Alessandro said.

Alessandro had asked the hotel receptionist the best route to the lake. She'd suggested heading down to the Quai d'Ouchy and had drawn him a map on a hotel compliments slip. He consulted it now.

'We need to go down this street,' he said, turning right, 'and then hopefully, just around this corner . . .'

They followed the bend in the road. The street widened and the houses fell away, and there was the lake down below, sparkling in the sunshine, closer and more vivid than it had been up at the hotel.

'My goodness,' Alessandro said. 'This is spectacular.'

Iris couldn't help but smile. It had been worth coming out just to see the look on his face right now. Carefree. Inspired. He leaned on the balustrade and seemed to soak up the view.

'It's pretty nice,' she said. She nudged his elbow. 'Are you comparing it to Venice?'

'I always compare places to Venice. We have the sea, but this water is a different blue. The meltwater has run off the mountains, cold and fresh, and into this lake.'

Iris smiled. 'That's very poetic.'

The wind blew his hair back and he turned his face to the warm sun. His scar was less visible in the fresh air. 'I think all perfumers are. What do you compare it to?'

'The Mediterranean, I suppose, but this feels cleaner, wider, more expansive.' She held out her arms. 'I can breathe here.'

Alessandro rested his elbow on the balustrade. 'You mean you can't breathe in other places?'

'London and Paris are so crowded and full of cars and buildings and noise. The air feels old somehow. But here . . . this is new air, freshly minted.'

Alessandro nodded. 'I know what you mean. It's like a second chance.'

Iris looked out over the lake, wishing they could stay here and pretend the war wasn't about to explode around them. Underneath everything was a sense of unease. War had been declared, but as yet nothing had happened. It was like waiting for a volcano to erupt.

Alessandro touched her arm. 'Come on, let's go and explore the town.'

Later, they sat in Plaza de la Palud, outside a café on the sunny side, and decided to have lunch. Posters on the walls encouraged vigilance. A battalion of troops marched through the square, a group of children running alongside, marvelling at the spectacle.

'The Swiss fear both sides,' Alessandro said. 'This country is the only break in the Maginot line and they're nervous of being used as a crossing place by either the Allies or the Germans. It's an awkward position to be in.'

Iris watched the soldiers disappear up the main street. 'It certainly explains why there's been a delay with the visas. I hope Raffaele and Isabella can sort something out soon.'

The waiter poured them both a glass of wine from the bottle Alessandro had ordered. Despite the turmoil of war hanging over everything like a dark cloud, spending the morning with Alessandro had been a moment of escape.

'Look, I don't want to pry,' Alessandro said, taking a sip of his wine. 'But I couldn't help overhearing what Henri said to you at the station, about it being to everyone's advantage if you marry him, including your family's perfumery.'

This was an unexpected change of subject. Iris blushed. 'I wish you hadn't heard that.'

'But I did,' Alessandro said, leaning forward, his face full of concern. 'Surely you're not going to let him force your hand like that, not if you don't want to marry him.'

'It's complicated,' Iris said. 'I'd rather not talk about it, if you don't mind.'

'I just can't bear the thought of your future being yoked to a man like that, who sees marriage as a business transaction.'

Iris shook her head. 'Please, let's not spoil the day discussing something which you couldn't possibly understand.'

Alessandro sighed. 'Oh, but I do understand. I understood about four months after I married my childhood sweetheart.'

Iris sucked in her breath. 'You're married?'

'Yes, and just like you with Henri, I'd known her all my life and it's what our parents wanted. I thought I was in love, and, although the stakes were vastly lower than I imagine yours are with Henri, there was money involved, and the uniting of my father's glass workshop with her family's.'

Iris shivered, heeding the warning in his tone and aware of the parallels with her own situation. 'So, what happened?'

'I had to go and fight Mussolini's stupid war in Ethiopia,' he said. 'I was injured, as you know, and when I finally got out of hospital and returned to Venice I discovered that Roberta had been unfaithful. Or rather, had always been unfaithful. She'd never really loved me and had been forced into the marriage to cover her father's debts. She moved in with her new lover and has been with him ever since.'

He picked up his glass of wine and downed the lot. Iris didn't know what to say.

'Don't pity me,' he said, seemingly anticipating her next words. 'That's not why I told you. If anything, let it serve as a warning. Don't let Henri or your family pressure you into a marriage that you don't want.'

His gaze was intense. Iris smiled to break the tension. 'You seem to forget that what a person might want from a marriage and what they get are rarely the same, especially for a woman. We live in an age when marriage is more about business than love.'

'I don't want that for you,' Alessandro said, reaching out his fingertips across the tablecloth so that they brushed her hand. 'That kiss in the perfumery, it meant something, Iris, you can't deny it.'

Iris pulled her hand back, startled by his touch. 'Love and passion are fine bottled in a perfume or remembered in a haze of nostalgia,' she said, trying to be matter of fact, 'but out in the real world, they're messy and treacherous.'

Alessandro nodded and sat back in his chair, as if accepting her rebuttal. 'I understand. I won't be like Henri and force you into anything. But just know that I'm here for you, whatever you choose. On this journey, you've got the chance to break loose of all the ties that bind you, at least for a while.'

Iris nodded. 'Thank you.' Then she stopped. 'What you just said. It's given me an idea for the top note of Amanti.'

'It has?' said Alessandro, smiling. 'And what is it?'

'Sage. That fresh, clean smell. The mountain air, the lake. People come to places like this to recuperate. It's like a tonic. It cleanses you of anything that has gone before and makes things new again. For people to become lovers, they need to start afresh, with each other, and with themselves.'

Alessandro raised his eyebrows. 'How is it that you can put my feelings into words like that?'

Iris smiled. 'Maybe it's what Raffaele meant when he said about learning to work together. Perhaps it gets to that point where it's hard to tell where one person's ideas begin and the other one's end.'

As her eyes met Alessandro's, Iris felt her axis shift. Somehow, without warning, his presence had become vital: to creating perfumes, to this journey, to her. The golden thread was almost taut.

20

Stella – Lausanne, July 1996

The train drew into the covered platform at Lausanne. The sky was bright blue, and the air looked alpine fresh. For much of the journey, while Bruno had worked, she had stared out of the window, wondering if she had made a mistake by not going back to London. Stepping off the train, dragging her suitcase behind her, Stella decided that now wasn't the time to ponder the future but to focus on the past, and hope that by doing so the future would take care of itself.

'The city hall is only a short walk from here,' Bruno said. He'd purchased a map from the kiosk on the platform. 'Perhaps we should start there and see if we can find out something about Iris and Henri's wedding.'

They made their way through the huge, high-ceilinged main foyer of the station. Outside, the streets were busy with people and cars, but the freedom of the mountains hovered just around the corner.

The Hôtel de Ville was an imposing building overlooking the Place de la Palud. A belfry tower rose up over the square and porticoes shaded the entrance.

Bruno explained the situation to the woman on the front desk. 'We'd be grateful if you have any information at all about a wedding that took place here, just after the war started in 1939.'

The woman nodded. 'The city hall was the scene of many gatherings and celebrations. We keep records going back a hundred years. We close in half an hour, but you could have a brief look if you can tell me what it is you need.'

'A wedding certificate,' Stella said. 'Dated 6 October 1939. A marriage took place here between Henri Levèque and Iris Penhallam.'

The woman made a note of the names and nodded. 'Please, take a seat.'

Stella and Bruno went over to the desk at the other side of the room. The leather seats creaked as they sat down. A few minutes later the woman came back with a folder in her hand. She handed it to Stella. 'Please bring this back when you've finished.'

Stella opened the folder. Bruno moved his chair closer, his arm brushing hers, sending a tingle over her skin. She leafed through the pages until she came to the September entries.

'Look at this . . .' she said. It was the marriage certificate.

Kanton Lausanne
Certificate of Marriage

This certifies that Henri Levèque (businessman) and Iris
Penhallam (perfumer)
were joined in marriage
on this day, 6th October 1939
At the Hôtel de Ville, Place de la Palud, Lausanne
By the power vested in me, Reverend T. Lempicker
Before the witnesses Isabella Curato (secretary at the
Swiss embassy)
and Raffaele di Fiore (perfumer of Paris)

Bruno stared at the certificate. 'Why is this woman Isabella's name on there? What connection could Iris or Henri possibly have to a secretary in the Swiss embassy? And more to the point, how did Raffaele get involved in all of this?'

'I don't know. None of it makes sense,' Stella said. 'Our only hope is that this woman Isabella or her descendants might still be here in Lausanne and can tell us something.'

Bruno closed the folder and shrugged. 'I've no idea.'

'We have to try to find Isabella Curato,' Stella said.

The woman came over. 'I'm afraid it's time for the city hall to close. Did you find what you were looking for?'

Stella nodded. 'Yes, we did, thank you.' She pointed at Isabella's name on the certificate. 'I don't suppose you know if this woman is still living here in Lausanne.'

The woman shook her head. 'I'm sorry. Isabella died ten years ago.'

'You knew her?'

'I knew of her. She was a remarkable woman. Her son still lives here in Lausanne, though. My husband is his accountant.'

Stella gripped the woman's hand. 'Please, could you arrange for us to see him?'

Stella and Bruno left the town hall and walked down towards the lake, following the woman's directions. Grand houses stretched out along the shoreline. The air was crisp and clear, and Stella was grateful for her warm sweater.

Eventually, they reached the address. Bruno pressed the buzzer at the side of a pair of huge security gates.

'Wow, this is some place,' Stella said, looking through the iron bars. 'It must have its own jetty on to the lake.'

The gate swung open and they walked up a long, winding drive at the end of which sat an imposing house. The grass and trees on either side were pristinely manicured. When they reached the front door a butler answered and showed them into a library, where a fire crackled in the fireplace. The walls were covered in bookshelves. A moment later, a man in his fifties entered and introduced himself as Laurence.

'Thank you so much for agreeing to see us,' Stella said.

'You're not the first people to come enquiring about my mother,' he said, gesturing to a large portrait above the fire. It depicted a tall woman with grey shoulder-length hair. She was sitting on a chair, serious-faced, and wearing a medal on one of her jacket lapels. 'That painting was commissioned after she was finally recognized for the work she did during the war.'

'Apologies to sound ignorant, but what did she do?' Bruno asked.

'Forgive me. I'd assumed you knew and that's why you wanted to visit,' Laurence said. 'She was involved in supplying Swiss visas for Jews in Germany, Austria and Italy, helping as many as she could to get out, over and above the quota set by the Swiss government. That's why it took so long for them to honour her. At the time, and for many years afterwards, she had to keep her work a secret.'

'How did word get out?' Stella asked, fascinated by the story.

'People came looking for her. Survivors, relatives, grandchildren, all keen to thank the woman who had saved family members from the Nazis and fascists. She was simply a footnote in history, but she did her part and is estimated to have saved hundreds of Jews.'

'That's extraordinary,' Stella said. 'But I'm not sure how your mother fits into our search. We're looking into my great-aunt's history. Her name was Iris Penhallam and she was here just after the war started with two Italian men, perfumers like she was. I can't understand why they needed to meet Isabella, unless it was for a visa for Raffaele.'

'I have the list of visas that she supplied, and for whom. She kept careful records,' Laurence said.

He fetched a sheaf of papers from the cabinet in the corner of the room. Names were listed alphabetically. Stella bent close to Bruno as they searched for Raffaele's name.

'There's nothing there,' Bruno said. 'It's impossible to know what the connection was between Iris and Isabella. Maybe she was just someone who acted as a witness at the time.'

'There must be more to it than that,' Stella said.

Laurence shook his head sympathetically. 'I'm sorry I can't be of more help.'

'It sounds as though your mother was a remarkable woman,' Bruno said.

Laurence nodded. 'She was. We've had visitors from all over the world who came to thank her for what she did. And their relatives too. Only last week, we met a Jewish family from the States. Their grandfather had passed away, but they wanted to pay their respects. The Swiss visa had saved him from being sent to Auschwitz.'

'She was very brave,' Stella said, glancing up at Isabella's portrait, 'to defy the Swiss government like that.'

'Yes,' Laurence replied. 'It is shocking how many countries in Europe, including Switzerland, closed their doors to Jewish refugees. So many more could have been helped. All the lives that could not be saved weighed heavily on my mother.'

Stella was silent for a moment, thinking about Isabella. She remembered Jacopo's letter. *I will be forever indebted to your sister, Iris, and what she did for me in the war. Her efforts, along with those of Alessandro Mori and Tommaso Ricci, saved my life.* That last sentence sent Stella's mind racing. If Isabella hadn't organized a visa for Raffaele, then perhaps it had been for someone else.

'Of course!' Stella exclaimed. 'Jacopo Calvetti. He was Raffaele's nephew.' She turned to Bruno. 'Remember the letter thanking Iris for helping to save his life? Maybe they were here to get a visa for Jacopo. Let's see if his name is on the list.'

Bruno eyes shone. 'That must be it,' he said.

Stella scoured through the names until she came to the surnames beginning with C. Row by row, she checked carefully.

'Look, there he is,' she exclaimed. 'Jacopo Calvetti was granted a visa on the fifth of September 1939. And also someone called Francesca Calvetti. I wonder if that was Jacopo's mother. Looks as though she was in her late forties, and Jacopo . . .' She worked it out from the date of birth. 'He would have been only eleven years old.'

Laurence smiled. 'The connections spread far and wide,' he said. 'By granting a resident permit and a visa, my mother was able to circumvent the strict border regulations that had arisen in 1938 and tightened even further when war was declared the following year.'

'But I don't understand,' Stella said to Bruno. 'I thought Raffaele, Iris and Alessandro went to Milan to create a collection of perfumes.'

Laurence nodded. 'For many people at this time there were two motivations for travelling – the public and the secret. Perhaps the legitimate reason of creating a collection of perfumes was a cover for also rescuing Raffaele's sister and nephew. The issuing of the visa, and the connection between the people you are asking about suggest this to be true.'

'Now Jacopo's letter starts to make sense,' Bruno said.

'Thank you for your help,' Stella said to Laurence. 'It's getting late. We'd better go and find somewhere to stay. There's a lot to think about.'

The Lausanne Palace was a sumptuous white building with pillars at the entrance. Each window had a jaunty red awning above it, which made the hotel look like a wedding cake covered in white icing and strawberries.

'This place looks far too expensive,' Stella said.

'It's only for one night, it's close to the station and this is where Iris probably stayed, according to the marriage announcement,' Bruno replied. 'Besides, we've tried all the B&Bs and everywhere is booked.'

Inside the hotel, it was even grander. A red-and-gold carpet swept through the atrium and up a magnificent wide staircase.

'I'm afraid we're almost completely full,' the man at reception said. 'There's an anniversary party taking place. But we've got a cancellation on a double room.'

That would mean sharing with Bruno. 'What shall we do?' Stella said.

'Don't worry, I'll sleep on the sofa,' Bruno said.

Stella wasn't sure if that would be enough to keep him off her mind. The very thought of being near him, in the dark, made her pulse race.

Bruno carried his rucksack and Stella's suitcase to the

lift. Their room was on the first floor. It was beautiful. A large window overlooked the lake and mountain. It was such a clear, bright scene that Stella felt her tension loosen.

'I hadn't realized how much I needed to see wide-open spaces like this until now.'

Bruno set down her suitcase. 'It's been a hard time for you. All the worries with the business, and seeing Iris for the first time.'

Stella nodded, thinking back to the dark days after her father's car accident.

'It's been a strange time ever since my father died. One thing after another has gone wrong. Hearing about Iris and the perfumes was a ray of hope. But somehow even that hasn't turned out the way I expected. I'd like to give her a call if that's okay, and see how she's doing.'

Bruno nodded. 'Of course. I'll go down and get us a table for dinner. Come and join me in the restaurant when you're ready.'

'Thank you.' After he'd gone, Stella sat on the bed and dialled the convalescent home. A moment later, the receptionist put her through to Iris's extension with a click.

Iris answered with a cautious 'Hello?'

'Iris, it's me, Stella.'

'Ah, I hoped you would ring,' Iris said.

'You wanted me to call?' Stella said, hoping that Iris had had a change of heart.

'Yes, you see there's something I think you should know.'

'I've already found it out,' Stella said. 'You weren't just here to create perfumes; you were here to rescue Jacopo and someone called Francesca Calvetti. I wonder if that was Jacopo's mother. That's why you stopped in Lausanne, to get the visas. What you were attempting to do was heroic.'

Iris's gentle breath came down the telephone line. 'Nothing about my actions was heroic,' she said, at last. 'That's what I wanted to tell you. It began that way, and then something went wrong. I don't know why, but I was dragged along by a current I couldn't control.'

'Has this got something to do with Henri?' Stella said, an ominous feeling in her stomach.

The line was silent. 'How do you know about him?' Iris whispered.

'Bruno found a newspaper announcement of your wedding in the online archives in France. Then we tracked down the marriage certificate at the town hall in Lausanne. We thought it was strange that you'd married him only a few weeks after embarking on your journey to Milan.'

Iris sighed. 'Then I must tell you the truth. It won't be long before you find it out for yourself. I wish it could stay buried, but I've decided that I'd rather you heard it from me than anyone else.'

Stella held her breath. 'You're going to tell me why you and Charles fell out so badly?'

'Yes,' Iris said, clearing her throat. 'But let me do it in my own time. You'll have lots of questions, and I might not be able to answer them all right away. You see . . .' Stella waited, anxious about what Iris was going to say. 'After the war, there were lots of trials, punishing people who had misbehaved in the war.' She hesitated. 'I was one of them. I was found guilty of embezzling Jews out of their businesses and property.'

The air seemed to freeze at Iris's words. Stella tried to take in what she had said. 'You stole from the Jews?'

'I was sentenced to ten years in prison,' Iris said, her voice heavy. 'I served every single one, but that doesn't atone for what happened. I wanted to tell you because this journey you're on to find the perfumes is a waste of time. You can't use these perfumes, not with my name attached. Charles knew that: it's why he cut ties with me. He was disgusted with me and knew that he had to protect Penhallam's against the taint of the scandal.'

Stella clutched the handset. 'But I don't understand. You came here to rescue Jacopo and his mother. You were helping Jews. How could your view of things have changed so much? What made you do it?'

Iris was in tears; Stella could hear it in her voice. 'I hate myself for what I did. I won't blame you if you hate me too. Now you know the truth, I'll understand if you just want to stop the search and have nothing more to do with me.'

Stella breathed hard, her mind racing. She was already halfway to Milan —they couldn't turn back now. 'I wish you'd told me sooner.'

'I was too ashamed.'

'What about Jacopo and Francesca? Jacopo was clearly very grateful to you in the letter he sent Charles,' Stella said. 'You must have been involved in going with Raffaele and Alessandro to fetch them from Milan?'

Iris sighed. 'Does it matter?'

'It matters to me. This is about more than just finding the perfumes, this is about my family history too. Please, Iris, I'd like to know.'

'Raffaele stayed in Lausanne, but Alessandro and I carried on,' Iris said. 'Nothing turned out the way I'd planned. I'm not trying to make excuses.'

'I don't believe that,' Stella said. Iris sounded as if she was rehearsing a script, not speaking from the heart. 'There's always a choice. None of what you've told me makes sense.

You were helping Jacopo, and yet you were imprisoned for taking advantage of the Jews. You were clearly in love with Alessandro, and yet you married this man called Henri.'

'In love with Alessandro?' Iris said. 'What makes you think that?'

'I read what you wrote about the third perfume, Amanti.'

'What did I write?' Iris whispered.

Stella reached for the notebook, opened it to the right page and read, '*Amanti. I don't even know how to describe it. It's the scent of another on your skin, their taste in your mouth, their warmth in your body. It's elemental, heady, all-consuming. But it also endures, like the flower in the hidden garden in Milan, Immortelle. No matter what happens, we are, and will always be, each other's.*'

A crackle sounded in the receiver as Iris breathed out.

'They're just words – they mean nothing,' she said with a sob. 'I've told you what you need to know. Please give up the search and go back to Penhallam's. You need to make your own perfumes, Stella, and leave mine alone.'

Before Stella could reply, the line went dead. She sat holding the receiver. So that was it. Iris had told her the truth. No wonder her grandfather had wanted nothing to do with Iris. The trial and her imprisonment must have been devastating to him personally, but also a public humiliation. Stella's father must have known the truth too. At last Stella understood. All those years of estrangement. It wasn't about some petty argument. Iris had done something unforgivable.

21

Iris – Lausanne to Milan, September 1939

By six the next evening, Iris was packed and ready to go. She took a small bottle of perfume from her bedside table and unscrewed the lid. Amanti still needed work, but she and Alessandro had spent all day working on an accord whilst Raffaele had been resting. The perfume seemed to sum up the feeling of renewal that being in Lausanne had brought. At midday, Isabella had arrived with the visas for Francesca and Jacopo. Iris, Raffaele and Alessandro were due to board the *Orient Express* when it arrived back in Lausanne from Paris at eight o'clock. Iris tucked the bottle in the travelling perfumer's case and went to see if Raffaele was ready.

His bedroom door was open. Alessandro was already there, but Raffaele was still in bed.

'What's wrong?' Iris said.

'My chest pains have come back,' Raffaele said. His face was white against the pillowcase and there were dark rings around his eyes.

'I've called for the doctor,' Alessandro said, 'but we haven't got long until the train departs.'

Raffaele tried to lift himself. 'I can't get up,' he said, grimacing with pain.

Iris rubbed his arm. 'You need to lie down; you mustn't exert yourself. This whole journey has been too much.'

'Then what do you suggest?' Raffaele said. 'I can't leave Francesca and Jacopo alone in Milan. I have to get them out.'

'I'll go and get your sister and Jacopo,' Alessandro said. 'Iris can look after you until I get back from Italy.'

Raffaele shook his head. 'Absolutely not. You are not going on your own. Without the cover of our perfume expedition, you'll be in danger. This is a two-person job, Alessandro, and you know it.'

Alessandro sucked in his breath and glanced at Iris.

'I want to come too,' Iris said firmly. 'Jacopo and Francesca have a better chance of escaping with me there too.'

'You have to take Iris with you,' Raffaele implored. 'I'll wait here at the hotel until you get back. The visas are in my suitcase – take them with you. Please, I don't want you to miss that train.'

Alessandro rubbed his forehead. 'Then I guess we have no choice. We'll bring Francesca and Jacopo back to you, I promise.'

After a hasty goodbye to Raffaele, Alessandro and Iris walked the short distance to the train station. It was nearly quarter to eight now. The *Orient Express* stood at the platform, steam billowing. It was a relief to have Alessandro's calm, decisive presence. He organized the baggage and presented the tickets as they got on the train.

'It's good to see you again. I insisted on working a double shift so I could be around to help,' Tommaso said, carrying their suitcases along the corridor. 'I've given you compartments next to each other. It's best if you keep a low profile as we head into Italy.'

'Thank you, my friend,' Alessandro said. He went into his compartment and Iris opened the door to hers. The guard blew his whistle. The train pulled out, the station slowly disappearing behind them. There was no going back. All that separated her from Alessandro was a door. For better or for worse, they were reliant on each other now, and heading to Milan together.

There was a tap at the interconnecting door before Alessandro came in.

'That wasn't quite the departure we'd expected,' he said. 'Are you feeling all right?'

'I'm worried about Raffaele, but I think it was the right decision for him to stay behind,' Iris said. 'I hope he can get some rest in Lausanne.'

'It's not ideal, just the two of us, but hopefully we can manage.'

Iris nodded. 'All we have to do is get Francesca and Jacopo out of Milan, and we can be on the train back to Switzerland later this evening.'

'I hope so.' Alessandro said, his eyes fixed on hers. 'I'm glad you've come too. Not just because this task will be easier with two of us, but selfishly because I didn't want to be parted from you.'

The air tightened between them. Out here, away from everything, there was no need to hide any more. 'It's probably best if you get some sleep,' Alessandro said. Before she could reply, he'd closed the connecting door between them.

Iris lay down, still in her clothes, on the bed, which had been made up ready for the evening. She didn't feel tired but she must have dozed off, because the next thing she remembered was hearing Alessandro and Tommaso talking next door. She checked her watch – it was approaching midnight – and got up and opened the door to Alessandro's room. 'What's going on?'

'The Italian border is coming up soon,' Tommaso said. 'Give me your passports and I'll hand them in. Since the war began, the border guards have started to come onboard the train. But I'll say you're still sleeping, and if I tell them you're a rich couple and slip them a bribe, hopefully they won't pursue it.'

'But what if they insist?' Iris asked.

'If there's anything of value you want to keep secure, you can place it in the drawer under the bed,' Tommaso said. 'There are spare blankets in there in case you're cold.'

'Thank you. I hope you can help us with the return journey too,' Iris said.

'We'll still need two compartments,' Alessandro said, 'but we won't be alone. Francesca and Jacopo will be with us.'

Tommaso nodded. 'Don't worry,' he said. 'You can count on me. I'm getting off the train with you at Milan. I'm owed a night's leave, and it's the only chance I have to see my sweetheart. Sit tight and don't come out of your compartment until I give the word, all right?'

He closed the door. The train slowed down. They were high in the mountains now. There wasn't a house in sight. 'What's happening?' Iris asked.

'Don't worry. We used to stop here all the time when I worked on the *Orient Express*. Normally the border guards are too lazy to be bothered to board the train. Let's hope they just want to get back to their game of chess.'

'But now that war has been declared, Tommaso said they're more vigilant. What if they search the compartment and see the visas? They'll know we're planning on bringing people out of Italy.'

'They won't,' he said. 'But just in case, let's draw the blinds. And put the visas in that drawer under the bed.'

Iris pulled the blind down. The mist and mountains disappeared. The room felt smaller. Gradually the train slowed to a stop. Iris held her breath. There were voices outside the window.

'You'll be wasting your time going onboard,' she heard Tommaso say. 'I have the passport for the occupant of this compartment.'

'We need to check: it's the government's orders since the war started,' the border guard replied. 'Kindly stand aside.'

Iris's heart ran cold. 'They're coming onboard.'

'Don't say a word,' Alessandro said. 'I'll think of something. We'll be all right, I promise . . . I can . . .'

His voice became breathless, his face a deathly pale. It was as if he were here but not here. He clutched his heart as if it was racing, panic rising in his eyes.

'Alessandro, what's wrong?' Iris said.

'I'm sorry,' he gasped. 'It happens when I'm afraid. A flashback to the war in Ethiopia. I was crushed under the truck, my leg immobile, hearing the enemy inspecting the vehicles abandoned all around, waiting for death. The bullet thudded into my cheek and—' He broke off, sweat pouring down his forehead. So that's how he'd got his scar.

There was no time to lose. Iris had to take control. She wiped his forehead with her handkerchief. He looked ashamed that she'd seen him falter.

'Iris . . .'

'Get into bed,' she said.

Her words seemed to jolt him out of his memories. 'What?'

'Take off your trousers and shirt. Quickly.'

Without questioning her logic, Alessandro did as she ordered. Taking a deep breath, Iris took off her blouse and skirt, flinging them to the floor, her heart thudding. She climbed into the narrow bed with him. The bare skin on his arms and legs touched her own, startlingly intimate and warm.

'What are you doing?' he said hoarsely.

'We have to pretend it's our honeymoon,' she said, pulling the cover over them both.

'But the papers won't match,' Alessandro said. 'We have different surnames.'

Iris thought quickly. 'All right, an illicit liaison then, between two work colleagues who are going to Milan on business. You stay here, buried under the covers. If they come in, let me do the talking.'

Iris lay on her back, holding her arm against her side, painfully aware of Alessandro's body warm next to her. She held her breath, listening for the border guards in the corridor.

'Pretend to be asleep,' she said in a low voice.

Alessandro turned over to face the wall. A second later, there was a brisk knock at the door. Iris didn't move. The knock came again. She stirred, yawning loudly, then called out, 'We're sleeping.'

'Sorry to wake you, signorina, we need to match passports to passengers. Kindly open the door.'

'Stay where you are,' she whispered to Alessandro. She swallowed, hoping she had the nerve to pull this off. She took off one of the blankets and draped it around her shoulders.

She opened the door. Two burly guards stood in the

corridor, stern looks on their faces, but they smiled when they caught sight of Iris half undressed.

'*Buongiorno*,' Iris said nervously.

She stood aside to let them see into the compartment, and Alessandro's shape under the covers.

'Ah,' one of the men said. 'You're obviously busy. We'll make this quick.'

Maybe this could work. She forced her breathing to slow.

The guard opened their passports. 'Miss Penhallam, and Signor Mori?' the man asked, and Iris nodded. 'And what is your business in Italy?'

'We're perfumers,' Iris said, thinking quickly. 'We're going to make a perfume for a client's wedding anniversary. It's good money, but if he thinks a fragrance is going to wipe out the memory of his past indiscretions, he's sadly mistaken. A woman never forgets, does she, gentlemen?'

The men laughed. 'My wife certainly doesn't,' one of them replied. 'Here are your papers. Safe travels in Italy.'

Iris closed the door and locked it. Thank goodness they'd believed her lies. The men's voices moved down the corridor.

The minutes ticked by. It seemed endless. Then, at last, a whistle blew. Doors slammed closed. The train started to move, slowly at first, then faster. Iris peeped out behind the blind. Only mountains and snow remained, visible in the moonlight.

'Thank God it's over,' she said, drawing the blanket tightly around herself and letting out her breath. Alertness still pumped through her body. But now it was hard to tell if it was the danger of getting caught or the danger of having Alessandro here like this.

Alessandro turned around slowly. 'You got us through,' he said, shaking his head. 'I'm so sorry – I don't know what happened to me.'

'It's all right. You panicked.'

She couldn't take her eyes off him. The covers had fallen away, his broad chest was exposed, his collar bone, the dark whorl of his chest hair as it travelled down his body and towards the shadow underneath.

Alessandro moved closer. He traced his finger along her bare shoulder and down her arm. 'You bewitched them, that's how you did it,' he said with a shy smile. 'Just like you've bewitched me.'

Iris shook her head. 'Nonsense . . .'

Alessandro's face grew serious. 'I mean it, Iris. You bewitched me from the first moment I met you.'

His hand slid along her arm. She shivered, hardly able to believe that this was happening. His touch was electric, creating tiny explosions under her skin. She didn't want them to stop.

She closed her eyes. 'We can't,' she murmured. The train rocked side to side. His hand explored under her hair, teasing apart the tendrils, massaging her neck, the tension of the day, and somehow making her melt inside.

'I'll stop if you want me to,' he said.

She didn't want him to. She wanted to have him even closer. 'Don't stop,' she said.

His arms were around her now, gently pulling her towards him. His breath was shallow; he was as nervous as she was. She opened her eyes. There he was. Only inches from her face. She touched the raised skin of his scar.

'Do you feel it too?' he whispered. 'If you don't, just tell me. I'll go back to my compartment and never mention this again.'

Iris hesitated, some part of her mind sounding an alarm bell. What was she doing? This journey was fraught with danger. She and Alessandro needed to keep their wits about them, not give in to their desire.

She sat up. 'Maybe we shouldn't. Not with everything that's going on. We can't risk putting our feelings for each other first.' She pulled the blanket tightly around her. 'We have to focus on getting Francesca and Jacopo.'

'Of course,' he said, lowering his eyes.

'It's not that . . .' Her words trailed off. She didn't know whether to follow her head or her longing.

'It's all right, I understand. I'll go.'

He got out of the bed, picked up his clothes and went to the connecting door. The sight of his almost naked body made Iris dissolve. But she steadfastly turned her eyes to the floor, only looking up when she heard the door click shut. He had gone, and immediately Iris felt an empty, cold ache where he'd touched her, and wondered how she would ever forget the feel of him next to her or satisfy the need that still raged within her.

22

Stella – Lausanne to Milan, July 1996

Stella woke early the next morning. She had slept badly. Her dreams were punctured by Iris's voice, the words she'd said last night on the phone.

The contradiction in Iris's story – helping Jews like Francesca and Jacopo, and then being convicted for stealing Jewish businesses – swirled around her head. She opened her eyes and saw that Bruno was lying just a few feet away on the sofa in boxer shorts and a white T-shirt. He had a sheet over him, but still the contours of his body were illuminated by the sun shining through the window.

Stella sighed, unable to go back to sleep. Bruno had listened when she had told him over dinner about Iris and her imprisonment. Then, as if sensing she needed some time alone to digest it all, had stayed in the hotel bar, while Stella tossed and turned, finally falling asleep to the midnight bells from the cathedral.

Now, he stirred. He lifted his head up, his eyes still sleepy. 'Morning,' he said. 'How are you feeling?'

'Pretty flat,' Stella said. She turned over, her head still on the pillow, to face him. 'I still can't believe what Iris told me. It renders the search for the perfumes completely pointless. I'm angry that we've wasted our time like this.'

Bruno rubbed his eyes. 'I guess it is pointless if you want the perfumes to revive Penhallam's. But maybe not so pointless if you want the perfumes so that you can understand Iris herself.'

Stella frowned. 'Why would I want to understand someone who embezzled Jewish businesses during the war?'

He raised his eyebrows, tucking his hands behind his head. 'Because I'm not sure she was entirely to blame.'

Stella sat up, pulling the covers around her. 'What makes you say that?'

'After you went to bed last night, I did a search on the internet,' he said. 'I know you said you didn't want me to, but things just didn't add up. I was interested in that man she married, Henri Levèque. I discovered that in 1946, according to a passenger list, he emigrated to Argentina.'

Stella took in his words. Somehow, talking about Iris made it easier to pretend that it was perfectly natural to be sharing a bedroom with Bruno. Which, of course, it wasn't, she thought, glancing at his bare arms and firm biceps.

'That still doesn't absolve Iris,' she said, getting back to the matter in hand. 'Maybe Henri couldn't stand the shame of being married to her.'

Bruno shook his head. 'South America was where collaborators and Nazis fled after the war. Over there, they were immune from prosecution. Nazi hunters pursued German perpetrators, but businessmen like Henri would have been small fry in comparison and left alone so long as they remained abroad.'

'So, you think Henri was involved in the thefts too?'

Bruno plumped his pillow and propped himself up. 'He must have been, or else why would he have fled? Perhaps he left Iris to take the blame. Think about it: Iris was more interested in making perfumes than the business side of things. Maybe she didn't know anything about it.'

'And if she *was* innocent,' Stella said, excitement in her voice, 'it means the perfumes would still be of use to Penhallam's if we could clear her name.'

'Exactly,' Bruno said.

'But Iris made no such claims about her innocence to me on the phone last night,' Stella said. 'Surely, if she'd done nothing wrong, she'd want to tell me that.'

'Maybe she's trying to put you off the search for another reason,' Bruno said. 'After all, she has no love for Penhallam's. Perhaps she just wants you to leave her perfumes out of any attempt to salvage the business.'

Stella rubbed her forehead. 'I'm still not sure if we can continue the search. We don't have any specific leads to follow in Milan.'

Bruno smiled. 'Ah yes we do. Do you remember that Jacopo mentioned a man called Tommaso Ricci in his letter?'

Stella nodded.

'Well, it turns out that he was an employee on the *Orient Express* in the years leading up to the Second World War. When we first discovered the letter, I asked one of my colleagues in the history department back in Venice to check out the name in the public records. I had an email from him yesterday. Among other things, he found out that Tommaso Ricci used to work on the *Orient Express*.'

'But that was years ago. How can that help us now?' Stella said.

'Look, I printed this out,' Bruno said. He got out of his makeshift bed and went to get a piece of paper from the desk. Stella swallowed as he came over and handed her the sheet of paper.

Stella read what it said, aware of the faint, lingering scent of Bruno's aftershave. Typed out were all the details about Tommaso, his date of birth, employment record and a list of addresses and telephone numbers. Stella's eyes darted to the one that said, 'current address'. 'This is in Milan,' she said.

'Yes, it is,' Bruno said, looking proud of himself, 'I gave the number a ring and Tommaso himself answered. He sounded pretty old and weak, but he's willing to see us tomorrow. That is . . . if you still want to go.' He pushed his hair back. 'I know I've overstepped the mark with looking all this up without you. Until now, I've generally followed your lead, but after what you told me yesterday I couldn't just let you give up without knowing more.'

Stella smiled. 'Well, this is exactly why I asked you to come along. This type of research is your speciality. I want to believe there's a chance Iris isn't guilty, but I'm just not sure . . .'

Bruno reached over and took hold of her hands, his touch full of strength and gentleness.

'You've taken such a leap of faith by coming this far in the first place,' Bruno said. 'No one would blame you for turning back. But if you do stop now, won't you always wonder? People like Tommaso and Iris aren't going to be around for ever.'

Stella looked at his steady brown eyes. It wasn't just his ability to research that she needed him for. It was Bruno's ability to challenge and strengthen her that Stella had come to rely on. He made her feel that they were in this together. For the first time in a long time, Stella didn't feel like she was battling things alone.

'You're right,' she said. 'We're here now, just a train ride away from Milan and Tommaso.'

Bruno smiled. 'Tommaso has arranged for us to travel the rest of the journey on the *Orient Express*. It seems he still has connections, and when I explained that we were travelling in Iris and Alessandro's footsteps, he insisted.'

Stella's eyes widened. The *Orient Express*. Just like Iris and Alessandro. Stella had the strangest feeling that she was following in more than just Iris's footsteps. Her life was almost becoming intertwined with her great-aunt's past, and, inescapably, she was drawing closer to Bruno too.

That evening, when the *Orient Express* pulled into Lausanne station, resplendent with shiny dark blue carriages and gold trim, Stella gasped at the beauty of it. It looked like it had emerged from a bygone era, so different from the modern TGV they had taken from Paris.

Bruno raised his eyebrows. Along with his rucksack, he carried a suit carrier over his shoulder and a shoebox in a bag.

'It's a good job we bought some new outfits,' he said. 'I didn't bring anything with me that would have been smart enough for this.'

They'd gone their separate ways during the day to find something suitable to wear to dinner that night. Stella had found a boutique and purchased a blue velvet dress and some black high-heeled slingbacks.

Afterwards, she'd spoken briefly to Arnold on the phone. Andrea had agreed to GPL buying 49 per cent of the business in return for bringing in a consultant to help at Penhallam's. It meant a huge injection of money, which was a relief, and the consultant could be good news for the business, but in the back of her mind Stella knew

Andrea would be looking for a return on her investment, and soon.

Now, one of the carriage doors opened and a smart conductor stepped out. 'I believe you are joining us here,' he said.

Stella could hardly wait to get onboard. She stepped up into the carriage, marvelling at the shiny brass rail on the door. It was such a romantic way to travel. Her heart thumped at the press of Bruno's hand on her back, guiding her along the corridor. She tried to imagine Iris boarding the train with Alessandro. It was like entering another world. She couldn't believe her good fortune at being able to experience such a luxurious form of travel.

'My name is Stephan,' the conductor said. 'If there's anything you need, please let me know. Sir, you have the compartment next door, but it's linked with a connecting door, which opens like this.'

He demonstrated, revealing a mirror image of Stella's compartment. Stella caught Bruno's eye and blushed. It suddenly struck her that a lot of the people travelling on this train would be couples. As if to emphasize that fact, the conductor disappeared down the corridor and re-emerged a moment later with a silver tray carrying two glasses of champagne.

'Oh, thank you,' Stella said, taking a glass.

'I'll let you unpack your things. The train will be departing in half an hour and dinner will be served then. You're welcome to have drinks in the bar beforehand.' Stephan bowed and left the room, closing the door behind him.

Bruno smiled. 'Well, this is definitely the way to travel. Look at how it's all been renovated. We must thank Tommaso when we see him.'

He smoothed his hand over the marquetry above the seat, which would double as a bed later that evening. Stella opened a cupboard and found a tiny white enamel sink with gold taps and running water.

'This kind of opulence is definitely out of my league.' She raised her glass. 'Well, here's to Tommaso and his generosity.' Bruno clinked her glass. 'Imagine what it would have been like back in 1939. Iris and Alessandro weren't just here to create perfumes. They were embarking on a dangerous task.'

Bruno nodded. 'And as Iris said, it was just the two of them. That would have been quite intense. I mean, the *Orient Express* is a very intimate setting.'

'It certainly is.' Stella took a large gulp of champagne. 'We'd better get ready for drinks.'

Bruno nodded. 'Okay. I'll meet you in the bar in ten minutes.'

He closed the interconnecting door behind him, and finally Stella let out a deep breath. This strange awareness between them threatened to make things awkward. That kiss in Paris had tipped them from being work colleagues into something more than just friends.

Ten minutes later, Stella made her way to the bar, wearing a dab of Primo Bacio. She carried a teal clutch bag that she had bought to go with the dress. Inside were the two tiny perfumes bottles they already had. A tannoy announced that the train would be leaving in twenty minutes.

It was dark outside, and the view of Lausanne station had been replaced by a reflection of what was going on inside the *Orient Express*. Rich, opulent scents floated along the corridor – intense perfumes, musky aftershaves, the fragrance of polish on wood. Stella emerged into a long open carriage. Women in long flowing dresses and men in dinner jackets congregated around a gleaming wooden bar at the far end. In between, dark blue upholstered chairs were laid out in intimate clusters and softly lit by polished brass wall lamps. Bruno stood up as she reached where he was sitting. He couldn't hide his smile.

'*Bellissima*,' he said. 'You look amazing.'

She'd put her hair up, letting a few tendrils curl down on to her neck. Despite everything, she'd wanted to look nice for Bruno.

'You look very smart too,' Stella said, feeling a ripple of warmth over her skin at the sight of him.

Her words didn't really do justice to how good he looked: clean-shaven, a black suit, dinner shirt and bow tie. But she wasn't going to make things even more awkward and tell him that. Instead, she accepted the waiter's suggestion of a gin and tonic.

'This is incredible,' Stella said, glancing around. Everyone looked so elegant.

'Is it what you expected?' Bruno asked.

Stella raised her eyebrows. 'It's even more.' A jovial hubbub of excited chatter enlivened the carriage. An older couple sitting on the seats opposite Stella and Bruno introduced themselves. It seemed that people were keen to socialize with their travelling companions. They chatted until one of the attendants announced that dinner was served.

Stella stood up, and at that moment, the whistle blew, catching her unawares. She swayed, only to be caught by Bruno in his strong arms. In that moment, desire shot through her as she felt the firm grip of his hand. Hurriedly, she pulled away.

'Thanks,' she said, smiling nervously. 'I was caught off guard.'

Bruno was still looking at her. 'I know what you mean.'

The dining room was resplendent with plush dining chairs, pleated lampshades and shiny cutlery laid out on white tablecloths. Each course was delicious. Mushroom soup, followed by seabass, and then a selection of cheeses. Stella put down her knife and wiped her mouth with her napkin. 'I've never eaten anything so wonderful in my life,' she said.

The company had been delightful too. She and Bruno had put all talk of perfumes and Penhallam's to one side and chatted about a range of other things, including speculating about the backgrounds and relationships of their fellow guests on the *Orient Express*.

'I think that lady over there is definitely his mistress,' Bruno said, subtly glancing at an older woman with dazzling emerald earrings and a matching necklace.

'And how would you know?' Stella teased. 'They might have been happily married for years.'

Bruno raised his glass to her. 'It's sometimes hard to tell a person's true status. When I was interviewed for my job at the university, I thought the dean was the caretaker. It was rather embarrassing.'

'I thought you were quite scruffy when you first arrived at Penhallam's,' Stella said, emboldened by the wine. 'I'd also imagined that Professor Silvestri would be a grey-haired gentleman with reading glasses.'

Bruno laughed. 'I'll try not to take offence at either of those statements.'

'Well, as you said, appearances can be deceiving.'

Bruno put down his glass and gazed at Stella. 'Do you want to know what I thought of you?'

A shiver ran over Stella's skin. Of course she did, and yet, maybe not. 'It depends if it's flattering or not,' she said, trying to make light of things.

Bruno's eyes looked very serious. 'How could it not be flattering? I arrived late, and you weren't there, and Amy asked me to wait in the shop. A few minutes later, you came back from a meeting or something. I remember the door opening and you stood there, wearing a black trouser suit, and looking so elegant, your long blonde hair loose around your shoulders. I actually did feel scruffy in comparison.'

He'd remembered a lot. Stella recalled the sudden thud in her chest at the sight of him leaning against the counter, an instant attraction that she'd quickly pushed aside.

Bruno smiled. 'I liked working in that basement, knowing you were around somewhere in the building. And those moments when you popped down, or I brought your morning coffee, were the best moments of the day.'

Stella didn't know what to say. Now was the chance to tell him what she'd felt, but the words wouldn't come out. Thankfully, the waiter came over and asked if they wanted some coffee.

'No, thank you,' Stella said, feeling flustered. 'To be honest, I'm actually quite tired. I think I'll head to bed now.'

'Me too,' Bruno said. 'It's been a long day.'

Stella led the way back along the carriages, conscious of Bruno walking just behind her. If she stopped now, and turned around . . . what would happen? She shouldn't have had all that wine, on top of the champagne and a gin and tonic. There was no point doing something reckless and ruining the rest of the trip.

Stella stopped outside the compartment.

'Stella,' Bruno said softly behind her. He touched her arm gently. It was all she could do not to turn around. She knew if she did and saw his deep brown eyes gazing at her, his chiselled jaw and full lips, she wouldn't be able to hold back.

Instead, she pretended she hadn't heard him and opened the door. And then she gasped.

'Oh my goodness,' she said.

Bruno peered over her shoulder. 'Christ!' he exclaimed.

The room had been ransacked. The covers had been torn off the bed and flung aside. Stella's suitcase was open, the clothes strewn all over the floor. The contents of her make-up bag had been tipped into the sink.

'I don't believe it,' Stella said. She rushed into the compartment, frantically searching for her bag, which contained Iris's notebook. It had to be here. She rifled through the jumble of clothes and bedding. 'It's gone, Bruno. The notebook's gone.'

23

Stella – Lausanne to Milan, July 1996

Thank God she had the perfumes in her clutch bag. But the notebook was vital too – it gave the background to each scent and some clues about where to find them. Without it, deciphering the ingredients and guessing the formulas would be even more difficult. Besides, it had been entrusted to her by Iris. Something so valuable and precious, and she'd lost it.

'Why would someone do this?' she said.

'I don't know,' Bruno said. 'Maybe they were looking for money.'

'But why my compartment?' It was a violation to think that someone had been through her belongings.

'Come on,' Bruno said. He opened the interconnecting door and took her into his compartment. 'You stay here. I'll go and find the attendant.' Stella stared back at the chaos in her compartment, trying to make sense of it all.

A few minutes later Bruno returned with Stephan.

'I'm so sorry this has happened,' he said. 'I'll make sure there's a thorough search of the train to see if we can locate your bag. We have a procedure for this, Mademoiselle Penhallam, and I assure you we will do everything we can to recover your belongings.'

Stella nodded, feeling shaken. 'Thank you.'

'Perhaps we could have a couple of glasses of brandy,' Bruno said. 'It's been quite a shock.'

'Of course,' Stephan said. 'I'll bring them now.'

After Stephan had brought the drinks Bruno closed the interconnecting door, hiding the mess in Stella's room. 'It's probably better if we don't sit looking at all that.'

Stella swallowed some of the brandy. It warmed her throat. 'I still don't understand. Who would have taken my bag? It's not as if I look like a wealthy passenger.'

Bruno sat down beside her. She was aware of his body next to hers, almost touching but not quite. 'It was probably just a random thing, someone taking a chance. The thief might have gone into other rooms – we don't know.'

He hesitated a moment, then put his arm around her. She rested her head on his shoulder, just as she'd been longing to do. His dinner jacket was smooth against her skin. He stroked her hair. 'Why don't you sleep in here? I'll take the top bunk and you can sleep on the bottom.'

'Are you sure?' She'd feel safer with Bruno.

He took her hand. 'Yes, I'm sure. Drink the rest of that brandy. I'll see how they're getting on with the search.'

While he was gone she put on her pyjamas and slipped under the white Egyptian cotton sheets. She lay tense and expectant, hearing footsteps and voices outside, until Bruno came back, carrying her handbag.

'Good news,' he said, sitting down on the bed. 'It was found in one of the toilet cubicles. Your wallet, passport and keys are in there.'

Stella sat up. 'What about the notebook?'

'There's no sign of it, I'm afraid,' Bruno said. 'The manager believes the thief may have got on and off before we even left Lausanne. We'll be able to report it properly when we get to Milan.'

'But it doesn't make sense. Why would they take Iris's old book? It's of no importance to anyone but me.'

Bruno bit his lip. 'I don't know. It certainly is strange. It seems that nobody else has been burgled.'

So, it was personal, or at least it felt that way.

'Iris is going to be furious,' Stella said. 'She entrusted me with that notebook, and now it's gone. It's going to make things even more difficult between us.'

'It's not your fault,' Bruno said. 'We couldn't have foreseen it.'

'And we need that notebook,' Stella said desperately. 'It was the only detailed record of the perfumes.'

'Can you remember some of it?' Bruno asked.

'Only the names of the perfumes,' Stella said. 'La Scintilla, Primo Bacio, Amanti, Tradimento and Solo Tu.'

'The Spark, First Kiss, Lovers, Betrayal, Only You,' Bruno said. 'The names of the perfumes are like clues to what happened. The more I think about it, the more certain I am that there was something between Iris and Alessandro. La Scintilla when they first met. First Kiss during their time in Paris. Lovers would have been created on their trip to Milan . . .'

Stella considered his theory. 'You mean it suggests they were involved with each other. But there was so much going on for Iris and Alessandro. Why would they be so foolish as to do that?' She shivered. 'And Tradimento. Betrayal. That doesn't bode well.'

'Perhaps they fell in love,' Bruno said. 'It's not always predictable how two people are going to feel . . .'

His eyes lingered on her face. 'What do you mean?' she said, a flicker of anticipation stirring up.

'I know we said we'd be sensible, but when I'm around

you, Stella, I don't feel sensible, I just want to follow my heart, and right now—'

'What?' Stella whispered, leaning towards him.

'I want to kiss you again.'

A hunger rose inside Stella that she didn't even know had been there. She wanted him, the feel of his arms around her, his tongue exploring her mouth, his scent, his fingers through her hair. The need for him had been lying dormant for so long that now it seemed to spread out from some deep, molten core inside.

'Then why don't you?' she said.

He moved closer and in a rush their mouths fused together. A kiss so deep and urgent it took Stella's breath away. She ran her hands across his shoulders, feeling his muscles ripple. She wanted to feel the weight of his body, the touch of his hand. He pressed against her, his lips still on hers, drinking her in.

'Are you sure you want this?' he whispered.

Stella tugged on his shirt, pulling him closer. 'Yes.'

He bit his lip, his breath shallow. 'Because it will change everything.'

Stella looked up into his eyes. They were deep brown and very serious. The realization hit her. The attraction they felt towards each other had started the minute they met. Bruno felt it too. To go any further would be to start something that Stella wasn't sure she could finish, but it was too late now. She didn't want this to stop.

'Maybe I'm willing to take that chance,' she said.

'Thank God,' Bruno said hoarsely, pulling her close.

At the sound of his voice vibrating against her skin something in Stella broke free. Desire took over. She undid the buttons of his shirt, one by one, her hands longing to touch him. Maybe she'd regret it afterwards, but right now she wanted him more than anything. Gently, he unbuttoned her pyjama top. His eyes drank her in.

'Come here,' he said huskily, tugging her hand.

This close, Stella could almost hear the thump of his heart. A warmth so strong radiated between them. He kissed her again, a kiss that trembled with desire, with all the pent-up feelings that had grown since their first kiss. He grasped her close, limbs entwined, his closeness an elixir that cleared her mind and focused her senses only on what was here, now. Bruno.

She wrapped her legs around him, longing to feel him hard and firm inside her. Stella heard the foil tear and he put something on, then found his way in, gently, watching to make sure she was all right. Stella clenched against him, feeling his length, her hips beginning to circle around him.

'Slower,' he gasped, turning on his side so they lay facing each other. Eyes locked on hers, he started to move, edging in and out with such exquisite restraint Stella thought she would die from wanting him.

'Please,' she whispered, 'don't stop.'

His lips found hers, his tongue finding its rhythm as the pressure inside her increased. She held him tightly, crying out as the molten core inside her exploded. Bruno drove himself deeper and deeper into her, tidal waves of warmth and pleasure rippling through her body, until he gasped her name and collapsed beside her.

Stella closed her eyes, suffused with a sense of bliss. She held Bruno close, feeling his heart beating fast, wondering what he was thinking. Maybe it had been a mistake, but it had been worth it, and there was no going back now.

24

Iris – Milan, September 1939

'Milan next stop,' a voice called. Iris had fallen asleep after Alessandro left, her cheek resting against the soft down pillow. Her neck ached and she opened her eyes, disorientated for a moment. And then she remembered. Alessandro. They had been so close, and then prudence had stepped in. Iris wasn't sure if she was relieved or disappointed at having come to her senses.

She rubbed her eyes. She peeped through the blinds. The sun was just beginning to rise. The landscape had changed completely. Fields stretched out as far as she could see. They must be nearly there.

Iris dreaded seeing Alessandro again, yet longed for him too. She gathered her make-up into her toiletry bag and blushed at the thought of what they'd nearly done. Iris had no experience to compare it to, but last night had felt natural, as if her body knew what to do. Until her head had intervened.

Of course, Alessandro had experience; he was married. He might have been separated from his wife, but he was still bound to her by law. Iris scooped up her clothes. And if he hadn't been married? What then? Surely it wouldn't have changed a thing. They were simply together for the sake of finding Jacopo and Francesca, that was all.

Her intimacy with Alessandro had shown Iris one thing,

however. She could never marry Henri. The thought of being close to him made her shudder. Her body couldn't lie, and neither would she.

Iris had nearly finished packing her bag when the interconnecting door opened. Alessandro stood there, the expression on his face unreadable.

'Iris,' he began, his voice serious.

Iris forced herself to smile. 'There's honestly no need to say anything,' she said briskly. 'We both rather lost our heads, didn't we?'

Her fingers trembled as she did up the clasps of her suitcase.

Alessandro took hold of her hand. 'I hope you don't think that I took advantage of you.'

The touch of his hand burned her skin and ignited the flame that still flickered inside.

'It's fine,' she said, in that same bright voice, which she hated because it sounded so false. She couldn't seem to relax around him now. 'You didn't take advantage. It was foolish of us to get swept away by the moment but, luckily, we stopped when we did, and now it's over I'd prefer it if you didn't mention it again.' She pulled her hand away. 'As you can see, I'm ready to disembark.'

Alessandro bit his lip. 'Yes, I see. Very well. I'm sorry if you regret what happened. I promise it won't happen again.'

'Good.' Iris swallowed. She longed to reach out and touch him, to feel his scent all around her, his lips pressing against hers. But it was better like this. Surely this was what he wanted too. To pretend it had never happened.

After breakfast in the railway café, they walked out into the narrow streets that opened out on to a huge, imposing piazza. The Duomo di Milano rose into the blue, cloudless sky like a white ice sculpture. Iris had never seen anything like it. The piazza was like a giant marble chess board surrounded by civic buildings, cafés and a hotel.

'So, who is this sweetheart of yours, Tommaso?' Alessandro asked. 'You never mentioned her before.'

'We met on the *Orient Express*, a couple of days after you went to Paris,' Tommaso said. 'Her father is a lawyer. Scuoldi. They're well known in Milan. He doesn't approve of me, and there's no way he'll let me marry Giulietta, but I live in hope.'

Alessandro put his arm around Tommaso's shoulders. 'I'm sure you'll find a way.'

'Where will we find Francesca and Jacopo?' Iris said. The piazza was enormous, with a maze of streets branching off it. 'They could be anywhere in Milan.'

'There's a café over there,' Tommaso said. 'There will be contacts there we can ask.'

'What sort of contacts?' Iris said.

Tommaso and Alessandro exchanged a glance. 'Maybe it's best if you wait outside. You could stroll around the piazza and look at the cathedral,' Alessandro said.

Iris shook her head. 'I want to come with you,' she said.

Alessandro hesitated. 'I'm just trying to keep you safe.'

Tommaso smiled. 'From what you told me about Iris's bravery with the border guards, it's Iris who has been keeping you safe.'

'Thank you,' Iris said to Tommaso.

Alessandro nodded. 'Good point. Come on, let's all stick together.'

Alessandro went over to the bar while Iris waited at a

table by the window with Tommaso. He smoked a cigarette, glancing around the café. Iris had never been to Italy before; she wanted to soak it all in. Underneath the beauty and grandeur, she was conscious of the hidden side. The watchful eyes, gossiping locals, armed policemen who weren't here just to keep law and order but to make dissidents disappear. Somewhere Francesca and Jacopo were hiding. Did they even know that Raffaele was sending someone to rescue them?

Her eyes drifted over to the bar, where Alessandro was talking to the barman, leaning forward and speaking in a low voice. He took an envelope out of his jacket and handed it over. The barman stowed it under the bar. They seemed to be bargaining about something. Hand gesticulations punctuated the conversation. At last, the barman nodded and the pair shook hands.

Alessandro came back to the table. He pulled out a chair and sat down. 'No news,' he said. 'He's going to ask around, so we'll just have to sit it out until he has something to tell us.'

'What did you give him in that envelope?' Iris said.

Alessandro shrugged. 'Just some papers, proof that we're trustworthy.'

Tommaso stubbed out the remains of his cigarette. 'Look, if you don't mind, while we wait to hear news, I'm going to see Giulietta. I'll be back in a couple of hours.'

Alessandro nodded. 'We'll meet you back here at nine.'

After Tommaso left, a silence spread across the table.

'We need to talk about yesterday,' Alessandro said.

His voice sounded uneasy. Iris longed for the comfortableness they'd fallen into the day before.

'I thought we had,' Iris said. It was awkward to sit with

him like this and pretend that nothing had happened, but she couldn't bear to discuss it yet. 'Would you mind if I popped over to the hotel? I need to send a telegram to Henri.'

She had to get it over and done with. Once she'd told Henri her decision, things with Alessandro would be easier to deal with.

'Of course,' Alessandro said despondently. 'I'll come with you.'

Ten minutes later and it was done. A short message explaining that while she hoped they would always be friends, she could never marry him. The capital letters typed on the sheet of paper were definite and clear. Iris nodded to the receptionist and experienced a moment of calm. She was free of that expectation at least.

Iris went back outside, where Alessandro was waiting.

'Are you going back to Paris?' he asked, his eyes full of anguish. 'Is that why you contacted Henri?'

Iris shook her head. 'No.'

'Then why the telegram?'

Iris hesitated. To admit the contents of the telegram would be to confess her true feelings. But seeing Alessandro's pained expression, she knew there was no sense hiding it. 'I had to tell Henri once and for all that I can't marry him.'

Alessandro stared at her. 'Thank God,' he said, his voice weak. 'After what you said this morning, I wasn't sure how you felt.'

'I didn't know what you felt either – I wish I'd let you explain. But whether you do care for me or not, one thing was certain: after last night, I can't marry Henri.'

Alessandro reached out to touch her arm. 'I do care. I

care too much,' he said. 'But you're like no one I've ever met. I'm not worthy of someone like you.'

Iris grasped his hand. It was time to be honest with him, and with herself. 'Isn't it clear from this morning that being close to you is what I want? I thought you wanted it too. Just because we didn't . . . well, it doesn't mean I didn't want to.'

Alessandro pulled her close, his touch sending a heat-wave through Iris's body. He murmured in her ear, his breath warm against her skin. 'I'm falling for you, Iris, and it scares me.'

Iris slid her hand across his chest. He wanted her. Suddenly the way forward seemed simple.

'I'm scared too,' she said, 'but we can't keep holding back. We need to put our hearts and souls into this, just like we do with our perfume-making, and make every moment count.'

'Do you really mean that?' Alessandro said.

Iris nodded, tugging his shirt. 'I do,' she whispered.

Alessandro leaned down and enveloped her in a kiss. Kissing in a public place. Charles would have been appalled. But as the kiss deepened, and took her breath away, everything else disappeared. The piazza, Milan, the war. There was only Alessandro.

He took her hand and they ambled through the city. It wasn't that they had forgotten the dangers, or the reason why they were in Milan; they had been offered this brief respite, so they chose to make the most of it.

'Come on,' Alessandro said. 'I want to show you some-thing.' He kissed the back of Iris's hand and led her down a side street. They turned a corner and Iris stared in surprise. There, in the middle of the city, was a garden.

'Orto Botanico di Brera. A hidden secret in Milan,' Alessandro said.

'It's beautiful,' Iris said.

The green, leafy plants offered cool shade and quiet compared to the hot streets, which were now starting to fill with people.

'I used to come here sometimes when the *Orient Express* was delayed and we had some time to kill.'

A sweet smell filled Iris's nostrils. 'What's that?' she asked, trying to work out which flower it was coming from.

Alessandro smiled. 'That's why I love this place. They've been growing medicinal plants here for two hundred years. Francesca told me it was one of the only places in Italy where I could find Immortelle.' He pointed to a plant covered with small, bright yellow flowers. 'It's known for surviving in the most difficult of places.'

'We don't have that oil in our ingredients,' Iris said, 'but if we did, I would add it to Amanti. It would make the perfect heart note. That heady, honey scent is irresistible.'

Alessandro smiled. 'You are irresistible,' he said. 'And I know where we can get some Immortelle. There's a perfumer not far from here.'

After purchasing the oil, Iris and Alessandro went back to the gardens and spent the afternoon making up accords. Iris passed her notebook to Alessandro, and he used her pen to write down the formulas. With bold strokes, he jotted the number of drops for each ingredient down one by one.

'Why do you do some numbers slanting left and others slanting right?' she asked, leaning against him to look at the page.

Alessandro looked up, surprise in his eyes. 'Oh, it's just a habit,' he said. 'It used to drive my father mad.'

'I don't mind it,' Iris said, pressing his hand.

Alessandro put the pen down and pulled her close. 'You know, this is the first perfume we've truly made together rather than merging our separate ones, and that makes it special.'

By the time they got back to the café it was nearly nine o'clock. Iris read through the formula for Amanti, sipping a glass of water, while Alessandro and Tommaso spoke to the barman. She hadn't written the brief for the perfume yet. She took out her pen and wrote it down, smiling as she remembered each of Alessandro's kisses. When she'd finished, she noticed that another man had joined Alessandro and Tommaso at the bar. The four of them were deep in conversation.

'That can't be right,' she heard Alessandro say.

The man who had joined them leaned towards Alessandro and muttered something in a low voice.

'What's going on?' Iris said when they came over. Alessandro sat down beside her and took her hand. His face was very grave.

'Francesca and Jacopo aren't here,' Alessandro said. 'They didn't make it out of Venice. Francesca was murdered at the perfumery, and Jacopo is stranded somewhere in Venice, hiding.'

Iris lifted her hand to her mouth. 'Francesca is dead?' she said. That wonderful, elegant woman who wore her long dark hair in a bun and spoke so eloquently about perfumes. Raffaele's sister. Alessandro's perfume teacher. 'Oh, Alessandro, this is terrible.'

He nodded, tears smarting his eyes. 'All she did was speak the truth about what those fascist bastards have done to our country.'

'Shh,' Tommaso said. 'You don't know who is listening.'

'I don't care,' Alessandro said, clenching his fist. 'If it hadn't been for Francesca I wouldn't have gone to Paris. Maybe if I'd stayed in Venice, I could have protected her and Jacopo.'

Tommaso bit his lip. 'What will you do now? Go back to Lausanne and tell Raffaele the news of his sister's death?'

Iris looked at Alessandro. She knew exactly what he was thinking because she was thinking the same thing.

'We can't go back yet,' she said, answering for them both. 'Francesca is gone, but Jacopo is still alive, alone and afraid somewhere in Venice. We have to get him out and bring him back.'

'Maybe you should return to Lausanne and support Raffaele. This isn't what we planned, and it could be very dangerous,' Alessandro said, squeezing her hand.

Iris shook her head. 'I'm not leaving you. Don't you realize? We're in this together.'

'If you're going to Venice, you'll need help, Alessandro,' Tommaso said. 'You can't manage this on your own. You'll need Iris with you, and some funds. You have to accept her help.'

'It's not that simple. You heard what he said.'

'I did,' said Tommaso, 'and I think you stand a better chance of pulling this off by having Iris with you. Look at how she diverted the border guards on the train. You need her brains.'

Alessandro bit his lip. 'I don't want to put you in this position, Iris. But I don't think there's another way. Tommaso's right. I need you to come with me. The *Orient Express* will be leaving in ten minutes. We have to act now.'

Iris nodded. 'Then let's do this and bring Jacopo home.'

Alessandro nodded gravely. He kissed Iris's hand, then got up and went back to speak to the man at the bar. The pair shook hands. Something had been settled. Iris didn't know what exactly, but if it meant bringing Jacopo home safely, then surely it was worth it.

25

Stella – Milan, July 1996

Stella woke to the sound of knocking at the door. She stretched out in the bed, expecting to feel Bruno next to her, but the space was empty. Stephan came in with a tray of croissants and coffee. He drew the blinds half up.

'We'll be arriving in Milan soon,' he said.

'Thank you,' Stella said, sitting up in bed. 'Has there been any sign of the notebook?'

'No, I'm afraid not, but we've arranged for you to talk to the police when you disembark.' Stephan left and closed the door.

If it hadn't been for the theft of the notebook, things might not have got out of hand with Bruno.

Stella closed her eyes. Last night had been incredible, but in the cold light of day she wasn't sure it had been wise to give in to her feelings like that. Maybe Bruno was regretting it too, and that's why he'd left the compartment without a word. He had a lot going on with his debts and looking after his sister. Stella was caught up in worries about Penhallam's. The more she thought about it, last night had been a mistake, especially when the purpose of this trip was to find the perfumes. And yet Stella felt a surge of warmth, thinking how wonderful it had felt to be close to him.

There was another knock, and Bruno came in. He was dressed and ready, with a businesslike expression on his face. Stella glanced at him nervously. His words and gestures would hopefully give her a clue about how he felt.

'I'm sorry about last night,' he said, clearly needing to get it off his chest. 'You were upset about your room being turned upside down, and I should have comforted you and left it there. I'm sorry that it went too far.'

Stella blushed. 'You don't have to be sorry; it was my fault too.'

Bruno cleared his throat. 'It's just that I'm not sure . . .'

Stella sensed that he was about to explain all the reasons why getting involved was not a good idea.

'It's fine,' she said, cutting in. 'Let's just pretend that last night never happened.'

Bruno stared at her. 'Never happened?'

'It was just the setting, the wine, the shock of the notebook being stolen – I don't think that either of us is looking for a relationship right now,' Stella said, preferring to say it before he did.

'I see,' Bruno said, his voice downbeat. 'Well, I'll leave you to get ready then.'

It was hard to tell if he was going along with what she said or if he really felt the same. Something in his eyes told Stella he was disappointed. But what could she do? She'd made the decision not to get involved, and he seemed to feel the same. It was better this way.

Stella stepped down from the carriage and into the huge, arching cavern of Milan train station. Bruno was a little reserved with her, not meeting her eyes and walking ahead. Things would hopefully settle down again soon. It was bound to be awkward. But it was impossible not to feel sick at heart about how things had turned out. Stella wondered if she'd been too hasty. She shoved her bag in one of the station lockers, annoyed at how much last night was playing on her mind. There were more important things to sort out, like the notebook.

The police weren't very hopeful about recovering it. A fan whirred hot air around the cramped police station at the end of the platform. Stella and Bruno sat on two hard plastic chairs and explained the situation.

'It's very unfortunate, but the culprit could be halfway across France by now,' the policeman said. 'Lausanne station has checked the surveillance cameras. There is footage of someone coming in and out of your carriage during the half-an-hour window before the train departed, but it's very grainy.'

'It would be worth circulating it across your network nonetheless,' Bruno said. 'Just in case.'

'A notebook is an unusual thing to steal,' the policeman said. 'Normally, it's money or valuables. It makes me wonder if the thief knew you had brought it on to the train and targeted you.'

'That's what we have speculated,' Stella said, 'but I can't think why it would have been of value to anyone else. It just contains information about perfumes.'

'We'll keep looking.' The policeman passed a form over the desk. 'Pop your address and contact number on here and sign at the bottom.'

Stella did as he asked.

Bruno rubbed his temples. 'Maybe when they realize it's worthless they'll hand it in.'

Stella sighed. 'I hope so.' They left the police station. Stella touched Bruno's arm. 'Is everything all right between us?'

Bruno smiled, but the smile didn't quite light up his eyes. 'Of course,' he said. 'Come on, let's go and see Tommaso. Hopefully, he can tell us more about Iris.'

Tommaso didn't live far from the station. Stella followed Bruno along the busy, dusty street, cars streaming past, until they reached Via Plinio.

He checked his notes. 'I think it's along here,' he said.

Halfway down the street they came to a house with a thick wooden door. Bruno rang the bell and the door whirred open. Their first glimpse beyond the entryway was of a cobbled courtyard full of potted plants and flowers. It was a rich, fecund contrast to the street outside. An older woman with sleek white hair and wearing wide-legged trousers and a white shirt greeted them.

'Hello, I'm Giulietta, Tommaso's wife. He's been intrigued ever since you called yesterday,' she said. 'Come up. He's out on the terrace.'

She led the way upstairs. The house was luxurious in an understated way. Marble staircase, discreet art on the walls and glinting chandeliers. The terrace, however, like the courtyard, was covered with plants, their bright yellow flowers releasing a sweet smell, and in among them sat an old grey-haired man in a wheelchair.

'They're here, my dear,' Giulietta said, kissing Tommaso's forehead. 'I'll go and get some coffee for us all.'

'Hello,' Stella said, warming to his bright smile and inquisitive eyes. 'Thank you so much for agreeing to see us.'

'It's my pleasure,' Tommaso said, studying her. 'I must say, you have such a look of Iris. Your hair is almost the same colour as hers, and your eyes are the same shape. But then I'm remembering the Iris from long ago. How is she now?'

Stella and Bruno sat down on the cushioned wicker sofa.

'She's not well,' Stella said. 'There was a fire in the hotel where she was staying in Paris and she's still recovering from the effects. The fire damaged her sense of smell.'

'That's terrible,' Tommaso said. 'Her nose was her life. She must have told you about her time with Raffaele and Alessandro and about making scents.'

'I'm afraid, in the few conversations I've had with her, she's been very reticent about the past. It obviously causes her a lot of pain. My grandfather didn't want anything to do with her after the trial.'

Tommaso nodded. 'Of course. I heard about her imprisonment. A terrible shame.'

Bruno leaned forward. 'Do you think she was guilty?'

Tommaso shrugged. 'I was still in contact with Alessandro then. He said very little about it all, but I do remember him saying that if a jury had found her guilty, it had to mean something. He was very distraught. I told him not to rush to judge Iris, not until he knew the facts from her. Not long after that, we lost contact. I haven't seen him since.'

'Do you know if he's still alive?' Stella asked.

'I've no idea, we lost touch,' Tommaso said. 'We'd been like brothers. I remember the year he met Iris. Something lit up inside him. That day we spent in Milan' – he smiled – 'they started off barely speaking because of some misunderstanding in the morning, but by the end of the day they radiated love. It was a joy to be around them . . . at least, until the war got in the way.'

'What do you mean?' Stella said.

Tommaso sighed. 'I don't know the full story,' he said. 'But I do know that soon after we left Venice, things became very difficult.'

'What's Venice got to do with it?'

'Iris and Alessandro had to find Francesca and Jacopo, as you already know. But we discovered that they never made it out of Venice. Francesca had been murdered and Jacopo was in hiding somewhere in Venice by himself. Alessandro and Iris decided to go and rescue him.'

So, the journey didn't stop here. 'It looks like we need to go to Venice then.'

Bruno nodded. It was hard to tell how he felt about this unexpected extension to their trip.

'Bruno mentioned on the phone that you want to find the perfumes that Iris and Alessandro made,' Tommaso said.

'Yes, Penhallam's is in financial difficulties. I need Iris's perfumes to revive its fortunes.'

Tommaso took off his glasses and pinched the bridge of his nose. 'Perhaps that's why Iris is being reticent. She might not want to help the family business that cast her out.'

Giulietta came out on to the terrace carrying a tray. 'Here we are,' she said. 'And then, I'm afraid, Tommaso will need a nap.'

'Of course,' Stella said. 'I'm sorry we've kept you for so long.' Giulietta handed her a cup of coffee. As she did so, Stella caught the aroma of Giulietta's perfume. 'That's a delicious scent. What is it?'

Tommaso smiled. 'That perfume was my gift to her the day I proposed,' he said. 'I never thought her father would let me marry her, but he was a self-made man and came from nothing so he took pity on my endeavours in the end.'

'Where did you get it from?' Stella said.

It was like nothing she'd ever smelled before. Clear and

fresh at first, but then it intensified with a golden, honeyed aroma, followed by a sensual, musky smell.

'Iris and Alessandro created it during their journey on the *Orient Express*,' Tommaso said, 'which made it extra special. Back then, when I proposed to Giulietta, I was just a lowly train conductor. I could never have afforded such a thing.'

Giulietta sniffed her wrist. 'I've worn it ever since,' she said, 'although this isn't the original, of course, I have a copy made up every year. I still have the old bottle and ask my perfumer to refill it every time.'

'So, you must be wearing Amanti,' Stella said incredulously.

Giulietta nodded. 'People still compliment me on it wherever I go. I have never smelled another fragrance like it.' She pointed to the yellow flowers blooming in the pots. 'That's why we grow these. Immortelle is one of the ingredients.'

Stella reached into her bag and took out La Scintilla and Primo Bacio. 'We found the first two perfumes that Iris and Alessandro made. I'd love to take a sample of Amanti, if you'll permit me.'

Giulietta went over to a cabinet and took out a small bottle. 'Here you are,' she said, handing it over. 'A piece of history. Guard it well.'

Tommaso looked at Stella gravely. 'You do realize that Amanti is more than just a perfume?' he said. 'It's the start of something, the coming together of two minds and two bodies. I don't want this perfume to end up mass produced on every shelf, a cheap imitation of what it once was.'

'That's not my intention,' Stella said.

'Maybe not, but does Iris know that?' Tommaso said.

'Iris poured her heart and soul into those fragrances, as did Alessandro. They were bottling emotions that essentially represented how they felt about each other. If you haven't got that deep emotional connection with the scents, then maybe you're not the right person to have them.'

Stella's heart felt heavy as they left the house. It was sobering to think how she had come across, grasping at finding the perfumes for Penhallam's rather than having Iris's best interests at heart. A few pigeons fluttered up from the pavement as they crossed the street.

'Tommaso was a bit hard on you,' Bruno said, 'but maybe he has a point. I've been focused on my book. You've been focused on Penhallam's. It's hard not to believe they are the most important things.'

'Well, they're important to us,' Stella said. 'I've worked my whole life to keep the business going. If there's a chance I can keep it running, I'm going to pursue it. I agree with what Tommaso said, but hopefully I can get to know Iris after this is all done.'

Bruno sighed. 'I know you're very driven and the business means everything to you, but Iris won't always be around, and here you are, walking where she walked. Maybe you need to clear your head of your obligations and live in the moment.'

Stella wondered if he was also referring to last night. Despite their conversation this morning, things felt very unsettled between her and Bruno.

'I understand what you're saying. It's just easier said than done.' She stopped at the leafy, wide street of Via Giovanni Battista Morgagni. A park ran through the middle, with children playing in the shade of the trees and friends sitting on the benches chatting. There was a phone box over by the tea and coffee stand.

'Would it be okay if I met you at the station?' she said. 'I need to check in with Arnold.'

Bruno nodded. 'Of course. The train leaves in an hour, so don't be long. I'll organize an extension of our tickets to Venice.'

Stella watched him walk across the square. Somehow the day was full of misunderstandings. Tommaso had certainly given her plenty to think about.

She put in some coins and dialled the number for Penhallam's. Arnold answered, his steady voice coming down the line.

'I'm so glad you've called,' Arnold said.

Stella held her breath. 'Is everything all right?'

'The consultant that GPL has installed to oversee their investment in Penhallam's is James.'

Stella puffed out her cheeks. 'Crikey. Now I understand why he broke up with me. This was obviously on the cards from the start. I knew it was a risk to let GPL invest that much, but I didn't anticipate them using James.'

'To be fair, he seems to recognize the awkwardness of the situation and wanted me to assure you that he'll have Penhallam's best interests at heart. But from what I can gather he's been asked to put forward a business plan that's quite different to what you had in mind.'

'How different?' Stella said, alarmed. 'I thought you explained to Andrea what I'm planning to do if I find the perfumes. Did you send her those marketing plans I emailed you from Lausanne?'

'I did, but the sticking point is that word "if". There's no guarantee that your search is going to be fruitful, and Andrea wants a commercially viable plan B on the table.'

Stella shook her head. 'So far, we've found three of the perfumes Iris and Alessandro created. They're incredible. The story is amazing too. It will all come together to create an exciting new campaign for Penhallam's.'

'I can talk to her again,' Arnold said, 'but she seemed set on this new plan. The idea is to bring in a new perfumer, someone who will shake things up a bit. GPL want to steer away from the past and focus on easy-wearing scents that will reach a mass market.'

Stella stared out at the trees and the cloudless blue sky. If Andrea got her way, all this hard work would be for nothing. Her father's legacy would lie in tatters. The very name of Penhallam's would be rendered empty.

This was exactly what Tommaso had warned her about: not to disregard the woman behind the perfumes for the sake of Penhallam's. If the perfumes were of no use to the business, did that mean that Stella was simply going to abandon them? If Stella went back to Penhallam's, with GPL breathing down her neck, then all this – the sense of discovery, of finding out the past, of getting to know Iris – would be all for nothing.

'When is the point of no return for this new business plan?' Stella said.

'It goes to the GPL board next week, but I warn you, Stella, James and Andrea are talking as if it's practically a done deal.'

'They can't make any decisions without me. I still own the larger share of Penhallam's.'

'True, but you're not in a strong position because of the finances. If you block this plan, I fear they'll withdraw their investment and the business will fold.'

Stella swallowed. She had to keep a grip on things. They were moving too fast. Maybe if she could find the other perfumes before next week, there would be something more concrete to support her argument.

'There's still a bit of time. Stall them as much as you can. Say that I want to be there when the decision is made, that it's my right as majority shareholder.'

'I'll do what I can,' Arnold said.

Stella put down the receiver. For so long she'd managed to stave off the hard choices about Penhallam's. Now it looked as if they were coming whether she liked it or not. She stepped out of the phone box and into the dappled sunlight. What would it feel like just to stop fighting for Penhallam's, to give in and let it go? The notion was exciting but also terrifying. The business had been around for generations.

Stella set off walking towards the station, lost in thought. But it wasn't just about the business now, it was about celebrating Iris's talents. All these years, her perfumes had remained hidden. Perhaps it was time to start thinking about the women behind Penhallam's and what they wanted and needed. Stella bit her lip. Maybe that also meant deciding what she wanted from the future too. That urge to create perfumes had lain dormant in her for years. There was no one around to stop her from exploring it now, only herself. Stella headed up the steps of the station, noticing the crowds of people setting off on their travels or arriving in Milan, and felt strangely calm. Being on this journey had opened things up in so many ways. It was time to look at all the possibilities for her life.

'I don't understand,' Bruno said, frowning, 'I thought you'd be more perturbed about it all.'

Stella took a sip of champagne and leaned on the bar on the *Orient Express*. The bubbles fizzed on her tongue. Tonight, she wore her long, dark blue gown again, and on her wrists she'd dabbed some of the Amanti that Tommaso's wife had given her.

'What you and Tommaso said put things into perspective,' she said. 'Penhallam's was the most important thing in the world to my father and grandfather. I've felt guilty about being the one who's in charge when it's going downhill. But after Arnold explained the situation with GPL I realized that even though I'll do everything I can to fight for Penhallam's I still have a choice. I always hoped I had a gift for creating perfumes, just like Iris said. But I've ignored it and, in the process, I've ignored Iris's place in all this as well. I need to take her feelings into consideration more, and value my instincts.'

Things were still difficult – she couldn't escape the situation that Penhallam's was in – but at least there were things she could take charge of: like her approach towards Iris. Bruno's eyes shone with admiration.

'I'm glad. You look less burdened by the weight of it all. But what does this mean for you and the search for the perfumes?'

Stella put down her glass. 'It will still continue. Like I said, I'm not giving up on Penhallam's. If anything, this feeling of not fearing the worst gives me the confidence to be bolder.'

Bruno reached over and touched her hand. 'You should tell Iris how you feel.'

Stella nodded. 'I will,' she said. 'As soon as we get to Venice. I hope she'll forgive the way I've chased after the perfumes instead of acknowledging what all this might mean for her. Especially when I tell her that the notebook has been stolen.'

'She'll understand,' Bruno said. His hand still lingered on hers. 'After everything that's happened today, do you still want to pretend that last night never took place?'

Stella put down her glass. While she was being honest, it was time to acknowledge how she really felt about Bruno. 'No, I don't,' she said, blushing, 'but I thought that was what you wanted.'

Bruno smiled. 'You never gave me a chance to explain. I was trying to be sensible and cautious, but I'm not sure that's what I want.'

His hand closed around hers. The press of his warm palm stirred her senses. She didn't feel like herself: the Stella that was careful and organized. She felt like someone else, cut loose from her moorings. Everything was heightened: the glittering mirrors behind the bar, the ornate velvet plush seats, the polished marquetry and the evening countryside speeding past outside. Even Bruno, dressed in his dinner jacket, looked like someone from another time.

Iris had been in this very situation with a man to whom she had been inescapably attracted. What had she done? Had she resisted temptation? Or had she gone with her heart?

'So, what are you saying?' Stella said.

Bruno shifted in his chair. 'I've had a hard time focusing on anything but work and my sister the last few years.'

Stella looked down at her glass. 'I thought that was the case. That's why I was hesitant today. I can't bear the thought of starting something that doesn't have a chance of surviving. I'm just as wary as you are of getting hurt.'

'But that's just it,' Bruno said. 'When I left you calling

Arnold, I realized that protecting myself means living only half a life.' The pianist played a soft jazz melody which mingled with the murmur of voices. 'Here we are, just the two of us. In what is possibly one of the most romantic settings in the world. And I think . . .'

He stopped, as if finding the right words.

'What do you think?' Stella said with a smile, a buzz of anticipation firing up inside her.

'I think we should make the most of it, come what may.'

The sleeping car was quiet, as most of the guests were now at dinner. Stella opened her door with trembling hands and led Bruno inside. She turned to face him, suddenly nervous. Was she being too reckless after all? This was Iris's story, not hers. And yet she felt bound up in Iris's journey in a way she hadn't done before.

Bruno seemed to sense her hesitancy. He took her hand. 'Come on,' he said, sitting down on the bed. 'I want to ask you something.' He lifted her wrist and inhaled her perfume. 'It smells beautiful to me, but I'd like to know what it smells like to you.'

'What do you mean?'

'I know you have the ability to deconstruct this scent, Stella. I've watched your face each time you've found one of the perfumes. You can read the words of this scent, almost subconsciously. I don't think you even realize you're doing it.'

Stella looked at him, surprised to hear him voice the unspoken feelings that had always hovered in her mind. It was true. She could smell the whole, so to speak, but also the parts of which the whole was composed.

She sniffed her wrist. 'Sage. Immortelle. Musk,' she said.

'I don't know how I know it, but I do.'

'Iris was right – you have a gift. You don't need the notebook; you just need the perfumes. If we can find the last two, you'll be able to interpret them yourself.'

Stella smiled. 'Do you really think so?'

Bruno smoothed his thumb across her cheek. 'Like you said, you have options. If it came to it, and I hope it won't, you could always start again. A new perfumery. One that's just yours, not your family's or anyone else's. Something with no history to it.'

Stella shook her head. 'I can't imagine it,' she said. And yet his words held weight. 'I'd have to train as a perfumer.'

'Then do that.'

Her thoughts raced ahead. 'I'm still hopeful I can save Penhallam's, but maybe it wouldn't hurt to have another plan in the pipeline.' She sighed. 'But I'd need a mentor. I've no experience on the perfume-making side myself.'

'You have Iris.'

Stella stared at him. 'She'd never do it.'

Bruno nodded. 'I think she would. Think about it, Stella. She was forced to cut loose from Penhallam's too. Charles didn't appreciate her creativity. Just as your father didn't nurture yours. Tell Iris your ideas. She'll be receptive. You have more in common with each other than you realize.'

Stella put her arms around his neck. 'How is that you're so wise all of a sudden?'

Bruno's expression turned serious. He held her close. 'Because you deserve to be happy. I don't want anything to stand in the way of that.'

He leaned forward and kissed her. His tongue tasted of champagne, his lips were soft, the kiss an exquisite promise of what was to come.

'I love kissing you,' he murmured.

She lifted her chin. 'Then don't stop.'

He kissed her again, deeper this time, a fire starting inside her at the touch of his lips. Could it really be this easy just to follow your heart and see what happened? All her life she'd kept her guard up. But today, right now, Stella felt it melt away.

'You smell divine,' Bruno said.

Stella smiled, losing herself in the warmth of his embrace. 'That's the Amanti.'

'No,' he said, pulling her down on to the bed, 'it's the Amanti on you . . .'

26

Iris – Milan to Venice, September 1939

The night train to Venice pulled out of Milan station. Iris sat in her compartment and watched the majestic buildings go past. The desperate tragedy of Francesca's death swept through her. Somewhere in Venice, Jacopo was waiting, alone and frightened. Iris undid the bottle of Amanti and inhaled it. Its strength and depth fortified her.

There was a knock on the door. Tommaso came in with a bowl of steaming soup. 'I thought you might need something to eat.'

Iris smiled. 'Thank you.'

Tommaso stopped and sniffed the air. 'What's that smell? It's wonderful.'

Iris held up the bottle. 'Do you like it? Alessandro and I worked on this new perfume today. It was Raffaele's idea to call it Amanti.'

Tommaso took the bottle and waved it under his nose. 'Lovers. That's quite a title for a scent, but it certainly delivers. I thought Alessandro was crazy to leave his job on the *Orient Express* for perfume-making, but I see now he has quite a talent. You both do.'

'I never thought I'd enjoy composing perfumes with someone else,' Iris said. 'But I couldn't have made this without him.'

At that moment Alessandro appeared through the

interconnecting door. His eyes were red. Iris had left him alone in his compartment for a while, knowing he would need time to let out his grief for Francesca in private.

'Couldn't have made what without me?' he said, taking Iris's hand.

'That perfume,' Tommaso said. He glanced at the bottle. 'Do you have any going spare? Next time I'm passing through Milan I'd like to gift it to Giulietta.'

'Of course,' Iris said. She decanted some of the liquid into an amber vial and handed it to Tommaso. 'Look after it,' she said. 'What you have in your hand is a unique limited edition.'

Tommaso smiled. 'It will be a gift to remember. Now, I'd better be getting back to work.'

After he left Alessandro sat down next to Iris. She smoothed her palm against his cheek.

'How are you feeling?' she asked.

'Wretched that she's gone. Angry with everyone who played a hand in her death.'

'I hate this world for what it does to innocent people,' Iris said.

'There are others who will protest in her place,' Alessandro said. 'People are tired of Mussolini. They don't want Italy to be like Germany. I'm just afraid the forces that control our lives are so powerful they will stamp out every dissenting voice. We mustn't let that happen.'

'We won't,' Iris said. 'Let's rescue Jacopo, and then maybe from Paris we can do something about it all. I don't want to be a bystander in this war.'

Alessandro embraced her. She relished the strength of his arms around her.

'I'm relieved that you're here with me.' He stroked her

hair. 'Every time I see you looking at me I have to pinch myself. That first time I saw you at Claridge's, you looked like a goddess, sweeping into that room in your blue velvet dress. You're like a dream, Iris.'

Iris shook her head. 'I'm no more a dream than you are. You speak my language, no matter that we're from different countries and different backgrounds.'

Alessandro smiled. 'Perfume. That's our language.' He picked up the bottle of Amanti. 'You know there's one test of this accord we haven't done yet.'

Iris felt a tingle of anticipation.

'What's that?' she said, raising her eyebrows. Alessandro got up and locked the door, then pulled down the blinds.

'We haven't explored how Amanti smells on you,' he said.

The room seemed to still. Alessandro opened the bottle and dabbed some of the liquid on his finger. He knelt down in front of Iris and took hold of her wrist. She shivered at his slow, deliberate movements. He turned her wrist over and softly rubbed a little of the liquid on to her skin. A sigh escaped her at the gentleness of his touch.

'You know how this works,' he said with a slow smile that made her heart contract. 'A perfume needs to be experienced on all the body's pulse points.'

He pushed up the sleeve of Iris's blouse and in the smooth crook of her elbow massaged another drop of Amanti. Iris felt her insides melt. Each touch was exquisite.

He came closer, sweeping her hair away from one side of her face. He leaned forward and kissed the delicate skin under her ear. 'Here,' he murmured, 'I can feel your pulse beneath my lips, Iris. It's getting faster.'

Iris sucked in her breath. He massaged some Amanti under her ear. His deliberate movements were unbearable.

Her core burned. She reached out her hands, clasping his shoulders.

'Alessandro, please, kiss me.'

He leaned back on his heels, a smile on his face. 'I'm not finished yet,' he said.

He slid off her shoes, one by one, then pushed up her skirt. She parted her legs, allowing him closer. With feathery movements he removed first one stocking, sliding it down her leg, then the other. He took another drop of Amanti and smoothed it on to the hidden place behind her knee, working the scent into her skin, his fingers gentle, his movements firm. She sighed, melting at his touch.

His hand moved upwards. He kept his eyes on hers, deep pools in which Iris lost herself as his fingers stroked closer and closer until they reached the warm place between her legs. Gently, he rubbed Amanti on to the pulse point near where the fire was burning.

Iris gasped. Alessandro's eyes locked on to hers, his pupils black with desire. His breath grew shallow. Iris couldn't wait any longer. She wrapped her legs around him and cupped his face with her hands. This moment, this man. They were all she wanted. The perfume surrounded them as their lips met.

Alessandro drew back. 'You know I said I was falling for you, Iris.'

Iris nodded, barely able to breathe for wanting him.

'Well, I've fallen.'

At the sound of his voice and the deep longing behind his words Iris felt the fire flare up inside her.

'Me too,' she whispered. And it was true. Nothing had ever felt like this before. Surely nothing ever would again. She lay back, watching Alessandro undo the buttons on her blouse and peel the skirt from her thighs. His touch was hypnotic. The train shuddered over the tracks. Iris inhaled the Amanti and it mingled with the scent of Alessandro. He slid his hand across the curve and swell of her breasts, making her skin come alive.

Her breath tightened. She pulled off his shirt, loosening his belt buckle. A sense of urgency filled her being. The war and the train thundering towards Venice suggested that time was running out, and yet somehow, with Alessandro, time seemed to stop.

He entered her slowly, kisses lapping her neck, hands exploring her body. And as she tightened around him, moving with his rhythm, catching the delicious sensation of every thrust, she knew that he was part of her, just like the Amanti, soaked into her being.

As the train hurtled across northern Italy they found their own rhythm. Iris cried out, aware of him calling out her name at the same time. She rested her head on his chest, feeling it rise and fall, his arms around her, closer than she'd ever been to anyone in her life. Doubts hovered at the edge of her mind, but she was too exhausted to consider them. Pleasurable aftershocks rippled through her body as she snuggled closer to Alessandro, grateful for this release, whatever it might mean, whatever might come next.

Tradimento
(Betrayal)

Top Note
Bergamot

❧

Heart Note
Jasmine

❧

Base Note
Oud

❧

27

Iris – Venice, September 1939

Iris awoke to the screech of the engine's whistle. She had slept so well, and now her body throbbed with the memory of Alessandro. She turned over and there he was, his brown eyes twinkling at her. 'Good morning,' he said.

'You're still here.'

He kissed her gently, his hands entwining hers. 'We're in this together, remember?'

'You've got ink on your fingers,' Iris said, kissing the back of his hand.

'I was just adding some quantities into your notebook for Amanti. I like what we created, but I wondered if we could try out some different accords when we're back in Paris.'

'Of course. We're working together now, after all.' Iris snuggled close to him, savouring his warmth. 'Are we nearly there?'

'I'm afraid so.'

'Why afraid?'

Alessandro stroked her bare shoulder. 'Because the outside world is about to come crashing in. Here on this train, I can pretend it's just you and me on an endless journey together. But in Venice . . .' He paused.

Iris lifted her head to look at him. The expression in his eyes was far away. 'I thought you wanted to see Venice again,' she said. 'It's your home.'

'I do. And I'm glad to have the opportunity to show it to you. But I wish it wasn't in these circumstances. I'm technically still married to Roberta, although I'm in the process of getting the marriage annulled. I intend to avoid seeing anyone I know, but it might be complicated if . . .'

A cold feeling crept over Iris. The outside world. Was it going to break this fragile thing between them? Their relationship was only just beginning.

She pulled the covers around her. 'I remember my last night in Mougins in 1935. I didn't want to leave. It had been the perfect summer. The last good memory of us all.'

'This isn't going to be our last memory,' Alessandro said. He stroked her arm. 'Mougins sounds like a special place.'

'It was,' Iris said. 'My father left the house to me. Not that I've had any opportunities to go back yet. But it's there, mine, a place to go to get away from everything.'

'Not me, I hope,' Alessandro said, smiling.

'Not you,' she said, kissing his collarbone and smiling up at him. 'Anyway, what I mean is I understand why you would be nervous about coming home.'

Alessandro nodded. 'It doesn't change how I feel about you.'

'Good.' But, inside, Iris wondered. This was his place, not hers. She sat up. 'Come on then, we'd better get ready.'

He kissed her cheek and headed back to his own compartment to get changed. Iris watched him go. They were here to save Jacopo: that was all that mattered. After which she would return to Paris and continue training to be a perfumer or help with the war effort. Whatever this was with Alessandro, an interlude or something more, she couldn't allow it to take over her life.

The train slowed down. Iris tucked her hair behind her

ears. It was like that old saying about strangers in a carriage exchanging confidences. The train wasn't a real place; it existed out of time. Just like the last few days.

The station teemed with people. A nun herded a group of children towards the door. Two men carried crates of clucking chickens. Soldiers patrolled the ticket office and businessmen hurried up and down the platform.

'This way,' Alessandro said, nodding towards the large entrance hall. Light flooded the space. Iris hauled her suitcase outside and stared in wonder.

In front of her was a quayside covered in black-and-white tiles, beyond which lay the waters of the Grand Canal, sparkling in the unbroken sunshine. The buildings on the other side of the canal clustered around a white domed church.

'Venice is even more beautiful than I'd imagined,' Iris said. She'd seen pictures of the city in a geography book in the school library, but nothing could have prepared her for this.

Alessandro wasn't concentrating on the view. 'We'd better get off the main street and head to Francesca's perfumery. It's too exposed here.'

'How will we get in?'

Alessandro drew out a key from his pocket. 'Francesca gave it to me as a parting gift in case I ever needed to return. She told me the perfumery was as much my home as hers.'

Alessandro led Iris along the canal and to a water taxi. In the shade of the station, it had been cool, but here the sun was hot on her skin. Iris climbed in and sat bobbing on the water. The engine started and the boat set off. Iris stared at the crumbling palaces and churches. Gondolas moved elegantly along the edge of the canal, decorated in bright colours. She caught glimpses of side canals, almost too narrow for a boat to pass through. Washing was strung out across the water from window to window. A cat curled up on a bridge, catching the sun as it went down. It all seemed so peaceful, but it was deceptive. This was the city where Francesca had been murdered.

The taxi turned off the Grand Canal and went through a maze of narrower water networks. Eventually it docked by a rickety wooden jetty. Alessandro paid the man and helped Iris out of the boat.

'We'd better get inside,' Alessandro said. He placed the key in the lock and opened the door.

Iris followed him in. The narrow hallway was dark. A room off to the right housed a double bed. A room on the left, a single bed. Iris paused at the doorway. She saw a desk, a teddy bear, toys scattered on the floor. Jacopo's room. He used to clutch that teddy in the late evenings, growing sleepy and leaning against Iris's side as the grown-ups talked over a nightcap in the garden at Mougins. Further along, she came to a kitchen. Alessandro opened the dresser drawers. He took out some candles and matches and lit the wick.

'So, this is where Raffaele grew up,' Iris said.

'And where Francesca was shot,' Alessandro said gravely, pointing to the window. Outside in the courtyard, Iris saw bullet marks in the brickwork. She drew her hand across her mouth.

'That's barbaric,' she whispered. How much had Jacopo witnessed? He was such a gentle boy, watching butterflies dance across the flowerbeds. Iris shivered at the horrors he might have glimpsed.

'That's what fascists are,' Alessandro said, gritting his teeth. 'Jacopo was lucky to escape.'

'Are we safe here?' Iris asked.

'We're safe enough, and hopefully we won't be here for long.'

'We don't even know where Jacopo is.'

Alessandro lit another candle. 'I need to ask around. Somone will know something.' He pointed towards another door. 'The perfumery is in there. That's where I learned with Francesca.'

Iris went over, intrigued, and opened the door. The room was very small and completely taken up by a large desk with shelves covered in bottles of perfume ingredients.

'It's all still here,' Iris said.

'Good, then I suggest you work on the next scent while I go out and discover where Jacopo is.'

'I want to come too. We're supposed to be doing this together.'

He stroked her cheek. 'It's too dangerous. You're obviously not Italian, with your blonde hair and blue eyes, and the bar will be full of men.' He kissed her lips gently. 'You're too striking to come to the places I need to visit.'

'But I want to help.'

'You will, when we go to find Jacopo. But I won't risk you coming with me tonight.' He kissed her forehead.

'Be careful.' Her heart ached to see him go.

After he'd gone, Iris went to Jacopo's room. The sight of his things, abandoned and forlorn, was unbearable. She picked up the teddy bear, inhaling the smell of clove and vanilla, and gave it a squeeze. It was awful to think he'd been parted from it, just when he was probably in most need of comfort.

'We'll find you,' she whispered. Wherever Jacopo was now, he must be terrified.

Iris took out her notebook and travelling perfumer's case and went into the perfumery. At least she could distract herself in here while Alessandro was gone. She held the candle aloft. There was a fine scattering of dust over every surface, and a vast array of scents, but some bottles appeared to be missing, a round, dark circle in the dust where a bottle had previously stood.

The next scent. What would it be? There was no brief from Raffaele this time. Instead, it would be completely up to Iris and Alessandro to create it. She thought for a moment, remembering what Raffaele had said. The perfume needed to express their true feelings, dreams and desires. Then it came to her. After Amanti, after being so close to Alessandro and now fearing the effect of the outside world on their relationship, what they needed most was trust.

Iris began to write.

That feeling when someone knows and accepts you entirely. When you have opened yourself up and so have they. Trust is clarity. Transparency. It's light as air, but deep as a cavern. Hard won and not easily extinguished. A steady flame. But can it survive the winds of fate? Only time will tell.

She had to trust what she felt for Alessandro, even if she couldn't explain it. It was real and still pulsed in her veins. The smell of his skin, the feel of him against her. She reached for the bergamot and jasmine. A top note and heart note that expressed the blossoming inside when she was close to Alessandro.

She was lost in thoughts about what else the scent should contain when she heard the scrape of a key in the back door.

Iris froze, hardly daring to breathe. With a swift movement, she blew out the candles and sat very still. Could it be Alessandro returning? Surely it was too soon. Her stomach clenched. Then she heard a click and the squeak of a door opening very slowly. Someone was coming into the building.

Iris stood up, grabbing the candlestick, just in case. She tiptoed towards the perfumery door and opened it.

To her astonishment, a little girl stood in the kitchen, her eyes wide open in terror at the sight of Iris.

'Don't hurt me!' the girl exclaimed in Italian, holding up her hands.

'*Che ci fai qui?*' Iris said, lowering the candlestick. The girl looked about six or seven years old.

'Francesca, peace be on her soul, let me take perfume ingredients and sell them to get food,' the girl said in Italian, fear in her voice.

'You knew Francesca?'

'Yes, I came to play with Jacopo every day after school,' she said. 'She wanted to help my family. That's why she let me have the perfumes. She said she couldn't trade any more but she still wanted to be useful. I'm not stealing, I promise.'

Iris crouched down, hoping to put her at ease. 'I believe you.' Why else would Francesca have given her a key? 'Do you know Jacopo? He's my friend too. I'm trying to find him.'

The girl hesitated, glancing towards Jacopo's room. She needed more reassurance to speak freely.

'I want to help him now that Francesca has gone,' Iris said. 'I need to take him to his uncle, where he can live safely.'

'*È vero?*' the girl said, wide-eyed.

Iris nodded and placed her hand over her heart as a vow. 'I promise it's true.'

'If I tell you where he is, will you let me take a bottle of perfume oil?' the girl said. 'My little brother is hungry.'

Iris nodded.

'I don't know the name of the place, but I can draw where it is,' the girl said. 'I'm good at drawing.'

Iris fetched her notebook and a pencil and placed them on the kitchen table. The girl picked up the pencil and began to draw.

An outline emerged; Iris guessed it was Venice from the shape. Wavy lines seemed to indicate the lagoon. It was a map. Further off, to what must be the north-east of the lagoon, the girl drew more islands. On one of these islands, she placed a cross. 'He's there,' she said.

'How do you know?'

The girl smiled. 'I was in the boat when my father took him there.'

Iris patted her arm, 'Thank you for telling me. Can you keep this a secret?' She placed her finger over her lip, hoping the girl would understand that she needed to stay quiet and not mention finding Iris in the house.

The girl nodded. 'I will. And the perfumes?' she asked.

Iris smiled. 'Come on, let's find what you were looking for.'

She led the girl into the perfumery. Straight away, the girl went over to the ingredients and picked out a bottle of vetiver. 'I can get a good price for this,' she said.

She tucked the bottle into her coat and scampered off. Iris heard the door close. At least she knew where Jacopo was likely to be hiding: the question now was how to get there.

Iris was engrossed in her work when Alessandro came back. She recognized his tread and waited for him to appear at the doorway. He looked downhearted.

'Nobody knows anything,' he said, 'or they're too scared to tell me. I tried all the usual places, but hardly anyone is left. The clampdown has been vicious. I don't know what we're going to do.'

He went into the kitchen and placed a bag on the table. 'I got some food, at least,' he said. 'Just bread and fruit. We can't cook anything; there's no wood, and people would notice if smoke started coming out of the chimney.' He sat down at the table.

Iris followed him into the kitchen. 'I had a visitor,' she said.

'Who?' Alessandro said, alarmed.

'I'm fine. It was a little girl. She was taking perfume to swap for food.'

'You shouldn't have let anyone in.'

'I didn't. She had a key. She was just as shocked to see me as I was to see her.'

'We can't stay here,' Alessandro said. 'She'll tell someone, and word will get round. It's not safe.'

'She promised to keep it secret so long as I didn't tell anyone about her taking the perfume ingredients. She also told me something else . . .'

Iris opened the notebook and showed him the girl's drawing. 'She drew this to show me where Jacopo is. Look.' She pointed at the map. 'Do you know this place?'

Alessandro studied the map. 'That's Isola del Deserto,' he said. 'One of the most remote places in the lagoon, at least an hour's boat ride from Venice. There's only a Franciscan monastery there.'

'It sounds like a safe place,' Iris said.

'Maybe. The Catholic Church is in league with the fascists, so it's hard to tell. It's going to be risky getting over there. The lagoon waters are patrolled. That is if this girl even knows what she's talking about.'

'I believe she does.'

He leaned back in the chair. 'The safest way would be to travel to Burano and then get a boat from there to the island. The waters can be treacherous.'

'How will we navigate them?' Iris said.

Alessandro raised his eyebrows. 'I'm from Burano. We can take Father's old boat to Isola del Deserto.'

He flicked back through the notebook and stumbled on what she'd written that night. 'I see you've started on the next scent,' he said, reading the words. *'But can it survive the winds of fate? Only time will tell.* Are you talking about us?'

Iris smiled. 'That's none of your business.'

His eyes grew serious. *'Fiducia*, trust,' he said. 'You can trust me. Whatever happens, I hope you can remember that.'

'What do you mean?'

'Things aren't always as straightforward as they seem. You see . . .'

There was a knock at the back door. Iris froze, her heart squeezed with fear.

'Wait here,' Alessandro said. 'I'll go and see who that is.'

He went down the hallway. The banging sounded again.

'You're going to have to let them in or he'll wake the whole neighbourhood,' Iris said.

Alessandro opened the door slowly, then stared, a grin breaking over his face.

'Filippo, my goodness, it's you?' It seemed they knew each other.

'Of course it's me,' the man said, giving Alessandro a hug. 'Lucinda said there was a perfumer here. A woman. I had to come and take a look.'

Alessandro turned to Iris. 'Filippo worked with Francesca, printing pamphlets. I got to know him when he came to hide them in the perfumery until it was safe to distribute them.' Alessandro closed the door. 'What are you doing here?'

'My daughter came home terrified,' he said. 'Said she'd drawn a map for a woman in the perfumery. If I'd known you were here, Alessandro, I would have come sooner.'

'That was your daughter?' Iris said. 'She said she knew where Jacopo is hiding.'

'It was me who got Jacopo out by boat when the *squadristi* raided the house and murdered his mother.' Filippo's eyes darkened. 'Bastards. They were merciless. I had just docked at the jetty when the shots rang out in the courtyard. I dragged Jacopo out and escaped with him just in time.'

'So, he really is on Isola del Deserto then?' Alessandro said.

Filippo nodded. 'It was the best place to hide him. But I can't keep him there much longer.'

'Could you take us to Burano tonight?' Alessandro asked. 'We'll head out to Isola del Deserto from there.'

'Of course. Whenever you're ready.'

Iris and Alessandro left their bags in the perfumery. Iris

put the perfume she'd started making in her perfumer's case. It didn't have a name yet, but the word Alessandro had used still hovered in her head. *Fiducia*. Trust. She thought Raffaele would approve. Whatever happened next with her and Alessandro, trust was a good place to start.

28

Stella – Venice, August 1996

The modernist grey of the Venice Santa Lucia station contrasted with the warm opulence of the *Orient Express*. Stella stepped out and was instantly assailed by the bustle of people in the main atrium.

'Bruno, Bruno.' A woman called out and waved frantically. Her grey hair, impeccably made-up eyes and twinset and pearls suggested that she was in her early sixties. Bruno walked over and gave her a hug.

'Mamma, this is Stella, from the perfumery in London. Stella, this is my mother, Luisa.'

Bruno's mother looked Stella up and down and then smiled. 'Wonderful to meet you,' she said. 'You were right, Bruno. She is beautiful.'

Bruno reddened and ducked his head. 'Mamma.'

'It's lovely to be here,' Stella said, secretly delighted that he'd told his mum about her. 'Thank you for letting me stay with you.'

'Of course – no problem. Come on, let's get you home.'

'How is Anna doing?' Bruno asked tentatively.

'I went to see her last week,' Luisa said. 'She was very subdued. The doctor said she's making good progress, but there was no light in her.'

'We have to trust that they know what they're doing,' Bruno said. Stella's heart ached for the helplessness in his voice. He placed his arm around Stella's waist. 'Come on, let's show you Venice.'

Bruno led her down the steps of the station to the glittering canal. It was crowded with tourists and people selling souvenirs on stalls. They joined the queue for the *vaporetto*. Stella held his hand as she stepped in, the water bobbing the boat up and down, the diesel engine chugging. The heat from the sun was almost unbearable.

Bruno found seats for his mother and Stella at the back of the boat. Stella sat down and admired her surroundings. It was like a dream: bridges interlaced the canals, water slapped against the stones and crowds bustled on the walkways, but nothing detracted from the timeless beauty of the place.

Luisa smiled. 'It takes some getting used to, being on the water. But it's the best way to see the city.' The *vaporetto* set off, steering clear of water taxis and gondolas at the edge of the canal. It made its way along the Grand Canal: palazzos passed by, each one more beautiful than the last. Just after the Rialto Bridge they got off and Stella followed Bruno and his mother back over the bridge, and through a maze of narrow streets to Calle Toscana.

At last they reached the house. Air-conditioning units hummed in every room; it was a relief to breathe in the cool air. Luisa showed Stella up to Bruno's room, insisting that he was going to sleep on the sofa downstairs.

'How has he been the last few weeks?' Luisa asked quietly. 'I know he worries about his sister.'

'He's mostly been concentrating on sorting out the basement at Penhallam's and, more recently, finding the perfumes,' Stella said. 'But he's told me a little about Anna. He obviously cares about her a lot.'

'I don't know where we'd be without Bruno's help,' Luisa said. 'He's so calm and level-headed, and generous to a fault. He works very hard to provide for us.'

Stella nodded. 'I hope we can finish our research and that he'll have enough material for the book.'

'He told me that you're a good team,' Luisa said. 'I'm sure your search for these perfumes will be successful.'

That reminded Stella. She needed to phone Iris.

'Is it all right if I give my great-aunt a call? I'd like to tell her we've arrived in Venice safely.'

'Of course, my dear.' Luisa brought the phone from her bedroom into Bruno's, the long extension cord stretching across the landing. 'I'll see you downstairs.'

Stella sat on the bed and dialled Iris's number.

Iris answered. 'Hello.' Her voice sounded clearer than when Stella had spoken to her from Lausanne.

'Iris, it's Stella. Before you hang up, there's something I need to say.'

Iris sighed. 'I said everything I had to say the last time we spoke.'

'Just five minutes, please. I'm in Venice, you see. After I spoke to you in Lausanne, we went to Milan and saw Tommaso.'

The line went quiet. 'Tommaso's still alive?'

'Yes.'

'Did he know about my imprisonment?'

'He did, but he wasn't quick to judge or anything.' Stella gripped the receiver. She had to say this right, to make Iris understand. 'In fact, speaking to him, I realized that I've gone about this whole thing all wrong. I should never have badgered you about the perfumes and helping Penhallam's. It was self-centred of me. I should have been focused on you, on us, on the relationship we never had but could still have. I'm sorry, Iris.'

Stella held her breath, waiting for a reply.

'That's a lot to take in,' Iris said. Was that the ghost of a smile in her voice? 'Does this mean you're no longer looking for the perfumes to revive Penhallam's?'

Stella smoothed her hand over the bedspread. 'I still want to find the perfumes, but I want to find them for us.' She took a deep breath. 'I've done a lot of thinking on this trip, and Bruno has helped me to see that I've been suppressing my natural talent and inclination for making perfumes to run the business. I don't want to do that any more. Instead, I want to learn from you, Iris.'

'But that's impossible. I can't smell anything, and I can no longer make perfume.'

'I could be your nose,' Stella said, hoping to convince her. 'You have all the knowledge, the powers of description, years of experience. That hasn't disappeared. If we worked together, we could remake these perfumes ourselves.'

The line was silent, then Iris spoke. 'I don't know, Stella. I'm still not comfortable with diving into the past, and you and I barely know each other.'

'That's why I want to do it. To get to know you. I'm already learning so much from the perfumes. It's incredible what you and Alessandro created. Amanti is like nothing I've ever smelled before.'

'You've found Amanti?' She cleared her throat. 'I didn't think it still existed.'

'Tommaso had some. He said you gave him a sample on the *Orient Express*. His wife went to a perfumery in Milan, and they've been remaking it for her, year after year. I can smell sage as the top note, immortelle as the heart note, and . . .

'Musk,' Iris said, finishing Stella's sentence. 'The base note that pulls it all together. My goodness. I forgot about the little sample I gave Tommaso. It was for his girlfriend, and now you say they're married. It's extraordinary.'

Stella was encouraged by the renewed energy in Iris's voice.

'So Bruno and I have come to Venice to find the fourth scent. The problem is that on the way here, the perfume notebook was stolen.' Stella bit her lip, afraid of what Iris's reaction might be. 'We've reported it to the transport police. They're looking into it, but I'm so sorry, I'm not sure we'll be able to find it.'

'I see,' Iris said quietly. 'Maybe the book being stolen is a sign. It was the root of all the problems, anyway. If I hadn't had it with me when we returned from Venice . . .'

'What do you mean?' Stella said.

Iris hesitated. 'You need to be careful, Stella. Don't follow in my footsteps too closely. I can remember arriving in Venice, my heart full of emotion, dreams for a future I'd never dared think was possible, a life with a man who understood me, who spoke the language of perfume like I did, who brought out the best in me and my talents . . .' She stopped, her voice catching. It sounded like she was on the edge of tears. 'But the next perfume didn't turn out the way I'd expected.'

Stella held her breath. She didn't understand the context of everything Iris was saying, but at least she was finally opening up a little.

'Why did you call it Tradimento?' She remembered the name from the notebook.

'We didn't name it until right at the end. When we were finished. If you go to Francesca di Fiore's old workshop, you might even find some – who knows? If Amanti can resurface, perhaps Tradimento can too. But that's why you need to be careful. Don't lose your heart like I did.'

'Why do you say that?'

'You're there with the Italian scholar, aren't you?' Iris asked. She gave a bitter laugh. 'You and Bruno are about to discover more than you might wish. About my life. About yourselves. Perhaps when you've done that, then we can talk about working together. I'm not sure you'll want to in the end.'

'But I already know about the prison sentence,' Stella protested. 'I'm determined to gather the facts and see what can be done to clear your name.'

'Oh, Stella. I may not have been guilty of those crimes, but I was guilty of something else, something worse,' Iris said.

'What?' Stella whispered, listening intently.

'Betrayal.'

Stella refused to let Iris's hollow voice get her down. 'You have to fight for this, Iris. Not succumb to defeat. It's never too late to make amends and sort things out. Tommaso has faith in you. So do I. You need to have faith in yourself too.'

'Maybe,' Iris said, her voice weary. 'You could almost make me believe that it's possible, this redemption of which you speak.'

Stella smiled, encouraged by this glimmer of hope. 'I want to share this journey with you. So much is becoming clear to me, Iris. I want it to become clear for you too.'

'Then perhaps it will, my dear.' Iris paused, then continued. 'If you go to the perfumery, look up and keep your eyes peeled – you never know what you might find. Good luck, Stella.'

The phone line went dead. Stella put the phone down

and closed her eyes. Iris was family. For the first time, Stella truly felt that. Finally they'd spoken properly, and although Iris was still cautious and mistrustful of the past, she seemed to be opening up in a way she hadn't done before. If only Stella could find Tradimento. Then she could take it back to Paris, the set of perfumes almost complete, and start her relationship with Iris afresh.

Over lunch, Stella filled Bruno in with what Iris had told her, and Luisa listened, quietly fascinated by it all. 'So where do you need to look for this perfume, Tradimento?'

'Francesca di Fiore's old perfumery in the Jewish Quarter,' Stella said. 'Have you heard of it?'

Luisa raised her eyebrows. 'Of course I have. Bruno told me all about it when he started his research,' she said, 'and it's been in the papers for the last few weeks.'

'How come?' Bruno said.

'Well, not the perfumery itself, but the old palazzo in which it's housed. It's been used for storage since the war but now it's being redeveloped into workshops for artists.'

'Then we can go and see it,' Stella said.

Luisa shook her head. 'It's been boarded up and no one's allowed in. The whole place is unstable. Maybe if you apply to the authorities, they can arrange a visit.'

'But that would take weeks,' Bruno said. 'We haven't got time for that.'

'Can you reach it by canal?' Stella asked.

Luisa frowned. 'There's a jetty at the back. I believe di Fiore's perfumery used to be on the ground floor. But the whole place is in poor repair. It's not worth the risk.'

Stella shrugged. 'I've come all this way. I have to see

inside it. Do you have a toolbox we could take? And a torch? We could go at night when it's dark . . .'

'You mean break in?' Bruno said.

'If it's the only option,' Stella said. 'It's worth a try.'

'*Dio mio*,' Luisa said, standing up and clearing away the plates. 'I don't want to hear any more. It's dangerous and foolhardy. But I can tell by your faces you're going to do it anyway.'

She turned on the tap. 'By the way, Bruno, have you decided what to do about that job offer? Surely you need to let them know soon.'

'What job offer?' Stella said. He'd only talked about the book, and needing the money for Anna's treatment.

'Harvard have offered him a contract to teach in America for a year. I'm so proud of him, and it could lead to something permanent,' Luisa said.

'Gosh,' Stella said. 'I had no idea. What an amazing opportunity.'

She was happy for him, of course, but if he moved to America it would spell the end for whatever had newly sprung up between them.

Bruno shrugged. 'The timing isn't great; I don't want to leave Mamma and Anna at the moment.'

'And we'd be sorry to see you go,' Luisa said, 'but you need to consider this seriously. Chances like this don't come round very often.'

Luisa threw a tea towel over to Bruno and he got up to help her with the dishes. This talk of Harvard reminded Stella that the deeper she fell for Bruno the more there was to lose. Perhaps it was time to pull back. As he smiled at her from across the kitchen, Stella's heart lurched. She wasn't sure she'd be able to.

That evening, at ten o'clock, Stella got ready to set off to the perfumery. It was strange to be in Bruno's old room. There were photos on his wall of when he was younger, at parties with friends, a pretty woman smiling next to him.

Stella sighed. She'd felt so close to Bruno on the *Orient Express*, but here, life and Bruno's future prospects, possibly in the States, got in the way. Would Stella even make it this far, a photo on his wall, or would things unravel once they'd finished the search?

She shrugged on her cardigan. It was even more essential now that they found the fourth perfume. At least things seemed more hopeful with Iris.

Bruno led her down to the canal. Rows of motorboats were tied up, bobbing in the waves. He stopped by a boat called *Barchetta Azzurra*. It was painted blue with a jaunty yellow awning.

'This is the one,' Bruno said, 'our little blue boat. We've had it for years. I taught Anna to drive it, and we used to go up and down the Lido. When I'm home I take it out most evenings after work. It's a lovely way to relax and forget about the stresses of the day.'

He helped Stella into the boat and they set off, white-capped waves rippling either side of them. Bruno steered the boat through the water, navigating the small canal until they were out on the Grand Canal. Stella sat back and admired the huge palazzos, which were illuminated with floodlights. Venice was stunning. She wondered what Iris had thought, coming here. At the very start of the war, it would still have been a fairly safe place for her to visit. But only months later Mussolini had joined with

Hitler and entered the fray, and the *Orient Express* had stopped running.

She'd been reading the train's history in the brochure as they'd travelled. The last *Orient Express* train had run in the new year of 1940. Iris and Alessandro had been lucky to seize that window of time.

A few minutes later Bruno turned into a narrow canal. It was darker down here; the light from the floodlit buildings didn't reach this far. Black water slapped the sides of the boat. Bruno slowed the engine down and turned on a headlight. Stella saw green algae marking the flood line on the buildings.

'This is it,' Bruno said, guiding the boat to a rickety-looking jetty by a boarded-up building. The water smelled foul. He tied the boat up against one of the posts.

'Let me just check it's not going to collapse,' Bruno said, stepping carefully on to the rotting wood. The jetty creaked and swayed but seemed to hold. He held out his hand. 'Come on. Bring the toolbox and we'll see if we can get in.'

The door at the end of the jetty was fastened with a padlock. An official-looking sign on the door had red letters spelling out that no entry was permitted.

Stella searched through the toolbox and found a hammer. 'We need to tap the sides until the pins come loose.'

Bruno glanced at her in surprise. 'I didn't expect you to know how to break open a padlock.'

'I discovered it one year when I wanted to open my dad's chest to see if my Christmas presents were in there,' Stella said.

A light went on in one of the rooms opposite. 'We'd better hurry,' Bruno said.

Stella tapped the padlock until the pins came out and

the padlock opened. She pushed the door and tiptoed into the gloomy darkness.

Bruno switched on the torch and closed the door behind them. The air smelled musty, as if bats and mice were now the sole occupants of this place. Stella opened the door on her left, which appeared to lead into a small room. It was empty save for a few sacks of concrete.

'The developers must have used this apartment to store building equipment,' Bruno said.

The next room was smaller and also empty. The corridor led through to a kitchen. There was an old oven that looked like it was from the seventies, with gas rings and a grill. Off the kitchen was another door, which Stella tried, but it was locked.

Bruno rummaged in the toolbox. He took out a screwdriver. 'I'll try removing the bolts and taking out the lock itself.'

'It seems you're just as proficient as I am at breaking into places,' Stella said. She shone the torch on to the door so he could see what he was doing. A few minutes later the bolts were out, and the door opened.

Electrical equipment – heaters, drills, tile-cutting machines – were stored in a corner of the room. But over on the other side was an old wooden table in the familiar shape of a perfumer's organ.

'Look,' Stella said excitedly. 'This is where Iris must have come with Alessandro. Francesca's perfumery.'

Any bottles of ingredients that had once stood here were long gone. Stella ran her hand over the wood. 'Nearly sixty years ago, Iris and Alessandro would have been right here where we are now. Isn't that incredible to think of?'

'Yes,' Bruno said. 'I wonder what it was like back then.

Jacopo's mother had been murdered and this place would have been deserted. Yet still they found time to work on the fourth perfume.'

'But where is it now?' Stella said. 'Iris said there might be some still in here.'

But there were no cupboards or shelves. The room was bare save for the equipment and the perfumer's organ. It was so long ago, perhaps it had all been cleared out.

'Are you sure she meant here?'

'I think so, although she was quite vague.'

Bruno looked behind the building materials. 'There's nothing here. What exactly did she say?'

Stella thought for a moment. 'She said to look up and keep your eyes peeled.' She lifted her eyes to the ceiling, wondering what Iris had meant. There was nothing but cobwebs up there. Stella scanned the rest of the wall, then stopped. Some of the bricks by the chimney were loose.

'That looks odd,' she said. She went to take a closer look and noticed that the mortar around one of the bricks was missing. She wiggled it with her fingers. The brick came free.

'It's a cavity,' she said. 'Look.'

'What's inside?'

Stella reached in and felt around. The stone was rough, then her fingers touched something dry and papery. She pulled out a sheet of paper and unfolded it. It was a drawing that looked like a map. 'It looks like a page from Iris's notebook. What does it mean?'

'Hold it the other way up,' Bruno said. 'That's Venice, and this is a route across the water going past Murano and then on to Burano. And then it looks as if the route heads to this place.' He pointed to the spot marked with a cross. 'Isola del Deserto.'

'Why would this have been drawn in Iris's notebook?' Stella said.

'I don't know, but the only way we'll find out is to go there,' Bruno replied. 'It's too far to go now. It's at least an hour and a half away, and my little boat won't have the power to take us there. We'll take a water bus to Burano tomorrow and then a water taxi to the island.'

'Okay.' Stella nodded. 'First thing in the morning.'

Bruno peered up at the little crevice again and shone his torch inside. Something glinted in the darkness.

'Wait a minute,' he said. 'There's something else in there.' He stood on tiptoe to reach inside. 'Look, it's a bottle.'

Stella gasped as she read the label.

'It's the fourth perfume. Tradimento. So Iris was right — it was hidden here.' She took the bottle and held it up into the light of the torch.

'There's barely any perfume left in it,' Bruno said.

Stella took the lid off and inhaled. 'I can smell something, but it's not enough to identify all the ingredients.'

Bruno bent down and sniffed. 'It's a very intense smell,' he said. He wrinkled his nose. 'Almost too much, if you know what I mean.'

'Iris said they didn't name this scent until right at the end. *When we were finished.* Her voice sounded bitter. Tradimento.'

'Betrayal,' he said.

'Yes.' A cold shiver ran over Stella. Until now, the names of the perfumes had had a special significance. Surely it was a bad omen that the fourth fragrance had been called Betrayal. But who had betrayed who? And why was the perfume bottle almost empty and left here in Venice? Iris had warned her about following too closely in her footsteps.

'I know what you're thinking,' he said. 'Just because

things ended with Alessandro and Iris, it doesn't mean the same will happen to us.'

Stella squeezed his hand. 'You don't know that.' Especially if he decided to take the job in America.

Bruno shook his head and pulled her close. 'I don't want this to be an interlude, Stella. I want to find a way to still see you after the search for the perfumes is over.'

'Let's see,' she said, trying to keep a protective distance. Nothing she'd experienced before could compare to this. His voice. His smell. His presence alone managed to over-throw any doubts her rational side cast in the way. But it was against her nature to fall for someone this hard. With everything that was going on, she needed to tread carefully.

29

Iris – Burano, September 1939

The motorboat bobbed on the water, the moonlight shining down from a clear, star-filled sky. Filippo sat at the helm, steering the boat across the open waters of the lagoon. Venice lay behind them, a pattern of lights and towers. Up ahead was the island of Murano, its lighthouse sending out a beam across the sea, through which the boat had to pass to reach another stretch of open water towards Burano. Iris had the map in her hand, the little girl's drawing showing the way.

Alessandro sat next to her, his hand resting on the rail at the side of the boat. He was gazing out across the water, his thoughts far away.

'Are you okay?' Iris said above the noise of the engine. She took his hand and squeezed it. At her touch, his shoulders relaxed. He lifted her hand to his mouth and kissed it.

'As long as you are with me,' he said, 'I'm okay. The sooner we're out of Venice safely with Jacopo, the better. I'm not sure what we'll find on Isola del Deserto. There might be more than we bargained for . . .'

He stopped and stared ahead. Bright lights appeared in the distance. Filippo slowed the engine.

'What's going on?' Alessandro called.

'It's a patrol,' Filippo said. 'If we get stopped, let me do the talking.'

Iris swallowed. Their first encounter with the Venetian authorities. She wasn't ready. Alessandro's words were still lingering in her head. What did he mean, more than they bargained for? There was no time to ask him. The patrol boat's light was getting closer.

'*Merda*,' Alessandro said under his breath. He slid his arm around Iris. 'Stay quiet. If they find out you're English it'll make them suspicious.'

'Maybe you should just kiss me and then they can't ask me any questions at all,' Iris said.

Alessandro smiled. 'That's not a bad idea.' He lifted his hand to her hair, stroking a tendril away. 'I've been wanting to kiss you again, although I had hoped for more romantic circumstances.'

A brusque voice called out. Filippo cut the engine. One of the men climbed onboard the boat. Iris kept her eyes fixed on Alessandro's. He closed his eyes and kissed her with such passion that she nearly lost her breath. Then, abruptly, a hand grabbed Alessandro's shoulder and pulled him away from her.

'What's going on here?' the man said. He was thickset and wore a black shirt.

'I'm taking this pair to Burano to see relatives,' Filippo said.

'I'm not asking you,' the man said. 'I'm asking him.' He jabbed his finger into Alessandro's chest.

'My mother's not very well and I got word to come and see her,' Alessandro said affably.

'And who's this?' the man said, looking at Iris disdainfully.

'My wife,' Alessandro said, 'and I'll thank you kindly not to speak to her that way.'

'Come on, Luigi, we need to head back to Venice,' the

man on the patrol boat called out to his companion.

'How did you get that scar?' the other man said, clearly not willing to let them go yet.'

'Fighting for my country,' Alessandro said defiantly.

'Hmmm,' the man said. He took out a notebook. 'Give me your name and your mother's address. I'll check it out when we get back.'

Alessandro swallowed. 'My name is Antonio Castelli. My mother lives on Calle Tibaldon, number 55.'

The man wrote it down carefully . Then he snapped his notebook closed. 'Now, be on your way.'

Iris breathed a sigh of relief as the patrol boat sped off towards Venice. Filippo started up the engine and they crossed over the dark open waters between Murano and Burano.

'That was quick thinking,' Iris said, looping her arm inside Alessandro's.

'Not really,' Alessandro said. 'I couldn't think of a single thing to say. The only address that popped into my head was Roberta's mother's. I used her surname too. I hope I won't have got them into any trouble.'

'Hopefully he won't bother checking,' Iris said.

Alessandro squeezed her hand. 'Let's pray he doesn't.'

It was nearly midnight by the time they got to Burano, yet Filippo wanted to take them to Isola del Deserto.

'I don't want to put you in any more danger,' Alessandro said. 'We'll be fine from here.'

The two men embraced, and Filippo shook Iris's hand. 'Let me know if there's anything else I can do.' He gestured towards the edge of the lagoon. 'The wind is up. Be careful out there.'

*

Iris and Alessandro walked through Burano. The streets were narrow and the houses painted in bright colours. Alessandro took her hand, his skin warm. Avoiding his mother's house, they made their way to the south side of the island. The moon shone with a pale light. The streets were empty; everyone was sleeping. A chilly breeze came in off the lagoon, and Iris pulled her cardigan tighter around her.

'We kept my father's boat,' Alessandro said as they reached the quayside. 'My mother doesn't leave the island, or if she does, she takes the *vaporetto*. But I didn't want to get rid of it. I have so many memories of going out fishing first thing. The sun barely up and the waters calm. Last time I was here I filled up the engine with petrol. Hopefully there will be enough to get us to the island and then back to Venice.'

He went over to a wooden motorboat and untied the tarpaulin. He jumped aboard and then helped Iris down.

'Will it start?' Iris asked.

'Let's hope so.'

He went over to the outboard motor and pulled the cord. The engine sounded loud in the still night air. Iris gripped the sides of the boat as Alessandro steered it out of the harbour. The island wasn't far. Alessandro pointed out the tall tower of the monastery and the silhouette of cypress trees. But seconds later a wind whipped up, and before Iris knew it the island was hidden by a mist that had rolled in on the strengthening breeze. Iris turned to Alessandro.

'Can you see where we're going?' she said, shouting above the roar of the wind.

'I know this stretch of water. Don't worry.'

Iris clung on to the sides of the boat. It was more than just a mist and wind. A storm was gathering pace. She was thrown back and forward in the boat. Soon Iris couldn't see a thing, not even the *bricole* that marked the safe route to the island. Alessandro slowed the engine. Sea spray broke over the boat, soaking them both.

'We're being blown off course. Hold on,' Alessandro said, fighting against the power of the water to steer the boat.

A huge wave crashed into the side. Alessandro was flung down, hitting his head against one of the wooden buttresses in the boat.

Iris tried to crawl towards him, but it was impossible. The boat was being thrown this way and that on the waves; all sense of direction was lost. Iris tried to hold on as the vessel rolled to the side, nearly tipping them both into the water. Then she heard a scraping sound along the bottom of the boat, the sickening sound of wood cracking. The hull was breaking apart. Water rushed in. The last thing Iris remembered was the boat flipping over, water pushing her down, down into the lagoon, and darkness enveloping her.

30

Iris – Isola del Deserto, September 1939

Iris shivered and opened her eyes. Her fingers felt gritty. She lifted her head. She was lying on some kind of sandbank. The sun was coming up; it must be early in the morning. Everything ached. The water lay calm and still. To her left was the island. She could see a stone wall behind which grew a row of cypress trees. She heard a moan and saw Alessandro lying by the wall. She made her way over to him.

'Alessandro, can you move?' They must have lain here for a few hours.

He nodded weakly. The cut on his head had dried. 'Damn storm,' he said. 'I'm sorry I couldn't control the boat. We might have both been lost. I can't bear to think what would have happened if you'd—'

'Don't,' Iris said. 'We're both here, almost in one piece, but we've lost the boat.'

Alessandro winced as she helped him up. He scrambled over the wall and helped Iris to the other side. Under the cypress trees it was cool and shady. Cicadas rattled in the trees. Pine needles lay on the floor and the air was heavy with the scent of sap.

She heard the crack of a twig. A monk stood a few feet away, hands clasped, wearing a dark brown robe, a rope belt tied in the middle.

'I thought I heard voices,' he said. 'What happened?'

'We got caught in the storm,' Alessandro said, 'and thrown on to a sandbar. This was the nearest place to find safety.'

'What were you doing this close to the island?'

'We understand that there is something here that needs returning,' Alessandro said.

The monk looked puzzled, then realization dawned. 'How do you know this?' he asked cautiously.

'Because we've come from Milan,' Alessandro said.

'Thank God,' the monk said. 'I can't hide them for ever.'

'What is going on, is Jacopo here?' Iris asked Alessandro.

'They're both here,' the monk replied.

'We've come to collect Jacopo, nobody else,' Iris said.

The monk and Alessandro exchanged a look.

'Come with me and I'll show you,' the monk said. He led them through the cypress trees towards the monastery, a sprawling red-brick building with terracotta tiles on the roof.

'Maybe we should wait here,' Iris said, not wanting to leave the cover of the trees. 'It might not be safe.'

'Everyone is at Matins,' the monk said, walking ahead.

Iris tugged on Alessandro's shirt. 'Can we trust him?'

Alessandro shrugged. 'From what Filippo told me, the monastery is known for being a safehouse. I don't think there's anything to worry about. Come on.'

The monk opened a heavy wooden door and took them into the silence of the monastery. Iris marvelled at the cool, flower-filled cloister and the feeling of tranquillity. He passed through a stone corridor and opened another door.

Light flooded in from diamond-leaded windows, and there he was: worn out, haggard, but still the same Jacopo that Iris remembered. He caught sight of Iris, surprise on his face.

'You're the last person I expected to see,' he said, running towards her. The he caught sight of Alessandro and gathered him into the hug too.

Iris squeezed Jacopo tight. He was taller, more solemn, than the little boy she'd played with in Mougins.

'I'm so sorry for everything you've been through,' she said. 'I can't imagine how horrifying it's been.'

Jacopo lowered his eyes. Tears spilled on to his cheeks. 'I hate them for what they did to her. I wanted to go back and save her, but the gunshot sounded and I heard her scream . . .' He clutched Iris, sobbing. 'She's gone. I'll never see her again. The monks say she's at peace with my father, but I just want them both back here so I'm not alone.'

'Oh, Jacopo, my love,' Iris said, holding him tight.

'You have your uncle,' Alessandro said, touching Jacopo's shoulder.

Iris nodded. 'That's right. Raffaele wanted to come with us, but it was too dangerous. He's waiting for you in Switzerland. He'll be so relieved to see you.'

Before Iris could say more another man entered the room, stocky and thickset with an alertness to his demeanour. He smiled as soon as he saw Alessandro.

'Are you the one who has come from Milan?' he said, enveloping Alessandro in an enormous bear hug and slapping him on the back. 'I had word you were on your way, but I didn't dare believe it.'

Alessandro glanced at Iris. 'Yes, that's me.'

'What's going on?' Iris said. She kept hold of Jacopo's hand. She had no idea who this man was, nor why he had been awaiting their arrival.

Alessandro avoided her gaze. 'Look, both of you, pack your things,' he said to Jacopo and Giovanni. 'If we can borrow a boat, we'll get you out of here within the hour.'

'Answer my question first,' Iris said.

'Not here,' Alessandro said, glancing at Jacopo.

Iris knelt down in front of the boy. 'You go and pack. I'm just going to be right outside this door, I promise.' Jacopo nodded. Iris followed Alessandro out towards the cloister. 'I don't understand,' she said as soon as they were out of earshot. 'We've come here to get Raffaele's nephew, and now there's someone called Giovanni who acts like he was expecting you.'

'I haven't been able to tell you any of this, not until now. It was too dangerous, and we didn't want to put you at risk. I tried to in the boat, but then the patrol came.'

Iris raised her chin. 'What do you mean, "we didn't want to put you at risk"?' she said. 'Who else knew that this man Giovanni would be here?'

Alessandro hung his head. He reached out for Iris's hand, but she pulled it away. 'Tommaso did. Look, this is going to be hard to explain, but promise you'll hear me out until the end.'

'Is anything you told me true?'

'I am a perfumer. I wanted to train under Raffaele. But that wasn't the only thing that led me to Paris.'

'What are you talking about?' Iris said, her heart growing cold.

'I didn't get this scar during the war in Ethiopia,' Alessandro said. 'I was injured in the Spanish Civil War. I went over to fight in one of the brigades from Giustizia e Libertà. We fought on the Aragon front. There were some victories. Our slogan was *Oggi in Spagna, domani in*

Italia – "Today in Spain, tomorrow in Italy." We wanted Mussolini to see that we meant business. But then I got injured at the start of last year.'

'All these secrets,' Iris said, her voice faint. 'I don't know what to believe.'

'This is the truth, Iris, you have to believe me. I was a mess after I came back from Spain. The scar became infected, and all I can remember is the darkness and the nightmares. When I recovered I was so weak, and lost.'

'Where does Roberta fit into this?' Iris said. 'I presume you do have a wife?'

Alessandro nodded. 'I recuperated on Burano, and married Roberta, like my mother wanted me to. I didn't have the energy to fight her entreaties to secure our financial situation.' He twisted his hands and looked away. 'Roberta soon lost interest in me and started seeing another man, a neighbour whose fortunes were rising on account of his involvement with the fascists. She thought I was pathetic and, to be honest, I was so low at that time, if Tommaso hadn't come along and convinced me to join him on the *Orient Express*, fighting for Italy's liberty a different way, I don't know what I'd have done. I still did jobs for Giustizia e Libertà, passing on whatever information I could to the organization in Paris, and somehow began to restore my sense of self-worth again.'

Iris closed her eyes. The anguish in his voice told her that his story had the ring of truth about it. She felt desperately sorry for what he'd been through. But still, he should have told her sooner. 'You lied to me.'

Alessandro nodded. 'I had to. When it became too dangerous for me to continue passing through Italy on the train, I contacted Raffaele to ask for a job at the perfumery.'

'You lied to him too?' Iris said.

Alessandro's cheeks flushed. 'Not exactly,' he said. 'You see, Raffaele has been a member of Giustizia e Libertà since 1929. He wasn't fit enough to fight, but he provided money which went towards purchasing guns and ammunition, first for the fight in Spain, and later in preparation for what we hoped might be an anti-fascist uprising in Italy.'

Iris felt nausea rise in her throat. 'He told me about leaving Italy,' she whispered, 'but I didn't know he was still involved. I thought the two of you were close because you're both Italian. But in fact, you lied to me and brought me here under false pretences.'

'The plan to rescue Jacopo and Francesca was my main priority, and that's the truth. Giovanni wasn't part of the original plan. Giustizia e Libertà agreed to fund our trip as far as Milan, if I brought letters from France to comrades inside Italy.'

Of course – Alessandro had handed documents over to the man behind the bar in the café. She'd naively assumed that Raffaele was paying for the trip and that Alessandro's contacts on the *Orient Express* had meant reduced fares for them all. Iris shook her head. She should have questioned the arrangements more closely, instead of blindly going along with things.

'When I found out that Francesca had been murdered and that Jacopo was still in Venice,' Alessandro continued, 'I had to make another deal with them. The communist group in Milan offered funds and assistance to rescue Jacopo if I agreed to rescue one of their main leaders, Giovanni Pascarella, at the same time.'

'And we're supposed to take Giovanni back with us,' Iris said, desperately trying to put the pieces together.

Alessandro nodded. 'Isabella gave us two visas, and false papers for the journey back. One of them was supposed to be for Francesca. I handed it over to the barman when we arrived in Milan, and he arranged for the local forger to rework the details for Giovanni.'

'So, Raffaele doesn't know about Giovanni?'

Alessandro shook his head. 'No, but if he did, I know he'd approve. He supports the fight against Mussolini too.'

The ground felt shaky. Everything she'd known up to now had been overturned. Iris couldn't look at him. It was too much to take in. He'd kept all this from her.

'I'm sorry,' she said. 'I need a moment to think this through. Tell Jacopo I won't be long.'

She walked quickly along the cloister towards the front door of the monastery. Her chest heaved with the betrayal. Rescuing a leader of Giustizia e Libertà had never been part of the mission. She had put her own life in danger to rescue Jacopo – that was her choice, a personal decision to save Raffaele's nephew. But Giovanni was not her responsibility.

She leaned against the wall, in the shadow of a buttress. Somehow she had to get Jacopo away from here and take him back to Lausanne herself. But how? She was furious with Alessandro for putting her in this position.

Down by the jetty, an engine throbbed. A boat was heading up the canal, preparing to dock.

Iris crouched down, her heart thudding. She watched as the driver steered the boat into position, then tied it to one of the posts. Two men sat in the boat; she recognized them at once. They were the Blackshirts from last night. They each carried a pistol in their belt and a truncheon hanging from a clip.

The men jumped off the boat and made their way towards the monastery. Iris's mind went blank with panic, and she pressed herself against the stone in the hope they wouldn't see her.

The men drew closer. She had to stop them. Jacopo must be protected. Iris looked at the state of her clothes. Her dress was covered in blood stains from Alessandro's head wound. Her shoes were dirty and covered in sand, and she was certain that her hair looked a mess after being tossed about at sea. Please God, let this work.

'Help, help!' Iris called, running out from the side of the building and on to the lawn, as if in fear for her life. Hopefully her cries would alert Alessandro to the danger.

The Blackshirts stopped and turned in her direction.

'Please, I beg you, you have to help me!' Iris shouted. 'I've been attacked and dumped on this island. In the name of Il Duce, you have to catch the bastard who did this to me.'

One of the Blackshirts came forward. 'I recognize you,' he said, touching her chin. 'You were on the boat we stopped last night.'

Iris nodded. 'He told me we were going to see his sick mother, and then he brought me out to the lagoon. He was very rough, and when I wouldn't give him what he wanted he left on another boat. I was left drifting around for hours, and then the storm came and washed me up here.'

'Antonio Castelli, he said his name was,' the man said. 'Turns out that was a false name.'

Iris shook her head. 'I didn't know, I promise. He lied to me. I never want to see him again, but please, you have to take me back to Venice. I beg you.'

The man hesitated. 'We've got business here first. Go and wait in the boat until we're finished.'

Iris forced herself to smile. 'Thank you. I'm very grateful.'

The blackshirt winked at her. 'I'll make sure you are.' He turned to the other man. 'Come on then, let's see if we can finally bag this fox.'

The pair trooped into the monastery and the heavy door closed with a bang. Please God, let Alessandro and the others have got the message, let Jacopo be safe. Iris skirted round the outside of the monastery, hoping to catch sight of them. She had just reached the corner wall when someone grabbed her hand.

'It's me, Alessandro,' a voice said. A small door opened in the outer wall. Jacopo and Giovanni were hiding in the shadows. 'You were magnificent,' Alessandro said. 'Thank you.'

Iris yanked her hand away. 'I didn't do it for you,' she said. 'I did it for Jacopo. Now follow me, quickly. I know where there's a boat. We can hide out at the perfumery.'

Alessandro considered her warily. 'So, you're going to help us all escape?'

'I'm going to help Jacopo,' Iris said. 'After that, you and Giovanni are on your own.'

31

Stella – Isola del Deserto, August 1996

The next day, Stella and Bruno took the vaporetto to Burano and then hired a motorboat to take them to the island. The driver set off, the boat, scudding over the water, towards Isola del Deserto. Stella felt the wind lift her hair and tasted salt on her lips. Bruno looked out over the water. Stella shuffled closer to him along the bench.

'You look lost in thought,' she said. 'Are you thinking about the job? It's worth considering. It would mean more money to help your sister.'

It would also spell the end for whatever feelings had sprung up between them, but Stella couldn't discourage him from this chance.

'True, but I'd have to move thousands of miles away, and I don't think I can do that right now, when Mum and Anna both need me around.'

'Perhaps your mum could cope better than you think.'

'It's not just leaving my family that's making me think twice,' Bruno said. 'I know it's very early days for you and me, and who knows where it might lead, but going to the States would make it impossible to find out.'

'Which is why I want you to count me out of your considerations. We could always stay in touch by email or phone, and like you say, we've barely begun,' she said. 'I don't want to influence you either way. It's up to you.'

What else could she say? If he stayed in Europe for her, he might end up regretting it and resenting her. The sunlight sparkled on the water. 'Come on, let's focus on what we're doing today,' she added, hoping to lighten the mood. 'We're nearly there.'

The boat grew closer to the island. Dark green cypress trees stood like a protective fence around the monastery. Stella searched the shoreline, wondering if this was the view that Iris would have seen all those years ago. The boat made its way around the island until it reached a cutting where a narrow canal led up to a jetty. The waves were calmer here, the wind quieter too.

'I'll be back in an hour or so,' the driver said as they disembarked.

The silence of the place was overwhelming. It was a relief to be far away from everything – the mainland, the complications. The air smelled clear, freshened by the sea breeze.

'Let's go and see what we can find,' Bruno said, taking her hand.

Stella walked alongside him up the winding path to the door of the monastery and rang the bell. A monk with grey curly hair and a bushy beard appeared.

'Good afternoon,' he said.

'We wondered if we could take a look around, if you don't mind?' Bruno said.

The monk frowned. 'We aren't open to visitors until later, when we do the tour.'

'I'm sorry. We didn't realize. It's just that I think my great-aunt was here before the war,' Stella explained. 'I'm retracing her steps. If we could just get a brief glimpse of the place . . . please.'

'I'm afraid you'll have to wait here and join the other

tourists when they arrive.' Bells sounded in the tower. 'You can sit here in the cloisters. I'll let you know when we're ready.'

The monk stood aside to let them in. Stella and Bruno entered a small cloister in which an abundance of flowers grew. It was cool here, the silence deep and still. The monk bowed and left them, disappearing through a heavy door.

'We could be waiting ages,' Stella said. 'Let's at least take a look at the chapel.'

'I don't think they'd be happy about that,' Bruno said.

'Come on. It'll be fine.'

Stella pushed open a heavy door. The light inside was dim, a few candles burning by an offertory. A deep, elemental smell hit her nostrils.

'Can you smell that?' she said. 'It's agarwood, but when it's distilled it's called oud. It's the base note in the bottle of Tradimento we found in the perfumery. I wonder if being here inspired Iris and Alessandro to use it.'

'It has the same intensity,' Bruno said.

'Exactly,' Stella said. 'There must have been a reason why Iris or Alessandro wanted oud to be the dominant note in Tradimento.'

Whatever had happened to tear Iris and Alessandro apart, it must have been more than just a lovers' quarrel. Stella felt protective of them, wishing she could go back in time and stop whatever had occurred from happening. Would she look back on this moment and feel the same thing about Bruno? He'd wanted to discuss his future with her on the boat coming over, but she'd shut him down. Maybe, one day, she'd regret not saying how she felt, but she couldn't bring herself to tell him that deep down, she wanted to see where things led too.

*

Voices could be heard outside the chapel. Bruno looked at Stella in alarm. She grabbed his hand and headed to a small side door. It opened into the monastery gardens.

'I hadn't put you down as someone who liked trespassing,' Bruno said with a smile. 'But it's become quite a common occurrence.'

'I wouldn't dream of it normally, but it's not like time is on our side.'

The gardens were beautiful, sheltered by the cypress trees that grew around the edge of the island. Stella and Bruno passed through a rose garden and a kitchen garden, heading away from the monastery. Under the trees, they came across a stone barn. Boxes containing bottles were stacked on the gravel outside.

She headed over to the window and peered inside. Through the dirty pane she could make out funnels and cast-iron distillation vats. Over to one side there were wooden crates designed to extract scent from petals in a process known as enfleurage.

'This looks like some kind of perfumery.'

Bruno took a bottle from one of the boxes. 'Look at this.'

He handed it to Stella. The label read: *Fedeltà a Dio*. Loyalty to God. She took off the stopper and sprayed the perfume on to her wrist. As soon as the molecules entered the air around her, Stella knew.

'My goodness,' she said, staring at Bruno in amazement. 'This is it. It's the same scent as we found in Francesca's perfumery. Tradimento.'

Bruno took the bottle from her and sniffed the nozzle. 'But how can that be? The formula was known only to Iris and Alessandro.'

Surely the connection had to be significant. 'We need to

find out where Fedeltà a Dio came from. Its formula must be the same as Tradimento, and then we can re-create it.' Her heart lit up with hope.

Bruno put a steadying hand around her shoulder. 'Let's not run away with ourselves. For all we know, Alessandro and Iris might have been influenced by this perfume, rather than the other way around. Without the formula there's no way of knowing the provenance of either scent.'

Stella shook her head. 'I'm too excited to be realistic right now,' she said. 'The similarity to Tradimento is too much of a coincidence. There has to be a link.'

Bruno smiled. 'When I first met you, you wanted concrete proof and hedged your bets. Now you're willing to hitch your wagon to a star.'

She felt the warmth of his hand against her skin. She was taking a leap of faith with the perfumes – why couldn't she do the same thing with Bruno, and tell him how she really felt? Was she just going to let him go without explaining her feelings? But what did she feel? It was impossible to pin it down.

'What's going on here?' a gruff voice said.

Stella turned round, startled. An old man dressed in workman's clothes and pushing a wheelbarrow stood at the side of the barn. He looked strong, despite his age.

'This is private land and, as far as I'm aware, the tour doesn't start for another hour,' he said, glowering at them both.

'I'm sorry,' Stella said, 'We just wanted to know a bit more about the perfume that's made here, Fedeltà a Dio.' She held up the bottle.

'Perfume hasn't been made here for a few years,' the man said. 'We're clearing this barn out to make a prayer room. Although I'd rather use it to store my gardening equipment.'

'You're not a monk then?' Stella asked.

'No, I'm the gardener. Now I suggest you head back to the monastery before you get into trouble. They don't like people wandering the gardens uninvited.'

'It's just that this perfume, Fedeltà a Dio, is remarkably similar to one that we've discovered in Venice,' Bruno said.

The man folded his arms. 'I'm not sure I follow.'

Stella took the nearly empty vial of Tradimento out of her bag and handed it to him. 'We found this in an old perfumery in Venice, and the traces inside are very similar to Fedeltà a Dio.'

The man twisted the vial round in his hand, reading the label carefully. Stella studied his face, his dark brown eyes and the faded scar on his forehead. He unscrewed the lid and inhaled. 'There is a resemblance. Perhaps it's one of the monastery bottles. Tourists used to buy them. The perfumery was in production from the late sixties until recently. I used to grow the ingredients for it here in the gardens. There must be plenty of half-empty bottles of Fedeltà a Dio around.'

'But this one was created in 1939,' Stella said. 'You see, it isn't the only perfume we've found.' She reached into her bag and took out the little bottles, cupping them in her hand. La Scintilla. Primo Bacio. Amanti. The glass bottles glinted in the sunlight.

'Where did you find these?' the man said.

Stella touched each bottle in turn. 'London. Paris. Milan. And as I said, the one you're holding we discovered here in Venice.' She took a deep breath, hoping he could enlighten her. 'Do you know where the formula for Fedeltà a Dio came from? I'm wondering if it was connected to two per-fumers, Iris Penhallam and Alessandro Mori, who visited this place and created the scents.'

The man shook his head. 'I've never heard of those people.'

'Do you think there would be any records?' Stella asked. 'It was September 1939; the war had just started. Alessandro and Iris had embarked on a journey to rescue Jacopo, the nephew of their perfume teacher, Raffaele. Perhaps you were living here then.'

'No, I came here after the war,' he said. 'I can't answer your questions, but I can tell you that there's no link between Fedeltà a Dio and your Tradimento. You're wast-ing your time looking here.'

'How can you be so sure?'

'Like I said, I grew the ingredients. Fedeltà a Dio uses a rose that only grows on this island and in the rose gar-dens of Villa Mocenigo in Alvisopoli, in the province of Venice,' the man explained. 'It's called *Rosa moceniga*, a rare variety from China that was brought over two centuries ago. Lucietta Mocenigo gifted a cutting to the monastery long ago. From what I can tell, Tradimento appears to be missing that vital ingredient.'

Stella reached for the vial and compared it again with the bottle of Fedeltà a Dio. Damn it, the gardener was right. Fedeltà a Dio had a sweetness that gave it an ethereal quality. The hint of scent in the vial was more earthy and intense.

The man took hold of the handles of the wheelbar-row, clearly keen for them to go. 'You should probably be heading back to the monastery. They'll be wondering where you are.'

Stella put the bottles back in her bag, struggling to hide

her disappointment. She'd been so certain the island would hold a clue to Tradimento's composition. 'I'm sorry we interrupted you, Signor . . .'

'My name is Signor Crosera.' He studied Stella. 'It matters greatly to you, finding a formula for your scent?' he asked, an unexpected hint of kindliness in his expression.

'Yes, it does,' Stella said. 'It's an important part of my great-aunt's past.'

'And who is your great-aunt?'

'Iris Penhallam. The woman who helped make the perfumes we found. We've only recently got to know each other, and I was hoping to bring all the perfumes back to her in Paris.'

Signor Crosera stared at Stella for a moment. 'I suggest your time is better spent with your great-aunt, instead of running after old perfumes from the past,' he said. 'Now if you don't mind, I still have a great deal of work to do.'

'If you remember anything, or if any information comes to light,' Stella said, taking out a receipt from her bag and scribbling on the back, 'here's the address of the retirement home where Iris is staying in Paris.' She gave him the sheet of paper.

Signor Crosera hesitated, then took it and put it in his pocket. 'I can't imagine I'll find anything, but I wish you luck.'

32

Iris – Venice, September 1939

Alessandro used the oars to push the boat off the jetty at Isola del Deserto and into the open water. Nobody heard or saw them leave. Iris kept watch on the island, but the heavy doors of the monastery remained closed.

When they were out of sight, Alessandro started the engine and steered the stolen boat away from Burano, round the back of Isola del Deserto and along the coast past Sant Erasmo, towards the opening where the lagoon met the sea. How long would it be before the Blackshirts realized that she'd gone, taking the suspected fugitives with her? It was unlikely that the monastery possessed a boat as powerful as this one. Hopefully, they had enough of a head start to outrun any pursuit.

Jacopo sat up front with Alessandro, the pair engrossed in conversation. Iris was still unable to take in the fact that he had lied to her. Every now and then he glanced back at her, his expression a mixture of guilt, regret and defiance. Iris looked out over the waves and guessed it must be nearly five o'clock by the dipping of the sun.

'Don't be cross with him,' Giovanni said. He moved around the bench and came to sit next to Iris. 'Britain is a democracy. You can't understand what it's like, growing up under a dictator. Alessandro's never known any different. He was only five when Mussolini came to power.'

'If Alessandro has never known democracy, then how does he know what to fight for?' Iris asked.

Giovanni smiled. 'That's a good question. I suppose my generation has played its part and tried to counter the fascists' educational brainwashing. It hasn't been easy. Many people have prospered under Il Duce. Fascism addresses the need for certainty and national pride. But luckily, people like Francesca and Alessandro recognized that our country could never really be great unless it was free. As long as we pass on that recognition to the next generation, there is hope.'

Iris bit her lip. 'That's all well and good, but I didn't sign up for a cause. I came here because of my loyalty to Raffaele, and because I couldn't bear to think of Jacopo being in danger.'

Up ahead, Jacopo was laughing at something Alessandro had told him. It was good to see the smile break on his face. For a moment, the grief he'd suffered disappeared and he looked like a carefree young boy again.

'They're honourable reasons for coming,' Giovanni said. 'I'm sorry you didn't know the full plan. What would you have chosen if you'd had the full facts available to you?'

'I don't know.' Would she have given up in Lausanne and gone back to Henri? Or turned back in Milan? It was impossible to know, since the choice had never been presented to her. But, deep down, Iris suspected that her desire to escape a future with Henri and her loyalty to Raffaele would have made her choose to come to Venice anyway.

Iris sighed. 'I would have respected Alessandro for taking me into his confidence and giving me the option to choose, although I would still have been upset that he'd told me so late in the day. What pains me now is that there *is* no choice. You are here with us, and our plans to leave Italy are infinitely more precarious.'

Giovanni nodded. 'I know. And for that I am sorry.'

'It's best if we don't travel together,' Iris said. 'We can't risk anything happening to Jacopo.'

'Perhaps that's wise,' Giovanni said. 'But I do not think Alessandro will be persuaded to let you go it alone. From what I've seen, he cares too much for you to let you out of his protection.'

'If he really cared for me so much, he wouldn't have lied about working for Giustizia e Libertà,' said Iris.

'You matter more than you think, Iris,' Giovanni said. 'Bear that in mind, whatever you decide to do next.'

When they arrived in Venice Alessandro brought the boat into the narrow canal by the perfumery. The shadows had lengthened now that the sun had gone down. Jacopo got out first, hesitating by the doorway. Iris climbed on to the jetty and took his hand.

'This must be very difficult,' she said.

He was returning to the place where his mother had been shot, and from where he had fled only a week ago.

'I couldn't save her,' Jacopo said, hiding his face against Iris.

'Oh, my dear, it wasn't your fault,' Iris said, stroking his hair. 'She wouldn't want you to blame yourself.'

Alessandro came over and knelt down next to Jacopo. 'Iris is right. Your mother would be relieved that you're alive. You have no reason to feel guilty.'

Jacopo took hold of Alessandro's hand too. The three of them went inside the perfumery whilst Giovanni secured the boat.

'Why don't we go and see what things you'd like to bring with you from your room? I've got space in my suitcase for a few mementoes,' Iris said, not wanting him to be alone.

Jacopo let go of Alessandro's hand; the boy looked solemn-eyed and older than his years. 'If you don't mind, I'd like to do it myself. I want to say a proper goodbye to everything.'

Iris nodded. She understood that feeling. She'd felt the same when her father died. But it broke her heart that Jacopo had to experience it at such a young age.

'What do you intend to do?' Alessandro asked Iris.

'We'll wait here until it's dark, and then Jacopo and I will go to the station and board the *Orient Express*.'

'I won't let you go alone.'

'It's not up for discussion,' Iris said, unable to meet his eye. 'I'm going to finish off the perfume and, when Jacopo is ready, we'll leave.' She headed to the perfumery before Alessandro could reply and closed the door, a lump in her throat.

Now wasn't the time to discuss how she felt. All she wanted was a few minutes of peace after everything that had happened. She took the vial out of her bag and inhaled the fragrance. It met her nostrils with a blast of the fresh notes of bergamot and jasmine. There was no base note yet to balance it out. She smiled bitterly to think that it had been inspired by trust. How empty that word sounded now.

But what would work as a base note? At the monastery, the scent of agarwood had dominated the chapel. She reached for the bottle of oud oil, made from the same source. It smelled of penitence, confession, guilt, which made it the perfect base note to add a darker mood to this scent. Isolo del Deserto was where Iris found out that

Alessandro had betrayed her. His intentions to his country had been honourable enough, but it was still a betrayal nonetheless. She added a few drops. Betrayal. That's what she would call the perfume now.

The door creaked open, and then closed. Iris turned, and there stood Alessandro.

'We can't leave it like this,' he said.

'I have nothing to say,' Iris said, clutching the bottle. 'I'm not sure I would believe anything you told me any more. It feels like from the moment I met you, you've been concealing the truth from me.'

Alessandro came over, his eyes full of anguish. 'Iris, please, you know that's not true. I've told you everything there is to know now.'

'Have you?' she said, staring into his eyes.

Alessandro moved his hand along the bench, almost but not quite touching Iris's fingers. Despite everything, static crackled between them.

'My heart was lost the minute I saw you in Claridge's,' he said. 'I've been fighting it ever since, but it was a losing battle.'

'What are you saying?' Iris said.

Alessandro took hold of her hand. 'I love you,' he said. 'Your talent, your bravery, the way you inspire me with perfume-making – with everything. If it wasn't for this war, and the state of Italy right now, it would be simple. After the annulment is granted, we'd be together, and nothing could stop us. But I have a duty to my country, a duty I decided on long before I met you.'

Iris put the bottle down on the worktop. 'The irony is that I probably would have understood about Giustizia e Libertà, maybe I could have even helped in some way, but you never gave me the chance. If you truly loved me, you would have told me the truth from the beginning and let me fall for the real Alessandro, not just a part of him.'

He bowed his head. 'I know. I made a mistake in thinking you wouldn't want anything to do with me if you knew, and for that I'm sorry. But I mean it, Iris. I love you, and when all this is over, I want us to be together.'

Iris felt her resistance soften. He was still Alessandro after all. Kind, determined, fearless, intelligent. Nothing had changed.

'If that's true, then you need to be honest with me,' she said. 'No more hiding things.'

Alessandro nodded. 'I will, I promise. But you've got to remember, keeping you in the dark was also a way to keep you safe.'

'I'm strong enough to cope with anything, if you are by my side,' Iris said.

Alessandro's eyes lit up with hope. 'Do you mean that?'

'Yes. You see, I love you too,' Iris said, her eyes drawn to the curve of his lips. In the kiss that followed she was lost in a future of possibilities, in the warmth of being cherished, of being near him.

After a moment, Alessandro looked down at the bench. 'What's this you've been making?' he said. He lifted the bottle to his nose and raised his eyebrows. 'I'm not sure I like the direction you've taken this in.'

Iris nudged his elbow. 'It was supposed to be about trust, but then you broke that. I was making something else to express how I felt. I called it Betrayal.'

'Tradimento,' he said gravely. 'I would never betray your trust. I was wrong to conceal the other reason for coming to Venice, but can't you see that I did it to protect you?'

Iris nodded. 'I think so.'

The perfume was all wrong now, in the light of what he'd told her. The oud felt like too much. Iris poured the contents of the bottle into the sink, thinking she could start over. Alessandro snatched the bottle from her just in time, when only a fragment was left.

'What are you doing?' she said. 'I want to make a new accord with you.'

Alessandro smiled and sniffed the drop of scent that remained. 'I actually think the oud works really well. It's the least volatile ingredient and remains on the skin long after the other scents have dissipated. We should add rose as well; their scent wafted across the monastery garden. It will soften the oud.' Alessandro ran his fingers along Iris's cheek. 'That's what I want. For us to remain on each other's skin for ever.'

Iris sighed. 'I hope we can,' she said, thinking of the journey that lay ahead. 'Maybe, through the perfumes, we will.'

Alessandro took the map the girl had drawn out of his pocket, and the bottle containing the remnants of Tradimento, and went over to the wall.

'Francesca used to hide communist pamphlets in here,' he said, working a stone loose to reveal a cavity behind. 'I'll put Tradimento here, along with the map. We'll come back to Venice one day, Iris, when the war is over, and finish this perfume. By then you'll truly see how faithful I've been to you down the years. It will be a perfume of fidelity, not betrayal.'

Iris took his hand, hoping he was right. Everything felt so fraught and uncertain. Would they even survive the war? Would the perfumery still be here? Somehow, his act of hiding the bottle felt like a leap of faith in a world of darkness.

'I hope so,' she said.

'Let's get Jacopo safely to Switzerland, and we'll both return to Paris. We can make this work, Iris.' He kissed her gently on the lips. 'Why don't you tell me how much oud you added, and I'll put the amount into your notebook, and my suggestions for the rose. That way, we won't forget.'

Iris handed him the notebook and leaned against his shoulder as he wrote down the figures. She loved the sight of his writing next to hers. If only everything could be as simple as this.

'*Tutti fuori*,' harsh voices shouted. Alessandro and Iris sprang apart. There was a clatter of boots out in the court-yard, and the sound of neighbours crying out. The furore could only mean one thing. Blackshirts. Iris stared at Alessandro in alarm.

'Get Jacopo,' Alessandro said. 'We've got to get out.'

Iris stuffed the notebook in her bag and ran through the apartment. Jacopo stood in his room, clutching his teddy bear, his face hollow at the loud noises. He'd been through this before, on the night his mother was killed. Iris took his hand. 'Don't worry, we're going to escape. Everything is going to be all right.'

'Giovanni is going to take you and Jacopo to the station,' Alessandro said, coming into the room with Iris's suitcase and travelling perfumer case. 'I'll create a distraction.'

'We can take the boat and all go together,' Iris said, not wanting to be parted from him.

'The boat's too conspicuous. They'll hear the engine. Head upstairs to the rooftops, and on to the next building.'

Iris grasped his arm. 'But you'll get caught.'

Alessandro shook his head. 'I want to be sure you get away. Don't worry, I'll meet you at the station before the *Orient Express* departs, I promise.'

'Come on,' Giovanni said, rushing in with his bag. 'We need to go.'

Iris kissed Alessandro briefly on the lips, then she followed Giovanni and Jacopo out of the apartment and up the stairs. Alessandro headed through the hall and into the courtyard.

'Move aside,' Iris heard one of the Blackshirts say.

There were sounds of a scuffle as Alessandro delayed the Blackshirts' advance. Iris, Giovanni and Jacopo fled upstairs to the rooftop, crossing the tiles to a ladder on the side of a neighbouring building. They climbed down, out on to the street, away from the perfumery.

Iris grabbed Giovanni's arm. 'We can't just leave him.'

'Don't worry. I'm sure Alessandro knows these streets like the back of his hand. He'll be all right.'

Iris wasn't so sure, but there was no going back now, and she had to keep Jacopo out of danger. Not daring to look back, Iris kept hold of Jacopo's hand and followed Giovanni through the busy streets towards the train station.

At last, they reached Santa Lucia. It was crowded with people who barely gave them a second glance. Giovanni led Iris and Jacopo towards the platform, where Tommaso was waiting.

'Where is Alessandro?' he asked.

'Coming soon, we hope,' Iris said. 'Meanwhile, we need to get on the *Orient Express*.'

The huge engine was already puffing steam, ready to go. They climbed up the steps into the train.

'You and Jacopo will be in a compartment,' Tommaso said to Iris. 'A governess and her student. Giovanni and Alessandro are going to be working with me as employees on the *Orient Express*. The uniform will make them invisible, and I can keep them safe.'

After depositing Giovanni in an empty compartment with a spare uniform, Tommaso took Iris to a carriage a couple of doors down. 'We leave in twenty minutes,' he said. 'Stay out of sight, and I'll let you know when we're on the move.' He pulled the blinds down. 'Keep the door locked, okay?'

After he'd gone, Iris locked the door. Jacopo was shaking uncontrollably. She needed to calm him down.

'What if Alessandro doesn't make it in time?' Jacopo said.

Iris didn't dare think about that. 'He'll be here,' she said, praying that he would.

Iris and Jacopo sat very still, listening as footsteps passed by their carriage and excited voices spoke. Iris couldn't relax, afraid that someone might find them here, and terrified that Alessandro wouldn't make it. Eventually, the noise died down. A whistle blew outside.

'We're about to go,' Iris said, unable to hide the panic in her voice. There was still no sign of Alessandro. They couldn't leave without him.

'Wait here,' she told Jacopo. She ran along the corridor and yanked down the window. Maybe if she could see him, she could get the train to stop. She hung her head out of the window, craning to see across the station.

'It's all right, Iris, I'm here,' a voice behind her said.

Alessandro. She turned around. There he was – he had a black eye and cuts on his cheeks. But he was here, and smiling at her. She flung her arms around him. 'You made it!'

'I managed to fight them off and then run. I wasn't far behind you, but the streets were busy, and I jumped onboard just as they blew the whistle,' he said.

'Thank God.' Her heart lifted with elation. They'd done it. Rescued Jacopo. Got on the train. They were as good as free and on their way back to Switzerland.

33

Stella – Venice to Lausanne, August 1996

The next morning, Stella went downstairs for breakfast feeling despondent. It seemed the only course of action now was to return to Paris. Tradimento would be forever unknowable without a proper sample of the liquid and without the missing notebook.

Bruno was already there in the kitchen. He poured her some orange juice. 'How are you feeling?' he said, kissing her forehead.

'I'm disappointed that Fedeltà a Dio and Tradimento don't match up,' she said.

She leaned against the kitchen counter, taking in the homely scene. Stella had got used to seeing Bruno every day, close enough to reach out and touch. What would it be like when they got back to Paris and everything was different again?

'I think it's a mistake to be put off by what Signor Crosera said. Whatever he thinks, Fedeltà a Dio shares the same antecedent as Tradimento,' Bruno said. 'With Iris's help, you can work on it.'

Stella smiled and touched his arm. 'I wouldn't have got far on this search without you,' she said. 'Do you think you've got enough material yet for your book?'

'Almost. Can you remember what the last scent was?' he asked.

'I can remember the name,' Stella said, thinking back to the notebook. 'It was called Solo Tu, but there were only a few lines of description. Maybe the scent was never made.'

'Only You. I wonder what the story behind it was. Maybe Iris can help with that scent too,' he said.

Stella shrugged. 'I'm not sure yet how much I can rely on her. She's still recovering from the fire and reluctant about delving into the past.'

'You know you can rely on me,' Bruno said. He took Stella's glass and placed it on the table. 'I called Harvard to say that I don't want to take the post. Not at the moment. They've agreed to let me defer it for a year. I'm going to travel back to Paris with you.'

Stella's eyes widened. 'Is that what you want?'

Bruno cupped Stella's face. 'I turned the job down not just because I need to stay close to Anna and my mum, I also want to discover what you and I could have together. If that's what you'd like too?'

His words made Stella's head spin. It was all happening so fast.

Bruno caught sight of her expression and smiled. 'Don't worry, I'm not trying to rush you into something. You've got lots to sort out in London, and I'll be working here, but we can at least see each other. No pressure.'

Stella smiled. 'Well, maybe a little bit of pressure. I know your decision not to go to the States yet isn't solely based on me, but I don't want you to regret it.'

He kissed her mouth and she sank into the warmth of his embrace, his firm lips on hers, his body pressed against her, his hand moving on her back.

'I don't want to let you go,' he whispered. 'Let's just see where this takes us.'

Stella's heart lifted. A new beginning. Who knew where it would lead, but for now, Bruno had chosen her, and she was glad of it.

Stella sat down in the plush velvet seat on the *Orient Express* and watched as Bruno said goodbye to his mum. He'd promised her they'd come back soon, and that next time he'd take Stella to visit Anna. He gave his mum one last embrace, then climbed aboard the train.

The guard blew the whistle and they started to move. As the train headed over the Ponte della Libertà, Stella rested her head against Bruno's shoulder. She had everything she could wish for. The three completed scents were in her bag. Iris was waiting for her in Paris and could hopefully help with Tradimento and Solo Tu. And she had Bruno.

On the mainland, the landscape sped past: red-roofed houses, churches clinging to hilltops, and endless vineyards. Bruno worked on his book while Stella let her thoughts wander, glad of this time to think about everything. It was strange to do the journey in reverse. To pass through Italy towards the Alps.

The train stopped in Milan to load on supplies. There was a knock at the door of Stella and Bruno's compartment.

'Shall we just ignore that?' Bruno whispered.

'Gladly,' Stella said, stretching out her legs.

But the conductor called out. 'Mademoiselle Penhallam, I have news of the notebook. Please could you disembark for a moment. The railway police would like to speak to you.'

Iris's notebook. Stella sprang up and opened the door. 'Have they found it?'

'If you could please come with me,' the conductor said.

'It should only take a few minutes. We're refuelling anyway, so there is time.'

Stella and Bruno followed the conductor off the train. Pigeons fluttered up towards the vast glass ceiling. Voices echoed in the cavernous station.

Bruno touched her arm. 'Stella, there's something I need to explain.'

'Can we talk about it later?' Stella said. There was no time now. She hurried after the conductor. He led the way to the railway office. Stella walked in and stared in surprise. There was James, sitting next to one of the policemen. 'What are you doing here?' she said.

'I flew out as soon as I could,' James said. 'GPL was offered a notebook for sale. It was on sale for an extortionate amount. I saw the Penhallam name on it, and knew I had to get it for you.' He opened his briefcase and took out a parcel.

Stella took the parcel in her hands, pulling back the paper. There it was. Iris's notebook. She showed it to Bruno. His face was pale. 'Thank God it's been found,' he said.

'How did you get this?' Stella said to James. In another room, a telephone rang. The air smelled of smoke and a half-full ashtray stood in the centre of the table.

'It was stolen by a dealer, Jacob Williams. He works for a collector who felt that the man he'd sent to do the job was not getting on with it as requested. Once he got the notebook and saw it was incomplete and without the formulas, the collector instructed Jacob to offer it to us for the highest price. GPL didn't want to buy it, but I knew how much it would mean to you. So, I bought it, as a peace offering.'

'You did?' Stella said.

'I felt so bad for telling Andrea and making things harder

for you at Penhallam's, I thought this might be a way to make it up to you.'

'Thanks, James, but I can't possibly accept it as a gift. I will pay you back, I promise. I'm so grateful that you've found it.'

Bruno rubbed the back of his neck. 'Stella, if I could just talk to you alone for a moment.'

'I don't think that's a good idea,' James said.

Stella looked between the two men. 'What's going on?'

'This collector is notorious in the perfume world for finding limited editions, forgotten texts and then spinning them back into the market,' James said. 'He collects to make a profit, not for the sake of the perfume.'

'I don't understand. You said that this man Jacob was sent by the collector to take the notebook after someone else had failed to do the job.'

Bruno groaned. 'Please, Stella . . .'

'Just let James explain,' Stella said.

'I had a chat with the collector, and he was happy to tell me what happened if I paid over the odds for the notebook. You see, the collector had first of all commissioned another man, an esteemed researcher and professor about whom no one would have any doubts or questions.'

'Who?' she asked, fearing the answer.

'Stella, it was me,' Bruno said, his eyes hollow and his face pale. 'When I accepted the job, I'd never met you. I had no personal connection with Penhallam's. I needed the money for Anna and thought I would wrestle with the moral dilemma if it ever came to it. But when I met you—'

'You,' Stella said, her voice barely a whisper. She couldn't take it in. Bruno had betrayed her. 'You said you were researching a book.'

'I was, I am . . .' Bruno said. 'But I was also doing this job for the collector at the same time. I thought I could balance both tasks and stay on your side. But it soon became obvious that I couldn't. That's why I rang the collector in Paris and told him it was off, I couldn't do it . . .'

Stella stared at him. That must have been the conversation she overheard in Paris, when he'd been talking on the telephone. All that time. Why hadn't he told her sooner? Just a moment ago they'd been so close. Now he was a stranger.

'You should have told me,' Stella said.

'I was going to tell you when we got back to Paris, I promise. I was too afraid to do it sooner, too afraid of losing you. I only hope that I can make you understand.'

Stella turned away. This was getting out of hand. She'd let her feelings for Bruno blind her, and now he'd let her down. Just like James had done. She should have kept her distance.

'It's too late for that now,' Stella said. She gathered up the notebook. 'I think I'd better return to the train, and perhaps you should go back to Venice. We can't continue this journey together any more.'

'I'll travel back with you,' James said. 'I don't want to leave you in this state.'

'Please, Stella, I beg you, give me a chance to explain,' Bruno said.

The desperation in his voice broke her heart but, right now, all she wanted to do was to get away. 'I don't know if that's possible,' Stella said, her voice catching, 'I'm sorry.'

Stella sat quietly in the compartment, watching the scenery of France flash by. After the revelation about Bruno she'd cried her eyes out, curled up on the seat, wishing the world would disappear. The rocking of the train must have lulled her to sleep. The oblivion had been blissful. But now came the pain of Bruno's betrayal, raw and throbbing.

James came in, his eyes full of pity. 'How are you feeling? Bruno looked wretched when we left him Milan, but to be fair, he should have told you how things stood. It looks like you became more than just work colleagues on this trip.'

Stella looked away. 'I suppose we did.'

Part of her still yearned to see him. Perhaps he could say something that would make things right again, although she doubted it was possible.

'I'm sorry about all of this,' James said, sitting down next to her.

'It's not your fault.'

'I shouldn't have told GPL about House of Fraser. It's made things harder for you.'

Stella patted his hand. 'Things were already hard. I made each decision by myself: taking out the loans, asking GPL to invest – everything happened because I decided it. If GPL hadn't invested, Penhallam's would have been finished.'

James shook his head. 'I don't understand how you can sound so calm.'

'Because I gave it my best shot,' Stella said with a shrug. 'It might not be enough to save Penhallam's, but at least I tried. I don't think my father or grandfather would blame me for that.'

'Well, Penhallam's is still there. At least you can come back now and negotiate with GPL on where we take things next. A total rebrand seems most likely, but if you come to the meeting, maybe you can convince Andrea otherwise.'

A rebrand. A new direction. Penhallam's would never really be hers, not now she'd opened the door to GPL.

Stella shook her head. 'The Penhallam's you're describing wouldn't be mine.'

'What are you saying?'

'That maybe it's time I considered selling Penhallam's and using the money to start something of my own. I've spent this whole trip far away from the one person who could actually tell me about what happened in 1939.'

'You mean Iris.'

Stella nodded. It was time to go back and get to know her great-aunt. Bruno was gone and there was nothing she could do to bring him back.

34

Iris – Venice to Lausanne, September 1939

Jacopo arranged the perfume ingredients in a row on the little table by the window. The glass bottles clinked together as the train rattled across northern Italy. 'When will we get to Switzerland?' he asked.

Iris put out her hand to stop one of the bottles sliding off. 'In a few hours, I hope. Raffaele and I have talked about you often, remembering those lovely summers in Mougins.'

Jacopo lifted out the bottles of Primo Bacio and Amanti, reading the labels. 'What are these?'

'Alessandro and I have been creating a series of scents for Raffaele, inspired by our journey. You can smell them if you like.'

Jacopo inhaled each one. 'They're lovely,' he said. His face crumpled and tears sprang to his eyes. 'They remind me of Mamma. Of all the scents she created. She won't be able to make them any more.'

'Oh, Jacopo.' Iris put her arms around the boy while he sobbed. All the tears he'd not had a chance to shed, the grief he'd not been able to feel, came out. He shuddered in Iris's arms, but she stayed silent, knowing from her own experience of grief that all he needed was a safe place to release the emotion.

At last, he lifted his head and wiped his face. 'I'm sorry.'

Iris shook her head. 'Never be sorry for showing how

you feel. This won't be the last time you cry for her, Jacopo, but, I promise, it will get easier eventually.'

He leaned his head against her shoulder, clearly worn out. Iris held him close and, as the train rocked back and forth, his eyes grew heavy and he fell asleep.

'Things are progressing well,' Alessandro said, bringing in a tray of food. Iris held her fingers to her lips and motioned to Jacopo.

'We'll be nearing the Swiss border in an hour or so,' Alessandro said, lowering his voice. 'That will be the test. Giovanni and I will wait in the stock room while Tommaso does the paperwork with the border guards. Let's pray there's no trouble.'

'And if there is?' Iris whispered back.

'Then we'll deal with it.' He squeezed her hand.

The alpine mountains crept closer. Iris was relieved, but also afraid. They had to get Jacopo safely across.

The train climbed higher and higher, snow dusting the surrounding landscape. Jacopo woke up and ate the food hungrily. The train began to slow. Iris pulled the blinds down in preparation for crossing the border. Hopefully Alessandro and Giovanni were safely out of sight. The carriage stopped with a clunk.

Iris stood by the window. It was tempting to pull back the blind to see what was happening, but that would be too risky.

'What's going on?' Jacopo whispered.

'I don't know,' Iris said. 'It's very quiet out there.'

She listened carefully, her neck taut. Something wasn't right.

'You need to hide,' Iris said. 'Just in case.'

Jacopo looked around the tiny compartment. 'Where? There's nowhere to go.'

'Under the seat there's a storage space where they keep the spare blankets. It's small, but you must get inside.'

Jacopo squeezed himself into the space and Iris put the bed back down.

Tommaso knocked on the door and came in. 'Nobody has boarded the train yet. I don't know why. I've been told to wait inside with the documents. Prepare yourselves.'

'I've hidden Jacopo under here,' Iris said. 'If anything happens, please get him safely to Raffaele.'

Tommaso nodded. 'Understood. Sit tight, Iris. Let's hope this is just railway company business and nothing else.' He closed the door.

Iris stood by the door, listening. Eventually she heard voices. Some men had boarded. She could hear them shouting at the other end of the carriage.

Gradually, the voices came nearer. 'Leave this one to me,' a familiar voice said. 'I don't want her mixed up in all of this. I've paid you well enough, and there's more if this concludes to my satisfaction.'

Henri. Iris put her hand on her chest. It couldn't be. What was he doing here? There was a tap at the door, and then it opened. Henri stood there, his coat over his shoulders, a cigarette in his hand. Behind him stood a man in a smart grey suit and three blackshirt thugs.

'Iris,' he said, his face visibly relieved. 'Thank God.' He turned to the men. 'Give me a minute with her. I'll get the information you need.'

The grey-suited man nodded. 'We'll be here, waiting. Be quick about it.'

Henri came into the compartment and shut the door. He stubbed his cigarette out in the sink. 'Christ, Iris, do you know what lengths I've been to to find you? Charles is frantic with worry, especially after your telegram from Milan.'

'You told him?' Iris said. 'I asked you not to.'

'And I respected your wishes, but as the days went by and there was no sign of you, I had to let him know. You sent that strange telegram about not wanting to get married and then disappeared. I've been worried sick. Your actions have consequences for those that love you, Iris, or did you forget that?'

'I'm sorry,' she said. 'I didn't mean to worry you all.'

Henri pursed his lips. 'I know you didn't set off on this trip just for the perfumes.'

'What do you mean?'

'Raffaele telegrammed me,' Henri said, straightening up. 'I was the only person he could think of with enough influence and motivation to sort this mess out. He had reports that his sister had not made it to Milan, and he was also desperately worried about your whereabouts. And that of his nephew. I was very displeased to hear that Raffaele was no longer chaperoning you and Alessandro, so I made it my business to get out here straight away.' He took hold of her shoulders, his grip firm. 'I've moved heaven and earth to find you, Iris. I hope you realize that.'

There was a bang on the door. 'Hurry up, we haven't got all day.'

'Why are those men outside?' Iris said, glancing fearfully at the door.

Henri ignored her question. 'I knew it was a mistake to let you come on your own. Look at how your bid for independence has turned out. Naivety and ignorance are dangerous things in a war, Iris. Apparently, Alessandro is wanted by the authorities in Italy. So is the man who is believed to be accompanying him, Giovanni Pascarella. You're guilty by association of harbouring and abetting known communists.'

Iris stared at him in panic. 'What are they going to do?'

Henri touched her cheek. 'I can make sure you're not embroiled in any of this. They only want Alessandro and Giovanni.' He looked pointedly at the under-the-bed storage. 'If you tell me where they are, no one will need to know anything about the stowaway you have hidden in there.'

'They don't know about Jacopo?' Iris whispered.

'Not yet. But the only way we can prevent them from searching this whole train, and your carriage in particular, is if you are willing to cooperate with the authorities.'

Iris's heart went cold. Here it was. The sacrifice he was going to ask of her. She could feel it coming like an avalanche. The choice that would start a succession of choices that would mean that her life, the life she'd dreamed of with Alessandro, would go in an entirely different direction.

'Tell me what I need to do,' she said, her voice flat. She'd come to Italy to save Jacopo. At all costs, she had to ensure he made it out alive.

Henri cupped her face, speaking slowly, as if to a child. 'It's simple. Just tell me, are they on this train?'

Iris hesitated. This couldn't be happening.

'Think of Jacopo,' Henri said. 'We can get him to Lausanne, you and I, but not unless you give those thugs outside what they want. Surely you don't have any loyalty to Alessandro. Not after he's dragged you into this mess with no thought for your safety or Jacopo's.'

Another bang came on the door. 'One more minute and we search the room,' the man shouted.

Iris tried to think. Everything felt so jumbled in her head. Jacopo was the innocent party in all of this. He was just a child. Alessandro had knowingly taken a risk by working for Giustizia e Libertà alongside the mission to rescue Jacopo. But still, her heart fractured at the thought of what she was about to do.

'For God's sake, Iris, we don't have much time.'

'They're on this train,' she said. The words felt detached from her mouth, as if they didn't belong to her.

'Good. Where are they?'

Iris opened her mouth, then stopped. She couldn't do it. She couldn't betray the man she loved, no matter what he'd done. The words just wouldn't come out. 'I can't . . .' she said, hanging her head.

'Yes, you damn well can,' Henri replied. 'That boy has a chance of life. Do you want to be responsible for his capture? Do you want to tell Raffaele that when you had a chance to save him, you didn't, because of some misguided feelings towards that scoundrel Alessandro? He's played you, Iris, don't you see? He never cared for you, not really. Men of that class don't know what it means to love – they don't have the refinement, or the morals. Do you want to save a man like that over Jacopo?'

The door burst open and the grey-suited man came in, followed by the Blackshirts. 'Time's up. I'm afraid we'll need to arrest your fiancée and search her compartment if she's not going to help us, as you promised.'

'She'll help you, won't you, Iris?' Henri said desperately. 'Tell them what they need to hear.'

Iris closed her eyes. Would Alessandro understand the pressure she was under? What would he do in her place? There was no choice. She had to save Jacopo. There was no alternative. These men were seconds away from ripping the compartment apart and finding him. She had to betray Alessandro.

'They're dressed as *Orient Express* staff,' she whispered. 'In the stock room. That's where you'll find them.'

The grey-suited man gestured to the Blackshirts. 'Take them off the train. I'll deal with them in a minute.' He turned back to Iris. 'We understand there's a perfume notebook in which Alessandro has been recording information to pass on to associates in Paris. We arrested a barman in Milan who talked under duress. I need that book now.'

Iris glanced at her bag. The perfume notebook. 'But that's impossible,' she said. 'It just contains my perfume notes. Nothing else.'

The man held out his hand. 'Let me see.'

Iris hesitated. All their hard work. She couldn't just hand it over. Henri picked up her bag and took out the notebook. 'For God's sake, Iris, just do as the man says. I've paid a lot of money to bribe them. I want us to get out in one piece.'

The man flicked through the notebook.

'But I need the book to make the perfumes,' Iris said.

'I'll only take out the bits I need,' the man said. He scoured the pages, then ripped out the parts that contained the formulas.

'But they're just measurements for ingredients,' Iris said, confused.

The man shook his head. 'On the contrary. Some of these numbers represent a code. See the way the digits are slanted differently. Most likely, it contains the names of those loyal to the anti-fascist cause and the locations of safehouses.'

'I had no idea,' Iris said. Her legs felt weak. All this, hidden among the perfumes they'd created, and he hadn't told her. Each page was a piece of evidence damning Alessandro.

'I told you,' Henri said. 'Iris was duped.'

The man nodded. 'Very well,' he said. 'You can bring her with you back to Paris. We're grateful for your assistance in this matter, Monsieur Levèque.'

Iris went to the window of the compartment. Alessandro and Giovanni had been hauled out next to the tracks. They stood in the snow with their hands resting on top of their heads.

'What's going to happen to them?' Iris said.

The grey-suited man shrugged. 'Officially, we'll say they resisted and tried to kill us, so it was only fair that we retaliated and shot them dead. Unofficially, my men will take them into the woods and finish them off.'

Iris wheeled round. 'No,' she said. 'Please, you can't kill him.'

'It's too late. I've already given the order. They'll wait until the train pulls off, of course. There's no point distressing the passengers more than we already have done.'

He nodded to Henri and went out of the compartment.

'Please, Henri, I beg you. This can't happen.'

Henri lit another cigarette. 'There's nothing I can do, Iris,' he said. 'You have to let him go.'

Iris turned towards him. 'Please, can't you do something for him? Prison – anything, just don't let him be killed.'

Henri sighed. 'I've already spent enough money on this trip without wasting it on saving that renegade,' he said. He inspected Iris, seeming to weigh up his options. 'But maybe I can persuade them to send him to a prison camp.

I have the funds. It just depends on what you are willing to do to secure his life.'

'What do you mean?'

Henri sucked on the cigarette and sent plumes of smoke into the air. 'I still want you to marry me. We can do it right away, in Lausanne. Charles will be so relieved, Penhallam's will have a steady source of income, and you . . . well, my dear, I will ensure you run the most successful perfumery in Paris,' Henri said, his eyes fixed on hers. 'Marry me, and then I will pay them to spare Alessandro.'

'Marry you?' Iris said. He still wanted her, after everything that had happened. She'd given herself to Alessandro, her heart, her body – how could she now marry Henri?

'It's a simple choice. Either you marry me, or Alessandro dies.'

Iris stared at him in dismay. There had been no mention of love. It was almost as if he was asking her to undertake a business transaction. 'This is what you ask of me?' she said.

'Indeed. Now, I need your answer quickly if I'm to prevent his death.'

What else could she do? Henri had money, power and influence. Iris had none. The only way to save the man she loved was to marry Henri. Iris nodded. 'Then I will do it. Everything you ask. I beg you, stop him from being killed.'

Henri kissed her forehead and went out after the grey-suited man. Iris swallowed and watched out of the window. She saw Henri talking to the man, further up the track. He took out some money and handed it to him. They both shook hands. Then she forced herself to look at Alessandro. He was staring at the ground, but at that moment he looked up at Iris. She placed her palm flat on the glass window, wishing she could touch him, longing to hold him in her arms, to take him away from this place to the life they'd dreamed of.

But he looked at her with such despair in his eyes that Iris gasped. He knew that she had betrayed him to the fascists. There was no love in his eyes, only pain. He shook his head a little, then closed his eyes. He didn't want to see her. If only she could explain and tell him why she'd done it, but the train was starting to move. She banged on the window, calling his name. But his eyes remained shut, as if he'd vowed never to look at her again. There was nothing she could do for him any more. The train picked up speed. Alessandro receded into the distance. It was over. He was gone. The final betrayal belonged to her.

Solo Tu
(Only You)

Top Note
Petitgrain

ରେ

Heart Note
Neroli

ରେ

Base Note
Iris

ରେ

35

Iris – Lausanne, October 1939

Iris stepped off the *Orient Express* on to the platform at Lausanne. Jacopo gripped her hand tightly, looking around at the hustle and bustle. She could only imagine how frightening it had been for him, waiting in the darkness of the underbed storage and hearing every word. After the ordeal, when the train was safely over the border into Switzerland and Henri had gone to the bar for a drink, she sat holding Jacopo, talking him through each perfume, hoping that he would find it as calming as she did. All the while, she couldn't get the harrowed expression on Alessandro's face out of her mind.

Now, Iris waited, gathering Jacopo close to her, anxiously looking out for Henri, who had gone to telephone Raffaele. Tommaso came over and stopped briefly. He had escaped detection and probably didn't want to draw attention to himself.

'Don't blame yourself,' he muttered. 'You had no choice. One day, please God, Alessandro will see that.' He nodded and walked off to help the other passengers with their luggage. Iris was grateful for his words but knew that nothing could erase the sense of guilt in her heart.

Henri emerged from the crowds. 'He's going to meet us at the hotel,' he said. 'Your uncle is hugely relieved that you're here safe and sound.' He ruffled Jacopo's hair and forced a smile at the boy.

'Thank you,' Iris said. There had been no time to talk to Henri since he'd paid off the Italian authorities to spare Alessandro's life. She had been so consumed with thoughts of Alessandro, the reality of what she'd agreed to hadn't yet sunk in.

Henri took her hand, looking sleek and successful in his camel coat and hat, and they walked towards the hotel. Iris's body felt leaden. It was impossible to think straight. She'd tried being independent and stepping away from the bonds of her family, but look where that had got her. If Henri hadn't been there, if he hadn't come to look for her – Iris and Jacopo might have been arrested too – or worse, they could all be dead. But then the cold dread hit her. Was it Henri who'd led the fascist police to them?

He noticed her stare, leaned down and whispered in her ear. 'You won't regret marrying me, my love.' And he lifted her hand and kissed it, his bristly moustache tickling her skin. Iris suppressed the urge to pull her hand away.

'Why were you on the train?' she asked.

'I told you,' Henri said. 'I'd travelled to the Swiss-Italian border, hoping to find you.'

'And were those men part of your plan?' Iris said, fearing her question would anger him.

Henri laughed. 'Don't be ridiculous. It was just a coincidence.' Then his smile disappeared. 'You should be grateful that I was there to protect you. You owe me a great deal,' he said. His tone was unexpectedly sharp. Then he smiled, and the moment passed.

When they entered the hotel lobby Jacopo gave out a cry. There, leaning on his walking stick and looking in much better health, was Raffaele, tears in his eyes, his arms opened wide to gather up the boy who ran over and flung himself into his uncle's arms. Raffaele hugged him tightly and smiled at Iris over Jacopo's head. 'Well done,' he said, 'I can't believe you've managed it.'

Iris smiled sadly. 'Not quite, Alessandro has been captured,' she said. 'And did you hear about Francesca?'

Raffaele nodded, still clutching Jacopo. 'A letter came from Milan, telling us what had happened. I guessed that you and Alessandro had continued on to Venice, but I had no idea. Henri was already planning to travel into Italy to find you. I had to confide in him and let him know about the plan to rescue Jacopo.' He turned to Henri, who was still holding Iris's hand firmly. 'I'd underestimated you, Henri. I'm very grateful for all that you've done.'

Henri bowed his head. 'You're welcome. I hope I've proven myself to you now, and that we can conclude that business of which we spoke.'

Raffaele nodded. 'Of course. I've arranged it with the embassy and my contact, Isabella, is willing to act as witness, on both fronts.'

'What business?' Iris said.

'Raffaele is taking the sensible course of action and travelling with Jacopo to America. I've persuaded him that you are the person in whom to temporarily entrust the running of his perfumery while he is away. I've had the contract drawn up. All he has to do is sign.'

'But . . .' Iris said, frowning.

'Come on, let's leave them to their reunion, Iris,' Henri said. 'We've got a wedding to plan.'

Up in the sumptuous hotel suite that Henri had booked Iris surveyed the ivory satin dress that was laid out for her.

'You'll feel better if you change out of those clothes and into something decent,' Henri said. 'I'll run you a bath.'

Iris caught sight of herself in the mirror. She looked incongruous in her grubby white blouse and plain blue skirt, but she couldn't bear to take them off. She'd been wearing them the last time she saw Alessandro. She smoothed out the skirt. Iris hated herself and knew that she would feel that way until things could be put right. But how could that ever be done?

The sound of running water came from the bathroom. Iris opened her travelling perfumer's case and looked at the three bottles of perfume. Tradimento, left behind in Venice, would never be finished, but at least she had these. She took out La Scintilla. It was the first one, a scent that represented the start of everything, the promise of what was to come.

She unscrewed the lid and held the bottle up to her nose, inhaling the fragrance. It was almost too painful to bear.

The running water stopped abruptly. Iris placed the bottle back into the case, waiting for Henri to come back in.

'It's piping hot,' he said.

'This isn't going to work, Henri.'

He squared his shoulders. 'We've already talked it through. It's what you agreed.'

'I had no choice. If I hadn't promised to marry you, then Alessandro . . .' She trailed off, unable to imagine it.

'Then Alessandro would be dead,' Henri said, finishing the sentence for her in calm, measured tones. 'Yes, that's right. And if you change your mind and renege on our agreement, then I'm afraid he might still be killed.'

There was the sharpness again. Henri's eyes were steely.

'You can't do that,' she said.

Henri came over to her. The coldness in his eyes hadn't relented. Iris took a step back, her heart thumping. He took hold of her wrists. His iron grip made her gasp.

'You're my fiancée, Iris. That was on the cards long before Alessandro came along,' he said. 'Surely you want Alessandro to live?'

Had he secretly always been like this, underneath his charming, kind exterior, or was it only now that he had cause to be jealous that this other Henri – controlling and possessive – had emerged?

'Of course,' she said, straining under his grasp.

'Then you know what to do.' Henri let go of Iris and turned to adjust his jacket in the mirror.

Iris drew in ragged breaths, waiting, fear entering her heart now that she knew this new, bolder Henri was here to stay.

'Please, Henri, have some pity. Not like this, I beg you,' she whispered. 'You could have any woman. Why me?'

Henri sighed. 'You know why. Your talent as a perfumer is unparalleled.'

'But it doesn't have to be marriage? I could work for you instead.'

Henri shook his head. 'An employment contract is not quite as binding as a marriage one,' he said. 'I love you, Iris, and I want us to get married. More importantly, Raffaele wants you to run his perfumery for him. Jewish laws are tightening. Many Jewish businesses are taking on Aryan partners. If I am married to you, then it means that I will be involved with the perfumery too. You know how much I've always wanted to have one. This will be the next best thing.' He waved his hand. 'At least, until Raffaele is able to return to Europe. But who knows when that will be?'

'But couldn't we wait to get married? Surely it doesn't have to be today,' Iris said, desperately wondering how she could change his mind.

'Oh, but it does,' he said. 'Raffaele intends to do the paperwork to hand over the perfumery before he goes to America. If we're not married, you'd be a woman of independent means, and I can't have that.'

Iris stared at him. 'Henri, I don't recognize you,' she said. 'Why are you behaving this way?'

'You left quite a mess behind when you disappeared to Venice,' Henri said, his voice hardening. 'Your brother doesn't know the full extent, but I could always inform him. Travelling unchaperoned around Italy. Your honour compromised. What man would have you now?'

'Please, don't tell Charles anything,' Iris said.

'No, of course I won't tell him, because we are going to be married, head back to Paris and you are going to make Raffaele's perfumery a success,' he said. He touched her cheek with his fingertips, almost as if he pitied her. 'There's no way out, Iris, because the last thing you want is to disappoint your family and let your beloved Alessandro die.'

Iris stared at Henri. What he said was true. The mess was all her fault, and now she was trapped. There'd be no escaping Henri until the war one day ended, and even then . . .

'Very well,' she said, her voice sounding far away. It was as if the room and her place in it were only a figment of her imagination. 'I won't argue any more.'

Henri smiled, took her hand gently and brought her over to the bed. 'You know, we'll have a good life,' he said. He pulled her on to his knee and brushed the hair out of her eyes. 'And you never really loved him, did you, not like you loved me?'

Iris winced at Henri's touch, but stayed still, not wanting to anger him. 'No,' she said, for it was the truth. She had adored Henri when she was too young to know better: dazzled by him, and unquestioning. The love she'd come to feel for Alessandro was quite different.

'Good,' Henri said, undoing the buttons on her blouse. She wanted to push him away but was too afraid. His arms gripped tightly around her waist. 'All you have to do is give yourself to me, be a devoted wife and an outstanding perfumer, and I'll take care of everything else.'

His hand moved lower, loosening her skirt expertly, soft kisses trailing the exposed skin. What choice did she have but to give in? Henri knew what he was doing. He was gentle and seductive, but her heart remained cold. She didn't protest, however, because if she did, she sensed he would force her. His power trembled in the wings, ready to take over if she should give but a murmur of resistance.

He took her hand and led her into the bathroom, where the water steamed, obscuring the mirror and window. 'In you get, my dear,' Henri said, 'I'll wash it all away, and you'll feel better.'

Iris climbed into the bath, the hot water stinging her skin. She lay down, motionless, hair trailing behind her, while Henri rolled up his sleeves. He dipped a flannel into the water and proceeded to scrub her legs, her thighs, her whole body. His strokes alternated between rough and gentle, the heat and his motions making her dizzy. The image of Alessandro's face, white with shock as he stared at her, flooded her mind, and Iris wanted to scream at the horror of it all.

But at that moment, Henri leaned over the side and

kissed her, his lips on hers, his tongue exploring her mouth, smothering her voice. Iris knew then that she would have to do this, she would have to give Henri what he wanted, because if she didn't, the man she loved would die.

36

Stella – Paris, August 1996

Paris felt different without Bruno. Stella closed the door of her hotel room and headed along the corridor. All the promise was gone – the anticipation of seeing him each day, the hope of something more. How could he have ruined all that by not telling her about his involvement with the collector? Stella punched the buttons on the lift. It was such a waste of all they'd experienced together. It had been foolish to fall so easily. Yet the anger was almost comforting, because when it died down, all she would feel was loss.

James hadn't stayed in Paris; instead he'd departed for the Eurostar when the *Orient Express* arrived back at the Gare de Lyon. Stella was grateful to him for returning the notebook, which was now safely stowed in her bag, but it was a relief to see him go. Things were simpler now. It was just Stella and Iris. Perhaps that's how it always should have been.

As she walked along the canal Stella hoped that at least Iris would be pleased to see her again.

'How is she?' Stella said to Monique when she reached the first floor.

Monique smiled. 'She's definitely on the mend. I've noticed a real improvement since you rang from Venice. She's pleased that you've come back and that your focus is on getting to know each other.'

Stella went into Iris's room. The curtains were open, sunlight streaming in and the window ajar, and Iris was sitting in a chair looking at the view. She turned to see who had come in and smiled when she saw it was Stella.

'You're back.' She glanced behind Stella. 'Where's Bruno?'

Stella sat down. 'What you said about trust was very pertinent. It turns out that Bruno had been working for a collector who wanted the perfumes for himself.'

Iris interlaced her fingers. 'Tradimento,' she said. 'I warned you to be careful. I'm sorry, Stella. I suppose this means he is no longer researching his book.'

Stella shrugged. 'I doubt it,' she said. 'I wouldn't give him permission to use what we've discovered so far anyway.'

Iris smiled. Was that a look of relief in her eyes?

'I'm glad,' she said. 'I've no wish to expose myself to criticism and condemnation any more than I have done already. I've managed to live a quiet life since my imprisonment. As you well know, I don't want people digging into my past. But I'm sorry that he betrayed you. You felt a lot for him.'

Iris's eyes were full of understanding as she reached for Stella's hand. Stella sighed. So much for putting on a brave face. The wound was clearly still raw and visible for Iris to see. 'Yes, when trust is broken it's irreparable, I fear. Bruno said he terminated his agreement with the collector not long after we arrived in Paris, once he realized what he was being asked to do, but he was too afraid to tell me about it.'

'Some things are hard to explain,' Iris said. 'Alessandro broke my trust, and I'm afraid I broke his too.'

'What do you mean?' Stella said, hoping Iris would say more. The breeze sent a ripple across the curtains. Traffic hummed outside.

'We went to rescue Jacopo from Venice, but I didn't realize that Alessandro was also doing secret work for the communists, who wanted to free Italy from Mussolini's dictatorship. It led to some complications in Venice.' Iris bit her lip. 'And then, on the journey back to Switzerland, I was forced to betray Alessandro to the authorities to save Jacopo's life. I've never forgiven myself for that.'

It was hard to imagine Iris having to undergo such an ordeal. She still looked frail, a blanket tucked over her legs. 'So, you did get Jacopo out?'

'Yes, thank God, I was able to do that. But in exchange for Alessandro's life, Henri forced me to marry him. He persuaded Raffaele to temporarily entrust the perfumery to me, and by marrying me, it meant he could be involved with the perfumery too. I didn't fully realize it at the time, but that was the start of it.'

'The start of what?' Stella said. She wanted Iris to keep talking. To know everything. Thank goodness she was opening up at last.

Iris tucked a strand of hair behind her ear. 'Of Henri forcefully appropriating Jewish businesses and putting them into my name. I should have kept an eye on things, but I was broken in those years after I married him. All my strength seemed to leave me. I felt like a shadow of myself. All the qualities I'd prized – my determination and, I suppose, a certain stubborn streak – had vanished. Instead, I was so tired I barely noticed what was going on around me. I'd made such a huge mistake in marrying Henri, but there was no way to undo it. My only refuge was in making perfumes.'

Stella sat back in the chair, digesting what Iris had told her. 'I knew you couldn't have been to blame for the crimes for which you were sentenced.'

'Maybe not directly. But I should have paid closer attention. That was the story of our marriage – Henri attended to the business side; I looked after the perfumes. It was all I'd ever been interested in. But it meant I was ignorant of what Henri was up to. I was too beset by grief and remorse to care, but I shouldn't have blindly signed the papers he put in front of me.'

Iris reached over and patted Stella's hand. Her skin was papery soft. 'Anyway, that's all in the past now. I'm so relieved you've broken free from Penhallam's. It sounds like you're about to begin an exciting chapter in your life. My sense of smell is frustratingly poor, but I've decided I will help you all I can once I'm better.'

Stella took her hand and squeezed it. 'Thank you,' she said. 'There's so much I want to learn from you. I want to work on the perfumes you made with Alessandro. I've got an idea to launch them with my own scents, based on the experiences of my journey. A collection called Past and Present. And your notebook has been recovered.' She took it out of her bag. 'Here it is. I want to make the last perfume with you, Solo Tu, and then the collection will be complete.'

The clouds covered the sun and the room filled with shadow. Iris clasped her silver locket. 'I don't think I can do that.'

'Why not?'

'I'm happy to work on new ideas, but I can't reawaken old wounds,' she said. 'That whole period during the war was very painful, and what came after isn't something I want to remember.'

'I want to do something about that too,' Stella said eagerly. 'It's clear that you were coerced into taking responsibility for Henri's crimes during the war. If we can track down Jacopo and consult with a lawyer, I've got a plan to try and get your name cleared. If that happens, then you won't need to be ashamed of the perfumes.'

'I'm not sure that's wise,' Iris said. 'It's best to leave things as they are.'

Iris clasped her hands together. She seemed to be retreating again. This was the moment to tread carefully, but somehow Stella had to make her great-aunt understand.

'But we need to let people know that it wasn't your fault,' she said. It didn't make sense. Why didn't Iris seem more enthusiastic about the plan? 'We need to tell the truth.'

'The truth?' Iris said, her face pale. 'No, it's too late. I thought you understood that you were giving up this nonsense about the perfumes and finally getting to know me, now, without all the encumbrances of the past.'

Stella shook her head. 'But how can I truly know you if you won't open up to me? I need to understand your story to make sense of my own. Otherwise, I'm lost.'

Iris sighed. Stella realized she'd pushed her too far. 'We're all lost, Stella. The sooner you realize it, the better.'

'I'm sorry, Iris. I only want to help.'

'As I have tried to explain a hundred times, I don't want your help with the past.' Iris twisted the locket in her fingers. 'I can't go with you on that journey. I'm sorry.'

Stella nodded. 'You're afraid, and I can understand that. But I have to keep going. I only hope that you'll change your mind.'

Iris shook her head. 'I won't,' she said. 'I can't.'

There was nothing else to say.

'Then I'll get going,' Stella said. 'I'm sorry if my actions have upset you.'

Iris said nothing. Stella picked up her bag and left.

Perhaps Iris was never going to let her in. The gap of years was just too great, Iris's mistrust of the past too unsurpassable. Stella still had the notebook and the perfumes, but she had lost Iris as a guide. Without her, the perfumes were meaningless.

Stella got back to her hotel, closed the door and sank down on to the bed, utterly spent. All she wanted to do was close her eyes and disappear from her problems in a deep sleep.

But the telephone next to the bed began to ring. Reluctantly, she picked it up. It was Arnold.

'Stella,' he said, 'I've been trying you all day. James said you're not coming back, that you're thinking of selling.'

'Yes,' Stella said, sitting on the edge of the bed. 'I'm sorry. I just can't face trying to keep rescuing something that seems to be sinking before my eyes. I've spent practically my whole life tied to Penhallam's. It's time I broke free.'

Arnold sighed. 'I know how hard this must be for you, but I have to say, in some ways, I'm relieved. I've seen how much pressure you've been under. It was almost an impossible task to alter the course of the business at this late stage. Your grandfather and father should have changed its direction years ago. It wasn't fair that you had to pick up the pieces.'

'It breaks my heart to leave Jermyn Street, but I have to face the reality of the situation. Penhallam's fate is out of my control. I'd like you to approach Andrea with a view to GPL buying us out.'

'Well, actually, it turns out that you do still have control over one thing. Just a minute, I've got it here somewhere . . .' Stella heard the sound of rummaging. 'Ah yes, here it is. While the intellectual property belongs to the company – the back catalogue of scents, names, formulas, etc. – the deeds to the building on Jermyn Street were separated from the business and placed in your name. So even though you're selling the company, you still get to keep the building.'

Stella straightened up. 'It's in my name?' she said. 'But how can that be?'

'Perhaps your father had an inkling of the way things were heading and wanted to secure some form of inheritance for you. I've double-checked it all. We can sell Penhallam's the business to GPL, but the building on Jermyn Street is yours.'

Stella blinked. This was incredible. Just when she thought she would have nothing left of Penhallam's, it turned out that she had the property in Jermyn Street. It was impossible to guess her father's motives, but the thought of him making a provision like that lifted her spirits.

'Thank you, Arnold. That is very good news indeed. I'm so relieved to think I still have a base in London, that the place where I grew up is still mine.' She felt a rush of joy. 'I've been thinking about retraining as a perfumer. I don't know how I'll manage it, but the idea that Jermyn Street could be my new perfumery, now that I know I own the deeds, gives me hope.'

'When are you coming back?' Arnold asked. 'There will be documents to sign for the sale, but I can always post them over.'

'I don't know. There's some unfinished business here. Iris isn't keen to revisit the past, she just wants to start over.'

Arnold was quiet for a moment. 'Maybe she has a point. If it's a choice between finding out about the past and knowing her, which would you choose?'

'That's just it, I can't seem to separate the two. When I'm with her, I just feel as if there's a massive elephant in the room that we're not discussing. I'm not sure you can have a relationship like that.'

'Hmm,' Arnold said. 'I see what you mean. Well, I hope you manage to work it out. I look forward to hearing all your plans when you get back.'

Stella said goodbye and put the phone down. The problem was that all her plans still hinged around Iris and her perfumes.

37

Iris – Paris, March 1946

Henri took Iris's arm as they walked across the Tuileries. He'd forced her out for some fresh air, saying that she looked a little peaky. She hadn't wanted to go: the less time spent in Henri's company, the better. His moods had soured even further since the war had ended, and he was preoccupied with the downturn in profits.

But it had done her good to feel the breeze down by the Seine and to see the city. Paris had been stripped of Nazi flags and was slowly returning to itself again. American soldiers still hung about the bars, much to Henri's consternation. But Iris liked their sing-song accents and friendly faces.

She walked ahead of Henri down the steps by the rose garden. The bushes were bare skeletons with no sign of buds yet. She'd just reached the gravel path at the bottom when she noticed a woman marching over to them, fists clenched, her face fuming.

'Isn't that . . .' Iris began, recognizing a former customer.

But there was barely time to think before the woman launched into a tirade. 'It's disgusting how you can walk about like this, after what you've done. Stealing from the Jews, making money from their misfortune. Is perfume worth more than someone's life?'

The woman spat on the ground at Iris's feet, whirling round to walk back the way she'd come.

Iris stared after the woman, stunned. 'What's she talking about?' she said to Henri. 'I need to go after her.'

Henri gripped her arm. 'I wouldn't do that if I were you.'

'Don't they realize that we've been looking after the businesses for Raffaele and the others?'

Henri shrugged. 'It's complicated to the outside world. They're all in such a rush to pass the blame and argue that they've been whiter than white in the war, they don't stop to consider the finer details.'

'Well, they must,' Iris said. 'It's harming business.'

Henri smiled. 'Don't worry, my dear. My lawyers have assured me that everything is watertight.'

'Good, because I think it's time we contacted Jacopo's guardian in New York and transferred the perfumery into his name,' Iris said.

News of Raffaele's death had come via telegram the year before. It had hit Iris hard; the thought of seeing Raffaele again one day had sustained her through the war. His loss was compounded by the grief she felt at losing Alessandro. Only perfume-making had got her through, and the thought that what she was doing was helping Jacopo. The telegram said that Jacopo had been taken in by the Italian Jewish community. Iris had written to him when she could, but no replies had ever been received.

'Indeed,' Henri said. 'All in good time.'

A few days later, Iris locked the door of the shop. It was nearly closing time, and the steady rain had made business slow. She went over to the till and opened it up. Since the end of the war in September 1945, Iris had been running the shop as well as the perfumery. One by one, the shop girls had left. Iris had imagined it was because their sweethearts had returned. But, since the woman's outburst, she was starting to wonder if there was another reason. Was it the same reason that kept customers away, even when the weather was sunny, and had caused suppliers to cancel deliveries?

Iris didn't know what to think. She knew Henri had sailed close to the wind during the occupation, dining with Nazis and encouraging them to frequent the perfumery to buy gifts for their families back in Germany. But he'd told her it was to secure the business and reminded her that Jacopo's only income came from the perfumery. She'd been there when Raffaele willingly signed over the running of the perfumery to her in Lausanne. But the woman's words came back to her: *Is perfume worth more than someone's life?* Just yesterday, the bakery she usually went to refused to serve her.

There wasn't much to cash up. Just a few notes and coins. The perfume she'd created for the wife of one of the German generals Henri liked to socialize with had sold surprisingly well in the months leading up to the end of the war. Critics had hailed its bold fragrance and initially there had been talk of exporting it to America. But the talk had tailed off and now Iris wondered if it was because of the allegations of collaboration and theft.

Iris wondered how to go about transferring the running of the perfumery back to Jacopo's guardian, and returning the other businesses Henri had wanted her to take on to their original owners. That would resolve the matter, at least in her own conscience. The trouble was that Henri had always taken care of the business side and money transfers to Jacopo and her brother, Charles, and the other perfumery owners. She didn't know where to start, and

Henri's drawers at home were always locked. But something had to be done. She couldn't sit by and do nothing while these rumours swirled.

A shadow at the window caught Iris's eye. Rain streamed down the windowpane. It made it hard to see who it was. It looked to be a man, scruffy with long hair and a bushy beard. Thank goodness the door was locked. Paris had been chaotic since the end of the war. Women's hair shaved off in the street for sleeping with the enemy. Neighbours accusing each other of betrayal. At least she was concealed here in the shadows. Hopefully the man would lose interest and leave with no hassle.

Unfortunately, he lingered, pressing his face up against the glass. Iris shrank back. He turned away, still blurred by rain. For a moment, she stopped breathing. There was something familiar about the set of his shoulders. His height, the shade of his hair. Then the man turned away, walking back down the street. A stab of certainty hit Iris. It was Alessandro. It had to be.

Iris twisted off her wedding ring and thrust it into the drawer. She rushed over and unlatched the door.

'Alessandro,' she shouted, to the retreating figure. 'Wait.'

The man stopped and turned around. The rain had plastered his hair down and he looked utterly bedraggled. But it was him. He stood for a moment, staring at her, then followed her into the shop, rainwater dripping on the tiles. Iris closed the door and turned to face him.

'Iris,' he said, the desperation in his voice breaking over her like the waves. 'Can you ever forgive me for how we said goodbye?'

Tears welled up. 'It's I who must ask you to forgive me,' she said. 'You have to understand. They said they'd take

Jacopo if I didn't tell them where you were. They already knew you were on the train. I couldn't do that, not to Jacopo, but all this time I've been aching inside that I had to betray you.'

'I know,' Alessandro said, 'I guessed as much.'

Iris tried to stifle the sobs that rose up. He was alive. He'd made it through. The man who'd haunted her dreams and her waking thoughts. The man she thought she'd lost. Here he was, standing right in front of her.

'I can't believe it's you,' Iris said. 'How did you know I'd be here?'

'I spent three years in a prison camp hating myself for what I'd put you through,' Alessandro said. 'Then when Italy capitulated and joined the Allies, I fought in the mountains with the resistance, longing only for the day when I could come and find you and tell you how sorry I am. Tommaso told me Raffaele had signed over the perfumery to you. This is the first chance I've had to visit Paris. I know I look a mess, but I couldn't wait another minute. I needed to see you.'

Iris swallowed. 'I don't know what to say. For such a long time, I've been so angry with you, and with myself. Your hidden life put us in danger, all of us – Jacopo and me, and you. If you hadn't been secretly working for the communists we could have all got out of there. Instead, I was forced to make a terrible decision. And the look in your eyes as the train pulled away made it clear that you blamed me for it.'

Alessandro bowed his head. 'I know. It was wrong of me. What else could you have done but tell them where I was hiding and hand the notebook over to keep Jacopo safe? I was just so devastated that the plan had come to nothing, that I'd been unable to do my bit for the war. But it wasn't your fault. Perhaps if I'd confided in you, you would have done things differently. Instead, I broke your trust and for that I am so sorry.'

Iris tried to gather emotions that fought inside her chest. All these years he'd wanted to find her. He had forgiven her for the choice she'd made on the train. They had both been victims of the war. Of circumstance. If he knew what she had done – marrying Henri to secure his life – would he forgive her that too?

'I never thought I'd see you again, but I never truly let you go.' She looked down at the floor, at the puddle of water at his feet.

'Even after you married Henri?'

Iris looked up, her cheeks burning red. 'How did you know?'

'Tommaso told me that too. He said it was the price you'd paid to save my life. I'm only glad to see you're no longer married to him.'

Iris rubbed the place where the ring had been, only moments ago. He seemed to assume her marriage to Henri was over.

'Alessandro . . .' she said, trying to find the right words. Perhaps she should have left the ring on. But instinct had made her take it off.

'It doesn't matter, Iris. There's no need to explain,' Alessandro said. 'All you need to do is look at me, then you'll know that I still love you, have always loved you. I'm a free man now, my marriage was annulled, and all I want is to beg your forgiveness and ask for a second chance.'

Iris looked up slowly. Alessandro's eyes locked on to hers. For a moment, she stared at him, and then, like a magnet pulled towards its twin, she moved towards him. She didn't want to talk or think about the past any more. She had done enough thinking. She simply wanted him to take her and make her his own again. He clasped her in his arms.

'Iris,' he breathed, kissing her face, her neck. She inhaled his scent, his breath on her skin, his lips crashing against hers. It was a kiss like no other. It was like being lost and coming home. His tongue entwined with hers, his body pressed against her, the contact igniting an inferno deep within.

'I've wanted you all this time,' he said, his hands moving down her back.

'Were there no others?' Iris whispered. The press of his shoulder blades, the hard muscles in his arms, his firm chest under his shirt.

'None,' Alessandro said. 'For me, there's only you. I've waited so long . . .'

He kissed her hungrily, his desire inflaming hers. A surge of strength rose up within her. He'd waited this long, for her. Forgiveness wasn't something either of them had to look for; it was simply there. He'd been loyal to her, and come all this way, and now . . .

'Let's go upstairs,' she whispered, tracing the line of his scar with her finger.

'Can we?' Alessandro's eyes implored her.

Henri was at a business meeting. He would head home after that. They'd kept Raffaele's flat above the shop for convenience. Sometimes Iris stayed over when she was working on a particularly complex fragrance. Sometimes, she just needed to get away from Henri for a while. It didn't bother Henri. Since 1944, he'd not gone near her, preferring the services of his mistress on the other side of town.

Iris led Alessandro up the stairs to the little room. On the dressing table was her travelling perfumer's case, the one that Raffaele had given her back in 1939. Next to it lay the perfume notebook.

'You still have it?' he said.

'Yes. They ripped out the pages you'd written on and let me take the rest.'

'What about the perfumes we made? Do you still have those?'

'Of course. La Scintilla. Primo Bacio. Amanti. But I couldn't bear to smell any of them. It was too painful. Tradimento is still in Venice, where we left it.'

'It's a pity we never got to finish them properly,' Alessandro said. He picked up the notebook and flicked through the pages.

'Wait here a minute,' Iris said. 'I have something to show you.'

She went to the kitchen and rummaged in one of the drawers. Where was it? After a few minutes, she found the photo and hurried back to Alessandro. He was holding a pen.

'Just jotting something in your notebook for you to read later,' he said. He put his hands around her waist and pulled her close. 'What have you got there?'

Iris handed him a photo. When the photographer had taken a picture of her and Henri after their wedding, she'd persuaded Henri to let him take one of Jacopo and Raffaele. It was in black and white, the lake and mountains in the background. Jacopo's face was brimming with happiness and Raffaele looked contented at last.

'So, it was all worth it,' Alessandro said, gazing at the photograph. 'They were reunited, thanks to you.'

'And you,' Iris said. 'We did it together.'

'I tried to track Raffaele down on the way over to France, but Isabella told me he'd passed away.'

'I know. Looking back, it seems he was only teaching us for a short while, and yet, even now, I owe so much of my career to the skills he shared with us. I learned enough to last a lifetime.'

'All that work, all those conversations,' Alessandro said, putting the photograph on the dressing table. 'Now that the war is over, I'd like to go back to creating perfumes. But I'm not sure I have the heart to.'

'Maybe now you will,' Iris said, slipping her arms around him.

Alessandro came closer. 'I love you,' he said.

Iris looked up at him, her eyes clear. 'I love you too.'

Something shifted in the room. A certainty that this moment counted for everything. Alessandro's eyes darkened. Iris held her breath as one by one he undid the buttons on her blouse. There was no hurry. Iris knew this was what they both wanted, without a shadow of a doubt. She stood still while he undressed her. Then, just as tenderly, she took off his jacket. Removed his shirt. Unbuckled his trousers. They stood in front of each other naked, held back only by the pleasure of looking at each other once again.

'Come on,' she said, smiling as she led him to the bed.

She traced her fingers across the taut muscles in his stomach. Alessandro sucked his breath. 'Are you sure you want this?' he said.

'I've never been surer of anything in my life,' Iris said.

The room dimmed as he drew closer. Iris's heart sang with the nearness of him. His touch against her skin, the depth of his kisses, the sweet smell that belonged only to him. The world shrank until there was only him, and the pulsing of his body fused with hers.

The fire swelled and burned exquisitely, radiating out warmth across every fibre of her being. With each movement, Iris cried out, the waves breaking over her, the rhythm holding her back with a delicious restraint and at the same time carrying her forward to the moment she knew would dissolve everything. As the tempo increased, Iris opened her eyes. Alessandro was there, holding her gaze. She reached up and kissed him as the moment rose and expanded and burst around her. The past was over. This was now. Henri didn't matter any more. Their lives could begin again.

She lay back as sweet oblivion pulsed through her body. Alessandro lay next to her, breathing deeply, still holding her tight. 'My love,' he whispered. 'Let's never be apart again.'

Suddenly the door opened and a cold breeze swept in. There, standing in the doorway, was Henri.

Iris drew back, pulling the covers around her. Alessandro must have registered the shock in her face. He turned round in the bed to face Henri.

'What the hell are you doing here?' he said.

'I might ask you the same thing,' Henri replied, his voice tight. 'Did you know you're in bed with my wife?'

Alessandro froze, then recoiled back. 'You're still married to him?'

Why hadn't she just told him straight away? She shouldn't have let him assume she was no longer married. And now Alessandro had found out from Henri.

'Of course she is,' Henri said. 'From the moment we had

our delightful ceremony in Lausanne, we've been inseparable, haven't we, Iris?'

Alessandro wrenched the covers back and grabbed his clothes. 'I thought it was over between you,' he said, throwing on his shirt. 'I would never have . . .'

'Oh, I'm sure you wouldn't,' Henri said. He shook his head at Iris. 'Don't look so shocked. I've been expecting Alessandro to crawl back to your door ever since the war ended. Get dressed, for God's sake. I'll be waiting in the kitchen.'

The door slammed shut.

'Alessandro,' Iris said, trying to take hold of his hand. 'Please let me explain. I had to make sure that Jacopo was provided for. That's why I've been running Raffaele's perfumery until the time it can be handed over to him. You have to believe me.'

Alessandro tucked in his shirt. 'All this time,' he said, 'I've been waiting for you. But you haven't been waiting for me.'

Iris stood up, the sheets wrapped around her. 'It's not like that. I'm doing it for Jacopo. If we separated, all my possessions would go to Henri, including the perfumery.'

Alessandro turned to face her. The hurt was palpable in his eyes. 'In the war, perhaps, I can understand you making that sacrifice. But the war is over and you've stayed married to him, for God's sake.'

He sounded so full of despair that Iris couldn't bear it.

'You don't know anything about it,' she said desperately. 'The war may be over, but not for me. Do you know what they're calling us? Traitors. Collaborators. I haven't got enough money to support myself, let alone send money to Jacopo. That's why I stay.'

Alessandro shook his head. 'He was your first love. How could I compete with that?'

'How can you say that?' she said.

'Because you're still his wife,' Alessandro said. 'You could have found a way to break free from Henri if you really wanted to. But maybe, deep down, you didn't have the desire to walk away. Instead, you gave up on me, on us.'

Alessandro picked up his bag and, without even looking at Iris, left the room. Iris stood looking at the space he'd left. Her heart emptied. She didn't even have the energy to call out after him. She listened as his footsteps receded down the stairs and then disappeared into a gaping silence, in which the only sound was her own heart beating.

At last, she went over to the perfume notebook and thumbed through the page to find what he'd written. On the next clean page, after Tradimento, he had written a new title: *Solo Tu*. Only You. The irony of it, after he had left her so abruptly. She held up the book and read the words he'd written underneath.

There is no place I'd rather be than in your arms. No voice I'd rather hear than your voice. No lips I'd rather kiss than your lips. Nothing I long to see as much as your smile. No one I'd rather come home to but you. For all the years that have passed, and all the years to come, there is only you.

Pain stabbed her heart. She *had* given up on Alessandro instead of fighting for what she knew to be right and true. Living in Paris during the occupation had been like limbo, draining her mind and soul of agency. She yanked a suitcase out from under the bed. She placed her perfume journal in first. Why had she stayed so long? Suddenly she felt wide awake, galvanized by the desire to get as far away from Paris as she could. Maybe there was still a way to prove to Alessandro how much she loved him.

The door opened. Henri leaned against the doorway, smoking a cigarette. In one hand, he held a brown manila file. 'So, he's gone.'

'Of course he's gone. That's what you wanted, isn't it?' Iris rummaged in the chest of drawers, looking for clothes to pack. 'Why did you come here anyway?'

'I came to give you fair warning,' he said, exhaling the smoke in a cloud.

Iris raised her head. 'Of what?'

'I'll be on a flight to South America in approximately two hours,' he said. He placed the file in front of Iris. 'Here are all the documents of ownership. All the businesses we took over during the war, they're all in your name. I'm afraid you will need to read the small print this time.'

'I don't understand.' Iris opened the file. Inside were documents relating to Raffaele di Fiore, Jarget, Klein, Floret and all the other perfumeries that Henri had looked after during the war.

'Investigations have opened into the unlawful appropriation of Jewish businesses by French collaborators.'

Iris swallowed. 'You mean . . . it's true, what they've been saying?'

'Yes, of course it is. But I wasn't stupid enough to put my name to all of this. It's your signature, Iris, that's on the paperwork,' he said, stubbing his cigarette out on the bedside table. 'So as a precaution, I'm getting out of the spotlight. Don't worry, I'll give you the name of my lawyers.'

Iris's brain scrambled into gear. 'Henri, you can't leave

like this. You organized all these deals – it's all your doing. I just signed them because you told me to, or else Jacopo wouldn't get his money, and nor would any of the others.'

'Ah, well, Jews look after their own. I'm sure he's doing fine in America,' Henri said. 'And you see, as you are a woman, they will be lenient on you, I'm sure, much more so than on me.'

The sight of him standing there, his immaculate overcoat, his smug face, it was more than she could bear. 'How can you leave? After everything I did for this perfumery, for you.'

Henri smiled. 'It's over, Iris, you'd better face it. The sins of omission are just as grave as the sins of an act performed. You know that as well as I do.' He nodded and, with that, he left.

Iris covered her heads with her hands. Moments ago, she and Alessandro had been so close. Now he was gone. And Henri was abandoning her to face the penalty for his crimes. Her eyes closed and she let the darkness take her.

38

Stella – Paris, August 1996

The next morning, Stella got up late and went down for breakfast just in time before the restaurant closed. It was strange to be back in the same hotel where she'd stayed with Bruno. She'd spent the last couple of hours scouring the notebook for any clues. The last perfume, Solo Tu, was unfinished. The hurried description at the top of the page suggested that this was as far as Alessandro and Iris had got with it. While she sat drinking a glass of orange juice, the receptionist came over with a sheaf of paper.

'Good morning, Mademoiselle Penhallam,' she said. 'This arrived for you by fax this morning.'

She handed Stella the piece of paper. The address at the top read the University of Venice. Stella put down her glass and pushed her plate away. It must be from Bruno. The movement of the waiters and the chatter of the other guests receded as she read his words.

Dear Stella

I can't get our last conversation out of my head. I'm so sorry for what happened and wish that I'd had chance to explain sooner. It must have come as a great shock, but I promise you, I aborted that job as soon as I got to know you and what the perfumes meant to you. Normally, I'm hunting for old samples that have no personal value. But this time it was different, and I wish I'd told you sooner about how I got involved.

I wish I hadn't left you and gone back to Venice. Now, I regret doing that. I hate to think of you in Paris without me. I want to be with you, Stella, not just to look for the perfumes, but to look ahead together. I wish I could be with you in Paris right now, but Anna has had a relapse and I need to be here for her.

Please, give me another chance. Let's meet again as soon as we can. I believe we can sort this out.

I also wanted to tell you that I had an email from Jacopo Calvetti's son. He's still alive and willing to provide testimony for Iris about how she helped him in the war. Here is his address so you can get in touch: 24 Amity Street, Cobble Hill, Brooklyn, New York, 11201.

And you don't need to take my advice on this, but if I was there with you in Paris, my next port of call would be the Archives de Paris, to check out the records for Iris's trial. Hopefully you'll find the missing piece of the jigsaw there.

I'm so sorry that I failed to tell you about the collector. I hope one day you will find it in your heart to forgive me this tradimento. In the meantime, I'm here in Venice. If there is anything else I can do to help you, please let me know.

Yours, Bruno

Stella stared at the letter. It still hurt, the fact that he'd not been honest with her. But hadn't she omitted to tell him things too: to tell him how much she cared for him? And now he'd written this letter, reaching out to her. Was she always going to be the one walking away? Or at some point, would she take the initiative and make the leap of faith herself?

It was fear that held her back, Stella realized. She put the letter down and took the notebook out of her bag, reading the first line of Solo Tu's description: *There is no place I'd rather be than in your arms.* That summed it up exactly. The longing she felt for Bruno. The problem was that Stella wasn't sure she had the courage to tell him.

But first she should finish this search for the truth about Iris. So far, Iris's experiences had taught Stella so much about herself. If she wanted to complete the circle, Stella needed to know exactly how Iris's journey had ended. It was good news that Jacopo was willing to help. But Iris was seemingly dead set against the idea of clearing her name. What was it about the trial documents that Iris was so frightened to face? Stella sighed. She would have to take the final steps of this journey on her own.

It was infuriating to think of following Bruno's advice, but he was right. Without Iris's cooperation, the obvious next step was to visit the Archives de Paris and look at the evidence from Iris's trial. She rang ahead and begged the clerk to let her book her slot, even though she didn't have an academic card. Thankfully, she was able to arrange a visit that afternoon.

The weather in Paris was grey and overcast so Stella took the Métro from Place de la République to the nineteenth arrondissement and emerged at Porte des Lilas. Rain peppered the pavement as she crossed the wide boulevard and hurried towards the archives. In front of her was a tall concrete building with scrubland all around and an air of neglect. It looked more like a prison than an archive. Stella headed up the path, hoping it contained what she was looking for.

'It will take a little while to fetch the document you've requested,' the woman on the desk said. She'd been helpful in finding the roll number linked to the evidence from Iris's trial.

There was nothing for it; she would have to wait. 'Can I use the database in the meantime?' Stella asked. 'I'd like to see if there is anything else of interest in the digital archives.'

'Of course,' the woman said. 'Right over there.'

Stella settled herself at one of the computers and opened up the database. Not all the records had been computerized, but a notice said that from 1900 to 1950 most of the items had been scanned. This was where Bruno must have looked when he discovered the wedding certificate.

Indeed, when Stella did a search for Iris Penhallam, the wedding certificate was the first item that came up, so Stella brought it up on the screen to view herself. She stared at Iris's and Henri's names, thinking of how Iris had married Henri to save Alessandro's life. It was such a brave thing to do, especially when she had been so clearly in love with Alessandro.

Stella went back to the other entries. There was a list of business transfer agreements seemingly used as evidence in the trial and all listed in Iris's name. Stella clicked on the first one.

Business Transfer Agreement

This business transfer agreement (Agreement) is effective as of October 1939
Between: Raffaele di Fiore (Seller), an individual with premises located at rue Bayard, Paris
And: Iris Penhallam (Purchaser), an individual with her main office located at 24 rue Rimbaud, Paris. The Purchaser and the

Seller shall be individually referred to as a Party, and collectively referred to as the Parties as the context may require.

Whereas:

A: The Seller is engaged in the business of making and selling perfumes

B: The Purchaser is a company incorporated on 6th October 1939 and engaged in the business of luxury goods.

C: The Seller has agreed to sell, and the Purchaser has agreed to purchase the business as a going concern on the terms and conditions of this Agreement.

Stella read through the twenty-page document. The date of the signatures was the same date as Iris's wedding day. Henri must have arranged both events to take place in Lausanne.

She leaned back in the chair and looked around at the tall concrete pillars and huge windows overlooking high-rise apartments. Why had Raffaele agreed to such a deal? He might have needed the money, but surely he would have been better off keeping the business and taking the profits? Then Stella remembered what Bruno had said about Jews not being allowed to own businesses. Unscrupulous French businessmen had taken advantage of this. According to the contract, in this case, it was Iris who had done so, as it was her signature at the bottom of the document.

Stella looked back at the front page. The company address was 24 rue Rimbaud, Paris. That was the address of Iris's husband, Henri. Stella typed his name into the archives. Some entries came up. Exploring further, Stella found a death certificate dated August 1965. The place of death was São Luís in Brazil, the cause pulmonary disease. Stella tapped her fingers on the desk, thinking things through. She knew from history lessons, and what Bruno had told her, that many Nazis and Nazi collaborators had fled to South America. Henri must have covered his tracks by ensuring that all the business transfers of Jewish businesses to Levèque Perfumes were in Iris's name.

If only Iris were willing to try and clear her name. There was plenty of evidence that could be reassessed. If only Bruno were here to talk it all through. There was no one else who could have understood like him.

The attendant tapped Stella on the shoulder. 'The trial papers have arrived,' she said.

Well, she would have to manage without him. Stella made her way over to the table where the papers were waiting. The sun was peeping out from behind the clouds. Hopefully it was a good omen.

The court papers confirmed Stella's suspicion that Henri had framed his wife for the theft of the Jewish businesses. Iris's lawyer, a M. Dupont, had seemingly done his best to prove his client's innocence, but the signatures on the documents were taken as irrefutable proof of Iris's complicity.

Stella sighed. It would be hard to overturn such a black-and-white conviction. Jacopo had just been a child when it happened.

Stella rubbed her eyes and turned to the last page, the judge's summation after the verdicts had been given. One line caught her eye and made her breath stop in her lungs.

It is against this backdrop, and regardless of the fact that you are pregnant, that I am sentencing you to ten years in prison.

Stella read the words again and blinked. This had come out of the blue. Iris had been pregnant. She'd been sentenced to ten years despite the fact that she was carrying a child. Stella couldn't bear to think of Iris's torment during the trial and after hearing that verdict. What had happened to the baby? Had it survived? There was only one way to find out.

Stella found a taxi and went as quickly as she could to the convalescent home, her mind racing with questions. Neither her grandfather nor her father had even mentioned that Iris had a child. Stella turned the corner, almost running in her haste to reach Iris. Tourists milled around stands displaying Eiffel Tower keyrings and fridge magnets. Stella dodged past them, impatient to ask Iris what had happened back in 1946, hoping that she would give the background to the notes from the trial.

But when she arrived, breathless and red-faced at the reception, Monique greeted her with a grave look on her face.

'Iris isn't here any more,' Monique said. 'She discharged herself this morning, and said she just wanted to go somewhere in France where she could be at peace. I tried to get her to wait for you, but the receptionist had already booked her a taxi. I don't know where she's gone.'

Stella shook her head in disbelief. 'She can't have just disappeared.'

'I'm sorry,' Monique said. 'Her address might be on the system, but I'd have to go through the *administratrice*, as she has access. And I know she won't be willing to give out personal information.'

Stella screwed up her eyes. Iris clearly didn't want to be found. Maybe she had already anticipated the questions that were now flying around Stella's head.

'What was the name of the taxi company?' Stella asked.

'It's the one we always use for transporting patients.' Monique looked up. 'Ah, I see, you're thinking that they can tell us Iris's destination.'

'Yes,' Stella said. 'Can you ring them now and find out?'

Monique picked up the telephone and spoke in rapid French to the taxi firm. Stella couldn't make out all the words, but her hopes rose when she saw Monique grab a pen and paper to write something down. Monique finished the call.

'The taxi company said he took her to the Gare de Lyon. She was chatting on the way about looking forward to seeing her garden at Les Beaux Vents in Mougins again.'

'Where's Mougins?' Stella said.

'It's in the south, I think, a little village not far from Cannes. I guess she must have caught the train down there. It takes about five hours.' She glanced at her watch. 'She should be there by now.'

Stella nodded. 'Mougins,' she said, thinking back over her conversations with Iris. She couldn't recall her ever mentioning it. 'Well, if that's where Iris has gone, then I need to go there too.'

39

Iris – Paris, November 1946

Iris sat in a cell behind the courtroom in the Palais de Justice de Paris and tried to breathe calmly. The jury was deciding on its verdict. One hour had passed since they had retreated to deliberate on all the evidence. Surely it was a good sign that they still weren't back yet.

She shifted on the hard wooden chair. Her hips ached. The bump that protruded from her stomach had grown so large it was painful to sit like this for long periods. The court had made some concessions to her state. Regular breaks. Access to a lavatory when she needed it. A cushion to sit on. But nothing had prepared Iris for the sheer exhaustion of undergoing a trial while pregnant.

Her lawyer, Michel Dupont, came in. 'How are you doing?'

Iris smiled. 'Okay. I just wish I knew what they were saying in there. Do you think we've done enough to convince them?'

Michel sighed. 'I hope so. But the fact remains that the money that was supposedly wired to Jacopo ended up in a bank account here in Paris doesn't look good. Your signature is on the papers. Your name is on the bank account. That was the prosecution's trump card. We said you'd done it all for Jacopo, but he doesn't appear to have benefited.'

'But neither did I,' Iris protested.

'It's true the amounts that are missing and are presumed to have found their way to Brazil far outweigh what you have accrued from all of this. But nonetheless, you had a pot of money that many in France would regard as a comfortable fortune. It's a pity Signor di Fiore is no longer alive to give a statement, and that Jacopo is too young to do so.'

Iris shook her head. 'I want to give Jacopo and the families who were swindled whatever money they need. What more can I do to convince the French state I wasn't involved?'

Michel shrugged. 'Nothing. You were an exemplary witness. Even under questioning you held your own and articulated the complexities of the situation and your marriage. I'm not convinced that every juror will be able to distinguish the grey areas. Temperatures are still running high after the war and, no matter what your reasoning, the fact is that a great many Jewish families have had their businesses stolen. I warned you it was going to be an uphill struggle.'

Iris slumped in the chair. 'I know you've always been straight with me. I don't hold out much hope. But tell me, what do you think is going to happen?'

Michel sighed. 'It's almost inevitable that you'll be found guilty, as I've explained before, but given that you're only a few months away from giving birth, your obvious naivety in the situation and your contrition, I think they'll commute the sentence to community service and a fine.'

Iris breathed out. Thank God. She couldn't bear the thought of having this baby in prison. Despite her exhaustion, the thought that she was carrying Alessandro's child inside her had been the only saving grace in all this.

In the days after Alessandro and Henri left, when the police came to arrest her and she was out on bail without any support but Michel's, Iris had thought her life not worth living. Charles had taken a hard line and was anxious to cut ties with her, not wanting to damage the Penhallam name. He'd paid her bail but made it clear that he wanted no further contact.

Iris had been plunged into despair after her arrest and had wondered if there was any point continuing. Life had never felt so dark. Then, one day, she'd woken up and felt a fluttering in her blood. A quickening she couldn't explain, that felt like holding a butterfly in her hand. That was six weeks after Alessandro had gone. And eight weeks since she'd had her last period. She'd opened the window of Raffaele's perfumery, looking up at the blue sky, and realized that whatever else was dark in her life, this new life, a ray of hope that had come out of her union with Alessandro, had to be protected at all costs.

'Is there anyone you want me to call?' Michel had said early on, when she'd been arrested. The thought of Alessandro had crossed her mind, but she wouldn't have even known how to reach him any more. He was gone. All the good things in her life were gone. Except this, the baby growing inside her. Somehow, despite everything, they had managed to make something exceptional.

The cell window slot slid back. 'The jury is back. It's time to go in,' a female guard said.

Michel stood up. 'Here we go,' he said. 'And whatever happens, good or bad, you'll be entitled to see me, and we can discuss what happens next.'

Iris nodded. 'Thank you for all your help.'

Michel had never questioned her innocence. He wasn't

the lawyer Henri had recommended but the pro bono lawyer offered by the courts. Iris had trusted him because, with his greying temples and round reading glasses, he'd reminded her of her father.

She walked into the wooden dock at the front of the courtroom. She looked at the jury. Was it possible to guess what they'd decided? None of them could look her in the eye. At last, the judge came in and asked the spokesperson to rise. Iris rested her hand on her bump. From deep inside, a gentle kick reminded her that the baby was there. She took a deep breath and tried to stay calm.

'On the charge of stealing the di Fiore Perfumery, how do you find the defendant?' the judge said.

'Guilty.'

'And in the matter of Jarget, Klein and Floret?'

'Also guilty, on three counts.'

Iris swallowed. Michel had prepared her for this. She knew the jury would have to find her guilty. What mattered now was the sentence the judge handed down. He was a difficult man to read, but notoriously fair, Michel had said, but in these uncertain times it was hard to tell how things would go.

The judge turned to Iris. 'Iris Penhallam, you have been found guilty of four counts of fraud and theft, and embezzling businesses to advance your own profits. Such crimes carry with them a sentence of five years each.'

He paused, rustling his notes. 'I accept your counsel's defence that you were at best naïve and at worst accommodating to your husband's business dealings. I also accept that you have had no previous convictions and have been fully accepting of your guilt in this matter.'

At this point he cleared his throat. Iris crossed her fingers. Please let him be lenient.

The judge turned to face the courtroom. 'However, as more details come to light of the horrors suffered by the Jews under the Nazis, of their untold suffering in the concentration camps and the process of ostracization that led to their systematic removal from French society, it means that we cannot simply view this case as a corporate matter. Indeed, the very background against which you and your husband were able to take advantage of these business is the antisemitic terror which reigned under occupation.'

Iris looked over to Michel. His face was white. As she heard the judge's words, Iris knew that she was in a great deal of trouble. Nobody believed that she was fully ignorant of what Henri had done. They didn't know that the marriage was loveless and born out of a desire to protect Jacopo. They assumed that she had known what she was doing and had profited from the death of those Jews whose businesses Henri had stolen.

'It is against this backdrop, and regardless of the fact that you are pregnant, that I am sentencing you to ten years in prison. All your assets will duly be stripped from you and returned to those families from which they were stolen. There will be no early release or parole. And this is my final judgement.'

The judge banged his gavel against the wood. The very sound of it struck terror into Iris's heart. She wouldn't contest this judgement. She would take the punishment for Henri's crimes and her own stupid blindness. But the baby didn't deserve this punishment. She couldn't let it suffer her fate. Somehow, she would have to let it go.

Three weeks later, Michel came to see Iris at Melun prison. A guard stood outside the cell. The bump bulged underneath her regulation prison wear. She was only a few weeks away from the due date.

'How are you?' Michel said.

Iris shrugged. 'They're more understanding about my situation than anyone was out there,' she said. 'Except for you, of course. There are a few women here, like me, because of crimes their husbands committed.'

'I'm glad they're treating you well.'

'And the doctor's been very kind. His conversations somehow make me feel human again, if only for the brief moments when he checks the baby's growth.'

'Ah yes. I need to speak to him once you've decided on which course to take. I'm glad he's been some comfort to you.'

Iris smiled weakly. 'I told him about Mougins – he knows the place,' she said. 'I described the garden and the Mediterranean just a short drive away and just the thought of it gave me peace. I need to remember that places like that still exist outside these walls and will still be there in ten years when I get out. Until then, I can visit them in my mind.'

Michel sighed. 'I hope you can sustain yourself on memories and dreams,' he said. 'You need to survive this. For the child's sake.'

Iris's hand drifted to her belly. 'Have you been to London?'

Michel nodded. 'I have, and I've talked to Charles.'

'What did he say?'

Michel leaned forward. 'He will only agree to take the baby if you relinquish all rights to the child. Charles and Jane will adopt the baby and raise it as their own and you must have no further contact.'

Iris clenched her fists. 'He has no right to ask that. I'm the child's mother. In ten years, I will be out and I can be a mother again.'

Michel spread his hands out over the tabletop. 'I know this isn't easy. If you were prepared to tell me about the father of the child, perhaps I could explore that avenue.'

Iris shook her head. She recalled Alessandro's face when he found out she was still married. The despair and the anger. She remembered his footsteps down the stairs, leaving her.

'No, I'm sorry. Our relationship is over. It's not an avenue that's open to me any more and I don't know where he is, anyway.'

'In that case, you have two choices,' Michel said in a calm, measured voice. 'One, after the birth, the child will be taken into a children's home, brought up by the French state and possibly returned to you when you are released. Or two, allow your brother to adopt the child and be raised as a Penhallam, with all that that entails – security, love, support and an education – but with the expectation that you are unlikely to ever have a relationship with the child even after you are released.'

Iris cradled her bump protectively. 'I can't let this child be raised by strangers.'

'Then you have only one option.'

Iris flinched at the thought of what she was about to do. She was trapped in every way, and this seemed the only solution. Charles might have his faults, but he would bring the child up well. Perhaps in ten years, when she got out, he would relent and let her see the child. It was the best hope she had.

'Let Charles have the baby,' she said, closing her eyes.

Michel touched her arm. 'Are you sure this is what you want to do?'

Iris hesitated. It was the most difficult decision of her life. She wanted to scream out, to break her hand against the stone walls, to wail at all the injustice and pain she'd had to go through and must still endure.

But she couldn't fall to pieces now. The baby needed her to be strong. She had to bury her emotions deep down if there was any chance of her surviving this ordeal.

Iris sucked in her breath. 'Yes,' she said. 'This is what I want.'

40

Stella – Mougins, September, 1996

Stella went to the Gare de Lyon the next morning and took the 11.22 train to Cannes. It sped non-stop southwards, through the lush fields of the Morvan and the mountains of the Ardèche, until the landscape changed to vineyards and hilltop towns.

Stella barely took in the scenery. Her mind was racing with questions for Iris. A baby. Why had she never said anything? Was that the real secret that Iris had wanted to keep hidden? As the miles dragged by, Stella's head ached. All she wanted was to know the truth. To finally hear it from Iris.

She arrived in Cannes just after four o'clock in the afternoon, inhaling the fresh sea breeze. The sky was azure and cloudless. Stella waited in line at the taxi rank and then found a driver to take her up to Mougins.

The taxi drove along the country road, which was surrounded by woods. Stella wound down the window and inhaled the scent of pines, olives and cypress trees. A medieval town appeared on the hillside. The driver steered the taxi up the steep incline and through the narrow streets. Restaurants and cafés were full of people making the most of the warm autumn sunshine. Stella clutched the map she'd printed out in Paris. It wouldn't be long before they reached the house.

At last, the car stopped. Stella paid the driver and got out, surveying the building in front of her. It was a tall townhouse with wisteria creeping up the stone walls and white shutters. Vine leaves grew over the porch. By the wooden door a sign read: Les Beaux Vents.

Stella knocked and waited. Eventually, the door opened. Iris stood there, dressed in blue jeans and a baggy white shirt. She was carrying a trowel, a red scarf in her hair. She stared at Stella, her face turning pale.

'You came all this way?' Iris said.

'Of course I did. You just disappeared.'

Iris swallowed. 'I know. I'm sorry. Come in. I was just about to have a coffee.'

She led Stella into an enormous kitchen. A cat napped by the stove. Dried flowers hung from the ceiling. The wooden shelves on the wall were covered in earthenware crockery and outside Stella could see a garden filled with a profusion of flowers. 'Why did you leave like that?' Stella said. 'You checked out of the convalescent home and didn't tell anyone where you were going.'

Iris brought the coffee pot and two cups over to the table and gestured for Stella to sit down. 'I panicked. When you started talking about the trial and looking at the court papers, I couldn't stay in Paris a minute longer. I was worried about what secrets you were going to unearth.'

Iris poured out the coffee. Stella took a sip; it was rich and bitter. 'You mean the baby,' she said.

Iris stared at Stella for a moment, then nodded. 'Yes, the baby,' she whispered. 'But it seems you've already found out.'

'Oh Iris,' Stella said, reaching for her hand. 'When I read those papers it was clear that you should never have been sent to prison. You were innocent. And you were eight months pregnant. The whole thing is unthinkable. I don't know how you coped.'

Iris shrugged. 'I had to. Not for myself. But for the baby.'

'Did the baby survive?' Stella asked gently.

Iris took a deep breath, then nodded. 'He did. I thought all the stress I'd undergone might have affected him. But he was a healthy nine pounds when he was born, nothing wrong with him at all. He was the most beautiful baby I'd ever seen,' Iris said, her voice breaking. 'I've not spoken about him to anyone since.'

Stella squeezed her hand. 'I know this is hard,' she said. Having a baby wasn't easy at the best of times, but in prison, after being convicted, Iris must have been distraught. 'What happened after he was born?'

Iris's face darkened. 'I don't know if I can bear to tell you,' she said, shrinking back.

'Please tell me, Iris. I think you've wanted to tell me all along, but you were too ashamed. Whatever it is, surely it's better out in the open.' She didn't want to rush Iris, but she simply had to know.

Iris hesitated then reached up and undid the chain around her neck. She gave the locket to Stella. 'If you open it up, you'll see.'

Stella undid the clasp. On either side were two photographs. One was a black-and-white image of a little boy; he didn't look happy to be dressed in formal clothes and made to pose. On the other side, there was a colour photograph of a little girl. She was sitting cross-legged on the grass, holding a rose, and a jam jar filled with water and rose petals. Recognition dawned.

'That's me,' she said.

Iris nodded.

'And this?' Stella said, trying to put the pieces together.

'Is Richard, your father.'

Stella stared at the photograph. She'd never seen it before, but as she peered closer she recognized the expression on the boy's face: observant, shy, impatient. It was her father. But what were these photos of Stella and her father doing in Iris's locket?

'I don't understand,' Stella said. 'He was your nephew; you barely even saw him.'

Iris smiled tightly. 'Not my nephew, not to begin with,' she said. 'He was my child. The one I gave birth to in Melun prison. This is the part I'm so ashamed of. I wanted to keep him. But they wouldn't let me. I had a choice. Hand him over to be cared for by the French state until I was released or give him to my brother.'

Here it was at last. The truth at the heart of everything. 'You mean Charles, my grandfather?' Stella said, taking it all in. 'Except, he's not my grandfather, he's my great-uncle, and you . . . must be my grandmother.'

'Yes,' Iris said. 'I am.'

'But I don't understand. I can't believe it,' Stella said. The details were muddled in her head.

'Charles and Jane had tried for years to have a child. He was happy to take your father, but only on one condition.'

Stella held her breath. 'What was that?'

'That I gave him up for adoption and promised never to see him again. He would be brought up as the son of Charles and Jane, sole heir to the Penhallam business, and would never, ever know that I was his mother, given the disgraceful things I'd been convicted of.'

'But you were innocent,' Stella said.

Iris rubbed her temples. 'It was my signature on those papers. Yes, Henri deceived me, but I was the name attached to those Jewish businesses. Charles disowned me, but he was willing to take my baby and look after him and so I let him. You have to understand what it was like then. I had no one else to turn to. I didn't want my son to be brought up in a children's home. However much Charles had come to despise me, I knew that he would take care of my son and love him and care for him as if he were his own.'

Stella cupped her hand around the warm mug. 'It must have been heartbreaking to give the child away.'

'It was. When I was released in 1956 I came straight over to England. All the time I was in prison I sent letters to Charles telling him I'd made a terrible mistake by giving my son away. I begged him to let me see him, even if I had to pretend I was a long-lost aunt; I implored him. He never replied. So when I got out of prison I came back to Jermyn Street, hoping to see my son.'

'What happened?' Stella said, listening intently to every word.

'Charles was furious. He told me I would never be allowed contact, that I didn't have a leg to stand on. I didn't care – I'd have torn the whole house down to find Richard. But Charles said something that made me change my mind. He said that at that very moment my son was at school, with his friends, and after school he was bringing two of them back for tea and Charles was going to take them to the cinema to see the latest film. He said that Richard had a life, and did I really want to be the one to shatter it, to annihilate everything he relied on, everything he believed to be true, just because of my selfishness?'

The anguish on Iris's face was plain, as if she were reliving the painful scene. 'So, you went away?'

Iris nodded, biting her lip. 'I had to; I could never have ruined your father's life like that. He had a good life with Charles and Jane. What could I offer him in return? Charles gave me the photo that you see in the locket and that was that.'

'But what about this photo of me?' Stella asked. 'How did you get it?'

'Your father gave it to me the day he brought you to visit me in Paris. I was never sure if he suspected there was more to our relationship or not. I caught him studying my face once or twice, just as you did when we first met. Charles and Jane would never have told him, but perhaps there was something in the back of his mind that made him wonder.'

'Why didn't you tell him?'

Iris sighed. 'Too many years had passed. I wanted to, but I thought of how hurt he would have been and I didn't have the courage. He never asked me either. But he was most insistent about giving me the photograph of you. I've always kept them close in this locket. I'd hoped that visit might be the start of getting to know you both as distant relatives at least, but after that a wall of silence returned. He never contacted me again.'

'And why didn't you tell me when I first came to see you in Paris?'

Iris's eyes sparkled with tears.

'For the same reason I couldn't tell your father. I was afraid you wouldn't want to know me,' she said. 'It was enough just to see you, to have you nearby. After you came back from Venice and wanted to spend time with me, I was so torn. I wanted more than anything to be close to you, but I was worried that if the truth came out – that I had abandoned your father and kept my real identity from you – you wouldn't want anything more to do with me.'

Stella clasped the locket. 'But I do,' she said. 'I've found something more precious than the perfumes. I've found you.'

She reached out to take Iris in her arms. Iris was tiny as a bird, frail and weak, but she hugged Stella tightly.

'Thank you, my dear,' Iris whispered. 'That means more than you could ever know.'

41

Iris – Mougins, October, 1996

Iris leaned back in the stripy deckchair on the beach at Cannes, wrapped in her coat and blanket, and watched Stella walk along the shoreline. Her granddaughter looked preoccupied, stopping now and then to gaze out at the sea. Perhaps she was thinking about Penhallam's, or that young man, Bruno, who had let her down. But whatever it was that made Stella frown sometimes, Iris was at least assured of her contentment that they were here together in Mougins. Iris felt it too.

Stella waved, her hair blowing in the wind. Iris waved back and inhaled, letting the salty air fill her lungs. It felt good to be able to do that again. Her throat still ached from time to time, and her sense of smell hadn't fully come back, but over the last few weeks, with Stella staying at the house in Mougins, something more far more important than smell had returned to Iris. A sense of peace.

It was as if the circle had been completed. Iris saw so much of herself in Stella. The sadness of her son's loss would never be repaired. She had only the memory of Richard just after he was born, and that afternoon in the garden with Stella as a toddler. But the line to her son continued in her granddaughter and Stella had shared memories of family holidays and funny experiences, and through those Iris felt closer to her son.

Other memories had come back too. As she savoured the time with Stella, Iris's thoughts had been drawn again and again to Alessandro. Not that her thoughts had ever been very far away from him, but just now, as Stella paused to look out at the horizon, barefoot in the gentle waves that broke in white foam along the sand, Iris wondered how much of Alessandro had been in her son and was now in Stella.

Alessandro had written to her in prison. It was a heart-felt note that apologized for leaving her in Paris that day, for not trying to understand her point of view or circum-stances and the reasons why she had done what she had done. He had followed the trial as best he could, he said, and wanted to write a dozen times, but none of his words seemed adequate. He'd felt impotent to protect her and, still, he knew that he could do nothing to help, other than tell her that he loved her and that he would wait for her. 'There is still only you,' he'd written at the very end of the letter.

What on earth could she say in reply? She loved him too, but how could she ever tell Alessandro that she'd given birth to his child and then given it away? And yet, if she saw him again, how could she hide it from him? Either way, the loss of that child would lie between them like poison, just like it ate away at Iris's heart. No, it was better to let Alessandro go, she'd resolved. He'd forget her. The years would pass. Not writing back would have left too many questions in his mind. So, Iris had written the hard-est words she'd ever had to write. 'It's over, Alessandro. Do not contact me again.' And, clearly respecting and understanding the seriousness of her request, Alessandro had obeyed.

Stella walked back towards Iris. This time together, tending the garden and working on perfumes, had done them both good, but occasionally Stella had looked pensive. Finally, she'd told Iris about Bruno and everything that had happened between them. And in turn, Iris had told Stella about what happened with Alessandro. Iris passed on the wisdom that had sustained her through the years: 'When something is over, perhaps it's best to let it go.' But now, seeing Stella frown as she fastened her cardigan tighter, Iris wondered if she'd been wrong to think this.

Stella packed up the flask and blanket and folded the deckchair for the beach attendant to collect. 'Are you ready?' she said.

Iris stood up and took her arm. 'You looked very thoughtful out there by the sea. What were you thinking of?'

'Oh, you know.'

'Bruno?'

'Yes. And Alessandro. I would have liked to have met him.'

Iris sighed. 'You remind me of him, sometimes,' she said. 'The way you pace and think. Your laughter. The sparkle in your eyes when you smile. His gift for seeing scent and putting combinations together with his visual imagination. I'm sorry, Stella. If I had known you would come into my life like this, perhaps I would have done things differently. But I didn't know. I just had to protect what little calm I had.'

Stella nodded. 'I know. But it was such a shame, such a waste of love.'

Iris smiled. 'Maybe it's old age that make me say this, but I don't believe any of it was wasted. The good parts are stored up inside.'

'But that's not enough,' Stella said, exasperated.

'Of course it's not,' Iris said. 'I'm an old woman – you're just at the beginning of your life. Perhaps I made a mistake, letting Alessandro go. Maybe we could have got through the pain of me telling him about the baby. Who knows? But I should have tried.' She took Stella's hand. 'Maybe you should try and talk to Bruno.'

Stella shrugged. 'Maybe.'

They climbed into Iris's battered Citroën and drove back through the forests to Mougins. A car was parked outside the house, one Iris didn't recognize. It looked to be a rental from the sticker in the back window. She noticed the side gate was ajar.

Iris pushed it open and ducked her head under the rose bushes that grew on the archway. There was someone at the bottom of the garden, looking at the flowers, but she couldn't see their face.

Stella followed her. 'Iris,' she said, her voice urgent. 'That man, he looks like the gardener from Isola del Deserto. What's he doing here? I'm sure it's him.'

Iris's mouth went dry. Her feet felt as if they couldn't move. Stella looked at her expectantly. Iris felt the wheels of time turning and knew she had to take the lead, for once. She'd been ill, and the fire had ravaged her throat and lungs, but that was no excuse. Until now, she'd left it all to others. From the moment she'd left Alessandro behind on the *Orient Express* and married Henri to save Jacopo, her life had not been her own. Where was that headstrong girl who'd defied Charles and travelled to Paris, who'd competed with such fire and passion with Alessandro to make the best perfumes, who'd risked her own life to reach Venice and rescue Jacopo? That girl had been lost for so many years. Only now, after being with Stella and remembering what it felt like to be young and purposeful, did she feel that flicker inside again.

'Could you go in and put the kettle on, my dear,' Iris said, her voice strong and clear. 'I need to speak to him.'

She stepped down the flagstone path that ran through the herb garden. The sun was shining, and it was one of those autumn days that felt like a left-over gift from summer. Her fingers brushed the herbs and, unconsciously, she brought her fingertips to her nose. Rosemary. For remembrance. The smell was clear and light. Oh, how she remembered! Every single thing fresh in her mind as if it were yesterday.

The sun shone in her eyes and, up ahead, the man by the herbaceous border was just a silhouette. But she recognized the outline of his shoulders and the turn of his head.

'Alessandro,' she said, her voice barely a whisper. But he moved, turning to face her, the sun dipping behind a cloud, and there he was, older, but still the man she remembered. His shoulders broad, his eyes still bright, and the scar still visible on his weathered skin.

'Iris,' he said.

Disbelief filled Iris's mind. He was here. 'How did you find me?' she said.

'I met someone who was looking for our perfumes. She said you were in Paris. I tried to forget about it, but her companion came back to visit me, begging for more information. I sent him on his way, but I couldn't stop thinking about you. I took leave from the monastery and travelled to Paris to find you. But when I arrived, you'd gone. You talked about this place in Mougins, so I came here.'

Iris swallowed. 'There's something I need to tell you.' For so long she'd carried the secret, but now it was time to let him know.

He shook his head. 'I think I know what it is. In Paris, I went to the archives and looked through the court papers. I wanted to see them for myself. Is it true? Did you have our child?'

Iris nodded, holding her hands to her face, tears springing to her eyes. 'I did, Alessandro, but I couldn't keep him. My brother took him, raised him as his own. The boy, Richard, is dead now. I'm so sorry.'

Alessandro bowed his head. 'You never thought of contacting me? I could have looked after him.'

'I know, I should have done that. But you don't know what it was like: the arrest, the trial, the imprisonment. I lost my mind, and didn't know how to reach you, and after our last meeting in Paris I thought you might say no, and that would have killed me. So, I did the safest thing I could think of at the time. But I am so sorry.'

Alessandro nodded. 'Perhaps I understand. After you sent me that note saying that it was over, I lost my mind too. I tried to find someone else, but it didn't work out. That's why I went to work in the monastery in 1966. That place, far away from everything, has been my home all these years. And I thought I'd found some kind of peace until, one day, a girl with the same smile as yours, claiming you were her great-aunt, walked on to the island.'

'Stella isn't my great-niece,' Iris said. 'She's my granddaughter. Our son Richard's child. She's here now. You can meet her soon.' She let the words sink into Alessandro's mind. 'She's your granddaughter too.'

He let out a deep breath and rubbed his forehead. '*Our*

granddaughter,' he said, astonished. 'Despite everything, something good was saved from the wreckage, something real was living all this time, our love in our child, and now in our granddaughter.'

He moved towards Iris. A tug deep inside her heart, a feeling from long ago, overwhelmed her. She moved towards him and, in a moment, she was in his arms. His smell was just the same. The strength of his chest. For a second, she was transported back, and the years disappeared into timelessness.

'My love,' he whispered against her cheek.

'Oh, Alessandro,' Iris said. 'There was only you for me too. There's been nobody else but you.'

He lifted her chin and stared into her eyes. 'Is it too late?' he said.

'I don't know. Perhaps that's not really the question to ask. We've both journeyed on such different paths that all we can be sure of right now is that we are here together. Let's just enjoy each moment and be grateful.'

Alessandro bent down and kissed her gently on the lips. His touch was like water after a long, long drought. 'Can I stay for a while? To spend time with you, and to get to know Stella.'

'Oh, Alessandro, I'd love that more than anything in the world. She's wonderful, but she's sickening for something. The man she was with in Venice, Bruno, they argued, and I fear she may let things go if she can't find the courage to solve the misunderstanding.'

'Like you and me.'

'Yes, but perhaps without all the difficulties we went through. She's the best of both of us. I wish we could help her.'

Alessandro thought for a moment. 'This man, Bruno, I know he loves her. I could tell by the way he spoke when he came back to see me at the monastery.'

'I wish she'd go to him. But what can we do? We can't interfere.'

'There is one thing we can do. Something we're good at,' he said, with a smile. 'We can create something for her.'

'What?' Iris asked, not following his thoughts

'Solo Tu. The last perfume.'

42

Stella – London and Venice, October 1996

Alessandro stopped the car outside Penhallam's on Jermyn Street. After spending a week together in Mougins, Stella had been summoned back to London for the completion of the sale, and Iris and Alessandro had insisted on coming with her.

An impatient horn beeped behind them. 'You'd better go in,' Alessandro said. 'I'll find somewhere to park.' The London traffic had been overwhelming, and Stella could tell he'd be glad when the car was safely stowed away.

'You can probably find a space to park further down,' she said. 'You'll need to put something in the meter.'

Iris was still sitting in the front seat, gazing up at the shop. Stella opened the door and helped her out. 'Are you feeling all right? It must feel strange to see the place again.'

'It does indeed,' Iris said.

Alessandro set off, and Iris followed Stella into Penhallam's, clutching her granddaughter's hand.

'It hasn't changed!' Iris exclaimed, tracing her finger over the counter. 'The day I left for Paris in 1939, I was convinced that one day I'd return as the perfumer. Sixty years later, and here I am again.'

Stella squeezed her hand. Who would have thought she'd be the one bringing Iris back here? A few months ago, her mind had been clouded by Penhallam's struggles and a sense of failure. With the sale of the business, a new challenge was about to start, and Stella would face it with Iris and Alessandro by her side.

'Good afternoon, Stella,' Amy said, coming out from the back of the shop. 'It's lovely to see you again.'

Arnold had arranged with Andrea that Amy would be employed with GPL on their trainee development programme. The girl had shown she was capable of learning more and, thankfully, now she would have the chance. Stella made the introductions, but Iris's gaze kept wandering all over the shop. It must have felt like stepping back in time.

'Arnold and James are in the perfumery,' Amy said. 'You can go right through.'

'I thought they'd be in the office. The perfumery is a mess.'

Amy smiled. 'I think you'll find it's a good deal more habitable than it used to be.'

Puzzled, Stella linked arms with Iris and walked to the back of the shop. The door to the perfumery stood open, the scent of fresh polish in the air.

'Oh, my goodness,' Stella said. The room had been cleared of boxes, the shelves restocked with bottles, and the perfumer's organ stood ready to use. 'I can't believe it.'

Arnold smiled. 'It was James's idea,' he said. 'He got an advance from GPL and arranged for the perfumery to be renovated.'

'I hope you like it, Stella,' James said. 'I know GPL is taking over the old Penhallam's, but this is for you. Andrea approved; she has a sneaking admiration for your determination. She's even pared back on some of the more radical plans for Penhallam's perfumes. You can rest assured that her modernization will build on the old scents that your ancestors created. She's planning a roll-out of national outlets with a vintage feel.'

'Goodness,' Iris said. 'What would Charles say about all that?'

Arnold held out his hand. 'You must be Iris Penhallam. I really am honoured to meet you.'

Iris smiled and shook his hand. 'I hear you've been very supportive to Stella,' she said. 'You, however' – she glared at James – 'I'm not so sure about, but I do have you to thank for retrieving my notebook.'

James cleared his throat. 'Yes, well, I hope Stella has forgiven me.'

'Just about,' Stella said. It was impossible not to; the perfumery looked wonderful.

'Shall we get the documents signed?' Arnold said. 'Then we can leave you to enjoy the perfumery in peace.'

He pushed the papers across the perfumer's organ for Stella to sign. She'd already read a copy that had been faxed over and had it checked by her solicitor.

Stella nodded. 'Yes, I'm ready for the next chapter to begin, although it does feel strange to finally let the company go.'

She took a deep breath and signed her name in the places marked with a cross.

Iris patted her arm. 'Well done, Stella,' she said. 'I know how hard that must have been. But now you are free. We both are.'

Arnold gathered the papers and put them in his briefcase.

'Have you thought of a name for your new perfumery?' James said.

GPL was keeping the trading name Penhallam's as part of the contract.

Stella smiled. 'Actually, I have, although I won't be ready to open for a year or so, until I'm fully trained as a perfumer.'

'What is it?' Arnold asked.

'I can't claim the credit for it,' Stella said. 'It was the article in *Le Figaro* that gave me the idea. Raffaele had planned to call the new collection of scents "The Perfumer's Secret". I've decided that when my perfumery opens, it will be called "The Perfumer's Secret" too.'

Iris smiled. 'That sounds perfect.'

Two weeks later, Iris and Alessandro were in the final stages of finishing Solo Tu. With Alessandro's help and the proceeds of the sale of Penhallam's to GPL, Stella had restocked the perfumery with ingredients. She'd been fascinated, absorbing so much new knowledge while seeing the fragrance come to life, but Iris and Alessandro had both been very mysterious about what it was supposed to represent.

'What do you think, Stella?' Iris reached over and handed Stella a vial. The windows of the perfumery on Jermyn Street had been flung open and the mild October air was smoky and damp.

Stella inhaled. Alessandro was sitting at the other side of the table, surrounded by amber glass bottles.

'It's delicious,' Stella said. 'But I'm not sure what you're aiming for. Can't you tell me the brief?'

Stella had mostly watched the creation of this scent from the sidelines, intrigued by the interaction between Alessandro and Iris, the back and forth of their debates and, occasionally, the fire of their disagreements. Iris's sense of smell was still not perfect, but Alessandro made up for what she missed.

Iris nudged Alessandro. 'You tell her.'

Alessandro reached for a scrap of paper in his pocket. 'I wrote this a long time ago,' he said, putting on his reading glasses and preparing to read it aloud. In that single movement, Stella was reminded of her father.

Alessandro cleared his throat.

There is no place I'd rather be than in your arms. No voice I'd rather hear than your voice. No lips I'd rather kiss than your lips. Nothing I long to see as much as your smile. No one I'd rather come home to but you. For all the years that have passed, and all the years to come, there is only you.

Alessandro put the paper down, took off his glasses and looked at Iris. Her eyes were full of tears, hearing his words. It sent a shiver down Stella's spine. She'd read the lines herself back in Paris. They still encapsulated her feelings for Bruno. Was she going to let him go, just like that?

'How did you know?' she said, glancing from one to the other.

'How did we know what?' Alessandro said.

'How you felt about each other?'

Iris smiled and reached for Alessandro's hand. 'It was when we first met. He was at the perfume convention I'd gone to, standing in the front row, about to hear Raffaele make his speech. He turned around and our eyes met. I knew from that moment.'

'Really?' Stella said. 'You knew right then?'

Iris laughed. 'Well, maybe not right then – at least, I didn't acknowledge it to myself.'

'It was the same for me,' Alessandro said. 'But I wrote these words the last time I saw Iris in 1946. We'd been apart during the war, and I thought our separation was over. I reacted angrily when I found out she was married to Henri.' He turned to Iris. 'When I wrote to you in prison and you didn't reply, I hated myself. I realized I'd left it too late. I should have been there for you.'

Iris shook her head. 'I didn't respond because I was too ashamed about having to give our baby away. I didn't want you to know, and that meant staying apart for ever. I thought I'd left it too late as well. But here you are.'

'Here I am,' Alessandro said, bending down and kissing her softly on the lips.

Stella smiled. 'Then maybe there's still hope for me and Bruno.'

'Of course,' Iris replied. 'That's what inspired us to finally make Solo Tu. Raffaele once told me, "Dreams don't die just because they don't come true. They die because we don't honour them." Don't you think it's worth giving Bruno a second chance?'

Stella shrugged. 'I don't know. He wrote to me when I got back to Paris to ask for my forgiveness, but I never responded.'

'Oh, Stella, don't hold it against him,' Iris said, 'not while you're still young and there's time for you both to be together. I made that mistake, albeit in different circumstances, but I wouldn't want it for you. Besides, Alessandro and I have been thinking . . .'

Alessandro smiled and took up the rest of Iris's sentence. 'We'd like you to ask Bruno to consider finishing his book. After much thought, we've decided we'd be happy to cooperate. In fact, telling our story after all this time would be something we'd both enjoy.'

'Really? After you fought so hard to keep it a secret?'

Iris sighed. 'What can I say? Maybe now that things have turned out well it casts a different light on the past, makes it more bearable. But you should be the one to approach Bruno – if you wish to.'

'He won't want to see me now.'

'Take him the new perfume, Solo Tu. It's designed to be a balance of masculine and feminine scents, perfect for a man or a woman,' Alessandro said. 'Sometimes it's easier to say what you feel with scents rather than with words. Show him what's in your heart.'

'But I don't know what that is,' Stella said desperately. 'I've no job. I need to earn some money, I'm completely adrift.'

'Nonsense,' Iris said. 'You're a perfumer's apprentice. You might have left it until rather late in the day, but you can easily catch up. Alessandro can teach you what he knows too, while he's here.'

'When do you head back to Venice?' Stella said.

'Soon. I need to tidy up my affairs at the monastery,' Alessandro said. 'I can't leave until a new gardener is found. But Iris and I have been thinking about Raffaele's old perfumery, the one you and Bruno broke into. We want to revive it. You can come and work there for us as our apprentice. It won't take long before you're ready to come back here and start making perfumes of your own.'

Iris smiled. 'I'll follow Alessandro in a couple of weeks. We'll see out the rest of our days making perfume together. Why don't you come with me?'

'I might,' Stella said, hesitant to commit just yet. There was a lot to think about. She inhaled the scent. 'The petitgrain is exquisite as the top note, and neroli strikes the right balance as the heart note, but I'm not sure ambergris is the right base note. It needs something woody and earthy.'

'What do you think it should be?' Iris said, leaning forward.

It was obvious.

'Iris absolute,' Stella said. 'My father planted irises in the flowerbed just outside the perfumery. I always thought it was ironic, given how little he spoke of you. He tended them every year without fail, despite my grandfather's objections. I think he did somehow know that you were his mother, even if he never found the courage to voice it.'

Iris took a deep breath. 'I never knew about the flowerbeds,' she said quietly. 'Very well, let's add some iris absolute, and then it will be finished.'

It was strange to see Venice from the air. Stella peered out of the window at the orange rooftops, snaking canals and wide-open sea beyond. The plane descended smoothly, but Stella had butterflies in her stomach. She hadn't phoned ahead to tell Bruno she was coming. It was easier without any build-up of expectation. The first time she spoke to him needed to be face to face.

'Can you see the island?' Iris asked.

Iris had slept for most of the two-hour flight, after a glass of Buck's Fizz at the airport. Now she was wide awake, leaning over Stella to look out for Isola del Deserto.

'Just about, in the distance,' Stella said. 'But don't worry, there'll be plenty of time to see everything. You're going to be living here. How does that feel?'

Iris laughed. 'Incredible. All those years, and I remember everything about our arrival and the city as if it were yesterday. Do you think it's possible that happy memories sink into the body and soul more than unhappy ones? Those ten years in prison are like a blank piece of paper in my mind. But that journey on the *Orient Express* with Alessandro, seeing Lausanne, Milan and Venice, is etched on my heart.'

Stella patted her hand. 'You're so different to the woman I met back in August,' she said. 'I hate to think what would have happened if you hadn't impetuously sent that notebook. I might never have known anything about all this.'

Iris nodded and sighed. 'Perhaps you would have worked it out from Jacopo's letter. I'm so glad that you persisted.'

Stella sat back in her seat. Would Bruno be glad that she'd persisted with him? It was impossible to know. Two months had passed since the fax he'd sent to her hotel in Paris. Only now did she have the courage to tell him how she felt. Hopefully it wasn't too late.

Alessandro picked them up from the airport in his car. Stella sat in the back, gazing out of the window as they crossed the long Ponte della Libertà from the mainland to Venice. Iris and Alessandro chatted about their plans for the perfumery. It was nice to hear their voices, but Stella was too preoccupied to join in.

Alessandro parked the car and Stella got out. 'You're sure you don't want us to come with you?' he said.

Stella smiled at her grandparents. They stood arm in

arm, concerned expressions on their faces. It was hard to believe they had spent all those years apart. They seemed to fit back together like the two sides of Iris's locket.

'I'll be fine,' she said. 'I'll head to the perfumery afterwards. I can't wait to see how the renovations are going.'

'Good luck,' Iris said, kissing her cheek.

Alessandro wrapped her in a big bear hug. 'Just tell him the truth,' he said. 'That's all you can do.'

Stella went off down the street, turning one last time before she reached the corner. Iris and Alessandro were heaving a suitcase out of the boot. It proved to be quite a struggle and the pair of them were laughing, their joy ringing in the air like church bells.

It was nearly five o'clock. Bruno would be finishing work at the university soon. Stella didn't want to find him there in the crowds of people. Instead, she headed down towards the canal near his house. Boats bobbed on their moorings. Where was it? She spotted the blue paint and yellow awning. *Barchetta Azzurra*. Bruno's boat.

She stood next to it, looking left and right along the canal. He'd told her that he always went out on the boat after work to take his stress away. Hopefully today was no exception. She waited, twisting her hands. Was that him? Brown curly hair, a familiar stride. She craned her neck over the crowd of tourists. Yes, it was. She straightened up expectantly.

But then, a woman waved. She had long dark hair and was wearing a red dress. Bruno caught sight of her and waved back, a huge smile on his face. The woman sprinted over, and Bruno lifted her in his arms, spinning round and round. He put her down, gazing into her eyes, and brushed back her hair with his hand.

Stella blinked away tears. This was unbearable. She had to get away. At that moment, Bruno, his arm around the woman, started walking towards the boat. Stella gripped her bag, the bottle of Solo Tu weighing it down. He mustn't see her here. But as she turned to bolt, Bruno called out, 'Stella? Is that you?'

Stella didn't wait a moment longer. She set off as fast as she could in the other direction, weaving in and out of the crowds, then sprinting up a side street, faster and faster, mortified that he'd seen her. She'd been such a fool to come here, to expose herself like this. She slowed down, gasping for breath. It was her own fault. She *had* left it too late. Bruno had moved on and met someone else.

'Stella,' Bruno called. She turned round. There he was, alone, bent double to catch his breath, his face red. 'What are you doing?'

'Nothing. I just thought . . . but it doesn't matter, I was in Venice, and I . . .' she stuttered, unable to put the jumble of thoughts into words.

She started walking, but he caught her up, grabbing her hand. 'Stella, what is it? You look like you've seen a ghost. Why did you run off like that?'

Stella dropped her eyes. She'd come all this way. There was nothing to lose now; it was clearly all lost. She might as well tell him, and then she could move on with her life and get used to the fact that Bruno would never be in it.

'I'm here with Iris and Alessandro,' she said. 'They found each other again, after all this time. You had visited the island again. The gardener was Alessandro and, after you left, he decided to go and find Iris. They made the last perfume together.' She reached into her bag and took the bottle out. 'I helped them – Iris and Alessandro have been training me. They want you to write your book and tell their story. And I wanted to tell you . . .'

She stopped, glancing into his eyes.

'What?' he whispered.

'That I'm sorry. I wanted to reply to the letter you sent me in Paris and tell you how I felt, but I was too scared. I wasn't sure if I could trust you, but being with Iris and Alessandro has made me see that some things are too precious to let go of.' She handed him the bottle. 'This is the perfume I made with Iris and Alessandro. It's called Solo Tu. And because there's no one I'd rather be with than you, I wanted you to have it.'

He took the bottle, turning it in his hands. 'Thank you, Stella.'

'And I know I've left it too late, but I wanted you to have it, and now, I'll let you get back to your girlfriend. You looked so happy, and I . . .' Her voice faltered.

Bruno clasped her hand. 'That woman you saw me with . . . it was Anna, my sister. She's out of rehab and she's better. We were going to take the boat out for a spin, like old times. Then I saw you. She's walking back home – she knew I had to follow you. She knows how much you mean to me.'

Stella stared at him. 'The woman you were hugging. That's your sister?'

Bruno nodded. 'Yes. There's only you for me,' he said. 'Now that Anna's back and settled, I was planning to come and find you. But you found me first.'

Stella's heart swelled. 'Oh, Bruno . . .' She took a deep breath. 'I love you.'

Bruno's eyes deepened. He came closer and kissed her lips. 'I love you too.' He was here, hers, the scent of his skin, the warmth of his body. There was no place else she'd rather be than in his arms.

'Can we start over?' he said, holding her close.

Stella thought of Iris and Alessandro, of all the years that had passed. Somehow, Iris had found a way to make a new beginning. Gazing into Bruno's eyes, Stella knew that she could too.

'I'd like that,' she said, 'more than anything. But there's something we need to do first.'

Bruno smiled. 'What's that?'

She tugged his hand gently, leading him up the street. 'I'd like you to meet my grandparents.'

Acknowledgements

I feel incredibly fortunate to have a second book published and I'm so grateful to you, the reader, for taking the time to read *The Perfumer's Secret*. I hope you enjoy it and get as swept away in reading it as I did in writing it. It's always a pleasure to hear from readers and you can find me on Instagram and Facebook (@fionaschneiderwriter) and on my website (www. fionaschneider.net). I'd be delighted if you got in touch.

The three themes that began this story, before I'd even written a word, were: perfume, the *Orient Express* and Venice. Exploring these subjects has taken me on an amazing journey.

First, I loved learning about perfume. I remember the first time I set foot inside the perfume shop Floris with its cabinets full of scent bottles. Seeing the museum at the back of the shop and the perfumery was a spark to my imagination. That day, I bought my first bottle of Honey Oud (after sampling all the scents) because I loved the combination of earthiness, strength and sweetness, and I imagined that it was exactly the kind of scent Iris would have created.

I have also enjoyed researching the history of Penhaligons and exploring their scents. The heavenly and mysterious Halfeti combines oud, bergamot and rose, three of my favourite ingredients. I could picture Alessandro experimenting with formulas and mixing accords to produce a perfume like this one.

I also attended the Apprentice and Expert masterclasses at EPC (Experimental Perfume Club) with founder and perfumer Emmanuelle Moeglin. Until that moment, I'd never realized how little I knew about the sense of smell nor how limited my lexicon of scents was. I spent a magical day sampling ingredients and writing formulas and came home with two bespoke scents that I'd created.

Second, it was wonderful to discover more about the *Orient Express* in my research. Through my son, Max, who used to volunteer on the Nene Valley Railway, I was fortunate to be able to look around two wagons-lits carriages that used to form part of the *Orient Express*. A day spent serving afternoon tea to passengers taught me about the logistics of working on a steam train and enabled me to absorb the ambience of the *Orient Express* restaurant carriage.

And finally, Venice. I first visited Venice many years ago. It rained every day, but it was still beautiful. Last summer, I went back with my family for an incredible week. The sun shone, just like it did when Stella was there. We explored the city and the islands, including Isola del Deserto, which can only be reached by hiring a private boat from Burano.

I'm grateful for all these experiences and for the many books that enabled me to find out about perfume, the *Orient Express* and Venice in modern times and during the Second World War. I loved embarking on a reading odyssey when researching this book, and I'm very thankful to those non-fiction writers whose knowledge has extended my own. In particular, I'd like to mention: *The Perfume Lover* by Denyse Beaulieu, *Orient Express: The Story of the World's Most Fabulous Train* by Michael Barsley, *Everyday Life in Fascist Venice, 1929–1940* by Kate Ferris and

The Jews in Mussolini's Italy: From Equality to Persecution by Michele Sarfatti.

So that explains how *The Perfumer's Secret* came into being in my imagination. As to how it comes to be in your hands now, well, that's all down to my wonderful publishers, Penguin Michael Joseph. Thank you to the whole team for having faith in this story and sending it out into the world.

Thank you in particular to my editor, Hannah Smith. I count my lucky stars that she has worked her editing genius on this book and enabled plot lines to deepen, characters to flourish, themes to be developed and the emotional heart of the story to beat true. Everything she suggests makes total sense and I'm grateful for her perception and insight. I'd also like to thank Nick Lowndes, Editorial Manager at Penguin Michael Joseph, for his work in coordinating the edits, and Sarah Day for copy-editing *The Perfumer's Secret* with great precision and detail.

Huge thanks also go to my supportive and talented agent, Rebecca Ritchie at A. M. Heath. She's an absolute pleasure to work with and I'm so grateful to have her in my corner. She is the best cheerleader a writer could ever want. It's wonderful to have a home at A. M. Heath.

Thank you to my mum, Susan Hall, who encouraged my writing from an early age, and to my brother, Mike, for the transatlantic conversations about writing, psychology and life that get right to the heart of things.

I'd also like to thank my amazing friends for being there through it all: Caroline and Dave Lamb, Alison and Paul Branston, Claire Smith, Caroline and Adrian Meadows, Michael Kaes and Annika Franck, Becky and James Scott, Gurdeep Kaur and Kal Singh, Sara and Adam Cole, Sarah and Martin Aldred, and Rachel and James Francis. I'd also like to thank my work colleagues for their enthusiastic support.

Finally, once again, my greatest thanks go to my family for their unfailing encouragement. Thank you to Max for your close reading of *The Perfumer's Secret* and insightful suggestions. Thank you to Karla for reminding me why writing and the life of the imagination matters. Thank you to Lukas for motivating me to keep going and for keeping my spirits up whenever they flagged. And thank you to my husband, Michael, who kept the home fires burning while I worked on *The Perfumer's Secret* and never let me forget that I'm a writer at heart. I love you all so much.